OF SEA AND SAND

THE KERRIGAN CHRONICLES, BOOK II

ALSO BY ANNIE DAYLON

Praise for *Of Sea and Seed*
The Kerrigan Chronicles, Book I

Daylon's talent is apparent in this engrossing opening to a projected series . . .
Intriguing characterizations . . . surprising level of suspense . . . a page-turner.
PUBLISHERS WEEKLY

. . . story of family secrets, deprivation, atonement, sins, and guilt. . . . memorable
characters who have met life's challenges with strength and stoicism . . . The
pages are so well rendered that the reader forgets time and tasks to be done.
LYNNE LEGROW, AMAZON TOP REVIEWER AND AWARD-WINNING BLOGGER OF FICTIONOPHILE

With insight, wit, and great understanding of the all-too-human emotions of guilt
and desire, Daylon draws the reader into a timeless story of yearning and loss.
PAUL BUTLER, AUTHOR OF *THE GOOD DOCTOR*

With the skill of a poet, Daylon weaves the tale of a Newfoundland outport family
in the early 20'h century. Her mastery of the written word brings the reader into the
lives of her characters as they deal with the truths and tragedies of everyday life . . .
RON YOUNG, FOUNDING EDITOR, *DOWNHOME* MAGAZINE

A longing for the sea, and from the sea...lives out of control since birth, torn by land
and by sea . . . souls steadily whipped by the rhetoric of religion. Pounding rhythms.
Exciting narrative. DARRELL DUKE, AUTHOR OF *THURSDAY'S STORM*

. . . you will draw in the scent of the land and the sea, your ear attuned to authentic
Newfoundland voices. The old-world characters are compelling in their secretive
lives and in acts of love gone wrong.
NELLIE P. STROWBRIDGE, AUTHOR OF *GHOST OF THE SOUTHERN CROSS*

Published by **McRAC Books**, British Columbia, Canada

Of Sea and Sand, The Kerrigan Chronicles, Book II
© 2021 by Angela A. Day (nom de plume: Annie Daylon)
All rights reserved.

For information, contact Annie Daylon: anniedaylon@shaw.ca or www.anniedaylon.com.

ISBN-978-1-7771814-0-6 (paperback)
ISBN-978-1-7771814-1-3 (html)
McRAC Books Trade Paperback Edition
First Printing: January 2021
Printed in the United States of America

Cover Photo: Newfoundland Coast, photo.com via canva.com
Cover Photo: Douglas C-47, Gary Blakeley via shutterstock.com
Newfoundland map design: Brian Rodda, www.roddawrites.com
Map photo © @FilipBjorkman

OF SEA AND SAND

THE KERRIGAN CHRONICLES, BOOK II

A novel by
Annie Daylon

McRAC Books
British Columbia, Canada

CAST OF CHARACTERS

Kathleen Kerrigan: Ghost, matriarch doomed to an afterlife of repeated telling of her story in atonement for mortal sin

Clara: Daughter of Kathleen, woman at cutting edge of social change, rum runner, wife, adulterer

Kevin: Son of Kathleen, widower

Kate: Granddaughter of Kathleen, daughter to Kevin

Dulcie Mullins: family friend, caregiver

Robert Caulins: British gentleman, rumrunner, husband of Clara

Patrick McMurty: Clara's lover

Tom Murphy: loyal friend of Kevin from the Burin Peninsula

DECEASED

Alphonse: Kathleen's husband, murdered

Jimmy: Kathleen's baby boy, murdered

Mavis: Kevin's wife, died in tidal wave

Jimmy, Marie, Johnny, Joseph: Kevin's children, died in tidal wave

. . . for love of Newfoundland and its Greatest Generation

Island of
Newfoundland

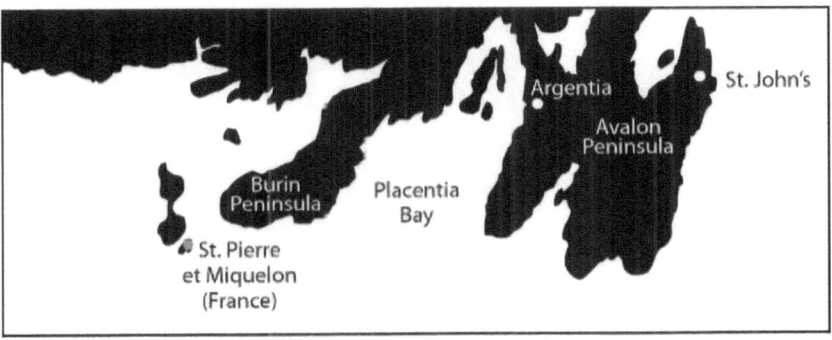

KATHLEEN

Every man is guilty of all the good he did not do.

VOLTAIRE

CHAPTER 1

———◆———

IT IS AN ARCHITECT, THE sea.

The North Atlantic is a meticulous artisan. On a clear day, a downward glance from gull or gannet reveals the contours of a chiselled island, its coastline the result of thousands of years of Atlantic artistry, its coves the producers of endless quantities of Atlantic food fish. An island utopia—Newfoundland.

On that same clear day, a landward glance from any seabird on a shoreline rock reveals smokeless chimneys, ragged clothing, and gaunt faces, proof of the poverty that creeps into every crevice. The beauty and bounty of this island hold no sway in the haunted eyes of its hungry.

It is 1932 and it is a time of nothing.

The stock market crash has fuelled a depression that fells forest, mining, and fishing-export industries. Unemployment is widespread. Newfoundland, a small, independent dominion within the British Empire, is one hundred million dollars in debt from the Great War with no hope of recovery. One third of the island's three hundred thousand residents are on the dole, a government relief system in which people are allotted food from a list—flour, pork, beans, cornmeal, split peas, cocoa, and molasses. Malnutrition and disease run rampant and infant mortality is at an all-time high.

During this dark time, my community of Argentia survives. Some residents seek assistance from the government and others leave to seek work. Most eke out a living at home, building their own, sewing their own and, blessed with good land, growing their own.

The breeze picks me up and shepherds me back, back to Argentia to continue my tale. I am Kathleen Kerrigan, mother to Kevin, Clara, and Jimmy, grandmother to Kate. Long past my living time, yet still here. A spectre and storyteller, who perhaps comes across like the Lord announcing Himself, but there's no help for it. My words are scripted.

Today I hold no thought of the scarceness that scrapes my island. The ocean gleams under the smile of the sun and I glow under the light that is the presence of my Clara, Kevin, and Kate. This wharf is a temporary stop for me, a respite from my ancient mariner journey. A familiar longing courses through me. Part of my penance, I suppose, craving the comfort of a cup of tea and a biscuit. No such luxury abides.

As Clara strolls the pier, there are the usual hoots and hollers from fishermen, creaks and groans from wharf planks, rattles and thumps of barrels and carts. Up ahead is the moon-faced Dulcie Mullins, her stubby legs pumping as she scurries to distribute her biscuit tins. Still warms my soul, does Dulcie, a gift of a woman who once tended to me, then cared for my daughter, and is now a constant in the raising of my granddaughter. Clara whispers something to Dulcie, accepts a biscuit tin and, smiling, moves on to the gangway of the *Elizabeth J*, where she meets her husband, Robert. The two are heading on possibly their last rum-running adventure, one in which Clara will land herself at the heart of a riot at the St. John's Colonial Building. But there I am, getting ahead of my story again. And, as always, it must be told in order straight through to the last dot of punctuation. Where was I? Oh yes, Clara and Robert. Their days as rumrunners are numbered. Rumours abound: the people are disgruntled with the lack of liquor, the prohibition laws will be repealed, and the need for illegal booze will no longer exist.

A carefree laugh pierces the clamour, the laugh of my six-year-old grandchild who is standing at her father's side, waving and calling to her Aunt Clara.

Clara rushes toward Kate, her face filled with the joy of greeting. Kate flies into her aunt's arms. They spin and laugh and dance their way toward the gangway.

Kevin leans into a barrel as he watches Clara and Kate, not a twitch of bitterness in him. He has overcome his possessiveness where Kate is concerned and has come to terms with his life in Argentia, a single parent of a single child. Kevin shifts into movement, his gait easy, and his shoulders relaxed. He nods at passing fishermen, stopping to talk to the pudding-faced Salty Joe Sallivan who sets down his salt-filled wheelbarrow and mops his brow with his flannel shirt sleeve.

"Mornin', Kevin b'y."

"Mornin', Joe."

"Mornin', Dulcie," says Joe.

Kevin turns slightly to see Dulcie standing beside him. He smiles.

"How's the family, Joe?" asks Dulcie.

"The diphtheria, you mean?"

Kevin raises an eyebrow. Dulcie nods her head.

"Diphtheria's done with, thanks be to God. The merchant took pity on me."

"How so, Joe?" Kevin asks.

Kevin's question jabs the air around me, sets it and me to quivering. I know what's coming.

"Well, I didn't catch enough cod to pay off me debts," says Joe, "but O'Brien gave the missus enough medicine for the two young 'uns anyway."

"Two, Joe?" says Dulcie. "I thought it was just the one."

"It was, last time I came across ya, me darlin'. But that was a while back."

"Thank the good Lord that things have come to rights, Joe. I'll keep an eye on the family for ya while you're offshore. Here's your biscuits." Dulcie plops a tin on top of the salt.

Grinning, Joe doffs his sod cap, grabs the handles of his wheelbarrow, and rumbles off.

"I still say it's a hard thing, the merchant deciding who gets the medicine," Dulcie says to Kevin, "but maybe O'Brien has a bigger heart than he lets on."

"Makes me wonder why my little brother didn't get medicine, though," says Kevin. "For the diphtheria, I mean."

Dulcie looks puzzled. "You must be remembering wrong, b'y. Jimmy's death was a crib death. No medicine in the world can fix that."

And there it is, as expected. A waft of wind latches onto Dulcie's words, swirling them through me and into the path of the sun. The sky darkens, a mere blink. Dulcie's comment has triggered a change. I lied to Kevin. Lies have consequences.

The puzzled look on Kevin's face transforms into a smile as Kate runs toward him. He grabs her hands and swings her through the air and she responds with squeals of delight. Then, along with Dulcie, they head out, Kate bouncing like an eager puppy.

At the end of the wharf, Dulcie leads Kate toward her own house and Kevin heads home. Curious about how Dulcie and little Kate will spend their time, I trail them. But curiosity has no follow-through when the universe has other plans.

As I slide through Dulcie's gate, the scene changes and I am at the foot of the lane leading to Kevin's house. I glide up the path and slip, like a wisp of smoke, through the keyhole of the side door.

Kevin is having a grand conversation with someone. Curious, that. Did he meet someone along the way? Was someone waiting here for him?

I ease into the kitchen, right up to Kevin who is slumped at the kitchen table, talking away to an empty chair. The name Mavis slips out, and I nod, understanding.

"Something's not right, Mavis," he says. "There's times my heart starts racing for no apparent reason whatsoever. I hunt all over the place, looking for a leak to plug, a fire to douse, a problem to fix. But I find nothing and am left standing like a fool, sweating from head to toe. I don't know why I'm still here . . ."

Unable to abide the heft of his grief, I pull back and back again, until I am huddled on the warming oven at the top of the stove, a foggy blob between two soggy woollen socks. Hovering there, I think on Mavis.

Never met the woman. At least, not in my living years. As ghost, I watched, joyful, when she was alive and a loving mother to my grandchildren. I watched again, heartsick, as the pregnant Mavis and four of her children were carried away in the raging foam of a tidal wave. Now, as I gaze at my son, that heartsickness reclaims me.

Kevin has gone silent, alternately staring at the empty chair and at the piece of whittling wood he holds. He pulls out a pocketknife and begins to carve. True to form, that. Always a project in hand, my Kevin, tying flies, polishing boots, knitting nets.

A gust of wind crops up, rattling the chimney flue. Kevin looks toward it, his head snapping with the speed of a sprung trap. "Mavis?" he says. The question hangs. His shoulders rise and fall, the whittling stalls. He whistles, poking a lilt into the eerie stillness, reminding me of times when, alone and berry picking on the barrens, I sang into the silence, a feeble attempt to ward off fairies.

Would that I could give Kevin back his life with Mavis and his children. He still has his surviving child, his miracle child, Kate. A miracle child maybe, but not his at all. Another lie, that.

I sigh as I consider the consequences of lies. I told Dulcie that Jimmy died of a crib death. Then I told Clara Jimmy died of diphtheria. A liar wants a good memory. I chide myself for the lack. Today, with Kevin as witness, my lies collided. In that instant, my respite ended. Now I, a ghost, must resume the telling of a tale in which I am a flesh-and-blood character. A bit of a muddle at times, but there's nothing for it but to get past the confusion. My Kevin will make his way to the home of the flesh-and-blood Kathleen. His questions will pour and her answers will propel him to the Burin Peninsula where a sliver of truth will spur him onward. A long, hard journey is on the horizon for my Kevin.

And, come heaven or hell, Kevin will dig to the depths of all the lies.

KEVIN

CHAPTER 2

———◆———

KEVIN AWOKE TO UTTER EMPTINESS, his head on the table, his hand on the hilt of his whittling knife. The hardness in his loins, a rarity, surprised him. It was the dream about Mavis that had done it, caused his blood to surge. Was there some manhood left in him after all? The question mocked. He instantly went limp. Sighing, he focused on recapturing his dream.

Was Mavis here? Beside the stove? Beside the door? Was that today? Yesterday? Countless, the times he had imagined, or dreamed, or just wished her here. And she was always on about the same thing. Airplanes. He shook his head. Why in the name of heaven would she be talking about that? The only things flying around here were gulls, mosquitoes, and sand-flies, and there were enough of them to scourge Egypt. The very notion of sandflies resurrected another sliver of a sentence from Mavis. What had she said about sand? About him leaving Argentia when all turned to sand? Was there any rhyme nor reason to that at all? His mind raced, searching for answers. There were none. Kevin's sigh was one of defeat.

Dropping his pocketknife onto the table, he lumbered to the side door which slammed back at him on the first push. When the hell had the wind come up? It was dead calm earlier. He shoved the door again and won out. His thoughts went to his sister at sea. Rum- running. A harsh trip in a gale. Merciless, the wind. But the *Elizabeth J* would have made it around the Cape by now and was probably holed up in St. John's harbour. Clara would be safe. Thank the Lord the rum running was coming to an end. The people wanted their beer and the laws would oblige them soon enough. Maybe

Clara would be content to come home and to remain there for a time. Maybe he'd talk to her about it. Not likely she'd listen. Stubborn woman.

Kevin latched the door to the storeroom and checked the chickens who'd hunkered down on their own. They'd get back to scratching and squawking once the wind let up. After a trip to the outhouse he returned to his chair in the kitchen. He retrieved his pocketknife and scraped at the grime beneath his fingernails. A wasted endeavour. The dirt was embedded. That's what happens when you let things sit.

He slid the knife into his pocket and brushed wood shavings from the table into one hand. At the stove, he lifted a lid and dropped the shavings in. The curls caught, flared, and crumbled. Kevin put the lid back and deposited the lifter on the top of the warming oven. What next? He felt the need to do something, to solve something. What was nagging at him? Had he let it sit too long?

It had been three years since the tidal wave on the Burin. Three years of living day to day, minute to minute, making a go of it for the sake of his miracle child, Kate. He'd come back to Argentia, to the beginning of things, with the hope of making sense of everything. Maybe it was time to do something about that, to talk to someone about the beginning of things. With his father dead and buried, that someone would be his mother.

For most of his life, Kevin had wrongly believed that his mother had killed his little brother, Jimmy. Kathleen had corrected him herself, her voice and eyes naked with truth. Still, something didn't fit. Clara said Jimmy died from the diphtheria. Dulcie said it was crib death. Which was it?

Perhaps under the guise of checking on things, he could pay his mother a visit. It was the job of a man, wasn't it, to check on his family? He snorted. Man indeed. Clara was the one who was keeping their mother warm and fed. But maybe Kathleen Kerrigan would have words that would put his mind at ease. If nothing else, the walk in the wind and the sea air would do him good. Dulcie Mullins would be bringing Kate home soon. Once Kate showed up, Kevin's heart and mind would be filled with the joy of her, and all else would be shoved to the background.

Now or never.

CHAPTER 3

———◆———

"MORNING, MOTHER," KEVIN SAID, THE odour of oil paint invading his senses as he strode into her kitchen. "What in the love of the Lord are you doing? Painting the cupboards?"

"Asked and answered." Kathleen held her brush above the paint can, which was sitting on a sawhorse she had lugged into the house. Cream-coloured paint streamed from her brush into its home. When the line was reduced to drips, she wiped the brush across the lip of the can. The well around the lip filled.

"You knows darn well I'd do the work for you if you asked," said Kevin.

"Nonsense. You've come for a mug up." Kathleen set her paintbrush crosswise on top of the can and stepped down from her wooden stool. "The kettle is full. I'll just move it over to the heat. Where's the little one this morning?" She grabbed a rag from a hook and wiped her hands.

"At Dulcie's." Kevin sniffed the air. "Could there homemade bread around here someplace?"

Kathleen chuckled. "Nothing wrong with your nose if you can smell that over the paint. Yes, there's bread in the pantry. Still warm. You're welcome to it."

Kevin nodded. "Some windy out there," he said. "Darn near lost my cap on the way over." He started toward the pantry. He halted. "You suppose the *Elizabeth J* will be able to keep upright in choppy seas?"

Kathleen's look was a knowing one. "Sure and a man of the sea like yourself didn't show up here to ask my opinion about schooners. If it's

Clara you're worried about, I wouldn't bother. That daughter of mine has more courage than most men."

"There's truth in that. The courage, I mean. Remember the day Clara followed me into the dory and I plucked her out of the drink?" There. Kevin had got to the beginning without much effort.

With a measured motion, Kathleen turned toward the stove. Did she suspect that he was here for information? Perhaps Kevin should let things be. Kathleen had given him one story about Jimmy's death. Was she able for a retelling? "I remember that day all too well," she said, not a flicker in her voice. "Saved her, you did."

"All's well that ends well," said Kevin quickly, uncertain about pushing on.

"Indeed."

The air hung, weighted, brooding. Should he abandon the conversation? If he didn't ask now—"Can we talk about Jimmy?" he blurted. Without waiting for a response, he hurried on. "All those years, thinking the wrong thing. Diphtheria, he had. Why didn't the rest of us get it too, I wonder?"

His mother turned back toward him, her face set in stone. "The Lord's ways are mysterious."

Kevin wasn't to be put off. "I don't know where I was the day Jimmy died. I just remember coming home and seeing him in your arms, blue."

Kathleen took Kevin's hand, led him to the table, and sat him down. "What is it, son? What is it you need me to say here? We had this conversation with Clara right in your own kitchen, remember? I told you about Jimmy, that I was preparing him for burial."

"Except that Dulcie said Jimmy died from crib death."

"Dulcie?"

"Yes, Dulcie. We were talking to Salty Joe about his young 'uns getting medicine from the merchant for the diphtheria. When he left, I wondered aloud why Jimmy didn't get medicine. And Dulcie said . . ."

"No need to go on." Kathleen sank onto the chair beside him. "How much do you remember about your father?"

Kevin walked out of his mother's house, stunned. His father, Alphonse? A murderer? By the time Kevin came to his senses, he was standing amid a cluster of white crosses in the cemetery. He stumbled toward his father's grave, beside which was the resting place of his baby brother, Jimmy. Kevin looked from one grave to the other. Father to son. Murderer to victim. How had Kathleen lived with this all these years? It was a wonder she hadn't murdered Alphonse with her own two hands. No one could blame her for it. Had Alphonse really killed Jimmy? This was far from what Kevin had in mind when he was trying to understand the beginning of things. But he had to admit that there was some sense to it.

At sixteen, Kevin had left home. Apparently, he didn't know much about his father. He remembered the drinking and the fists, but he hadn't realized the cost of war. His father, shell-shocked, had returned without a grain of sense left in him. The man had killed his own son so the boy wouldn't have to grow up, go to war, and see the things Alphonse himself had seen. Dying boys calling for their mothers.

Kevin shivered as he thought of Clara as a little girl and wondered what he had left her to. But Alphonse surely would not have harmed Clara. A girl child was different than a boy. A father has to protect a girl child.

Kevin himself hadn't protected his own family but a man can't control everything, certainly not the devil sea. Kevin's heart ached as he glanced over the horizon. His thoughts ran through memories of his life in his own saltbox house with Mavis and his children, and his heart filled with longing. Perhaps it was not this cemetery but another that he should be visiting. Maybe, just maybe, he should go to Burin to visit the graves of Mavis and his children. Mavis was trying to tell him something, he was sure of that. Maybe, if he went back . . .

What about Kate? Should he take her?

Six-year-old Kate had ceased wondering if their soggy house on the Burin got lonesome without them. Her nightmares about raging tides had vanished. She accepted, without question, his rowing off in the dory. So, should he leave her here or take her to the Burin?

Kevin had sworn that as long as God sent him no more trouble, he'd never leave Kate's side. God had kept his promise. Kate was happy. Dulcie Mullins was a grand caregiver. So was Clara. Kathleen too, now that he was willing to allow it.

With a sigh, Kevin conceded that he could not tamper with Kate's happiness, could not risk awakening dark memories in his daughter. If he was going back to visit the graves, he was going alone. Dulcie and his mother and Clara would take care of Kate. But he would have to talk to Kate about this. And he would have to go soon, before doubts entered. Maybe he should go to the Burin on the very next coastal boat, be there and back before Clara returned from rum running.

Kevin hawked up a wad of spit and spewed it onto his father's grave marker. He genuflected beside Jimmy's resting place and made the sign of the cross. He was not much of a religious man anymore, but Mavis would have approved of the gesture. "At least Alphonse got his comeuppance, Jimmy," said Kevin. "Thanks be to God."

Kevin made it home without remembering a step of the route. There was no sign of Kate. He sat on a sawhorse in the yard. Absentmindedly, he picked up a wood plane and pulled at a curl of wood lodged in the blade. He released the shaving into the wind. Blond and curled, it was. Like Jimmy's hair. Not a blond in the family yet little Jimmy had blond hair.

Kevin grabbed a board and began to use the plane. Sliding, sliding. He remembered the morning he had followed Clara to the Silver Cliff mine. There was some detail about that memory he was trying to get to. It wasn't about what she was hiding there; he never did find out. Someday, maybe. But that wasn't it now. There was something else. What was it? He had caught up with her at the mine. There was that sound, the drip of water, the image of the baby Jimmy, blue in his mother's arms. The truth about Jimmy's death. Or Clara's truth. Did Clara know what really happened to Jimmy? He had said something to her, and she had replied, "You can't do that." What had he said? The plane hit a knot in the wood and jerked to a stop. What he had said was that he had left Kate in the care of Alphonse. Why was Clara so upset about that? Had Kate been safe with Alphonse on that day? Nothing untoward had happened, had it? Kevin had returned home with Clara. Alphonse had gone fishing. Kathleen was there. Kate was fine. The plane began moving again. Yes, Kate was fine. Maybe going back to the beginning of things meant looking at all that had happened while he was away, including what had happened in Clara's life. Were there secrets? Possibly. Maybe there would be answers in whatever she was hiding in the silver mine.

A lighthearted laugh broke through his musings. He looked up to see Kate skipping up the path, followed by the panting Dulcie Mullins. As Kevin stepped up to meet them, he dropped the plane but not his train of thought.

Maybe he should visit Silver Cliff while Clara was at sea. What was that sister of his up to anyway?

KATHLEEN

CHAPTER 4

———◆———

It is a paradox, the sea.

During this time of rumble and outrage, the North Atlantic, nonchalant, rolls on, set on creating at will. Within its swell are all the makings for good and evil, encompassing every possibility from the brightest of angels to the darkest of demons.

I cherish its angels.

For a time, the Atlantic bestowed blessings upon my son Kevin and his family, lulling them into a contented life on the Burin Peninsula. It continued that kindness, slipping its fingers onto the Argentia shore, summoning my unwed daughter Clara to the Burin. There Clara's dark secret—her unborn child—flourished within her and erupted from her into the arms of Kevin's wife who took the baby as one of her own. The sea obligingly ushered the shamed Clara back to Argentia, to the silence of her mother, me, locked in a dark room, to the sourness of her father, Alphonse, shell-shocked by a dark war.

Again displaying good grace, the ocean swept in a suitor for my fallen daughter. When Clara walked down the aisle toward Robert Caulins, the living me—the actual architect of this marriage—did not attend the event. Instead, I exiled Clara from my home. A stone-cold act. A necessary act. I had to liberate Clara from the grip of her abusive father. My gratitude for the solution from the sea was boundless. Then. But there's no such thing as getting too comfortable with the kindness of the sea.

I recoil from its demons.

The Atlantic upends vessels, revelling in the groans of seams ripped from wood like ligament from bone, rejoicing at the wails of seamen doomed to a watery grave. On days like these, the ocean carves fine lines on human faces, ridges permanently etched on widows who have spent their whole lives in vigilance.

Offshore malice alone does not satisfy the Atlantic. The ocean begets monster waves like the green tidal wall that swooped onto the shore of the Burin Peninsula and swallowed Kevin's family, belching back one child, the very one that Clara had birthed, the one that Kevin believed was his own. This same ocean allowed for the death of my son Jimmy at the hands of my husband. Was the Atlantic good, perhaps repentant, when it slid in to act as my accomplice in the murder of that husband?

A paradox indeed, the sea. Does it move with intention? Does it act on a whim?

I think both.

Time slips forward and I find myself sitting in a bubble of rain outside the Majestic Theatre in St. John's, the meeting point for those attending a planned, peaceful demonstration. Indeed, it starts peacefully enough. From the Majestic Theatre, protestors form a procession and inch their way through the streets of St. John's: New Gower Street to Queen Street to Water Street to Prescott Street to Duckworth Street to Cochrane Street to Military Road to the final destination, the Colonial Building.

On the periphery of this procession, I see a familiar figure, my daughter, Clara, and I settle into this scene like a penny into a pocket. Why is she in this soggy crowd, threading her way through clusters of dissenters and beggars and urchins? Why is she not luxuriating at the Newfoundland Hotel? I lean in as she lends an ear to the voices of merchants who gather in batches on corners to rail against Prime Minister Richard Squires and his cronies. The men clear their throats in a chorus of coughs and then start flapping their jaws. Clara is wide-eyed as the gist of their conversation reaches her.

"Had enough of Squires stealing from the pockets of the people. I hope they lynch him."

"Get enough liquor into this crowd and they might do just that."

"That would take a lot of rum."

"A lot of rum is what we've got." The men break into guffaws.

With a shrug of distaste, Clara scurries past. She moves into the heart of the crowd where she meets up with a man. Not her husband, this man. A stranger. But the smile she gives him is one of intimacy. This is obviously a tryst. And what better place? The unruly mob provides stealth, an opportunity to hide in plain sight. I sense a familiarity about this stranger but if there is memory there, I cannot summon it.

A soaring rum bottle elicits a roar from the crowd. I move a breath or two back while a man in a black serge overcoat and black felt fedora rushes toward the flying flask, hands raised. The crowd lurches, tossing Clara about. She looks up, catches sight of the airborne bottle and then of the face of the man who is grabbing at it. The startled look on Clara's face is one of recognition. The man is her parish priest, Father Mahony.

Am I cruel to long for the entertainment of an encounter between my daughter and her priest? Clara, ensconced in secrets, will try to avoid him. A useless endeavour, her attempt to manipulate fate.

When the projectile reaches its apogee, people scatter like startled pigeons. The priest doesn't catch the missile but does manage to snatch one small, unaware boy out of its descending path. The bottle hits the ground, shattering on a stone, and shards of glass fly like shrapnel. Drops of golden liquid burst forth, adding a mist of colour to the driving rain. The air is rank with the odour of rum. An anxious mother jumps forward, reclaims her child from the grip of the priest, and melts back into the mob, all the while scolding the boy.

Father Mahony blinks and then refocuses on the crowd, his eyes darting this way and that. He starts off in one direction, is blocked, and goes in another. He stumbles over a discarded liquor crate which he then upends and stands on. He is searching, his intent clear by the side-to-side motion of his head. When his head jerks to a stop, I know he has spotted my Clara.

The priest abandons his perch. I soar over the group and spot him scrambling to the top of a knoll. Using his hand as a visor, he again scans the crowd. While he is seeking Clara, she is watching him. When their eyes meet, she clamps her hand over her mouth.

Intriguing, this. My Clara, caught contemplating adultery, is wedged in a mob. Just how will she extricate herself?

Father Mahony widens his eyes and then narrows them to slits. I'm sure he is wondering what Clara, a member of his parish, a married woman, a slip of the thing, is doing in the midst of this mayhem, talking to a strange man who is not her husband.

The crowd sways. The air writhes. The flushed face of Father Mahony is slippery with sweat. He re-enters the throng and is jostled about. Keeping an eye on Clara, he edges his way toward her. Partway along, she meets his gaze for an instant. She whispers into the ear of her companion who immediately disappears into the crowd.

The wind teases the wide brim of Clara's blue felt hat, but it holds firm. She raises one hand to tuck in wayward coils of hair, then stands tall, aloof. She turns away from the priest, no doubt hoping to dissuade him from approaching. I wonder what on earth she is thinking. When, if ever, has that priest been deterred by gestures of dismissal?

True to form, Father Mahony moves closer, extends his hand, and touches Clara's shoulder.

She swerves. "Father!" She raises her hand to her mouth.

Would that I could roll my eyes. The likes of her. A guilty woman, caught, feigning innocence.

"What on earth are you doing here, Father?" Clara glances nervously about. Lowering her hand, she takes a deep breath. "I mean, it's such a surprise to see you."

"Likewise, my child. This is not a safe place, Clara." The wind, the rain, and the racket drown his words. He places a hand on Clara's arm and motions for her to follow him. He leads her past the edge of the crowd to an alcove in front of a clothing shop. "As I was saying, Clara, it's not safe here." Leaning in, the priest jabs a finger at her. "Where is your husband?"

"Robert? He is at the hotel, Father. I was just out for a stroll and I came upon this. I'm beside myself with the fear and the smell." Clara fans her face with her gloved hand. Amusing. Perhaps my daughter should vie for a career on the stage.

"You should return to the hotel until things settle," says the priest. "I'm sure that this situation will resolve itself peacefully," he adds, his eyes streaking with the lie. There will be no peace on this day. The priest knows it and so do I.

Sod caps tilt backwards as their wearers imbibe rum from bottles that are passed through the crowd. When a deafening howl rises from the front, the people at the back push forward. Father Mahony turns toward the ruckus, an inattentive moment during which Clara slips away. Would that I could follow but my plot is set in stone. I sail along with the priest. With his arms straight out in front of him, Father Mahony attempts to plough his way through the mob.

No doubt it is the stench of booze that causes his nostrils to curl. Soon his arms are curled as well for elbows are needed as he is jostled about like an empty dory in a stormy ocean. Horses snort, panicking, as their riders—police officers—gallop the periphery, trying to prevent people from climbing the steps of the Colonial Building whose elegant façade of white Irish limestone, Ionic columns and stone steps sit in jagged contrast to the ragged horde stuck in the muck and drizzle. Police on foot are wildly slapping batons, hitting indiscriminate targets. The mob batters the building, hurling sticks and stones, any projectile they can lay hands on, shattering pane after pane of glass that has shepherded the sunlight into the Colonial Building for decades.

A horde rushes up the steps, penetrating the doors with a crude battering ram. They storm forward, unstoppable now, swarming like ants on a mission. Seconds later desks, chairs, books, and papers fly through the doors. An upright grand piano sails out and slams its way down the steps, parting a sea of irate people. The crowd pauses, collectively startled. During this break in the forward rush, Father Aloysius Mahony scuttles up the steps. Behind him the crowd thunders and surges, a giant wave bent on annihilation.

Father Mahony does not look back. Inside the building, he faces more steps, a central staircase, and continues to climb. Clinging to the banister, occasionally looping fingers into iron railings, he makes his way up the stairs to the chambers of the Prime Minister. He pounds on the door which opens a slit. A hand reaches out, pulls him inside, and the door is slammed and locked behind him.

Panting, Father Mahony looks around. Prime Minister Richard Squires is there as are some cabinet ministers. Who is that chatty, skinny man, yapping like a crackie, fedora clamped on his head? This question is answered when someone addresses the undernourished bag of bones as Smallwood. There are other men, maybe twenty or so, all clergy, Catholic and Protestant alike. All, including Squires and his men, are dressed in black.

"The mob won't hurt the clergy," one minister says. "If we make a protective ring around the Prime Minister, we can get him to the motorcar. If that doesn't work, we'll get him into a neighbourhood house. No time to waste! Let's go."

The clergy forms a tight circle around Squires. Father Mahony, being closest to the exit, opens the door on cue, and they all pound through it, down the stairs, to the outside. The motorcar awaits.

"There goes Squires now," someone yells. "Lynch him!"

With that, the alternate plan comes into play. Some clergymen hold back the crowd while a small group, Father Mahony included, runs with Squires in tow. They bang on the door of a house on Colonial Street. The door flies open. They rush inside and slam it, a mob on their heels. Father Mahony grabs Squires and pulls him through the back door to Bannerman Street and pushes him into a taxi. The priest stands, watching, as the taxi speeds off. He places a hand on his chest and takes deep breaths. "What am I doing, ensuring the safety of a scoundrel politician?" Shuddering, he wipes his hands on his coat and starts to turn but something catches his attention. He comes to a standstill. What is he looking at?

I glance in the direction of his stare and catch sight of Clara's blue hat. Mrs. Clara Caulins is entering Bannerman Park. A concerned frown flickers across the priest's face and this I understand. Darkness is encroaching and a multitude of angry drunkards are just yards away. What on earth is Clara doing? Why is she here? Would that I could ask her myself.

Father Mahony takes after her, my shadow resting on his shoulders. As he scurries along, the cries of the mob fade until there are no sounds but the rustle of leaves and the steady fall of footsteps, his and Clara's. He slows his pace. When she slips behind a grove of trees, he speeds up again. He is just a yard or two away from the grove when she giggles. On the heels of that giggle comes a man's voice. Father Mahony stops. In the dead of night he lets out a silent sigh. I guess he could march into the centre of Clara's shenanigans and shame her in the name of God and the Church. Perhaps if I had a riding crop, I could urge the good priest onward. But he apparently has nothing of the kind in mind. He makes the sign of the cross and leaves.

Father Mahony's departure marks the end of my sojourn here. As I slip away into some nebulous cloud, I wonder if Father Mahony assumes that Clara will visit him in the confessional. Perhaps she will. Will he absolve her of adultery in exchange for a rosary? Maybe it will take a few rosaries to wipe that slate clean. That's the way it works, isn't it? A trip to the confessional to eradicate conscious acts of sin?

It strikes me as amusing that, for the lack of a *mea culpa*, I am doomed to this penance: watching, telling, repeating.

CLARA

CHAPTER 5

—◆—

THE INSTANT THE ROAR OF the crowd seized Father Mahony's attention, Clara bolted. She couldn't resist giggling as she wove a path through the drunken masses. It had been no trouble at all, escaping Father Mahony's scrutiny.

"I'll meet you in Bannerman Park," she had whispered to Patrick earlier and then shooed him away. With that, he was gone. Other men might stiffen at the mere idea of a woman giving directions. Not Patrick. If that man had a smidge of ego he didn't show it, not now, not ever. Convenient, at the moment, this lack on his part. It fleetingly occurred to Clara that Patrick had slipped away without a drop of concern for her safety. Not the gentlemanly thing to do. But how could she hold that against him? She detested the idea of any man hovering, treating her as if she couldn't handle things on her own. She couldn't have it both ways, now could she?

As Clara approached Bannerman Park, she questioned her own independent nature. Was she beyond bold or just plain stupid? There were pods of inebriated young men about, staggering, screaming, smashing bottles. At one point, she was certain she was being followed, but she convinced herself that she had been listening to too many of her mother's stories of fairies and ghosts and banshees and she kept on.

She had met Patrick in Bannerman Park before and hurried to their predetermined rendezvous, a copse of birch trees.

"Over here, Clara." Patrick emerged, a shadow.

When he reached for her, she responded with a snicker.

Patrick put a finger to his lips. "Shh. People might hear you."

"People might hear me? Over this ruckus? What people?" she said. He backed her into the trunk of a tree, its crisp, papery bark crackling in resistance. He pressed himself against her, locking his mouth on hers. She emerged from the kiss, breasts heaving. She placed a hand on Patrick's chest. "What people?"

He leaned in again.

Clara shook her head.

"Doesn't matter. We're not staying." Patrick grabbed her hand. They ran across the park, away from the clamour of demonstrators and drunkards.

"Where are we going?"

Patrick did not answer. Still gripping Clara's hand, he slowed and came to a full stop in front of a dark, narrow house.

Clara cast her glance from the bottom to the top. The house was tall, very tall, with a sloping mansard roof and dormer windows on the second, no, on the third floor. Three floors? Why would anyone need three floors?

Patrick began moving again, heading up the pathway and around the back to the basement door. He turned the knob. Clara followed him inside. Patrick pulled Clara into his arms and closed the door behind them. Despite the dimness of the interior, he made no effort to search for a light.

"Where are we? Who owns this place?" Clara asked.

"It doesn't matter. There's no one home."

"How do you know?"

"The owners are out, protecting the Prime Minister. They won't be back. These are the servants' quarters."

"Servants? How on earth can people afford servants?"

"Many can't. But these houses were built with servants' quarters regardless. A relic from the Victorian era. The British aristocracy would be lost without servants' quarters."

"But aren't we trespassing?"

"Not likely. I live here."

Clara took a step back. "You? In servants' quarters?"

Patrick shrugged. "Rum running has risk. Vessels get seized. Money dissipates. This is a way to get by until the wind changes."

"So you work for these people?"

"Chauffeur." He doffed an imaginary cap and offered a sweeping bow. "At your service, madam." He opened his arms wide.

Clara paused. Did it matter to her how he made a living? No answer came to her, nothing at all. Shrugging, she slipped into his arms and slid with him to the floor.

Two hours later, Clara and Patrick crept back across Bannerman Park. An eerie silence surrounded them. The riot was over, the rioters gone. But the remnants? The park was strewn with glass and boards and bottles and pieces of a piano that had had all the music beaten out of it. Clara bumped her shoe against a section of soundboard which uttered a dying twang. She sighed her way past it, treading carefully the rest of the way.

When they reached a relatively safe street within view of Clara's lodgings, Clara went ahead alone. She opened the door of the Newfoundland Hotel and looked back just in time to catch a glimpse of Patrick as he slid into the night. A sense of loss cropped up but she didn't dwell on it. It was time to change her focus to Robert.

Clara's head was buzzing with lies to tell her husband: *I got caught up in the riot. I took refuge in a church.* Feigning breathlessness, she entered their suite. "Robert?" She looked around. "Robert?"

No sign of him. Her smile turned to a chuckle as she wiggled out of her clothes and into her nightgown. Abandoning her night-time bath in favour of a sprinkle, she dove for the bed. Body curled, eyes tight, she sighed into sleep.

CHAPTER 6

———◆———

THE FOGHORN WAILED ITS MORNING warning, and the grey menace crept in, first fingering, and then masking the windows of the Newfoundland Hotel. With the view of the harbour obliterated, Clara wrapped her hands around the comfort of her coffee cup and eyed her husband, all the while remembering her encounter with Patrick. His lust, her lust, and the explosive gift of release bestowed by Patrick, his attentive hands, lips, and tongue. Her thoughts triggered pleasure and she shivered.

"Clara?"

Clara gave a start and felt her face redden. Dear Jesus. Was Robert reading her mind? Sitting on the chesterfield, shaking his head, he was staring at the words above the fold on the front page of *The Daily News*. "Have you seen this?" He waved the paper at her, creating a ripple of air that sent the steam from her coffee wafting into her face.

Clara, grinning inwardly, took a deep breath, inhaling the aroma of coffee. She took a cautious step forward and read the headline aloud, "Premier Escapes Wrath Mob through Protection of Clergy."

An image of Father Mahony jumped into her mind. Hadn't he said something about helping the Prime Minister? Was he involved in the escape plan? "A terrible thing," she said and then bit down on her tongue.

"Terrible is an understatement." Robert continued to peruse the article aloud, flinging details like the wind tosses leaves. "Windows smashed, stoves flung, a piano heaved down the steps. Ten thousand in damages. They did all but swing from the gas chandeliers. At least those weren't destroyed." He hesitated. He looked at her, his face as veiled as the fogged window. He cleared his throat. "All because people don't know their place."

The hair on the back of Clara's neck prickled. "What do you mean, don't know their place?"

"The system is working fine. People should leave well enough alone."

"There's nothing fine about people in poverty." Her fingers whitened around her cup, the rippling coffee a match for the tremor inside her. "You've seen with your own two eyes what life is like for people in outport communities. Women and children in rags and starving. We should be helping them."

"Why on earth should we do that? Giving underlings help or money is tantamount to giving them ideas. There's no need for them to get above themselves." Robert sniffed. His body stiffened.

Clara blinked. Underlings. Did he mean what he was saying? She squinted her eyes, scrutinizing, waiting, but he offered no retraction. His words endured, rigid as his posture.

So strange, this behaviour from her husband whom she knew to be kind. Not at all content to accept what he was saying, Clara moved closer. "Robert," she said, her voice tender, "it's not like you to light into the poor like that. Is there something you want to talk about?" She touched his arm.

"There's no excuse for mob behaviour. There's always a way to make a living." Robert brushed her hand away.

Stung, Clara stepped back. "You mean by breaking the law? The way you do?"

Robert smiled. "You mean the way *we* do. Be careful there, sailor, or I'll have no choice but to take you off the payroll." He shook his newspaper to straighten the fold. "Should have had housekeeping iron this paper," he said as he turned the page and buried his head.

Silenced and distanced, Clara returned to the window and stared into the fog. A memory arose through the grey, a recent event at the hotel. Robert and his rum-running comrades were grouped and cackling like gulls on a rock, congratulating themselves on padding their wallets. How would they feel if Prohibition were repealed? "Rum running won't last forever," she said, more to herself than to him.

"Probably a good thing." Robert spoke without raising his head from the paper. "It's time I started thinking about going home to England."

"England?" Clara asked.

No response.

Clara did not ask again. It was worth noting that he had just said "I", not "we." Clearly he had no plans to take her with him. Was he trying to push her away? More importantly, did she care? She searched her soul. With him, she had a good life, a moneyed life. Could she manage without him? She almost laughed out loud. Of course she could. But what would her husband do, not about her or his marriage to her, but about his precious schooner? Sail it to England? Not likely. Sell it to locals? Not if she had anything to do with it.

The fog on the window developed shape now, the shape of a woman at the helm of a schooner. Captain Clara Kerrigan Caulins.

Clara turned slowly toward her husband who was still lost in the newspaper. She had convinced this reluctant man to allow her aboard his schooner and had since become a well-respected member of his crew.

Would Robert leave her and return to England? She shrugged. Would he teach her to navigate the schooner? She nodded.

KEVIN

CHAPTER 7

———◆———

KEVIN'S SLEEP HAD BEEN FITFUL, filled with images of Mavis and his children in the graveyard far away. He awoke at first light, a decision locked in. He was going to visit the Burin. Not a whim or a want, this idea. It was a need. He felt compelled to face his losses. Yes, he was going to the Burin. But how was he going to tell Kate?

Kevin crawled out of bed, stumbled into his trousers, and pulled up the suspenders, snapping them into place. Running a hand over his stubble of a beard, he headed for the washstand, then sidestepped it. Shaving could wait. He went to Kate's room, where the door was ajar. He nudged it. The well-oiled hinges offered no resistance and the door swung wide. Kevin stared at Kate, deep in sleep, her hair tousled, her tiny frame buried in a rose-covered quilt. He edged forward to the foot of her bed and sat. How was he going to tell his fragile six-year-old that he was going to the Burin without her?

Kate stirred.

Kevin braced himself.

Kate rolled over, grabbed onto her Mrs. Fan doll, and exhaled deeply. She did not open her eyes.

Kevin waited, not moving a muscle. Daylight crept through a crack in the curtains and streaked its way across the top of the bed. Still, he waited. The crow of a rooster reinforced the arrival of morning. Still no further movement from Kate. Looked like it would be shave first, talk later. With a heavy sigh, Kevin headed for the door.

"When are you going away, Daddy?"

As the words dropped, Kevin stopped, motionless as a moored boat on a glass sea. Had he heard right? Should he ask her to repeat it? He tried to ask but couldn't form the words.

"You don't have to stay here on account of me," continued Kate.

Kevin managed a slow turn.

"Mommy dreamed it to me."

"Mommy?" The word jolted Kevin and he asked, "Exactly what did Mommy dream to you?"

"When are you going, Daddy?"

"What did Mommy—?"

"It's okay, Daddy."

"What's okay?"

"It's okay for you to go."

"Go where?"

"Back to the old house. Back to visit Mommy."

"Oh." Kevin paused, giving himself time to absorb Kate's words, time to choose his own words carefully. He himself had been in the presence of the spirit of Mavis and he was all the better for it. Heaven forbid he utter anything now that made light of his daughter's dream. Kevin focused on Kate's brown eyes that were clear and true and waiting for him to respond. He leaned in. "You don't want to go with me, Katie girl?" he whispered.

"Uh uh. Like I told you, Mommy dreamed it to me. You go and see the people and the house and the garden with the little white crosses. I'm staying here with Mrs. Dulcie and Nanny. Aunt Clara too when she comes off the schooner."

"I'll be back from Burin before Aunt Clara comes home."

"I know." Kate yawned, and curled up, hugging Mrs. Fan to her chest. "I'm still sleepy."

"You go back to sleep. I'll call you for breakfast." Kevin tucked her in, a sense of ease flooding him, body and soul. He smiled. Were all men oblivious or was it just him? He had been shaken by the mere idea of revealing news of his pending departure, thinking that Kate would be beside herself with the fright of it. He had planned to comfort her, to reassure her.

Turned out that she, this tiny girl-child, had reassured him.

CHAPTER 8

A COUPLE OF DAYS BEFORE Kevin was scheduled to take the coastal boat to the Burin Peninsula, he hiked his way to the silver mine. Good timing for sleuthing. Rumrunner Clara was at sea and six-year-old Kate was keeping Nanny company. Kate's words, not his. He grinned at the thought.

As he scuffed along and skirted potholes, Kevin remembered the day he had trailed Clara to the mine. He had stopped her just inside the entrance. An error in hindsight, his not waiting until she revealed her hiding place. What was she doing there that day? Couldn't have been dropping off anything. She was carrying nothing other than an oil lantern. Had she gone to check on her treasures? To pick up something? He had no clue. But he did recall one thing she said: she wasn't going that far in.

He arrived just after sunup, light crawling into the mine opening, water dripping down its notched walls. He trod carefully, stepping over tracks and ties and bits of metal. There wasn't as much rubble as last time. Had someone been picking up scrap? For what purpose? It was common knowledge that rumrunners had used this place to store booze. Was there any evidence left? Not much. No broken crates or burlap sacks. A smattering of sawdust here and there, that was all. Thieves definitely had had the run of the place. No wonder the rumrunners had abandoned the use of the mine. Perhaps Clara had abandoned it too. Perhaps she had already taken whatever she had been hiding. He shrugged and went on with the task, inspecting the wet wall, holding his oil lamp up to the seams, using his other hand to poke and pry. When he reached a tall barricade of dirt and rock, one that blocked forward motion, he crossed in front of it to the other side. Another wall to explore. He was working his way back to the opening now. Would he find the hiding place on this side? Had he already missed it? Would it be high or low? If Clara had wanted to remain unseen, she would likely bend, not reach. He focused on the lower part of the wall, which was mostly rock. He ran his hand across it until he found a loose stone. Carefully, lest it trigger a slide, he extracted it. Sure enough, there was something behind it. A leather case.

Treasure in hand, Kevin made his way to the entrance. He sat on a boulder, opened the case, and pulled out two packets. One contained money. He put that back. Not his money. Not his business. That was rum-running money and Clara probably put it here to keep it out of the hands of the authorities. They could raid her house. An unlikely event, but not unheard of in the rum-running world. He opened the second pack. In that, he found a bundle of letters tied by a wide ribbon. The ribbon looked familiar, the black colour, the ribbed texture. An image of Mavis' sewing box cropped up. He dismissed it, returning his attention to the letters in his hand. So many letters. He removed the ribbon and fanned through them. All the envelopes were addressed in cursive writing, circles and curlicues that triggered disappointment. Kevin couldn't read cursive writing. The only thing he could do was recognize names and Clara's name was front and centre on every envelope. In the upper left-hand corner was another name he recognized: Mavis. Kevin trembled. His Mavis had written these letters. He clutched the envelopes tightly, attempting to squeeze out some semblance of her. But nothing came. The only sense of her would be in the words she wrote and he couldn't read them. He stared at the envelopes through tears of frustration.

Kevin had never regretted his lack of schooling; a man could get by without it. But now? He was desperate to decipher these letters. He slid the first one from the bundle and opened it. He could read the date: 1921. An old letter, written to Clara when she was just a girl.

Mavis had read Clara's letters aloud to him around this time. Kevin smiled at the memory of Mavis taking the letters from her sewing basket.

At first, he hadn't wanted her to read them at all. He had stood rigid in the kitchen, ready to break into a run. Mavis had emptied everything from her sewing basket and placed the items on the table. He saw those items in his mind now, the needles, the colourful spools of thread, the travel sewing kit that she had brought from Boston. At the time, the items were a blur, but now he remembered clearly the tiny gold-plated oval sewing box with the hinged lid and the pink floral design on top, a gift from Mavis' employer when they were leaving Boston. He had scooped up a stray reel of thread while Mavis removed the black ribbon that bound those letters. A black ribbon just like the one that held Clara's bundle of letters together. What had Mavis called that ribbon? A grosgrain ribbon?

He dismissed the memory as he folded the first letter and returned it to its place. Moving to the bottom of the pile, he removed another. Once again, the writing confounded him, but this one was written in 1926, perhaps while Kevin was away in Boston after he had lost his dory to the sea, or perhaps while he was on the sealing ship. This one had no postmark at all. That was odd. How did Clara get a letter that had no postmark? He shrugged. The post office must have made a mistake. There were several letters after that, the last one mailed in November of 1929, just before the tidal wave. The date surprised him. Mavis was writing letters to Clara right up to the time of the tidal wave? Why hadn't Mavis told him about these letters?

Kevin wanted more information but there was none to be had, not here, not unless he could read what he was holding in his hands. He pictured Dulcie teaching Kate to print and to read and his mother filling Kate's ears with stories. Maybe he should pay more attention, learn to read and write himself. How could he do that? It would be embarrassing as hell to have to ask for help with such basic matters. But maybe he could avoid learning entirely. Perhaps he could get someone to read the letters to him? Was there anyone he could ask, anyone he could trust?

What about Robert? Kevin shook his head. He couldn't ask Robert for help deciphering letters that Clara clearly wanted kept secret.

What about his mother? No. Kathleen would never betray Clara.

What about . . . No, there was no one else in Argentia. Tongues would wag. He shifted his attention to his upcoming trip.

What about on the Burin? It was possible someone there would read these letters to him. The Burin. That was it. Not likely that Tom Murphy, his old friend, could read. But Tom's wife? Different matter entirely. Kevin set his lantern down, fanned the letters out, and then counted them. Twenty-five. Would Tom's wife read them? Kevin could be gone to the Burin and back before Clara sailed into Argentia.

Should he take these letters with him on his journey?

CHAPTER 9

As THE COASTAL BOAT SCUDDED along the shores of the Burin Peninsula, Kevin stood on deck, eyeing every cove and inlet. There was no denying what had happened here, not with the evidence coming at him in chunks. Many stages and wharves and houses were new, replaced with aid from the South Coast Disaster Committee. Many holes gaped where old stages and wharves and houses had stood. No hint of renewal. Were the people waiting for money? Surely be to God they had none. All their savings had been stashed in mattresses which the sea had stolen from under them. Perhaps people had just lost all hope. Kevin knew firsthand the depth of their grief. His loved ones were numbered among the dead—twenty-seven, twenty-eight, perhaps twenty-nine souls lost, depending on who you listened to. There was death for the cod fishery, too, with no sign of rebirth for three years. And now the whole world was in trouble. Depression everywhere.

The bitterness of it all broke into his thoughts dredging up buried memories of him legging it along the landwash, struggling to get home amid the wreckage. Kevin let the jagged images run until the fetid stench and dizzying dread from that day filtered into the present like it belonged. He crimped his nose and closed his eyes, willing it all away, breathing it all away. When images faded to black, he turned his back on the shoreline and looked at it no more until the boat docked at the government wharf in Burin. Then he began the walk to his former community.

The church was still there, clinging to its rock base, towering over every scurrying thing, pointing at an endless sky. Beyond the church, around a bend on a rise on the other side of the road, was Tom Murphy's house. its chimney sending up a welcoming curl of grey smoke. Eagerness claimed Kevin's step as he marched up the dirt path to the back door. He lifted the latch and poked his head in. "Anybody home?" he called.

"Come in. Come in." Tom Murphy's wife, a voice that set Kevin right at ease. There was comfort in the familiar. "Be minding my clean floors, now," she added.

Kevin wiped his boots on the woven mat inside the porch door, adding a muddied streak to the red-and-white nap. The air was sweet with the smell of jam, perhaps rhubarb or strawberry or a mingling of the two. His mouth watered. A sudden clattering of a pot lid brought Mrs. Murphy's voice again, this time in the form of a plea to God and all the saints. Chuckling, Kevin stepped into the kitchen where a spitting cauldron was oozing pink foam onto a hot stove. Tom Murphy's missus, potholder in hand, removed the cauldron's dancing lid and stuck a long wooden spoon into the pot. Stirring vigorously, she turned her head, not all the way around, just enough to get her words out. "Ye'll have to hold onto yer horses, whoever ye are."

In silence, Kevin waited. Mrs. Murphy was grey-haired now, unruly strands sprouting from her topknot. She was as plump as ever, her black dress straining to hold her in, her apron strings dangling at her sides destined never to meet. He watched as she withdrew the spoon from the jam, set it aside, and replaced the pot lid, angling it against future outbursts. "Well, jam or no jam, that pot will be spotless by the time the rhubarb's done boiling its innards." She stepped back from her labour, taking time to gander past the bottom of her black dress to her stockings that were rolled down to her ankles. With a shrug and a sigh, she swung around. At the sight of him she stopped. "Dear Father in heaven. It's the lamb to his home." She shot him a grin.

"Good to see you, Mrs. Murphy."

"Never mind the Mrs. Murphy now at all." She grabbed the bottom edge of her apron and dabbed at the beads of sweat on her forehead. "It's Mary-Tom, sure you knows that as well as you're standing there."

Kevin smiled, remembering. It was Mary-Tom, not to be confused with the other Mrs. Mary Murphy married to Tom's brother, John. Mary-Tom and Mary-John. "I don't think I ever thanked you proper for what you did for me and Kate."

"No thanks is needed, my love. How is the little one, your Kate? Did you bring her along?"

Kevin shook his head. "Someday. Maybe. But I had to come back myself. Trying to make some sense of things, I suppose."

Mary-Tom's eyes glistened, the kindness in them bridging distance and time. "But she's doing okay? Kate?"

"Kate's the finest kind. Her grandmother and Mrs. Dulcie Mullins take good care of her when I'm not around."

"And your sister too, I'm sure."

"Yes, Clara too," Kevin said, his insides suddenly prickling like a caution. He didn't know what that was about but, whatever it was, it sparked a question, one which he dropped flat into the conversation. "When did I tell you about my sister?"

"Never did." Mary-Tom's answer was quick. "But your Mavis. Now that was another matter entirely. We nattered on a lot, me and your Mavis, God rest her soul." She made the sign of the cross and Kevin mirrored it. "It was Mavis who told me about your sister in Argentia."

Opportunity was right in front of Kevin now and he had no intention of letting it slide past. "Did Mavis ever tell you about letters she got from Clara?" He put his hand deep into his coat pocket and fingered the letters.

"Oh yes. Kept them in her sewing basket, if I remembers correctly. I'd stop by for a mug up or she would show up at me door and bring them along."

"What was in the letters?"

"Nothing much. The usual stuff about the family."

The usual stuff. No harm in bringing the letters into view. Kevin tugged at them. As envelopes peeked around the edge of his coat, Mary-Tom jumped back, bumping into the stove, too close to the cauldron.

"Careful there, miss_us," said Kevin, knowing he'd triggered something, not knowing what.

Mary-Tom rubbed her hands down the sides of her dress, missing the apron entirely, perhaps forgetting she was wearing one. "Sure, you'd think I'd be knowing my way around my own kitchen." She fiddled with a delinquent strand of hair, poking it behind her ear. "Tom'll be some glad to see you. He should be back any minute. Where's my manners at all? You showing up to the house after all this time and not being offered as much as a cup of tea. You must be half-starved. I got leftovers for supper and I'll be fixing you some of that." She busied herself at the table, grabbing a fistful of mottled red-and-green rhubarb stalks and tossing them to one side. She scurried into the pantry and then back to the stove where she slid the cauldron to a back burner.

The kitchen door flew open.

"Tom, you're home." Mary-Tom let out a relieved laugh and pointed a jam-stained finger at Kevin. "Will you look what the cat dragged in?" She disappeared into the pantry.

Kevin slid the letters back into his pocket as he stepped up to greet his old friend. He looked into Tom's face which, as far as Kevin could fathom, hadn't changed. Fine lines set like those in boulders. Indelible. He shook Tom's stump of a hand without a thought or a glance. Even with the trials the world had dumped upon Tom Murphy, there was sturdiness in that handshake. The man was rooted in the soil and the sea.

"Yer lookin' good, Tom,' Kevin said.

"How are ya gettin' on?" Tom tilted his head.

Kevin sensed an answer of sorts form inside him. On the edge of something, didn't know what. He shrugged. "I've a like to say I'm the finest kind but I'll be telling you no stories. I'm walking and talking, b'y, walking and talking."

Tom thumped a hand on Kevin's shoulder. "Let's you and me go to the storeroom out back. Odds and sods to see."

"We're off to the storeroom," he called to his wife who was still in the pantry. "Then to the merchant's. Be back in time for supper."

"Takin' your flask, are ya?" she called back.

"No flies on you, Missus." Tom guffawed his way to the door. Kevin followed.

"Supper will be here and a bed will be ready for ya, Kevin, when me old fella brings you back," called Mary-Tom.

Kevin opened his mouth to protest but sighed it shut. He needed lodgings and the woman wouldn't take no for an answer. "Mighty good of ya."

Once outside, Tom produced the flask and took a swig. Kevin refused an offer.

They plodded to the back of Tom's house. Tom unfastened the storeroom latch and swung the door wide. "I salvaged what I could," he said. "Yours to take."

Kevin stepped inside, every nerve strung tight. Sunlight flooded in, giving life and form to dust motes and sawdust. He ran his eyes over each item in the neat pile on his right. All recognizable. Butter churn, galvanized tub, chipped dishes, sewing machine, twisted flatware, wrought-iron headboards and footboards, three-legged milking stool, rusted flat-iron, blackened kettle, corroded tools. Kevin blinked. "Yours to keep," he said.

"You might be wanting this." Tom plucked a small item from the shelf inside the door. He blew the dust off it.

Kevin opened his hand and Tom dropped in a tiny sewing kit. The very thing Kevin had recently been thinking about was now tumbling into his palm. Sighing, he put the sewing kit into his pocket. Perhaps he would give it to Kate. A memory of her mother.

Tom and Kevin headed down the hill to the road. A clear day this, sunshine poking from behind clouds. A breeze was picking up and dust devils were dancing along the side of the road, swirling, disappearing. Kevin remembered another day like this, the day he had returned from his stint as an ironworker in Boston. He'd been gnawing on the idea of staying home and fishing inshore then and had voiced his worries to Tom. A casual talk over a hand-rolled smoke, the upshot of which was that work rules a man.

On that day, Tom had been working on building a dory, the usual thing. Tom was always hammering or sanding. Today there was no sign of boat building. "Not making a dory?" Kevin asked.

"No."

"No need for it?"

"Built or repaired as many as I could after the tidal wave. Inshore fishing grounds are not yielding. A little now and then but not enough to hold a community. Will be a decade or more before it all comes back. Maybe the Lord will come up with something that offers work to the men. Meantime, those who has the heart for it has to go where the work is. Living is working. Working and living. Same thing."

Kevin could have finished those words for Tom. That was exactly what Tom had said to him long ago. "You ever get the sense that you should be working and living someplace else?" Kevin asked.

Tom shook his head. "Me sons had to go away to work. Want to give them a home to come back to as long as I can. You?"

"Something's nagging at me. Don't know what."

"Time and tide, b'y. You'll know soon enough."

When the merchant store appeared before them, Kevin looked up in surprise. Guess Tom really needed some things after all.

Kevin had come to hate merchant stores. In the merchant store in Argentia, he had learned about Clara being at sea, rum running. And, long before that, in this very Burin store, he had heard men groaning about the stock market crash in New York City and the poverty that the crash was going to bring to Newfoundlanders. Kevin had scoffed at those men, thinking they were stunned. How could the people of Newfoundland be harmed by the goings-on in New York City? Turned out he was the stunned one.

Now here he was, back at the Burin store. He eyed his surroundings warily. God only knew what was lurking here today.

Tom approached the counter, Kevin on his heels. Artemius Nolan's wife was there, head bent over a ledger, her jaw clenched and grinding. Except for a few silver threads in her hair, she was the same angular woman

Kevin remembered. She looked up. "Good day to ya, Tom. Now what can I be helping you with?" She glanced at Kevin and opened her eyes wide. "Sweet merciful heavens. It's Kevin Kerrigan. Never thought I'd see the likes of you again."

"Good day, Mrs. Nolan." Kevin doffed his cap.

"Mercedes. Call me Mercedes. A good day indeed. Let me get Artemius. He'll be wanting to set eyes on ya."

As she rushed off, Kevin attempted to thwart a grin but his amusement won out. Artemius Nolan? Wanting to see him? Must be a cold day in hell. Kevin looked at Tom, who merely folded his arms and shrugged. "Guess I'll be waiting on me tarpaper for a while," Tom said.

"Guess so." It struck Kevin that Tom should be grinning too. Where was the lighter side of Tom? Was it possible that Tom was after more than tarpaper? Kevin considered asking. He didn't.

It took a couple of minutes but, sure enough, Mercedes returned, husband in tow. Artemius wiped his hands on a rag dangling from his pocket and then extended a hand to Kevin. "Good to see you, son. Good to see you. And I want you to know that all debt has been erased. You don't have to worry about anything you might be owing to this merchant store."

Debt? Kevin hadn't given it a thought. He had run from Burin, barely alive, his soul as empty as his pockets. Nothing left but his daughter Kate.

As if reading his mind, Mercedes Nolan chimed in. "And Kate, the little one, Kate? How is she doing?"

"Best kind. Best kind." Kevin appreciated the interest in his daughter, but there was something else behind Mrs. Nolan's eyes, something he couldn't fathom. She locked her gaze onto him, staring until he squirmed with the need to get out from under it.

A jingle of the bell above the store door announced the entry of another customer. Mrs. Nolan elbowed her husband. "Artemius, you take care of the next one and I'll finish up here."

"Now, Mercedes," said Artemius, "You must be all in. Sure you been hard at it since the crack of dawn. Why don't you rest up a bit? I'll help Tom."

"Nonsense. Off with ya."

With a worn sigh, Artemius obeyed.

"What was it you wanted, Tom?" asked Mercedes, never taking her eyes off Kevin.

"Tarpaper, at least five yards of it," Tom said. "Me roof is needing some work."

"Got all the tar you need, do ya?" she asked.

Kevin shifted his weight from one foot to the other. Was there any rhyme or reason to Mercedes Nolan? She was intent on something and whatever it was, it was coming at him, and it was coming fast. Could he handle it at all?

"Don't need any tar," Tom said.

"Oh." Mercedes paused like she was making up her mind. It was abrupt, her turning full on Kevin. "A good woman, Mavis Kerrigan, God rest her soul," Mercedes said, her voice shrill, eager. "A remarkable woman. Raising that little Kate like she was one of her own." Mercedes stopped dead.

The words swirled around Kevin. He knew there was meaning in them, he even knew what that meaning was, but he couldn't let it in. A blow like that could stagger a man. Kevin leaned on the oak counter, grateful for its sturdiness. He couldn't look at Mercedes Nolan. Instead, he let his eyes travel along the ten-foot counter from the cash register to the weigh scales to the wrapping-paper roll dispenser to the cast-iron twine caddy. It was the spool of twine that snagged Kevin's attention.

He had once clipped some of that twine, carted it home, and used it to firm up a Christmas tree that was threatening to topple. He was living the memory now, whiffing the scent of pine, extending a tight strand of twine from the top of the tree beneath the tin-foil star to the top of the wall above the front-room window. The Christmas tree was out of choices after that. It had to stay put for the duration.

Kevin returned his gaze to Mercedes, to the streak of regret in her eyes. When she opened her mouth to speak, Tom spoke, cutting her off. "Don't need another thing this morning," he said.

Kevin took his hand off the store counter. He stepped back. Easy enough. No threat of toppling. "I'll be waiting outside, Tom," he said.

"Good enough, b'y. Good enough. Be right out."

Fresh air slapped Kevin and he welcomed it, breathing deep. His mind took over, travelling through all he knew and then searching, spinning off in all directions. He paced from the store doorstep to the store corner, back to the step and to the corner again. He stopped. He'd stay put and wait for Tom. That's what he'd do. Wait for Tom. He turned to face the ocean. He hated the ocean. He loved the goddamned ocean. He kicked at a stone that ricocheted off a wooden bucket and clunked back onto the ground right beside his boot. Kevin sniffed. No point in kicking stuff away if it was going to find its own way back. He'd just focus on the sea and the wind and waiting.

It was unexpected, the sound of voices coming at him from the side of the merchant store. Artemius and Mercedes. Kevin took a step to the right, just past the corner, out of view, but within earshot.

"Do you suppose he ever knew?" said Artemius.

The wind picked up. The bell above the store door clanged. The door slammed. And Tom was standing beside Kevin, a roll of tarpaper under his arm. "Good to go," he said.

Kevin placed a hand on Tom's arm. "Wait," he whispered.

The voices continued.

"Not a chance," said Mercedes. "Not with that look on his face. But he knows now, thanks to me and my big mouth. I should have listened to you, let you serve them. When I'm tired, I says things I shouldn't. What was I thinking? Sure Kate was born while Kevin was at sea. Nobody told him nothing. God forgive me."

"Don't be too hard on yourself, Mercedes. You're a good woman. You didn't mean no harm."

"I couldn't hold a candle to Mavis Kerrigan."

Kevin faltered. He withdrew the hand he had placed on Tom's arm and just stood there, staring at his friend. Tom offered no reaction, no surprise. Kevin knew the why of that right away. What was news to Kevin was no news to Tom. Kevin could see that in Tom Murphy's eyes, which were as clear as the light of a full moon. "Is that why you brought me here?"

Tom did not answer.

Kevin abruptly turned, kicking up dust as he sped along the road. Tom was right behind him. "You knew this?" Kevin said, spinning to face Tom.

"I knew, b'y, I knew. Struggled with the telling. Couldn't just drop it on you after the tidal wave. How the hell would you have gone on? Sure enough, I took you there today on purpose. Mercedes got a mouth on her, everyone knows that. I guess I figured whatever choices you make from here on should be sitting on truth."

Kevin turned, ready to march off again. This time it was Tom who reached out, latching on to Kevin's arm with two pincer-like fingers. "Before ya goes off half-cocked, think on this," Tom said. "Mavis was a fine and generous woman and that's what saved you, Kevin b'y. Saved you. You would have done yourself in if it hadn't been for Kate. Maybe Mavis knew what she was doing, taking in that baby. If Mavis didn't, then the good Lord did."

"Don't hold much to religion anymore, Tom."

"That may be so, but maybe the Lord needs you for a reason. And, like I said, Kate and your Mavis saved you. A loving God had a hand in this to be sure."

"God, my arse!" Kevin stormed away.

CHAPTER 10

———◆———

KEVIN STOOD IN FRONT OF the low-slung cemetery gate staring at a row of white crosses on the far side of the graveyard, one large cross, four small, all framed in by a stunted post-and-rail fence. The sleeping place of his family. They were waiting for him. He wasn't moving. He'd been here a while, stuck. Didn't know how long.

The open cemetery gate kicked into motion. Propelled by offshore wind, it slammed into its broken latch and fell back again, angled, creaking, taunting. Was he going in or what? His right foot started, retreated. With his cap clutched to his chest, he looked up from his dark dilemma into the afternoon sun. The sun remained steady. Kevin blinked. With a sigh, he stepped around the gate and trudged across the rolling slope through trampled grasses and spring buttercups. He heard a muttering of the rosary and turned to see a withered man leaning into a knobby cane and hovering over an unkempt grave. In hunched silence, Kevin moved on.

The five crosses, white-washed to a glare, were backed against one edge of the fence that bounded them, the edge that Kevin reached first. He paused, remembering the day he left Burin. That day the graves were individual, fresh mounds of moulded earth, giving off the damp smell of spring planting. Now all five graves lay beneath a carpet of young grass, the smell of fresh earth erased and replaced by that of salt air. So smooth was the plot's surface that Kevin would be hard-pressed to tell where one grave left off and the next began. It was the way a family should be, he supposed, united, their graves carefully tended. There was certainly no sign of neglect here, thanks to Tom Murphy. It was Tom who helped care for Kevin's family when they were alive. It was Tom who was caring for the family plot now. A good man, Tom Murphy.

Kevin sucked in a deep breath, just to make sure he could still do that, breathe. Nothing felt real, not the revelation by Mercedes Nolan, the confirmation by Tom, and certainly not the graves in front of him now. With a raised foot he nudged the low fence rail. Rock solid. He moved along the perimeter, brushing his trouser leg against the fence, keeping rail and reality close as he went to the opposite side where he stopped and stared at the names of his five loves lost. The sun coming up and going down for nearly three years and him still missing them. What was it Tom said? That God had a hand in this? That explanation didn't sit with Kevin. Sure enough, the Catholic in him knew the Catechism. Like everyone else, he had scraped and splintered his knees on wooden kneelers, praying to the God who had given up His Own Son, His Only Son, for the good of all mankind. It was not the Catholic in Kevin but the father in him who was having none of this. The father in Kevin would not have sacrificed one child. Not one. Never mind four. What kind of God would do such a thing? Was Kevin himself a better father than God? And how far gone was he at all that he was challenging the doings of the Lord God Almighty? Did it even matter? He wasn't putting a stop to his thoughts, not with the graves firm in front of him and no sign of God anywhere. If that Almighty God were to show Himself, Kevin would have at Him. No doubt about it. He'd tear the face off any so-called caring God who had ripped away most of his family. And, if Mercedes spoke the truth, if Kate was not Kevin's daughter, then the loving God that Tom had spoken of had taken not most, but *all* of Kevin's family, all of them, every single one. Yes, Kevin Kerrigan himself should have been God. If he were God, he would have done better. If he were God, if he were God, if he were God . . .

But he wasn't God, now was he? He was just a man or what was left of one, back rounded, hands on knees, lungs wheezing while the remnants of his anger receded into the wind. His blasphemy was spent now, gone. Everything gone but the fear, the underlying and ingrained fear of retribution. *God'll get you fer that, my son.* Perhaps it wouldn't be God who'd be showing up here, but Satan himself with hell on his heels. Kevin slowly straightened his back. He caught himself looking all around. The only movement was that of the old man who had been praying the rosary and was now shuffling his way out of the cemetery. Certainly not a devil, that one. But if the Devil had presented himself, what would it matter? Could hell be any worse than this?

Kevin stepped over the low rail. He focused on the large cross in the centre of the row, Mavis' cross, and dropped to his knees at the foot of her grave. "What did you do, Mavis? Took in a child and never said a word? Where's the reason in that? What have you got to say for yourself?"

The wind whipped through the graveyard but whispered no answers.

"Tom was right, I suppose. I would have done myself in if not for Kate. A man's got to have a purpose. What do I do now, Mavis Kerrigan?"

Still nothing.

"Are you after hearing me at all, Mavis?"

The silence kept on.

Emptied of questions, Kevin stared blankly at the cross. He'd always leaned on Mavis. Life, death, made no never mind. But she had no answers for him now. The only answer he got here in Burin, one that he didn't expect and didn't want, came from Mercedes Nolan. With a groan, he rose and made his way toward the markers of his children—Jimmy, Marie, Joseph, Johnny. At each gentle touch on a little white cross, a jagged ache ripped through him. The last cross he touched was that of Mavis. No ache this time. Just the wondering. Why had she lied to him? And more than that, should he chase the lie? Should he let it sit?

Kevin dragged himself away from the graves and out of the graveyard. Then he began the trek toward his saltbox house. On the way, he came upon new houses, new stages and wharves, bright builds, pictures of success. Some success. Was there no end to the lies in this life? The truth of it was that the people were good hands at carpentry and had used their talents to turn government money into hope. But what hope was there? *There's no point blessing the fish until they get to the land.* And there were no fish handy enough for the people to get at. The tidal wave had seen to that. Maybe in time the ocean would reverse its crime, would see fit to bring back enough cod to revive the inshore fishery. But now? New buildings meant nothing. Kevin's thoughts fell from the new to the old, to his own house. Had it fallen asunder? As he got closer, he braced himself for what he might see.

The house was still there, clinging to its foundation, listing like a grounded ship waiting for some merciful tide to haul it under. The path to the front door didn't quite meet up with the door anymore, but the path still had most of its border of rocks. Kevin stumbled forward until he could reach out a hand and run it along distressed clapboards that were peeling and greying from tragedy and neglect. Dare he go inside? He was rigid with apprehension. He shut his eyes tight and inhaled. Remembered aromas of homemade bread and salt beef and cabbage leached through the walls. Would someone be at home? Mavis?

He stood for a long time, eyes closed, longing for ghosts.

CHAPTER 11

ON THE COASTAL BOAT ON the way back to Argentia, Kevin stood in the stern, focused on, mesmerized by, the froth of the wake. His mind rambled through memory, landing on the day that he had let his attention slide and the sea had gulped him down. He could again hear the rumble of the encroaching schooner, see it burst through the fog on a collision course with his dory. The deathly groan of wood, the extreme cold of water, the desperate scream of lungs. If he'd attempted to gasp for breath then, the ocean would have filled him up, done him in. But he couldn't, wouldn't let that happen, not when his mind was packed with images of home and family. He did what he had to do, mustered up the guts to grab his knife and release his snagged sweater from the sinking dory.

Today was different. The spray of the wake. The pull of the water. No accident here, but an invitation. So easy. So easy. A simple splash would release him from all responsibility. He was conscious of a stinging sensation in his gut, the seeming rupture of a seam, the promise of freedom hissing through the slit. What a relief it would be to stop all the worries. He leaned toward the water. Was it all a lie? The love from Mavis? Why didn't she tell him that she had taken in a child? Whose child was Kate anyway? And, if Mavis had told him all this, would his life have been any different? Would he have abandoned three-year-old Kate? Left her in Burin and gone off on his own? Would he have loved her less? Had he loved his other children more?

The questions were piling up, creating more tangle than he could handle. So he stopped asking, just let his mind go quiet, kept his eyes on the swirling white water. Leaning in, leaning in.

The ferry suddenly slowed, thrusting him a little more forward, then knocking him onto the deck. Backwash slid over him, smacking him with the cold. Kevin scrambled to his feet, all the while cursing the sogginess seeping into his clothes. Served him right, getting too close to the edge.

A few passengers darted toward him. "Are ya all right, b'y? Are ya all right?" Mortified, soaked to the skin, he shooed them away like he would a bunch of gluttonous gulls. Sure enough, they moved off but not before they threw disgruntled looks his way.

Kevin took up a place at the stern, a few feet back from his original position. He stood there, rigid, stubborn, ignoring the gawkers. None of their damn business if he wanted to do himself in. When the ferry bumped the dock, he didn't budge. It was not until the gangway clunked into place that he tore through the clump of passengers and hurried toward shore.

As he stepped onto the Argentia dock, he caught sight of the *Elizabeth J* moored at the opposite end of the wharf. Was that Robert, standing on the pier, staring right at him? Kevin's heart quickened. How in God's name had the schooner got back ahead of him? One thing for sure, Kevin couldn't face Robert right now, not with Clara's stolen letters in his pocket. What kind of idiot was he, taking those letters in the first place? He turned, pretending he hadn't noticed his brother-in-law and then ran full tilt, abandoning the sway of the wharf in favour of solid ground.

His clothes clammy and clinging, Kevin made a beeline for the silver mine. Any man with half a brain would go home first, wouldn't he? Get himself dried out? But Kevin couldn't go home. Not yet. Not until he had returned Clara's letters, Clara's now slightly damp letters, to their original hiding place. He doubted that his sister would head directly to the mine, but it was a possibility, one that he couldn't risk. And, if he had the strength to go home at all, he couldn't risk taking the letters there either. It would be one thing for Clara to notice the letters missing from the mine, another thing entirely for Kate to happen upon them at home. Heaven forbid. Yes, the thing to do was to put the letters back where they belonged. Right now. Maybe at some point he could learn to read, go back and reclaim the letters and unlock their secrets. He sniffed. Slim and none, the chances of that. He was a man stuck in ignorance.

At the mine, after a last, longing look at the letters, he shoved them into their pouch, squirrelled the package into its alcove, and then slinked toward home. A low blanket of fog was drifting in fast, so fast it would soon cover the entire headland of Argentia. Kevin slowed his motion until the fog swallowed him, making his every action secret, making him feel safe and smug. Mother Nature was on his side today, giving him this grey cloak. What better way to hide the sin of spying on his sister? The thought stopped him dead, killing his smugness and replacing it with guilt that prickled his nerves. Was he sinful in what he was doing? Or was he blameless, just a man doing what he could? The lack of a handy answer had him rubbing his forehead. Perhaps he should just have done with all of this, give it up, forget he ever found those letters. And perhaps he should have done himself in on the ferry when he had the chance. Was that what he really wanted? To do himself in? And if he did, what difference did being on the ferry make? He could create other chances. Dangerous thoughts, sinful thoughts. He broke into a run, an attempt to flee the thoughts, but they ran with him, all the way to his home. He couldn't face Dulcie now, he couldn't face Kate. Dear God, Kate wasn't even his to face.

Kevin stumbled toward the storeroom. He plopped down on a milking stool in a dark corner, the only light a streak through a crack in the door, and let thoughts swirl until he thought they would derail him. When he couldn't sit still anymore, he grabbed a bottle of rum from a nearby alcove. The bottle fumbled its way into his hands and up to his lips. He tilted his head. One quick gulp. That's all he wanted. That done, he slid his flannel sleeve across his mouth but when the scrape of damp fabric against the stubble of beard came at him like a thin wail, he took another gulp of rum. And another. And another. Finally, quiet descended. His breath was working again, still fitful, but working. He kept drinking, slow and steady, the only sure way to numb the evil. But the evil was as stubborn as a weed, determined to find a slit and slither through. As Kevin fixated on the far corner of the storeroom where he kept his shotgun, he played with a single thought that had been in the back of his mind for years, the idea of doing himself in. He had always managed to bury that thought. For Kate. For his daughter, Kate. But Kate wasn't his and the demons were dancing now, all reasons for angels gone. In a dismissive motion, he dropped the bottle and claimed the gun. Amid sobs that sounded like they were far off, he cocked the rifle, reclaimed his perch, and jammed the barrel under his chin. There was nothing else for it. He would see it through.

"Kevin?"

Was he dead? Was he in heaven? More likely hell. Who was calling him?

"Kevin?"

Was that Robert? What was he doing here? Shouldn't he be on the schooner? Wasn't the captain always the last to leave the boat?

"I saw you careening away from the dock." That was definitely Robert. Kevin did not move.

"Decided to pay you a call." A breeze crept across Kevin's face as Robert crouched low in front of him. A hand clasped Kevin's wrist, another wrestled Kevin's finger from the trigger of the gun.

"Where's Clara?" Kevin asked vaguely.

Robert let out a slow breath. The smell of pipe tobacco drifted between them. "That woman has the idea that she can learn to navigate," Robert said, his voice quiet, steady. "She's checking instruments and charts on board."

As Robert talked, Kevin was aware of the gun being removed from his hand, of Robert standing up and moving away. The sound of the shotgun being unloaded made Kevin sigh. His way out had just gone to dust.

Sure enough, Robert returned, without the gun, stooped and leaned in, face to face. Too close. Angry now. "What the fuck are you doing?" Robert spat the words. "How could you think of doing this to your family?"

Kevin let out a wail. The sobbing came then, all on its own. He couldn't stop it. He dropped prone onto the floorboards and howled. On and on and on. Was there no end to the pain? Perhaps Robert wouldn't even be there when it ended, if it ended. Kevin cried until his throat was raw. "I . . . I . . . I . . ." His attempt at speaking was stifled by hoarseness. He felt a hand on his back. Surprising, the comfort of a hand on his back.

"We'll go to my house," Robert said. "We'll stay there for a while before Kate and Dulcie get back. Clara won't be home for hours. We can get something to eat and get to the bottom of this."

"There's no bottom," Kevin protested. "Only lies." Still, he offered no resistance when Robert helped him up. "Don't tell Clara," Kevin said and the blackness hit him.

The next thing he knew he was at Robert and Clara's house. In the kitchen, at the table, the aroma of hot coffee drifting up his nose, Robert's face staring at his.

"Good, you're awake," said Robert. "Now what the hell is going on?"

Kevin's head pounded with every syllable Robert uttered. He dropped his eyes to the table. "I don't suppose you're going to be letting me out of here unless I account for myself?"

"You have that right."

Kevin shrugged. He coughed. "Went to the Burin just to check things out." He clutched his coffee mug and stared into its greasy blackness. "Found out that Kate isn't my own child, that my wife Mavis took her in without telling me."

"And . . ."

"And I've been all these years living for Kate, the miracle child they called her. And all this time, she wasn't even mine. That so-called daughter of mine was the only thing keeping me alive." He put the mug down and looked at Robert. "What the hell am I supposed to do now?"

"Whatever it is, the answer isn't the shotgun."

"Remains to be seen."

Robert sat in silence, his jaw set. He leaned in, his eyes searching Kevin's face. "So, Mavis lied to you?"

Kevin gave a brisk nod.

"Tell me," Robert said, "do you love Kate any less because Mavis lied?"

The ruptured seam in Kevin's gut flared, burning. He sat bolt upright and paused in position, allowing a single image of Kate to enter his mind. It goaded him at first, creating more pain, but as he sat he felt a welling up, a groundswell. His love for Kate was there. Always there. And that was the truth of it. He loved Kate when he believed she was his by blood. He loved her now. Had anything changed?

"What would Mavis say about all of this?" A gentle prompt from Robert.

"Mavis?" Kevin sucked in a breath. Before he could exhale, her voice sounded inside his head.

The child needed a home.

"The child needed a home," Kevin repeated.

Robert nodded. "What else?"

So you'll be going home to Kate.

"That I should be going home. To Kate."

"Good idea," said Robert.

And stay there until Argentia falls to sand.

"And stay there until Argentia falls to sand."

"What are you on about? What sand?"

"I haven't the foggiest." Kevin sat in stillness for a moment and then, with a deep breath, he denounced the tear in his gut, suturing it shut. "Mavis may be dead but she's got better eyes than I do. Something's coming. I don't know what but she does." A sudden realization hit and he looked deep into the eyes of his brother-in-law. "Sweet Jesus, Robert! What if I had used the shotgun and Kate had found me?"

"You didn't. No need to dwell."

"But I would have if you hadn't shown up." He retreated to silence for a moment. "Are you going to tell Clara about this?" he asked.

"To what end?"

"That's no answer."

"Won't say a word."

Kevin let out a sigh. "You saved my life. Can't thank you enough."

"No thanks necessary." Robert leaned back. "Drink your coffee. When you're ready, we'll get you home. Good enough?"

"Good enough." Kevin raised the coffee to his lips. He was going home, to Kate. Home, where Mavis's puzzling words would eventually have meaning. Home. Definitely the best place for him for now. All he could do was be there, one foot inside the mystery. And wait.

KATHLEEN

CHAPTER 12

IT IS AN ARCHIVE, THE sea.

With its unceasing cycle of rise and rain, the North Atlantic holds within its basin every drop of data and every dream of man from the dawn of time, harbouring all details of life and land from the obvious to the mysterious. It marks the passage of days in a peaceful rhythm of waves.

Unlike the sea, I hold the data for only one life. Mine. It is with an underlying grumble that I bide my time through summer glow, fall fade, and winter pall. The New Year nips, grips. People hunker down until spring yawns. A full cycle of seasons, packed with events, passes while the ocean and I abide.

All the while, deep down, change is churning and the sea can barely contain its secrets. An upwelling is on the horizon.

On the local stage, the corrupt government of Newfoundland has imploded. Not a steadfast soul left to run it. Partly the fault of the St. John's merchants who had groomed their sons for politics but then, lusting for glory, shipped those same sons right into the insanity of the Great War. Did the Atlantic even belch a warning when it provided those young men passage? And, if it had, would any puffed-up paternal merchant have paid heed? Doubtful. Over seven hundred Newfoundlanders went over the top into No Man's Land at the Battle of Beaumont Hamel and dropped there, mowed down by machine guns and artillery. Dead within a half-hour without firing a single defensive shot. A crippling loss for Newfoundland whose failing government leaders eventually implored Canada and Great Britain for a Commission of Government. Now, six men have been appointed to take over. No votes. No voice of the people at all.

On the world stage, a man named Hitler is chancellor of the faraway country of Germany. Seemingly an inconsequential piece of news, this, mostly ignored by members of my island community. Among my own family, it is only Clara's Robert who appears troubled. The Kathleen that I was then paid no heed. But now? As ghost, I observe all and notice that the usually sedate Robert fidgets as he awaits radio reports. His demeanour flips from calm to dour as he reads newspaper headlines. On some level, he knows the threat, the consequences, but he withholds all concern. A few surface ripples. Nothing more.

Within my offspring, changes abound, some open, some secret. Once again there are possible threats, hardly comparable to the political but crucial to my story.

The door to truth is edging open for Kevin, threatening Clara's secrets.

The door to leadership is ripe for Clara, threatening the men who would deny it to her.

The door to her First Holy Communion is open for Kate. Like all little ones, she knows the difference between right and wrong, and must engage in this rite of passage, being marched off to the priest to confess her sins. Innumerable transgressions, no doubt.

It is not only Kate but all sinners who travel the penitent's path for it is the Easter season, the season of first sacraments, a time of death and renewal. On Ash Wednesday the priest marks the people's foreheads with a cross of ashes to symbolize their nothingness. *Remember man thou art but dust and unto dust thou shalt return.* What follows is forty days of Lent during which the faithful keep their heads low, walk the Stations of the Cross, and give up a favourite food or drink, some form of sacrifice aimed at replicating the forty-day sacrifice of Jesus in the desert. The irony amuses me. It is no sacrifice for this community to give up food in March, always known as the long hungry month of March, when storerooms have already surrendered most of their goods. A turnip, a carrot, an occasional potato are all that bump around in the bottom of bins once piled high with the fall harvest. Still the dark, hungry, monotonous month serves its purpose, I suppose, as it stirs guilt in the adults who have sinned, bestowing upon them a desire to confess. To start anew.

Or to keep buried the demons that haunt.

CLARA

CHAPTER 13

———◆———

It did Clara's heart good, being in the warmth of her mother's kitchen and watching Kathleen and Dulcie fussing as they fitted Kate for her First Communion dress. Kate, eyes shining, ringlets dancing, bounced on her perch, a wooden chair that had been pulled from the side of the table and planted in the centre of the room. She clutched both sides of her white dress which was so big that it appeared to have swallowed her whole. "How am I supposed to be wearing the likes of this?" Kate spread the skirt wide as she attempted a curtsy.

"Be still, child," said Kathleen. "You'll take a tumble."

"It's big because it was my dress," said Clara. "My wedding dress."

"And mine before that," said Kathleen, her voice strained.

Clara looked at her mother and saw Kathleen's pained expression. Did she object to the use of this dress for First Communion? Perhaps Clara should have asked her opinion before offering up the dress. Perhaps she should have given some weight to the tragedy of the union between Kathleen and Alphonse. Was the dress dredging up bad memories for her mother? Damn it all. Clara definitely should have asked. Should she ask now? Dithering only increased her edginess. She was still wavering when Kathleen said, "It's no odds to you, is it, Clara? It is your dress. Mine first, yes. But you fixed it up grand. I didn't get much of a look at it on your wedding day . . ." Her voice faded and her enquiring look changed to remorse. "I'm sure we could find something else among those bolts of cloth you lugged from town."

Relief tumbled over Clara. Her mother's concern was only for Clara, nothing to do with bad memories or buried demons. Clara reached out a hand and touched Kathleen's arm. Light. A butterfly landing. "It's fine, Mom," she said. "Don't give it a second thought."

Kathleen smiled.

Feeling easy now, Clara turned her attention to the dress.

"A lot of work but we'll get her done," said Dulcie.

Lured by a dangling thread, Clara stepped forward. She wound the thread around her finger and in a single, quick motion, snapped it. "It will be grand when we finish." She turned to Kate. "Are you looking forward to your First Holy Communion, Kate?"

Kate promptly stuck out her tongue and kept it out while she tried to talk.

"What in God's name are you saying, child?" Dulcie asked.

Kate pulled her tongue in. "Is my tongue flat enough? My teacher said that if your tongue's not flat enough, the Sacred Host will fall off."

A trio of laughs filled the room.

"Ye are all laughing at me," cried Kate.

"Your tongue is perfect," Clara said, "and we're not laughing at you. We're remembering, that's all."

Kathleen nodded. "Yes, remembering. First Communions bring out the fear in everyone."

"Don't you pay your teacher no never mind now at all," said Dulcie. "Like your nanny said, First Communions are scary."

"But you're too old to remember," said Kate.

Dulcie laughed. "You're a dance, now aren't you? Maybe I'm old now but I was young once. Ask anybody."

"And dare we ask about your first Confession, Kate?" said Clara as she removed her wedding veil from a box and placed it on Kate's head. "Have you had it yet?"

"Yes." Kate crinkled her nose and tossed her head. The veil went flying and Clara swooped in on it, snatching it just before it met up with the stove.

"In all my born days, I never saw a veil take wing before," said Dulcie.

"I didn't mean it," said Kate, eyes wide.

"Nothing to worry about." Kathleen took the veil from Clara and returned it to the top of Kate's head. "I take it confession wasn't much to your liking?"

Kate muttered something unintelligible.

"What's that you say, child?" Dulcie asked.

"Didn't have no sins. So I made some up." She lowered her head.

"You lied to the priest?" Dulcie said, her voice sharp like a blade. "Don't want to hear tell of that. We all has to learn to confess our sins."

Kathleen moved closer to Kate, elbowing Dulcie in the process.

Dulcie flinched.

Clara raised her eyebrows. Would Kathleen explain her action?

Kathleen said nothing.

The silenced Dulcie stooped low and focused her attention on basting the hem of the dress.

Clara suppressed the urge to speak. She wasn't interested in pacifying Dulcie, only in querying Kate. But the air was turbulent, in need of time to settle. Clara let the seconds tick to minutes. Then, curiosity piqued, eyes on Kathleen, she whispered a question. "Kate, do you think you should have invented sins?"

Kate sighed as she shook her head. "It made me feel dark. Like a black hole right here." She put her hand on her midriff. "My teacher said it is a sin to tell a lie," she said, her voice beginning to quiver. She looked her grandmother straight in the eye. "Am I going to hell?"

A decisive "no" clipped the tip of Clara's tongue but she bit it back. Kate had addressed her nanny, not Clara. Kathleen was a better one to ask anyway, wasn't she? If anyone here knew about hell, it was Kathleen. Clara looked at her mother, wondering, wondering. Had Kathleen ever visited a confessional, ever confessed to the killing of Alphonse? Certainly not here, never here in Argentia where the priest knew everyone by face and voice and footfall in the aisle. But surely be to goodness, she had confessed somewhere. St. John's, maybe?

Kathleen returned Clara's gaze, eyes fixed and certain to the point where Clara squirmed. Was her mother reading her thoughts?

When Kathleen spoke, she addressed only Kate. "You are not going to hell," Kathleen said. "Not even close to it. No one here is going to hell."

Kate's relief was visible, sliding over her like a waterfall, sweeping away all signs of tension. Clara stepped back and plopped onto a chair, eyes on the dress, mind on Kathleen's words: "No one here is going to hell." Did Kathleen Kerrigan believe she had committed no sin? Or had she confessed it as sin and moved past it? Would Clara ever know?

"The whole thing was scary," said Kate, not done with the confession story. "The teacher stood by the back pew and we all had to sit there. Waiting and waiting. When I got my turn and saw the inside of the confession box, I almost tore for the hills. Black as a coal bucket in there. But Miss made me go in and she closed the door behind me. And I knelt down like I was supposed to. Then that tiny gate flew open with a slap." She clapped her hands together. "The priest talked and I said what I was supposed to, the 'Bless me Father' bit." She again looked to her grandmother. "Then I folded my hands and bowed my head like this." Kate entwined her fingers and lowered her head, chin to chest. White veil and brown curls swept her shoulders. Folds of the wedding dress obscured her body, making her look even smaller.

Kathleen reached both hands to Kate's shoulders and gave them a gentle squeeze.

Kate looked up. "Priests are like God, aren't they, Nanny?"

"Priests are people, child," said Kathleen with cast-iron certainty and with a hint of annoyance. "No more, no less. Some good as saints. Some crooked as sin itself. You listen to them. You take in what's right. Then you do what you must."

Clara let out a heartfelt sigh. She shared Kathleen's sentiments, wanting Kate to think for herself, wanting her to step aside, not toe the line of serving, bowing, and obeying blindly as so many did. How could people be so wrong, for so long? Clara shook her head, a tiny movement, one that went by without notice.

Kathleen pinched the wedding dress, enormous on the child, in at the sides. "Her name was Kate . . ."

Kate grinned. "Story, story, story."

"Don't be wiggling, child," said Dulcie, "or I'll be sticking you with a pin. That'd be my undoing, it would, seeing your lovely face screwed up with the pain." Dulcie's words were worrying but her voice was lilting. She basted the hem without pause, the stitches equally sized and evenly spaced.

"Can I be of any help?" asked Clara with no intention of rising from her chair. Something was about to surface and she wasn't going to miss it.

"You just stay put," said Dulcie. "Sure and it must be hard enough to see your wedding dress cut to pieces without your having to do it yourself."

"Where's my story?" said Kate.

Clara smiled to herself. God bless little Kate.

"Her name was Kate," Kathleen began.

"Just like you," Kate quipped.

"And I'm sure she had a smile on her face and a sparkle in her eye," said Kathleen.

"Just like you," said the group in concert.

"This brings to mind Mass on Sunday," said Dulcie.

Kate blinked. "What about Mass?"

"You know," Dulcie explained, "when the priest says '*Dominus vobiscum*' and everybody answers . . ."

"*Et cum spiritu tuo*," said all four.

Kate went right back to her earlier chant, "Story, story, story."

Clara nodded. Yes, a story. *The good kind, not the scary kind.* And just like that, she flitted back to childhood as she always did when Kathleen was on the verge of a story. She folded her hands and leaned back, ready to fall into the magic of folklore or fairy tale. Particularly curious on this day, in this story, would be the moral. Something about sins and confessions and truth and lies?

"This Kate lived long before you. In Ireland. She did not have a white dress for her wedding. Wedding dresses were not white then."

"Were they blue?" Kate's eyes suddenly brightened. "Can I have a blue dress?"

Kathleen shook her head. "Women often just wore their best dresses, different colours, none of them white. That all changed after Queen Victoria wore a white dress. Every woman wanted white after that."

"Now don't that beat all," said Dulcie. "I guess if white's good enough for royalty, it's good enough for the rest of us."

"I guess so, Dulcie. But the Kate in my story only had her best dress, a brown wool dress, for her wedding day. After she was married, she wore it only on special occasions. When it showed its age, she wore it while she was putting up preserves in the storeroom, figuring her apron would keep it clean. So there she was one day, in the storeroom, paying no attention to anything other than the task at hand when the whole place suddenly turned dark, like the confession box. She turned. The doorway was blocked by the shadow, the outline of a man, a big man, the light aback of him, and she couldn't see his face. She was beside herself with the fear."

Clara sat up. In the past, she had worried needlessly about the content of her mother's stories. But was her concern misplaced now? What the hell was Kathleen doing? The opening to this story resounded with truth. It was familiar. Too familiar. Too much like the story she had told Clara three years ago. But the horror of Kathleen being interfered with took place in Newfoundland, not in Ireland. In the shed, not the storeroom. What devilish story was her mother telling?

"The fear was justified because the giant was evil, taking everything that Kate had preserved her whole life."

"He stole all the jam, Nanny? All the blueberry jam?"

"Every last bit of it," replied Kathleen without a breath of hesitation. "There wasn't an article of bakeapple, blueberry, or strawberry jam left by the time he was finished with the place. The cupboard was broken into and robbed of every bit of sweetness that Kate had spent ages building up. All the berry picking on the barrens, the washing and the cleaning of the fruit, the boiling of it. All gone to waste. And the strawberry stains all over her dress." Kathleen paused for a minute. "Now, Kate," she said, "do you think the Kate in my story needed to go to confession to tell about the stolen jam?"

Kate shook her head. "She didn't steal nothing."

"Anything," corrected Kathleen. "She didn't steal anything. And you are right. But she thought it was her own fault because she left the door open. She was ashamed to tell, but she told the priest. And he said it was all her fault because she left the door open. He gave her penance, hours of prayers."

"Did she do it? Her penance?" asked Kate.

Kathleen nodded. "There was nothing left for her but to do what the priest told her."

Kate was silent. "But the priest was wrong."

Kathleen nodded again. "Yes. The Kate of my story stewed over it until she settled on the truth of it. After that, when things were not her fault, she did not confess. If she had absolutely no sins to tell, she told nothing. She did not lie." Kathleen toyed with a ringlet of Kate's hair.

"No lies?" asked Kate.

"No lies."

Kate was silent for a moment. "No lies," she repeated. She reached out and touched her grandmother's arm. "What about the dress? Did the Kate in your story get a new dress?"

"You can always make a new dress," said Kathleen, "and you can always get on with things. She did both."

Kate's eyes were wide as she whispered question her next question. "Did she get her jam back, Nanny?"

"No, child," Kathleen said, her expression soft, "sometimes when sweet things are taken from you, they never come back."

"I'm sorry, Nanny."

"You have nothing to be sorry about."

"I won't be telling no more lies, Nanny."

"I know."

Dulcie finished her stitching and snapped the thread. "Good as done. Seams are tucked and hem is basted."

"Well done, Dulcie," Clara said without looking. She couldn't take her eyes off her mother. Kathleen had reshaped her own pain into a life lesson for her granddaughter. She had done what she needed to do and moved on. No lies, therefore no guilt, and no confession. Did that mean no *mea culpa* for the demise of Alphonse?

Clara thought about her own life, a life of adultery, one lie after another. Discomfort crowded in. She clamped a lid on thinking and feeling before her own demons owned her. She would continue to lie. Her demons would remain buried.

KEVIN

CHAPTER 14

———◆———

ON THE MORNING OF THE day of Kate's Communion dress fitting, Kevin was on the north side of Argentia, tarpapering a roof. Not a paying job, just a helping one since the house's owner was laid up for a time. Shocking how a stray kick from a mule can darn near lay waste to a man.

Kevin was lagging in the work due to an assault from the wind. He had suspected Mother Nature was up to something, had sniffed it in the air, but banked on getting the work done ahead of it.

At first, the wind toyed, dancing a jig and curling the unsecured ends of the tarpaper. As it gained strength, it prodded the ocean which rippled and billowed and ruptured into whitecaps. Somewhat annoyed, Kevin continued working. When rollers thundered to shore, Kevin glanced up to see strands of seaweed slapping at boulders and seagulls struggling against the currents. Kevin bent his head and leaned in, hammering faster. The wind sneered, staggering him. He checked his balance. An attempt at a deep breath brought a mouthful of grit. High wind indeed if the topsoil was flying off the fields. When he pulled out a handkerchief to wrap around his face, the wind snatched it away. Grumbling, Kevin gave in. Nature had the upper hand. He took comfort in knowing that a sudden storm wouldn't stay long. *Long foretold, long last. Short notice, soon past.*

Grabbing his hammer and roll of tarpaper, Kevin descended the ladder, rung by rung. Couldn't help but note that sand was piling against the front door of the house. Good decision to let the job alone for now.

In jig time, the very doorknob would be buried. Kevin called in at the back door, promising to return on the morrow.

In the afternoon, when nature had finished her snit, when Kate had gone to her grandmother's to be fitted for her First Communion dress, Kevin went to work in his own yard, coaxing wood into gunwales for a dory. He was thinking on First Communions past, the fuss of preparation with his eldest children, Jimmy and Marie. A painful memory, one that obliterated any desire to be involved with this first for Kate. Yes, he would show up at the event, but other than that, he was willing to let the women take over. Right now, on this day, their preoccupation with Kate's First Holy Communion was a blessing. He had time to himself, time to spend working with his hands. Nothing like chopping, sawing, and carving to keep a man level. That was important to him, keeping busy, keeping level.

As he was about to screw the final C-clamp into place on the gunwales, he caught a glimmer out of the corner of his eye. He glanced up. The clamp tumbled from his hand. Was he seeing things? He blinked. A thin pole pierced the low-lying cloud, a pole with a flag at the top. A pole that sure as hell wasn't on the north side this morning while he was tarpapering. The only thing blowing there this morning was the wind. The Stars and Stripes had no business in these parts. Why would an American flag be flying here in Newfoundland? Hand to brow, Kevin took a step back. He tripped on a stone and instantly recovered but when he searched the sky again, the flag was gone and all the good was gone out of him.

Kevin had heard stories about a flagstaff, a ghost flagstaff, and had attributed the stories to the demons in the storytellers' flasks. But he himself had just seen the flag and he wasn't drunk. Not that he wasn't tempted. Would love to be drunk, but he wasn't getting drunk. The last time he hit the bottle he nearly did himself in. The shame of it tore at him. If it hadn't been for Robert . . .

A tremor set itself up in his gut and made its way through him. His lips were dry. He stumbled his way into the root cellar and, slamming the door behind him, he holed up in a corner, back rigid against an empty vegetable bin. When the cellar door fell open, he jumped up, shut it tight, and reclaimed his hiding place. Didn't want no light coming in here. And no ghost flags either. No room in his narrow existence for demons or ghosts. Things were going along fine. Robert had gotten through to him about his staying where he was and he was doing it, staying put. It was enough that the ghost of Mavis showed up in his dreams. God help him. He couldn't handle any more ghosts.

The more he thought about ghosts, the darker the root cellar seemed. "What of it, God? What's going on here?" No answers were forthcoming. He sat still until he could sit still no more. Then he jumped from the dirt floor, bolted through the door, and resumed his labour. He retrieved the tossed C-Clamp and placed it in line with the others, screwing it tight. A dory would be useless if its gunwales fell apart. He stepped back. It was looking good, this boat. What now? What else could he do to this dory? Nothing. There was just the waiting for the gunwales to set up. What would he do next? He had to do something. He eyed a pile of logs, stripped trees that were next in line for the wood box. That would do it. He'd knock them down to size.

He heaved a log between two sawhorses and claimed his bucksaw. He jolted into action, back and forth, back and forth, a steady rhythm. Movement was good. Movement kept his mind off things. But the saw jammed on a knot. Damn. He jumped back, leaving the stuck saw vibrating and humming, and swung his way toward the house. In a strange repetition of things past, things he did before the tidal wave, he checked for cracks inside and out, and shored up windows and doors and fences and gates, all the while yammering at God and the saints. At one point, he aimed a fist at the sky. "Are you up there, God?" The sky darkened. Son of a bitch. Kevin circled the house in search of more chores but could find none. Still needing to move, he scurried about like an alarmed cockroach seeking shelter. Where could he go? Finally, he lurched toward Clara's house. She wouldn't be home, of course. All hands were at Kathleen's. All the women that is. What about Robert? Could he talk to Robert about a ghost flag? Would Robert think Kevin had lost his mind? Robert had hauled Kevin from the brink before and hadn't judged him. Robert hadn't told anyone either. Robert. Could Robert help him again? Should Kevin go there now? Damn it all. He had nowhere else to go. Now was as good a time as any.

In the kitchen, at Robert and Clara's, all was silent. A chime sounded, startling Kevin. The clock on the mantel in the front room. Three chimes then back to stillness. He heard movement upstairs. "Robert?" he called. Kevin waited for a moment, then called again. This time there was a thump of footsteps overhead, then on the stairs.

"Kevin. How are you doing?" Robert appeared in the doorway, eyeglasses on the bridge of his nose, his left hand clutching a book. He extended his right hand as he walked forward.

"Finest kind, I suppose, b'y." Kevin shook Robert's hand and then glanced past him.

"Clara's not here. Communion dress, remember? I expect her to make a day of it."

Kevin nodded. Stymied now, he just stood. What the hell was he doing here? What should he say? His intended topic—a ghost flag—seemed ridiculous. He looked at the book in Robert's hand. "What are you reading?" he asked and instantly felt fear clutch at his gut. Good Lord, what had he done? Now the talk would be about books, big books, books as thick as his own skull. He should hightail it out of here while he had the chance. But no. His boots were stuck to the floor like they had a mind of their own.

"Oh, this, an old favourite. *A Tale of Two Cities.* Was settling in for a re-read but you may borrow it if you wish." Robert held the book out.

Kevin waved the offer away. "I'm too busy for—" In mid-sentence he stopped, his jaw dropped, his practised response failing him. He couldn't read that book or any book beyond a first-grade primer, but he was suddenly overcome with want. He wanted to read that book. Any book. Every book. What was he on about at all? Clara's letters? He wasn't sure. Kevin raised his head and met Robert's eyes full on. Something shifted inside him, slowly, deliberately, like a motor switching gears. All thoughts of ghosts and flags and letters were gone.

Robert maintained his offer, still holding the book in the space between them. Kevin locked his eyes on the book. He took it in his hand. He liked the feel of it, firm, solid, and smooth. He returned his glance to Robert. "Well, truth be told, b'y, I would love to read it but I can't. It's a hard thing for a man to admit, not being able to read and write." He ran trembling fingers over the book's brown leather cover. "It's harder still as Kate gets older. Don't want her thinking I'm dumber than a bag of beach rocks." Kevin's face was burning him but he kept going, digging deeper. "I'm actually looking to learn reading and writing too, handwriting, if you would—"

"Be happy to oblige, old man. Clara will help too, if—"

"Don't want Clara knowing nothing." The words were quick, too quick. Kevin managed a weak grin. 'She's a smart one, smug too, that sister of mine."

Robert clapped a hand on Kevin's shoulder. "No problem. None at all. Ready to get started?"

Kevin looked at Robert quizzically. "Now?"

"As good a time as any."

As good a time as any. Exactly what Kevin had said to himself a few minutes ago, the very words that got him here. He nodded, a simple gesture that turned turmoil to quiet and left Kevin stumped with the wonder of it all. It wasn't the ghost flag he had come to talk about at all. Not today. That discussion would come another time. That discussion would be with his sister. Being here with Robert now wasn't about ghosts and flags and demons. Unless the demon he was banishing was ignorance.

It was a curious thing, a man starting down one road, ending up on another, and knowing that he had landed in the right place.

CHAPTER 15

———◆———

THROUGHOUT THE FOLLOWING YEAR, KEVIN leaned into learning as he would into oars, giving everything he could muster. Always a book in toolbox or tackle box, always a pencil tucked behind his ear. At the merchant store, he lingered in line, spending time cracking the code of letters sprawled across labels. The mere sight of new tins and boxes and signs could set him to smiling.

He had placed the ghost flag issue on the back burner, expecting it to return to the fore. It did, a glimpse here, a flutter there. With each occurrence, he thought of, but put off, discussing the flag with Clara. When the sightings became more frequent and the bother bulged like a blister, Kevin readied himself to put words to his worry.

Prospects for a heart-to-heart with Clara seemed slim and none since that sister of his was always at sea. It was the doggone repeal of Prohibition that did that, allowed the *Elizabeth J* to sail without wreath of darkness. Clara and Robert were on the high seas both night and day now, no fear of consequences.

Kevin tasked himself with keeping track of their comings and goings, with finding a crack in Clara's schedule. Patience won out on that one. Today, Clara was arriving in Argentia on the coastal boat, alone. Robert was staying in St. John's for business meetings and would sail the schooner home at a later date.

Clara's house was chilled and Kevin immediately set to the job of warming the place up for her arrival. Unlatching the door of the stove, he piled in tinder from the wood box in the corner. He opened a stove lid and dropped in a lit match. When the fire blazed, he added splits, slammed the door, and replaced the lid.

Now what? On a shelf beside the warming oven sat an egg timer, one shaped like an hourglass. He lifted it, flipped it, and watched the sand drain from top to bottom. When the last grain of sand dropped, marking three minutes, he repeated the procedure, again watching time drain away, minutes to seconds to nothing. Like life, wasn't it? What was it Mavis had said about sand? He should stay here until all turned to sand? He shrugged. Still no meaning in that. *What about ghost flags, Mavis?* A stirring of air lifted strands of Kevin's hair and sent shivers across his shoulders. The egg timer slipped from his hand, shattering as it hit the edge of the stove. Sand spilled, sliding down the side of the stove and skittering across the floor. Kevin groaned. No chance of repair here. What was the good of being able to fix things when they are destroyed beyond all hope? Grabbing the broom and the dustpan, he set about gathering shards and slivers and granules of grit. He resolved to buy his sister a replacement egg timer.

Kevin set the broom back in its corner. What next? Perhaps he could sand the new door he and Robert were crafting in the workshop. But no. The two men should work on that together. The door was a surprise for Clara, a secret, as hushed and hidden as Kevin's literacy lessons. No need for Clara to know about the door or the learning. So what then? What chores could he do? Nothing seemed evident. He plopped into a chair that promptly wobbled. Kevin grinned.

This chair was the first of Robert's carpentry projects to make it into the house. A minor flaw, the wobble, and Kevin set about repairing it. He would never say a word about the fix, but he would teach Robert how to cut multiple pieces of wood the same length. A halfway-decent carpenter squares up ends and clamps pieces together before using the saw. The next chair Robert made would not wobble.

As Kevin worked, a light rain set in, tapping at the kitchen window. A comfortable rhythm. He was finishing the chair repair when he heard familiar footsteps on the path. Clara. He smiled, contented. The kitchen was warm and she would be hankering for a bit of heat.

The hinges creaked and the door grunted as Clara attempted to push through. Why hadn't he noticed those annoyances? Hadn't he been looking for chores? No matter. He made a mental note: oil hinges and plane edges. Sprinting across the room, he whipped the door open.

"Kevin!" Clara dropped her suitcase. "So good to see you."

Kevin nodded. "Likewise. How was the trip?"

"All good. Still delivering booze around the bay. Not to the States anymore. No Prohibition, no need." Clara removed her coat, hung it on a hook in the porch, and strode into the kitchen. "Grand to come home to a warm house." She lifted a lid on the Waterloo stove and peered inside. "Thanks, Kev. Want some tea?" she asked. "I've brought Purity crackers." She grabbed the kettle and headed to the pump in the pantry.

"I'll do that." Kevin was on her heels. He primed the pump until water gushed, quickly filling the kettle. Together they returned to the kitchen, Kevin to his original seat at the table. Clara pulled out a chair but then abandoned it. She marched to her suitcase, and from it retrieved a bright red package of Purity Cream Crackers. Kevin offered a faint smile when she put them on the table. "Store-bought?"

"Store-bought or nothing, I'm afraid." Clara slid the crackers toward him. "No time for baking in my line of work." She headed to the cupboard, opened the glass doors, and took out two teacups. "How's Kate?" she asked as she placed the cups on the table. "Can't believe it's been a year since her First Communion. Seems like yesterday."

"Kate's right as rain. Growing like a weed." The answer came easy and the mention of First Communion was right in line with his purpose. It was last year, while Kate was being fitted for her First Communion dress, that Kevin had first seen the ghost flag. "Things are as good as they can be." He drummed his fingers on the table. "Mauzy day today. The usual grey." He let out a deep breath. "Clara . . ."

She looked at him, eyebrows raised.

"Clara . . ."

Clara's look changed from question to concern. "What is it, Kevin?"

"Have you ever seen a flag, a big flag, flying high on a staff, over on the north side?"

"What on earth are you on about?"

The question was cast. No reeling it back. Kevin leaned in. "Bear with me here. The flagstaff. Have you seen it?"

Clara eased back into her chair. "I've heard about it, Kevin," she said, her voice low, tolerant. "People used to tell stories about it, don't you remember? But those stories are like the folktales that Mom tells. The flag is not real."

Thwarted, Kevin sank into silence. How could he move forward with this?

"Are you telling me that you've seen the flagstaff?" Clara asked, the question coming like a nudge.

There was relief in Kevin's sigh. "Sounds like my senses took wing, don't it?" He shrugged. "Perhaps they have. I've seen the flag a few times. It's gnawing at me. Something bad always turns up when I get to feeling like this. It's like the day our brother Jimmy was born."

"What about it?"

"I was sitting on the doorstep and, the second Jimmy let out his first scream, a raven landed on the shed and screamed back. I darn near jumped out of my skin. I shooed the bird away but I knew it would be back. I was sure it had come for him. For Jimmy. I watched and watched, tried to do my best to protect him, but one day I was away from the house and, when I came home, Jimmy was dead."

Clara reached across the table and put her hand on his.

He brushed it away.

"It was not your fault," Clara said softly, looking straight at him. "Jimmy's death had nothing to do with you." Her eyes were suddenly riddled with alarm. "You do know the truth of that, don't you?"

Kevin jumped to put a stop to her fear. "Don't worry. You're not breaching no secrets. Mom told me the truth about Alphonse and Jimmy."

Clara dropped her head into her hands. "Thank God."

"But I still blame myself," continued Kevin. "If I had been there . . . It seems that whenever I turn away, people die."

"Not true, Kevin. You kept me safe. Remember the dory?"

Kevin waved a hand through the air. "But even that day I knew something was off. Not the first time you tried to be a stowaway." He shuddered. "There are signs. Always signs." He folded his arms, leaned back until his chair was balanced on its hind legs, and began a slow rock, back and forth, back and forth, a silent marking of time. "On the day of the tidal wave," he said and then stopped. Did he want to tell this?

"Go on," said Clara.

Kevin leaned forward. The two front legs of his chair met the floor with a singular, satisfying thump. No wobble. He dove into the telling. "I was safe from the water that day, in the heart of the woods, chopping for the winter. The ground shook. I ignored it, thinking a tree had fallen someplace. When a flock of birds tore from the woods, screaming their way to the sky, I knew something wasn't right. But I didn't dwell. I didn't run. I settled on thinking that a falling tree had startled the birds. But my innards knew different. A sleepless night, that one. In the morning, scared out of my wits, I trudged home. I kept hoping nothing was wrong but then I got home and nothing was left. Nothing except Kate." He halted again, waiting for a word from Clara. Something about Kate, maybe?

Clara again reached for his hand. This time he didn't resist. She held his hand tight.

So she wasn't offering information. Just comfort. Enough, he supposed. "Something is brewing now," he continued. "I don't know what. I saw the flagstaff a year ago. And that strange feeling came with it. When that feeling first came, I lost my brother. It came again and I lost my family. What could happen now? I made a deal with God. I would take care of Kate if he gave me no more trouble."

"I don't think God will give you any more trouble, Kevin. He will watch over you." She released her grip on his hand.

A tinge of sadness grazed Kevin, a scraping across his chest. "Nothing watching over me other than a cloud or a crow." He sighed. Should he tell

Clara what he knew about Kate, that Kate was not his, that she had been taken in by the kind-hearted Mavis? No, he wasn't telling that. Not now. "I'm sticking to the deal I made with God or the sky or whatever it was, but trouble's coming. I don't know what and I don't know when but, mark my words, it's coming." He looked up at Clara, who was staring at him, her eyes blank.

Kevin turned his attention to the red Purity box on the table. With trembling fingers, he opened the box, retrieved a single cracker, and snapped off tiny pieces, each of which he placed on his saucer. When he had ringed his teacup with the pieces, he brushed his fingers together, adding more crumbs to the smattering he had already created on the table. Seconds passed in silence while Kevin traced lines through the sandy pile of crumbs. With a single swipe, he brushed the crumbs to the floor. What had he gone and done that for? "I'll get the broom."

Clara shook her head. "I'll deal with the crumbs later."

"Second mess today." He nodded toward the stove. "I broke your egg timer. Will get you a new one."

"Not important." Clara's expression was still blank. "But the flagstaff—I don't know what to tell you, Kevin," she finally said. "Lots of people say they have seen the flagstaff. That's been going on since the last century. Nothing has ever come of it. Maybe it was just a shadow, a cloud crossing the sun."

A wave of fatigue anchored Kevin to the chair.

The kettle screamed from the stove. Clara rose, grabbed a potholder, and poured boiling water into the teapot. He watched while she warmed the pot, emptied the water, and made tea. A ritual. She placed the pot on the table and fetched sugar and milk. She sat.

"With prohibition over," she said, her voice smooth, "the days of rum running are ended. That husband of mine is talking a lot about England these days. About what's going on in Europe, and that man Hitler. I think Patrick wants to go home to England."

Kevin frowned. "Who the hell is Patrick?"

"Robert." Clara's answer fell out of her, just dropped straight to the floor. Or so it seemed as that's where she cast her eyes. She cleared her throat before raising her head. "I meant Robert, of course." Nothing smooth about her now, squirming in her chair, fiddling with her hair, her face red as a boiled beet.

Damn it all. Did Clara have another man tucked away in some port? Uneasiness sank into him. Jesus. He knew the answer to that. The flame on her face gave her away. But he didn't want to know any of this. This was Clara's secret. He didn't come here to stick his nose into Clara's business and he didn't want to deal with the likes of this. But then she spoke and he knew he was in it, whether he wanted to be or not.

"Kevin," she said, her voice a quiet prayer, "please don't say anything to Robert. It would cost me my marriage."

Kevin hesitated. He stared at his sister whose eyes widened, alarmed. She placed a hand on his arm. "Please," she repeated.

In his whole life, Kevin had never seen his sister beg. Until now. What was he supposed to do here, caught up like this? Yes, he and Robert were friends, but Clara? Clara was his sister.

He nodded and watched the tension rolling off her, easy, like snow releasing its grip on a roofline in the springtime.

"It would cost me the schooner too," Clara added. "I need to make a living, Kevin."

"I see."

"England is Robert's homeland," she continued.

"I won't say a word." He was done with this topic. "As for the ghost flag," he added, hoping to bounce the conversation back to its start.

"As I was saying, England is Robert's home," Clara said.

Damn. England again. Kevin didn't need to hear this, did he? Perhaps England and Hitler and Germany had something to do with the ghost flag-staff. He held back, waiting for a thread. Clara picked up her spoon and added sugar to her tea. Calm now, she stirred slowly. "There is a lot of talk about this Hitler, and Robert listens to the radio and reads the newspapers from across the pond. Robert is wrapped up in all of this. His England."

"Is he going to his England? If he does, will you go?"

Clara shook her head. "I'm not wanted." A shadow crossed her face, gone in an instant.

What was it, Kevin wondered? What would make her want another man? Whatever it was, Kevin was making no judgment about it. Robert had helped him when he needed help. God only knew what was going on in Robert's life. And God only knows what goes on between a man and a woman when the rest of the world is turned away. She was still talking. He tuned in.

" . . . short of our people going to England to support the British, like they did in the Great War, I don't see how any strange flags could be raised here."

"Oh," he said. Seemed she hadn't forgotten his concern after all. "Well, I saw the flagstaff. I saw a flag. Something's coming. I don't know when and I don't know what, but something's coming." He paused. Should he talk to Clara about him leaving Argentia? What would Clara say? Did Mavis write to Clara about the fact that Kate was taken in? Did Clara know who Kate's mother was? Should he ask? He took aim. "Only thing I know for sure is that Mavis and God wanted me to take care of Kate. Maybe I should take Kate away, leave now before trouble ends up on our doorstep." Now he was back to the waiting game. Not revealing anything. Just waiting.

All this while, Clara continued stirring, not a hitch in her movement, the only sound a steady clink of the spoon meeting the cup. "You can't do that," she said. She removed the spoon and placed it on the saucer.

"I have to keep her safe," he said, still fishing. "She's all I have left. If I have to take her away from here, then I will."

"But you also have me." Clara's words came through a clenched jaw. "I'm your family, too. Kate lost her home and most of her family once. She's so young, Kevin. You shouldn't move her away based on a ghost story. If anything happens, whatever it is, surely we can manage it together. You and me and Mrs. Mullins and Mom. You can't just take off. If Robert leaves, I'll need some help managing things."

Kevin snorted. "You are the most capable woman I know. You're already the talk of the place with all the stuff you get up to." He leaned toward her. "Do you think I don't know that you and that husband of yours ran the grandest rum-running operation on the coast? I'm sure you have contacts and business partners all over this continent, likely in Europe, too. Don't try to be a right poor little thing in front of me, Clara Kerrigan Caulins. I know better."

Clara smiled. "Yes, I know a lot of people." Her face turned somber as she met his eyes. "I may never have children of my own, Kevin."

Kevin shifted with a whole other form of discomfort. He wasn't talking about women's stuff.

"Somehow I had hoped to be closer to Kate, maybe to help her more." Clara apparently was not done with this conversation.

"I didn't want me and Kate to be a burden to you," he offered. "That's why I took on Mrs. Mullins." There was a lot more to it, but that was enough to cover it. "I still think of you as my younger sister, you know. My baby sister. To tell the truth of it, I'm glad the rum running is almost done for. I was beside myself for a while there, with the worry of it. All your gallivanting around, from the sea to the silver mine." He tilted his head. "You never did tell me what you were doing at the silver mine, now did you?"

"I guess I didn't." Clara's smile was glib.

"And you're not going to?"

"I guess I'm not."

"Perhaps I'll head there and have a look for myself." Inwardly, Kevin cringed. What was the matter with him at all? He'd just issued a reason for her to collect her treasures from the mine.

Clara slapped a hand on the table, rattling the teacups. "You'll do no such thing. Won't find a darn thing anyway. All been taken care of." She fidgeted with the edge of the tablecloth for a minute and then leaned in. "Don't leave Argentia, Kevin." Her voice was soft, pleading. "This is your home, my home, and now Kate's home. Yes, I will still go to and from St. John's on occasion, but I will be here when you need me. If Robert leaves, I will captain the *Elizabeth J* and run goods and supplies to the outports. But I will help with Kate too."

"Robert mentioned that you were learning to navigate. You'd make a good captain." He was filled up then, done with the talking. He stood.

"You're leaving?"

"Best be off now." He aimed for the porch and removed his coat from a hook. When he turned, Clara was standing beside him. "How about if you join Kate and me for supper this evening?" he said, not knowing why he offered. "Mrs. Mullins left a roast beef dinner warming on the stove." He shrugged on his coat and grabbed his cap.

Clara smiled. "I'll be over later. Mind if I bring a gift for Kate?"

"You're spoiling the child."

"What's an aunt for?"

At the door, Kevin paused and turned. "I'll stay, Clara. For your sake and for Kate's. I'll stay."

Clara's eyes filled with tears and she threw her arms around Kevin. He resisted, then relented, lifting his arms in embrace. When Clara pulled away, she wiped her eyes with the back of her hand. "Thanks, Kev," she said.

Kevin patted her shoulder, stepped back, and toyed with the edge of his cap. "I noticed the door grumbling a bit when you tried to get in. Be happy to oil that hinge and plane the edge before I leave." He was on solid ground now, away from feeling, onto fixing.

"I think I can manage it before I return to the galley," said Clara.

Kevin sniffed. "Galley, my arse. You belong at the helm. Well, if it's the helm women wants, as far as I'm concerned, they can be having it. It's a burden, sometimes, being at the helm . . ." As his voice faded, his spirit drifted with it. He snapped his fingers, a deliberate return to the moment. "Okay, so we're staying, for the time being anyway. Just stop spoiling Kate," he said as he left the house.

"What's an aunt for?" she repeated as she closed the door behind him.

Kevin shivered as he walked away. Sometimes, when the light faded inside him, it scared him. What would he do if he couldn't snap it back on? Would he choose to leave this helm he talked about? What's a man for? To take care of his family. His family now was Kate, Clara, and his mother. Who else was there? And what if he had nothing left to give any of them?

He chased the questions away by whistling a jig.

CLARA

CHAPTER 16

———◆———

CLARA TRUDGED HER WAY TO the silver mine. A final trip, during which she mulled over her morning conversation with Kevin.

What kind of fool was she at all, letting Patrick's name drop out of her mouth like that? Caught. Just like that. Hovering in dread. Would Kevin tell Robert? When Kevin promised secrecy, Clara bought into his words and settled into relief. But her nerves were rattling again now. This new concern had nothing to do with adultery and everything to do with the silver mine. Why had Kevin mentioned the mine? Clara sure as hell didn't want him, or anyone else for that matter, poking around there. It was not the hidden money that concerned her. The source of Clara's unease was the letters. Letters from Mavis. Letters about Kate. She knew Kevin couldn't read a lick of handwriting but what if he found those letters and took them home? What if Kate herself got at them? Perish the thought. Clara picked up her pace.

Today she would reclaim everything from the mine, including the money. With Prohibition gone, she was free to store money in her own home, still hidden, but in her own home. That money was her security. She had a solid situation with Robert but she wouldn't let her life hinge on his. Homesickness seemed to be eating at Robert. It was there in his wistfulness, in his longing for his old life in England. Maybe there was nothing to concern herself with. Maybe it was all in her head but Clara wasn't about to relinquish her general distrust for men. Men like her father Alphonse Kerrigan. Clara hawked a blob of phlegm and spat onto a gnarled fence post. She smirked: not the least bit ladylike. She sniffed as she spun about, eyeing the rocky path and the green meadows and the stunted fir trees. It wouldn't do to have someone trailing her. Confirming that the only movement was that of wind, plucking at ocean swells and frolicking through overgrown grass, she proceeded.

The mine hadn't changed any since Clara's last visit a few weeks back. It was still dark, slippery, the plopping and trickling sounds of water finding ground, the flapping of birds with nests near the entry, the blackness of the interior. Clara lit her lantern and trotted in, stepping over rails and ridges, sloshing through puddles, slogging through mud. Her feet were soaked in seconds but she paid that no mind. She steadied herself by leaning into a jagged and bumpy wall, cold and slimy to the touch. At her hidey-hole, she removed the lodged rock and pulled out a leather pouch containing a wad of cash and a stack of letters. The leather was smudged and had a mouldy smell. Had it gotten wet? She shrugged. Anything that had been stashed in this damp cave would likely reek after a while. She divided the money into even-sized bunches and pocketed them in her petticoat, one that she had made after visiting the island of St. Pierre for the first time. It amused her now to remember the maid in the restaurant selling petticoats with hidden pockets to store illegal bottles of rum.

Her cash stowed, Clara tucked the letters securely into her bodice. Determined to leave no evidence, determined to keep her nook available, she jammed the rock back into place and turned toward the exit.

A few steps outside the mine she extinguished her lantern.

"What the hell are you doing here, missy?"

Clara swivelled. Her skirt slapped her legs, triggering disconcerting images of paper money fluttering around her like discarded leaves in autumn. Thankfully, her petticoat held true to its purpose. A relief, that. She looked at Salty Joe Sallivan who stood in her path, shoulders slumped, shovel in hand, his beady eyes glinting from his pudding face. She was instantly taken back to the day on the wharf when she had slammed into Salty Joe, causing him to upend his wheelbarrow. Clara, dressed as a man at the time, her first time in that disguise, had been quick to duck behind a mackerel barrel. Salty Joe had not found her out. But that was then. And now? Well, the best account of herself in this situation would be no account at all, wouldn't it? "Could be asking you the same," she said. "Nothing doing on the wharf today, Joe?"

"I'm digging up stuff." He raised his shovel.

"What stuff, Joe?" she asked, intent on keeping him on about his own deeds and away from hers.

"Anything I can lay me hands on to help me build my new storeroom," said Joe. "Lots of metal and wood in this place, doing no good for nobody. Such a shame, such a waste. I remembers a time . . ."

Clara tuned him out, but feigned interest, moving closer and then slipping past him, all the while nodding as he nattered on. Before he caught on, she was well on her way down the path, waving goodbye, never having given the why of her presence.

Safely away from Salty Joe, Clara turned her thoughts back to Kevin. Earlier she'd been annoyed with him but now she was grateful to him. His inquiry about her doings at the mine triggered her to show up, to collect her belongings. Had she delayed the visit, Salty Joe might have had himself one very beneficial expedition.

At home, safe and sound, Clara opened all her treasures. She counted the money. She counted the letters. Everything was there, every bit of money earned, every piece of paper received from Mavis. But where would she put all of it? Clara headed up the stairs, marched into her bedroom, and dumped the letters and cash on the top of the bed. She dragged a chair into the closet, stepped up and reached high, pulling down a hatbox. The one that contained her blue, felt, wide-brimmed hat. Box in hand, she returned to the bed, removed the tissue from the bowl of the hat, and replaced it with money and letters. She returned the hat to the box and the box to the shelf, to the back of the shelf where no husband would be curious to look and no child would be able to reach.

She brushed her hands together. Now hadn't Kevin said something about a roast beef dinner?

KEVIN

CHAPTER 17

—◆—

KEVIN AND ROBERT CONTINUED WITH literacy lessons disguised as carpentry sessions. Turned out to be a fine ruse. Every now and then a new shelf, table, or chair appeared and made its way into one of the three family houses. Kevin never did say anything about repairing the first chair, the wobbly one that Robert had made, but perhaps Robert noticed the gesture anyway because a short while later, Kevin found a well-thumbed book in his toolbox—Robert's copy of *A Tale of Two Cities*. Kevin still wasn't able to read it properly, but he liked the promise of it. He often lifted the top tray from the toolbox just to stare at the book concealed underneath. Someday.

Many evenings, when Kate was asleep and the light from the kitchen window faded, Kevin lit the kerosene table lamp and drew it close while he practised forming his letters. He sneaked into Kate's school bag and pulled out her books, reading simple stories about David and Ann and about how those two children bought a box of colourful thread for their mother's birthday. This twigged his memory of Mavis' travel sewing kit which he had recovered on his trip to the Burin. Would he give that kit to Kate? Maybe. Maybe not. For the time being, he would hold it, cherish it, and picture Mavis using it. He sighed the thoughts away and went back to reading Kate's books.

When Kate completed the third grade, Kevin was in the background, doing the same. When Kate asked about the ink stains on his fingers, he muttered about soot from the stove or polish from his boots. When Kate pointed out marks on the kitchen tablecloth, he replaced the oilcloth and, from that point on, left no evidence, not an inkblot nor an eraser crumb. When the wick in the table lamp, Kevin's learning lamp, required frequent replacement, Kevin beamed. All the work was worth it. He was gaining hold. Yes, he was accepting help from Robert here, but it wasn't charity. Once, only once, had Kevin taken charitable help from Robert. That was all for Kate who deserved to have her own home after the ocean shattered their lives. Now was different. Now the men were bartering. Kevin could build anything. Robert, as it turned out, could only pay to have something built. A fair trade.

It was a fine fall day when Kate headed off to her first day in the fourth grade. Kevin bid her goodbye and headed toward Clara's, to the back of the house, to Robert's workshop. In Kevin's mind, it was an outbuilding, like a shed or a store, but Robert called it a workshop. The name of it made no never mind to Kevin.

It was a joiner's pride, this workshop, its walls salvaged from a barn, then sanded, scrubbed, and sealed. On the wall to his right was a single window that looked out at the sea, a proper view for any sailor toiling at the workbench beneath. Flanking the window on both sides were two rows of shelves containing wood planes and kerosene lamps and preserve jars pilfered from the kitchen, proper things for holding nails and screws. Below the shelves on one side was a wooden trunk, its lid up for easy access to sledgehammers and axes, their heads down for safety. On the other side was a table on which sat a long wooden toolbox for gathering and carrying the tools of the day and in front of which were two barrels shaped into chairs. The space on the walls above the bench displayed saws of all kinds, hand saws and buck saws and coping saws.

The opposite wall was home to the heart of the place, the potbelly stove with its box for wood and its cupboard for teacups, handy for boil-ups. Just beyond that was Kevin's treasured alcove, his library, hidden behind a sliding barn door. Everything was here: a stepladder, a rusted first-aid kit, even a mousetrap tucked beneath the workbench in case any rodent dared gnaw its way in.

Kevin placed his toolbox on the desk, sat, and pulled out *A Tale of Two Cities*. He hesitated. Was he even ready for this? Getting into any story was hard. Seems like they all held never-ending accounts of green valleys and forested hills. But this one was different, something about the best of times and the worst of times. A long sentence. But he could have a long wait for Robert. He started. He stumbled. He got up, lit a fire, sat back down, and started again. Yes, it was the longest sentence he had ever seen but he staggered his way to the end of it and he kept going. After a while he fell into the rhythm of the reading, accompanied by crackle of the fire and the cadence of the sea. At the sound of Robert's footsteps, as Kevin put the book aside, he felt a note of disappointment that caught him off guard. He smiled. There was joy in reading.

A brief hello, a boiled kettle, a cup of tea. All part of the routine now. Then the learning. Literacy before carpentry, the advantage of which was that they were less likely to be interrupted at the beginning of their sessions, less likely to be caught. Secrecy was still important to Kevin.

Kevin had graduated from printing to the cursive alphabet. He could now handwrite the names of all of his family members, both the ones on earth and the ones in heaven. Today he wanted to write big words, long sentences of all types, but time was marching. The two hours allotted to literacy was up and it was time for two hours at carpentry. Kevin guided Robert in shaping a table leg while Robert quizzed Kevin on a book they had read. The work flew, and when Robert held up the finished table leg to admire his handiwork, Kevin realized the true benefit of bartering. Here and now, he was Robert's equal, proud of Robert's handiwork and proud of himself as teacher. "Well done, b'y," he said to Robert.

"Not so bad yourself," replied Robert, his grin spread wider than Kevin had ever witnessed. Robert extended a hand. Without hesitation, Kevin responded, locking hands and eyes with Robert. A memory fired, that of his friend Tom Murphy on the Burin and of the bond they shared. Was Kevin ripe for another such friendship? Should his relationship with Robert stay with reading and writing and building and nothing more? Robert was nodding his head. Was there already a bond here? "Jesus," Kevin said, the warmth inside him surfacing in the form of a smile. "You're a good man to my sister, Robert," he offered.

"I'm her husband," Robert replied. They released hands.

Kevin pressed on. "You're good to Kate, too."

"A lovely girl, your Kate."

"Humph. My Kate."

Robert's eyes were alight with concern. "You told me about Kate, about Mavis taking her in. You doing all right?"

Kevin took in a deep breath, sucking a mixed scent of sea and sawdust. When he breathed out, words fell out of him. "Between you and me and the lamppost?"

"We're friends, aren't we?"

Kevin contemplated. Friends. He nodded slowly. "I needed book-learning because I came across letters from Mavis to Clara. Letters that I couldn't make no sense of at all. Letters that could likely tell me who Kate's mother is. I stole those letters. Couldn't find anyone to read them to me so I put them back where I found them."

"But you can read now. You going back to get them?"

Kevin shook his head. "Wrong the first time. Two wrongs won't make it right."

Robert set the completed table leg aside. "Clara has never said anything to me about Kate," he said slowly. "Not a word." He slid a hand across his workbench. Sawdust snowed to the floor. "Have you asked Clara about the letters?" He brushed dust from his hands.

"Can't. Can't tell her I was spying on her."

"You expect me to ask?"

"Well . . ."

Robert put a hand up, palm out. "I wasn't offering to do that. Clara can keep her secrets to herself. As for you, ask her, don't ask her. No judgment here. He looked thoughtful. "Positively no judgment. People who live in glass houses . . ." He sighed, loud and long.

"What are you talking about?"

"We all keep things to ourselves," Robert said in a voice so quiet it brought to Kevin's mind the times he himself had spent on his knees, telling his sins to the priest. What was Robert about to confess? A sense of alarm hit Kevin, bringing heat to his face. He pulled at the collar of his flannel shirt. God help him. He was already harbouring his sister's secret, that of her having an affair.

"Everyone has secrets, Kevin," said Robert.

Did Kevin want to hear this? Could he harbour any more secrets? Perhaps he could organize thoughts into slots the way he organized his tools. A compartment for every secret. Was he able for that? "You've been keeping my secrets," he said, certain that the weight of his doubt was as plain as his words. "I suppose I can hold yours."

"Duly noted." Robert went quiet. "Perhaps another time."

Relieved, maybe a little disappointed, Kevin gave a brief nod.

"Kate was off to school this morning, wasn't she?" asked Robert. "What grade is she in now?'

"Fourth," Kevin replied, relief completely taking over. The talk had returned to the ease of the everyday. Then Clara popped her head through the door and the conversation ended entirely.

"Hello, you two," she said. "What are you on about?"

Robert grabbed the newly-formed table leg and hurried toward Clara. "Look at this, Clara."

Kevin felt his heart pick up pace. He glanced toward the back of the workshop. The books were hidden. He looked at Clara's open expression which echoed the greeting from her lips. No need for alarm. She suspected nothing. He leaned on the workbench, watching the couple while he considered his brother-in-law's potential secrets.

Robert was a good man, the finest kind. Kevin hadn't gone looking for a bond with Robert. It just showed up. Wouldn't it be the proper thing to accept it? As Kevin pondered, he toyed with a chisel from the workbench, all the while wondering if he could dislodge doubt the way he gouged flaws from wood. Why not? With a shrug, he chose to let go, just let doubt slip away. Calmness instantly settled in. The proper thing indeed.

If Robert decided to confide, Kevin would lean in.

CHAPTER 18

———◆———

WITH BOOK-LEARNING TOPPING KEVIN'S LIST of skills as carpenter, fisherman, sailor, and machinist, his pride rose like mist. A fair wind would come and the jobs would sail in. And sail in they did, the first a few miles away in Jerseyside where a master shipbuilder had three schooners under construction. Kevin eased through the hiring for that one, paperwork and all. It seemed too soon, the completion of the work, but Kevin kept an eye out, looking for the next job and it came. There was a cottage hospital on the build in Argentia. Following that and handy to it, was the construction of the herring factory. Life for Kevin was the best kind now, no thought to trouble. Perhaps he should have been just a little afraid because, when he wasn't paying attention, trouble dropped right out of the mouth of Salty Joe Sallivan's wife.

Mrs. Sallivan was a crusty, bitter soul, always fired up about God knows what. Her husband spent his days bent over a salt-laden wheelbarrow and had the curved spine to prove it. In Kevin's mind, the man's rounded back had more to do with wife than work. That woman screeched the hymns in the church, scoured the sacristy to a shine, and harped on her husband something fierce. Not Kevin's business though, none of it. *Say nothing and saw wood.* Kevin made a point of stepping aside when he saw her coming.

At the merchant store one day, Kevin didn't step fast enough. Mrs. Sallivan was ahead of him in the line, pounding on the counter, yelling "Serve me" while the merchant's wife was busy serving someone else. Kevin was taken aback. What on earth possessed people to go on like that?

When Mrs. Sallivan turned suddenly, Kevin fixed his gaze on the wall of tinned goods behind the counter. She sidled up to him, stabbed a finger at his face, and prattled in his ear. "You're not fooling me, Kevin Kerrigan. I knows you can't read them labels."

Kevin snapped his head toward her, glaring, barely managing to hold his tongue. No point in saying anything. She'd be done and gone soon enough. But the woman hovered, met his glare, and curled her lip. "Your sister Clara," she spat, "she's some fool if she thinks that Caulins fella don't got no other woman." With a self-satisfied nod, Mrs. Sallivan plunged her hands into her gloves and snatched up her brown paper package. Then she stomped out, banging the door in the process. The bell above the door sprang into a jangle and a rush of chilled air swept into the room.

Kevin remained silent, but not so the merchant's wife. "Knock the door right off its hinges, why don't ya?" she yelled from behind the counter. A strapping woman, the merchant's wife. She had wide eyes and thick lips and a pimpled face that was currently puckered with anger. Kevin looked at the two red pencils that jutted like devil's horns from her knot of dark hair. Certain there were more comments coming from her and not wanting to hear tell of any of them, he hesitated before moving to the counter.

The merchant's wife planted her hands on her hips and gave him a knowing look. "Cold enough to clip you, that woman," she said. Then she rolled her eyes, yanked a pencil from her hair, and swapped her frown for a grin. "Now what are ya after today, Kevin, b'y?"

Kevin smiled. Not a devil at all, this woman, but one who'd just had a devil of a time. He stepped up, bought the sandpaper he'd come for, and made his way home.

When the shadow of evening put an end to the labour of the day, he set to thinking about Mrs. Sallivan. How had she conjured up such a bit of spite? Perhaps Salty Joe got wind of a rumour from Robert's crew. If so, if the rumour was true, was it any odds to Kevin? Clara was his sister, his family. Did he have any responsibility here? He sniffed. Clara herself had another man in a backroom someplace. Not Kevin's business, none of it. But curiosity was clawing. Who was Robert Caulins? What possessed him to leave his native Great Britain in favour of an isolated place like Newfoundland? Was it money? No end to the things men did for the love of money. He glanced at the clock. He and Robert were meeting tomorrow. Another skills session.

Kevin stood in the doorway of the workshop, staring at Robert who was bent over a lathe in the centre of the space, shaping spindles for the back of a chair. Robert looked at home with the wood turning, his left foot steady on the treadle, his black boot coated with a layer of dust. Unnoticed, Kevin lingered in the doorway, letting a bit of sun warm the back of him while he turned things over in his mind. What harm would there be in mentioning the rumour? He fidgeted as he eyed his surroundings.

Kevin took a deep breath and let it slide out. He reached a hand toward the captain's bell beside the door, grabbed the rope, and jerked it.

The single clang grabbed Robert's attention. "Good morning," he said without stopping his work.

"Rumour is that you got another woman somewhere," said Kevin.

Robert removed his foot from the treadle and its steady drone faded into silence. He raised the spindle he'd been working on to eye level, spinning it through his fingers, examining every crevice. Here a puff of breath, there a swipe of sandpaper, in the air a haze of dust. With slow, easy movement, Robert set the spindle onto the workbench and turned toward Kevin. "Close the door."

CHAPTER 19

—◆—

"I WONDERED WHEN WE'D GET to this," Robert said as he sagged against the workbench. "I was gathering the nerve to tell you before but Clara showed up and the opportunity flew out. After that? Second thoughts. You're her brother. Devoted to your family, as it should be. So I said nothing."

"Perhaps I should be doing the same thing myself," Kevin sighed. "Saying nothing, I mean."

Robert shook his head. "To everything a season. It's time." He closed his eyes for a moment, perhaps needing to rest. "You mentioned a rumour?"

"From the wharf, I reckon."

"My crew." Robert sighed. "Ironically, I hired them because they were not from Newfoundland. Come-from-aways, the lot of them, like myself. I figured strangers wouldn't gossip with locals."

"All it takes on a wharf is an idle word."

"Apparently." Fatigue lined Robert's face. He stumbled toward the barrel chairs, rolled one from under the table, and dropped into it. He indicated toward the other.

Kevin remained in the doorway. A sentry of sorts. He had no liking to move.

"Good enough," said Robert. With his head lowered and his arms folded, he started in. "I told Clara that the *Elizabeth J* is named after my mother. It's not." He stopped. He looked up.

"Who then?"

Robert hardened his gaze. "It's named after my wife."

Every muscle in Kevin's body tightened. He instantly put a hand up, palm out. *You can't see all you see and you can't hear all you hear.* Did he want to hear this? Not a chance in hell, but a question shot right out of him anyway. "Are you telling me you're married to someone else?"

"Yes and no."

Kevin felt a vile taste in his mouth. He stared past Robert to the kettle on the potbelly stove, a kettle so blackened there wasn't a hint of shine left on it. Had he misjudged Robert, seeing decency that was long gone? Was it ever there at all? He looked back at the man, waiting.

"My wife left me," Robert said. "And her name is not Elizabeth. It's Elsheva." He paused again, giving Kevin a direct stare.

If there was meaning in that stare, Kevin didn't twig to it. Elizabeth. Elsheva. The name made no difference. "What about Clara?"

"The name Elsheva is Hebrew, Kevin."

"Why the hell did you marry Clara?"

"Elsheva left me."

"So? Why did you marry Clara? Is your marriage to my sister even legal?"

"Please." Robert raised both hands. "Sit down. I'll explain. You do what you will. Good enough?"

A reluctant Kevin stumbled into motion, edged toward the second barrel chair, and rolled it from under the table. It clunked into position. Kevin paused, then moved it again, slightly farther away from Robert, farther away from the words that were about to forge a path between the two. He sat. In silence, he surveyed his friend.

Robert, always a giant in Kevin's eyes, looked trivial in this instant, a greying man in overalls, one strap unhooked and dangling, his face as red as his flannel shirt, which was matted with sweat. Pulling a handkerchief from his pocket, Robert mopped his brow.

"Elsheva is a learned woman, a linguist. Speaks German, English, and French. Italian too, if I remember correctly. She wouldn't stay in London where my titled and entitled relatives treated her as less because she was Jewish. She went home to Germany. To Berlin. She took our three children." His eyes teared up. "Fool that I was, I let her go." Drops spilled onto his cheeks.

Kevin couldn't watch tears falling, not on a man, at least not this man. He focused instead on the mousetrap beneath the workbench, a trap that was set, a clump of cheese sitting there, lying in wait. "You telling me," he said, stepping cautiously, stretching his words to match his misgivings, "you telling me that your family up and left and you just let them go?"

Robert shrugged. "When I came to my senses, it was too late. Other than responding to a couple of letters, Elsheva would have nothing to do with me." He wiped the handkerchief across his eyes and then used it to swipe at dust on his boot. "When the rum running came," he said in a raspy voice, "I opted for life on the sea."

"Life on the sea." Kevin glanced through the window toward the ocean. The tide was coming in, a grey billow. Kevin himself had opted for life on the sea, leaving his mother and father and sister when he was a mere sixteen. Determined to get by on his own hooks. A child. Not a man. But he would never have allowed his wife and children to sail away, now would he? He sniffed. Did it matter? The ocean took them anyway. The Atlantic had seemed like a friend and then it turned on him. He turned toward Robert. "Mind telling me when this happened?"

"1925."

"And you married Clara in '26?"

Robert nodded.

"You divorced Elsheva?"

Robert shook his head. "Never got around to that."

Kevin stared at him, hoping to hear a retraction. The gulls set to screeching, but Robert? Not a word. "Jesus H. Christ," Kevin muttered.

"Indeed."

"Three? Did you say three children? How old were they?"

"The girl was a couple of months. The twin boys were just over a year."

Kevin did some quick calculations. "So twelve and thirteen now? Not much older than Kate?"

Another nod.

"And not a word out of the lot of them?"

Robert opened his mouth, then opted to swallow. He shook his head.

"So why not just leave it be?"

"Do you pay attention to what's going on in the world? To the radio? To the newspaper? Jewish people in Germany have been deprived of citizenship. Conscription is back. Hitler has amassed tanks and planes and there's mass exodus going on in Europe. Elsheva and I may be estranged, but I want to make sure they get out of Germany."

"What kind of fool notion is that?"

"The only notion I have. I've tried to dismiss it but I can't." He turned his attention to the floor. "I've already been trying to find them, to help them. I have contacts." With a shudder, Robert chucked his handkerchief into a corner. He ran smudged fingers through his thinning hair. "A good woman, your sister. Deserved better than she got." He jumped to his feet. "Your father Alphonse met me on the wharf, ready to hand her off to a husband like she was a head of cattle." Robert paced the floor, each stomping step creating a tiny cloud of dust. "Perhaps I was trying to rescue her, to make up for what I failed to do for my own wife." He came to a standstill. "How arrogant can a man be?"

"You think your sins are back to haunt you?"

Robert nodded. "Sins get heavier, the weight of them can break a man who has nowhere to put them, no way to change them." He looked at Kevin, eyes sagging with apology.

"There's more to the truth of why I married Clara. You deserve my honesty. I needed a home base in a small place with a safe harbour, a place to stash money. The truth is that I used Clara's situation to my advantage. And once I'd done that, put my moral compass aside, her past didn't matter." Robert let out a long sigh.

Kevin turned to him. "Did you tell Clara all this?"

Robert shook his head. "Started to. But, in the end, I cared more than I wanted to."

Kevin pulled back, his gut churning. How was he supposed to feel about this? Shouldn't he be outraged with this man who had used his sister? Nothing inside him pointed to anger, not so much as a clenched jaw. Why not? A memory ringed his brain, then stumbled in, that of the name Patrick tumbling from Clara's lips, that of Clara turning red in the face from the slip of her tongue, that of Clara begging Kevin not to say anything to Robert about it. Kevin recalled her exact words. "Would cost me my marriage." Now Kevin wondered how she'd feel if she knew she wasn't married at all, neither in the eyes of the Church nor the law.

"Surely you know that I have been kind to Clara. Sometimes distant, but always kind." His face took on a plea. "I don't want her to know about this, about Elsheva. I don't want Clara to be hurt."

"It's a bit late for that, isn't it? Clara already has it in her mind that you want to leave. Said something about you missing home, going back to England."

"Home?" With a heavy sigh, Robert dropped back into his barrel chair. "I guess England is home but it's not really mine. Not anymore. Too much time and ocean between England and me. And the island of Newfoundland, grand as it is, is yours, not mine. It's not home I'm concerned about now."

"So you're not going to England?"

"England is a stepping stone. I have to get to Germany. Maybe this year. Lots of people travelling to Berlin to the Olympics."

"Olympics? In Berlin?" It all seemed too much to Kevin. The wind was picking up outside, the gulls were clambering in from the sea. The bit of sun he'd felt earlier had given way to a bitter chill. A storm was on the way. Berlin? "Why the hell are you telling me this? Clara is my sister, for Christ's sake."

"You asked."

Kevin let out a long sigh. "Well, things can't be too bad if the Olympics are in Berlin. The whole world will be watching Germany. Perhaps you should wait, see how things turn out."

"Perhaps." Robert went quiet. "Kevin," he said, his voice a mere whisper, "if you'd had a chance to get ahead of the wave that took your family . . ." He looked up, his eyes vacant.

Instantly Kevin's protest vanished, all questions draining away like deck water through a ship's scuppers. He rose from his chair and was struck by a dizzying sensation, the air around him a swirl of memory and regret. Steadying himself, he aimed toward the desk at the back of the workshop, pausing to place a quiet hand on Robert's shoulder. He just stood there.

"I have a bad feeling about this Hitler business," said Robert.

Kevin stayed very still.

"I have to get them out but I have to find them first,' said Robert. "Eleven years. I have to find them."

Kevin removed his hand from Robert's shoulder. He slumped as he headed to the writing desk at the back.

"Wait," said Robert.

Kevin stopped.

"It may be a year or two before I go, but when I go, I won't likely be back. I can't tell Clara. Maybe I'm a coward, but that's the way it is. Clara's a strong woman, but this? Another family? I can't tell her. I can't watch myself do that. But I have to leave. My children . . ."

Kevin looked directly at Robert. "Your secret is safe," he said.

Desperation crowded Robert's eyes. He did not look convinced.

Kevin harked back to a time he himself was the desperate one, when the rum had a hold on him, when he nearly made away with himself. It was Robert who pulled him back from the edge. "Your secret is safe," Kevin repeated, his words a vow, as solid as a signed contract. "And if you need help, just ask."

Kevin continued to the back, to the reading desk, leaving the slicing door of the alcove open, keeping an eye on Robert.

Robert sat motionless for a long time. When a crack from the mouse-trap split the silence, Robert plodded his way toward the workbench, disposed of the dead mouse, and reset the trap.

Shortly after that, the lathe went back to its hum.

KATHLEEN

CHAPTER 20

◆

IT IS A PASSAGEWAY, THE sea.

The North Atlantic bustles with liners and schooners and coasters scudding the fiords and bays and harbours of the island of Newfoundland. The sea welcomes all vessels, those carrying fishermen, those ferrying fish, those transporting the privileged, and those conveying the penniless. She receives ships with grace and even greets skiffs, mere dots against the billow, some with eager passengers bound for Sunday Mass, others with beleaguered occupants bent upon medical aid. So cordial the sea, who brings lovers and families together. So cruel the sea, who rips lovers and families apart. The Atlantic is the passageway, the only way, and as evidenced in her constant swell, she revels in her power.

In my living years, as I witnessed my loved ones set sail, I cringed with the silent agony of those who have no choice but to cede to the rule of the sea. Now adrift in the afterlife, I bear witness to all vessels brave enough to spill onto the Atlantic. Still powerless, I watch and wait in the background while my spirit twists in the wind. The agony persists.

I observe my Clara as she skips on and off the schooner, as lighthearted in her leaving as in her homecoming. I scrutinize Robert who, unlike Clara, sags his way on and off the gangway. This discrepancy is a foreboding, the signal of a brittle snap. Not now, this break, but in time there will come a lone trip along the ocean corridor for Robert. A dark shadow passes through me and a dark thought emerges. How dare he abandon my Clara? I fervently wish him a watery tomb. The air is heavy and still and I wallow in it, up to my eyes in penitent sighs. Perhaps I could be kinder to Robert. Yet, as ghost, each and every time I tell this story, I experience the same feelings, the same wishes, in the same order.

The breeze picks up, nudging me, a reminder to move on. So I refrain from regret and choose to observe the comings and goings of skiffs and ships and daughter and son.

And son-in-law.

Camouflaged in a film of fog, I slide up beside my Clara and her husband as they approach the island of St. Pierre. The sea is surprisingly slick and smooth in this season when storms can arise, and the schooner, guided by a groan of foghorn and a steady hand upon the wheel, slips slowly into dock. I hug tight to Clara's shoulder as the two alight from the vessel.

It is nostalgia that has these two sailing the sea to this old haunt. But the world here now, as revealed piece by piece in the lifting of the fog, is not the world of their memory. With Prohibition gone, there are few people, fewer sailors, all ambling, not scurrying as they did in the glory days when whisky barrels and heavy boots rocked the pier. No more do residents sell booze from every building but the church. No longer do women's steps jangle from the jiggling bottles veiled in skirts. The longshoremen who abandoned cod for cargo have returned to jigging in dories, and the stench of fish guts has replaced the aroma of sawdust that was used to cushion bottles.

As Clara eyes the long line of abandoned warehouses in front of her, her face is blank, a reflection of their emptiness. "So sad, isn't it?" she whispers to Robert.

Robert says nothing.

I remain with them, hovering, as they leave St. Pierre, as the *Elizabeth J.* navigates the Cape of St. Mary's on its way to St. John's. I watch Clara who in turn watches every slow, deliberate, and seemingly reluctant move her husband makes. When he swerves away midsentence and heads into the wheelhouse, she doesn't trail him. Instead, she stands feet wide apart, fists on hips. She maintains this deck posture, letting the wind blow through her hair, likely letting all manner of thoughts spin through her head. As the schooner pitches with the swell of the sea, my Clara lurches to the gunwale and retches into the foam. A gust of wind jolts me. My sailor daughter seasick? She hauls her hand across her mouth and I can tell by the sour look on her face that acid is burning her gullet. Clara knows that change is coming. All through their journey, even after they land in St. John's, she continues her traipsing to and from the gunwales. Useless as I am, I cling to her side unnoticed, wishing I could do more than observe her suffering.

In St. John's, Clara studies her husband as he stares through the window of their hotel room, his arms folded, his body swaying, his meerschaum pipe emitting intermittent puffs of smoke. I notice his thinness and wonder, does she? It's easy enough to hide weight loss at sea when sweaters and slickers shield one's frame. My Clara steals a glance at her husband's breakfast plate. Every triangle of buttered toast remains intact. His pot of orange marmalade is untouched. His teacup is full, milky, and no doubt cold.

A look of guilt crosses Clara's face. She turns her eyes to him again. I'm sure she sees it now, his thinning body and his greying hair. Surely some form of wifely duty is about to well into words.

Clara slips up behind Robert and follows his gaze. A British ship, the object of his attention, is navigating the harbour, its Union Jack unfurled and whipping in the wind. Clara edges closer, so close her face brushes the linen of his shirt.

Robert flinches.

She steps back. "Are you missing your homeland, Robert?" she says, her voice tentative.

"Whatever makes you think that?" His words are firm, a barricade.

She points past him, at the British ship.

Robert's rigid posture softens a little, then a little more. Moving to a side table, he gingerly sets his pipe down. A sigh comes, followed by a nod. "I miss my homeland," he says.

"I think I might like England."

The air seems a jacket colder, catching her words and holding them in a draught that has emerged through some undetected crack in the window casing. Clara's breath is a sharp intake. She is clearly testing the waters here. Dare she continue?

The back of Robert's neck turns a peculiar shade of red. "There's no point in discussing this now. I won't go for a while." He tugs at his collar. "Besides, it's one thing to hug the shore as we sail into outports. It's another thing entirely to take on the Atlantic."

"But surely you're not talking about crossing the ocean in the schooner?" says Clara. "That's what passenger ships are for. I would love—"

Robert jerks into motion, storming across the floor and snatching his overcoat from the closet. He thrusts his arms through its sleeves. "I'll be back in a couple of hours," he says without casting a glance in Clara's direction.

I hang in the wrinkle of air between them.

"You don't want me to go to England with you, do you?" Clara spits the words which sear through me to her target.

Robert's hands twitch and he shoves them into his pockets.

My daughter assumes the satisfied look of someone who knows she has landed a successful blow. A silent, simmering gap ensues. Will it bubble up, boil over? Clara must know she could lose the schooner by challenging him here and now. Is she pondering her own foolishness? It matters little for the words have been flung. As I look from one to the other, Clara stiffens, ramrod straight, and folds her arms.

Robert does a slow turn, his eyes searching her face.

The retaliation Clara seems to have braced for does not come. Robert does not lash out. Instead, I am witness to a man dissolving, his body sagging, his face turning ashen.

The air aches. I ache. How tired is this man that he can be furious one minute and flattened the next?

"I will go back to England and I will go alone," he says. "Trouble is brewing in Europe. My homeland could be facing war. I must and will go back. But you? War is no place for a woman." With a hint of a nod, he exits. The door sighs closed behind him.

As Clara slowly returns to the window and stares through it, I ponder his parting words. Didn't he once use those same words to describe the sea, telling Clara the sea was no place for a woman? Then, I disagreed with him. Now, the mother in me wholeheartedly supports his view. War is no place for my Clara.

My concern fades with the passing of days, for Robert doesn't take himself, or anyone else, anywhere. Not for a long time. Quiet and sullen, he keeps whatever qualms or plans he may have close to the vest. As months slide into years and worries of war whirl, Robert remains in Argentia, holding steady for some sign that it's time to go.

When that sign comes, true to his word, Robert does not take my daughter.

However, he does attach a towline to my son.

KEVIN

CHAPTER 21

———◆———

Kevin had finished installing storm windows and was now hard at it, putting up storm doors, vital chores that would see him and Kate through the winter. After this, he planned to hang doors and windows on his mother's house and then on his sister's. Robert would help him with that last one.

Thoughts of working with Robert again brought a sense of contentment to Kevin. Not so long ago, the two had installed a bright red, hand-carved door at the Caulins' home. A lot of effort, but there was joy in the job, and the delight on Clara's face was worth it. A good deed if ever there was one. Yes, Kevin enjoyed working with Robert.

While checking hinges on the back door, Kevin heard footsteps behind him. He shot a bit of oil into the upper hinge before he turned. "Robert. Good to see ya, b'y. What are ya at?"

"Planning to leave. That's what I'm at."

Kevin paused, holding the oil can in mid-air while the words fell over him like needles of rain prickling his skin. It had been a long time since he'd heard words of leaving from Robert. "Come on in, b'y," he said, placing the oil can on the step. He then led the way to the kitchen. At the table, he pulled out a chair for Robert who quietly sat. Kevin plopped into a chair opposite.

Robert stared at the table.

Kevin dug in for the wait. On some level, he had hoped that the situation with Robert's other family had resolved itself or that Robert had somehow forgotten about it. A foolish thought there. Kevin would never have forgotten about his own family.

"*Kristallnacht*," Robert muttered.

Kevin leaned in. "What?"

"*Kristallnacht*, a German word. It means 'Night of the Broken Glass,' the night when the streets glittered with shattered glass from storefront windows."

Silence fell again, and again Kevin waited. Robert lowered his head, then glanced up, his eyelids drooping, his eyes mere slits. The corners of his mouth and his shoulders sagged like they were being dragged by an undertow. Even Robert's clothes, usually neat, were wilting. Kevin would have to be blind not to see that the man was drowning in his past, and had to face it now. Robert needed to talk about it, about his other family.

"Apparently some young frustrated Jewish man shot a German and the Nazis retaliated with a vengeance," Robert said. "The Nazis destroyed Jewish synagogues and Jewish-owned stores and Jewish cemeteries. At least a hundred were killed and they arrested thirty thousand Jewish men. I don't know if Elsheva is safe, if the children . . ." His voice broke. He cleared his throat. "This is the first time the Nazis have rounded up Jewish people like cattle and herded them off. It won't be the last."

As the wave of information came at Kevin, he leaned back in his chair and closed his eyes. Images of broken glass and broken bodies flew before him. He opened his eyes and looked out his own window, one of the new-ly-installed windows. Was all of this horror going on while he himself was putting up storm windows to guard against the destruction of winter? It was impulsive, his reaching his hand and placing it on Robert's forearm.

Robert pulled away. "Don't be too kind, Kev. Not now."

"Good enough." Kevin sat back. "Does Clara know you're planning to leave?"

Robert nodded. "But she doesn't know exactly why." He retrieved an envelope from his coat pocket. His fingers trembled as he thrust it toward Kevin. "After I leave, will you give her this letter?"

Kevin took the sealed letter. He turned it over and over in his hands. "You leaving right away?"

Robert shrugged. "Not until spring."

"What's in this letter?"

"Truth."

With a sigh, Kevin placed the letter on the table in front of him. "You want her to have it as soon as you leave?"

"When the time is right. You'll do it?"

"Do my best."

Stumbling to his feet, Robert shuffled toward the door.

Kevin made no attempt to follow. "Robert," he said, his voice low.

The shuffling stopped.

"I owe you my life, Robert." He looked up and saw that Robert was staring directly at him. "If you need me . . ."

Robert nodded. The new storm door offered not a squeak of resistance as Robert plodded through.

Kevin stared at the letter. He would deliver it. Eventually. How much did Clara need to know? Would any of this matter to her? And what odds was it to him? He had chores to do. Windows, doors, hinges. Shrugging, he shoved the letter into the bib pocket of his overalls. Seconds later, oil can in hand, he was back on task.

CLARA

CHAPTER 22

—◆—

As CLARA WAS LAYING THE table, the noon church bells sounded, a reminder to the faithful to pray the Angelus. She made do with the sign of the cross and continued with her task. The back door creaked open. "Is Kevin coming to help you put up the storm windows today?" she called.

"Maybe later," said Robert, entering the kitchen. As he seated himself at the table, the chill of November sat down with him and Clara shivered as she ladled pea soup into bowls. She placed the bowls on the table and pulled on a wool cardigan before she joined him.

"Winter's coming," she said. "The windows need to be seen to before an Atlantic storm cracks the casings and shatters the glass."

Robert's glance was quick and pained, like she'd pierced him somehow. Puzzled, Clara bit her lip, watching him stir his soup, the air now heavy with all-too-familiar silence. Her sigh was, by design, soundless.

Conversation between them had faded by degrees, folded into a habit of greetings and send-offs and remarks about the weather. Seasons coming and going while his thoughts were God only knew where, while hers were on dreams about her lover.

As Clara sipped her soup, she slipped into memory, recalling the day she married Robert, the day her father gave her away like she was livestock. She had wanted the church floor to swallow her whole. But she had stood there and gone through with it. And, in the time that followed, this gentleman, Robert, filled her life with conversation, music, literature, and even skill at sea. And now?

And now there was a constant hush, one on which Clara would never comment. How could she? What had she ever given Robert? Nothing. Not loyalty. Certainly not children. Perhaps his current conduct was a sign of regret. Why ever had he married her anyway?

Robert dipped a chunk of dumpling into his soup, chewed, and swallowed, repeating the actions until his spoon brayed its way across an empty bowl. He turned toward her, stared for a moment. "You will do a great job at the helm of the schooner, Clara," he said.

The words surprised Clara, even created a glow in her. She parted her lips to breathe a thank you but stopped dead, stifled by a rush of truth. There was no compliment in Robert's statement. He wasn't flattering her at all. Robert was leaving her. He had hinted at it in the past, at missing England, at going back. Many times. But this time? This was a certainty.

Mouth agape, she gazed at him. After a brisk nod, he walked away from the table, his steps quick, sure. The den door creaked open, clicked shut. She flinched. Easy for him to retreat to his pipe, books, his radio. Not at all satisfied, she followed, pushed open the den door, and leaned into the jamb. "Why wasn't a man like you taken?"

"What?" Perched in his wingback chair, pipe in one hand, pouch in the other, Robert stared at her.

"You heard me the first time."

"At one point, I guess I was."

"I need more than that. Why did you marry me?"

Robert sighed. "I rescued you, Clara. You know the answer to that as well as I do. Your father . . ."

"There's nothing you can tell me about my father," she said, voice raised, heart racing. She took a deep breath. "That's all you have to say then? A rescue?"

Robert fumbled with his tobacco pouch, stuffing his pipe. The aroma of tobacco wafted. He struck a match, brought it to the pipe bowl, and sucked. The bowl glowed. He huffed out a stream of smoke. "That's all I have to say," he said, his voice clipped and cold.

Bitten, Clara stepped back.

Robert rose from his chair, walked to the door, and closed it. *Click.*

Stung, Clara gasped. Had he really just closed the door in her face? Clara reached for the doorknob. She hesitated, withdrew her hand, and slogged her way back to the kitchen. She reclaimed her chair and let her thoughts run. When would Robert go to England? Would he return? Did that matter? He was leaving her. She put a hand over her heart. Yes, he was leaving her and telling her she'd do a great job with the schooner. She paused, letting that sink in. Did he mean that he was leaving her the schooner? Dear Father in heaven! Robert was leaving her the schooner. Clara sat back in her chair. Wasn't that what she always wanted? Yes, and yet she couldn't force herself to smile.

As the days shortened into winter, Robert remained in Argentia, silent and plodding and hiding in his den, and continued on that way through both the storms and the celebrations of the holiday season. It was not until the days lengthened into spring that he told Clara his plans. "I'm going to England next week," he said, an announcement, not an invitation to discussion. He then turned heel and walked away.

It was unexpected, the pang Clara felt when the time came to see her husband off. Throngs of people were milling about on Harvey's Wharf in St. John's, people like Robert and herself—passengers bound for Britain and well-wishers saying goodbye. Could Clara bring herself to say goodbye to this man standing beside her, this man who had been at her side for years? Should she insist that he stay? That this was his home? Would she truly miss him or was she just lying to herself? She sucked in a breath and let it slide out, slow and soundless. It was Robert who spoke first.

"Before I go," he said and then paused, casting his eyes low. "Before I go, I want to tell you . . ." He let the words fade away.

With a tremble, Clara grabbed his arm. Robert drew her close, cupping a hand around her chin. "Life is full of secrets, Clara. You are a good wife. Loyal and loving. Perhaps I will be back. But if war breaks out . . ." With that he brushed his lips across hers and headed for the gangway.

Clara scrutinized the lanky Robert as he walked away, his brown leather suitcase at his side. It was not so unusual, his walking away. How many mornings had she watched Robert leave for the schooner? But he always came back. Would he come back this time? Another spasm of pain. Dear God, for all her sins, she depended on Robert, her husband, her companion. Should she run to him? Tell him she loved him? That she would wait for him? Why didn't he turn and wave? He always turned to wave.

Panic clutched Clara and she tore after him, calling his name, calling and calling his name. When he stopped, a few yards in front of her, she came to an abrupt halt. Panting, she stared at him, looking for some welcoming sign. He put the suitcase on the wharf and spread his arms wide. Clara lurched into an all-out run and then jumped. He caught her and twirled her, much in the same way that he had when they had danced at the galas at the Newfoundland Hotel. Clara flared her lips into the widest possible smile. She was still smiling when Robert plunked her down and still smiling when the wind attempted to lift her blue felt hat. She clamped a hand on top of the hat, holding it firm, and she leaned her head back to meet Robert's eyes. It was then that her smile died. Robert's face was as grim as a requiem.

"I have to leave, Clara. I have to see what is happening, what is coming to my homeland. But I want you to know that I care for you. Perhaps I didn't right away, when we met, but I do now."

Clara, awash with guilt, opened her mouth to blurt her wrongdoings. *Bless me, Father for I have sinned . . .* Her thoughts writhed with words of confession, with admission of adultery, but she could not voice those thoughts. Robert said he loved her. Robert was leaving, possibly to war. Robert had been good to her. She let out a deep breath. "Whatever happens, I'll be here for you when you get back. I'll wait for you, Robert." The promise strangled her, cutting her breath short. *Liar. Adulterer.*

Robert drew her into his arms once again. "I love you, Clara," he said.

"I love you, too," said Clara. It was what he wanted to hear, wasn't it?

He released her from his embrace and turned away. Sadness dragged at Clara and she dropped her arms to her sides. It wasn't really a lie, was it, the love part? She did love him, after a fashion. Not the way she loved

Patrick, the very sight of whom made her whole body shiver with desire that women were not even supposed to think about. But she did lie about being the waiting wife.

Robert strode across the gangway onto the vessel. He'd be gone soon, wouldn't he? Gone. The thought triggered a flutter in Clara's heart. Much to her surprise, there was little, if any, sense of loss in that fluttering heart. A tiny gasp flew from her and she touched her fingertips to her parted lips. What kind of woman was she at all? What kind of woman was happy to see her husband go to war? She didn't want to consider the dark answer to that question but the answer slapped her anyway. Heat rushed to her face. She herself was that kind of woman, the kind who cheated on her husband. For a few moments, Clara allowed herself to indulge in thoughts of Patrick.

With Robert gone, she would see Patrick more often. The only obstacle was that Patrick lived here, in St. John's, and Clara spent most of her time at sea or at home. But she had met Patrick at home, in Argentia, hadn't she? Would he consider living there, now that there was no husband cluttering the path to her front door? The idea flitted, a pleasant sensation, and then floundered. There'd be no end to the chin wagging. Clara couldn't subject Kate or Kathleen or herself, for that matter, to the gossip. No there'd be none of that. Sighing, she returned her attention to the departing ship.

The deckhands tossed and hauled lines. Clara tapped a foot. The crew hauled in the gangway and the ship's horn sounded. Engines churned. Almost there. A space appeared between the dock and the port side of the vessel. The water swished its resistance, the crowd waved at passengers, and goodbyes floated in the air.

Clara put her hand above her eyes and searched for Robert on the deck. There he was, leaning on the railing. She raised her arm and, using as much effort as she would if she were extracting water from a reluctant pump, she waved. She continued to wave until the ship entered The Narrows, until it passed the lighthouse at Fort Amherst, until the crowd onshore began to disperse. Then she stood there, both arms folded around her torso while people strolled about. She swayed gently as she wondered what would become of Robert, what he was going home to. Everyone had secrets, he had said. What of his secrets? Was he trying to tell her something? If so, why had he not shared with her? A glance around showed gaping cavities in the crowd. It was time for her to leave but her body was heavy with unwillingness. Then someone called her name and she swerved. Instantly, the weight lifted.

"Patrick," she said. She stared, drinking in his tall, lean body, his steel-blue eyes, and thick, fair hair. All this despite his attire, that of a longshoreman, woollen coat, overalls, and salt-and-pepper cap. Where was his chauffeur's uniform? Didn't matter. Clara's body shivered, the way it always did when she saw him. The longing came too, a physical longing that Clara had no name for. Flushed with heat, she lowered her head so that she was now staring at Patrick's scuffed boots.

"Come with me," he said, his hand reaching into her line of vision.

Staring at his outstretched hand, Clara stood motionless. Patrick was waiting for her while she was supposed to be waiting for her husband, Robert. She glanced toward the ship one last time. It was far off now, through The Narrows and into open water. Robert was gone.

Clara did not take Patrick's hand. She did walk to him, stand beside him, and inhale the scent of him. He nodded, comprehending, and dropped his hand to his side. Together, they strolled, their destination known—his lodgings in the lowest level of the three-story house not far from Bannerman Park. A long walk, mostly uphill. A quiet walk, during which concerns about Robert drifted into Clara's mind. She didn't hold onto the disquiet, just dismissed it, piece by piece, the way a breeze plucks tufts of mist from a mountain top. As they neared Patrick's residence, Clara, her mind clear, her heart present, grabbed Patrick's key from his hand, raced to the door, and hurried into his bathroom. From her purse, she pulled a comb and a small bottle of eau de toilette. She dropped her felt hat to the floor, loosened her hair from its dignified bun, and let it cascade. She combed and fluffed, a push here, a pull there, until curled tendrils draped evenly over her shoulders. She dabbed scent on her neck, her breasts, and her wrists.

When Patrick entered his bedroom, she was posed by the bed, hand on the bedpost, blouse unbuttoned. Patrick did not take his eyes off her as he closed the door.

Clara afforded herself the pleasure of taking him in. When, at sixteen, she first encountered this man, she was so short she had to tilt her head back to see his blue eyes. She'd gained a couple of inches in height but she was still looking up at, and getting lost in, those eyes.

Patrick tossed his jacket onto an overstuffed chair in the corner. "It has been too long," he said, his voice a hoarse whisper. He scooped her up and dropped her onto the bed.

When darkness fell and Patrick slipped into slumber, Clara stared into the blackness and contemplated. She owned one truth: the man beside her was the man she wanted. She would continue to sin. Maybe one day, she and Patrick would be permanently linked. But today? Reaching out, she ran her fingertips along his arm. She pushed her breasts up against his back. He turned.

The next morning, as Captain Clara Caulins guided her schooner from the bowl of St. John's harbour through The Narrows and into open water, her enthusiasm knew no bounds. It had been long, the wait to be a woman at the helm, and today, with sun blazing and sea shining, she owned the role. She indulged in thinking that the Atlantic was welcoming her, perhaps experiencing the same delight she was. Indeed, it seemed that the ocean had just opened its arms and drawn the *Elizabeth J* in. Silly thoughts, perhaps. The Atlantic couldn't care less who was at the helm. Right here and right now, it was the opinion of the crew that counted. And for the most part, her crew, Robert's original crew, were loyal.

There was one disgruntled employee, a new and gnarled hire named Beady whose round eyes bulged with disbelief when Clara boarded the vessel and took the helm from Niall, her first mate. This newcomer had assumed Niall, the man who'd hired him, was captain of the *Elizabeth J*. No surprise there: a man's reaction in a man's world. Beady said nothing untoward at the time but, as he went about hauling lines, he uttered a litany of muttered complaints that did not escape the mate's attention.

"The likes of him," Niall reported to Clara, "flapping his jaws about the bad luck of a woman at the helm of a boat. Figures we'll all be done in by a hurricane. Superstitious arse. Gave him a piece of my mind."

"What piece would that be, Niall?" asked Clara.

"Told him it would take more than a bit of wind to conquer Clara Caulins. Told him about you at the helm with the Coast Guard on our tail. Told him you sailed this vessel like you stole it."

"It was Robert who was at the helm that night," she said.

"But Beady don't need to know that, now do he?" Niall ran a hand through his bushy red hair. With a grin and a salute, he headed abaft.

Clara laughed as she headed to the wheelhouse.

CHAPTER 23

———◆———

REELING FROM THE SUCCESS OF her first stint as captain, Clara crossed the threshold of her home, flew up the stairs, and flung open all the second-floor windows to release the stale air. Barrelling back to the first floor, she repeated the procedure. She had just opened the latch on the kitchen window when the shriek of a gull tore through her like a nail ripping a hole in a sweater. Clara eyed the bird as it eased off a fence and took to the sky. A memory crawled in. There was a time when she had assumed the life of a bird to be a lonely one. But in the wake of Robert's leaving, now that she herself was alone, she pondered that assumption. Did alone mean lonely? The answer was there and the answer was no. Alone meant free. Robert had given her a gift.

This house was hers.

The schooner was hers.

Clara Caulins was free to sail, free to captain, free to love a man of her choosing. No more worry about Robert catching her in the middle of a sensual daydream, her face flooded with heat as she struggled to recover her place in their conversation.

Clara abandoned her perch at the window and curled up on the daybed to consider this gift, this freedom. Was it real? Undoubtedly. But it was a bubble, one that time would burst. Then there would be consequences. She'd have to be stupid not to expect that. God had the Commandments on His side. Squirming, she engaged in her old habit of pushing unwanted thoughts down, hard. She would focus her thinking on St. John's and on

Patrick. From time to time, she would show up, and be swept up, in Patrick's arms. And that would be that. In fact, this, the tail end of the sailing season would be forever marked in her memory by a series of liaisons with Patrick, the starting point of which was Robert's departure. When the sailing was over, when the schooner was stored and the crew dispersed, Clara would turn her mind to home and to a life without liaisons.

KATHLEEN

—◆—

CHAPTER 24

IT IS A BAROMETER, THE sea.

The North Atlantic is a gauge for a global wave of change. In the spring of 1939, the sea lands Robert in England to begin a search for family. In June, it ferries King George VI to North America to secure the support of allies. My island is a stop on this royal tour: King George thanks the Newfoundland Regiment for its service during the Great War.

Meanwhile, Great Britain's Prime Minister Neville Chamberlain's year-old policy of reconciliation has not brought peace. Instead, it seems to have emboldened Hitler. Fascism screams to the forefront in Europe. In September, Germany invades Poland and Great Britain declares war against Germany.

In a rising tide of fear, Operation Pied Piper evacuates London children to the countryside. While they flock to safety like seagulls fleeing a storm at sea, their anguished parents are left to enlist or lie low, attempting to remain calm, readying for bombardment.

But after all the preparation and desperation and evacuation, nothing happens. No winds of war, not a ripple. In fact, with fishing reduced in many places, with embargos on shipments to Germany and France, the sea appears becalmed. There is no evidence of fighting along a reinforced Maginot Line in France, and there is much talk among the citizens of a phoney war. Some Londoners bring their children home.

On the other side of the Atlantic in my island home, all are aware of the outbreak of war in Europe. News travels on the radio, in the newspaper, and on the wind to every outport and cove of the rocky coast of Newfoundland. For the second time in the first half of the twentieth century, Newfoundlanders are preparing to cross the Pond to support Great Britain. Many young men gather on docks and stages to discuss joining up. To others, like my son, the war is something heard about on the radio, or read about in the paper—a news report.

KEVIN

CHAPTER 25

It was November of the year of Robert's departure when Kevin stripped away the little library at the back of Robert's workshop. As he worked, he thought about Robert's foresight. How had Robert been so quick to know about what was coming? About the war in Europe? Would he hear from Robert? Would Robert be back? Kevin had no idea.

As he looked over Robert's tools which still hung at the ready, Kevin considered using them but, with his carpentry companion gone, he didn't have the heart for it. Each step a sigh, he boarded up the building and hunkered down for the blanket of winter.

The traditions of the season kicked in and Kevin picked up his pace. He harnessed horse and sleigh, headed into the crisp forest, and felled trees for each of three houses. On the ride home the weighted sleigh creaked, the wintry wind nipped, and the familiar smell of the sea filled him. Spirits soaring, he delivered his cargo, tree by tree, injecting each home with the overwhelming aroma of pine. He embedded the cut trees in rock-filled buckets and used twine to tie the tops to strategically-placed nails in the walls so there'd be no toppling. Clara and Kathleen and Kate decorated all three trees with wool and buttons and store-bought ornaments and also used every bit of shiny tinfoil that had been collected over the year. Kevin created wreaths for their doors by twisting wire into circles, wrapping the circles with boughs, and tying them with red ribbons poached with permission from sewing boxes.

Christmas Eve and Midnight Mass rolled into Christmas Day with the dinner and the dropping-in to visit. It seemed moments until the New Year was upon him, moments until Ash Wednesday marked his forehead with the cross of sacrifice, and a brief time until Easter marked the end of Lent. With the long drawl of winter over and done with, work was on the horizon. Kevin could handle the work.

On a breezy spring day, Kevin was poised at the top of a recently erected house frame, checking measurements for the alignment of the roof. Was someone calling his name? He paused. Amid all this hammering and sawing ruckus, a man couldn't hear himself think. He rose from his stooped position. A gust of wind slammed him. As he checked his balance, the sound of his name came to him again. He peered over the side of the roof. "What in the name of the Lord Thunderin' Jesus do ye want?" he yelled down. It was then that he spotted the priest.

"God forgive me for swearin'," Kevin said and instantly made the sign of the cross. No need to rile the priest.

"Never you mind that now," called Father Mahony. "Your young Kate is at the hospital with an injury to her head."

Kevin jumped to the nearest corner post and shimmied down. "What are you on about, Father? What happened?" An all-too-familiar feeling of dread swept through him but he stopped it dead. Not that, never that.

"Kate was out playing. Hurt her head. I was at your house when she came running home, crying, so I drove her and Mrs. Mullins to the hospital. She'll be fine, my son. Likely in need of a few stitches, that's all. I'll give you a lift to the hospital if you can be leaving the job site."

"Let 'em try and stop me." Kevin was already on the running board of the car, door swung wide. "Let's get going."

Father Mahony got behind the wheel.

Kevin sat, clutching the door handle, paying no never mind to the priest who nattered on. All Kevin cared about was that he had to get to his Kate. Mavis had made her *his* Kate, hadn't she?

At the hospital, Kevin shot out of the motorcar before it had completely stopped, blasted through the doors into a stench of antiseptic that knocked his breath back, and almost slammed into Dulcie.

Dulcie put her hand to her heart. "Sure you just about scared the life out of me."

"Where is she?" Kevin had no time for apologies.

"I gave her name at the counter," panted Dulcie. "She has to wait for the doctor. And she's right over there." Dulcie pointed to the waiting room.

Kevin turned. There was Kate, perched on the edge of a wooden chair, her right hand pressing a towel to her head. The edges of the towel were sun-bleached white but the centre was a spreading pool of red. Heart pounding, Kevin ran across the polished, porridge-coloured linoleum. He took a breath. He spoke softly. "Kate, I'm here."

Kate looked up. She blinked, her eyes blank.

Had she heard him at all? Kevin put his hands on Kate's shoulders and locked eyes with hers. "Kate, I'm here."

This time Kate responded, a sniff and a hiccup. "Look what happened." She lifted the towel. After a glance at the injury, Kevin breathed more easily. The cut didn't seem too deep. He guided Kate's hand back so that the towel was again resting where it should be.

"You'll be fine," said Kevin, making sure his voice was soothing, not worrying. Kate didn't need any more upset. "We just need to wait for the doctor."

"I think I got blood in the Father's motorcar."

"Blood in the motorcar is no concern of mine," boomed Father Mahony's voice as he strode up. "Tell your father what happened, child."

"Tommy dared me to stand still," said Kate, her voice trembling, "while he pushed a wheelbarrow toward me. He promised he would come to a dead stop and would not hit me. He lied. My head slammed the ground."

"That was a risky game," said Kevin, dying to get his hands on the likes of Tommy, whoever he was. "Do you think he really had it in him to hurt you?"

Kate shook her head. "When he saw the blood, he ran home screaming for his mommy."

Dulcie plopped onto a chair beside Kate. "You can't be doing what young fellas tell ya just to impress them, if that's what you were at, young lady."

"Humph," said Kevin. Dulcie could be right here. Kate was fourteen and there was no end to the antics young ones got up to. But now was no time to give Kate a talking to. Kevin stared at the blank, beige wall opposite while he gathered his thoughts. "Perhaps," he offered quietly, "I should have a word with Tommy and his mother."

"No need," said the priest. "I'll talk to the culprit. Do you want me to run Mrs. Mullins over to get Clara for the paperwork? I'm sure you have to be getting back on the building job."

Kevin smiled to himself. He could fill in any hospital papers himself but he had no need to broadcast that. He would let the priest believe what he believed. Besides, Clara would want to be here. As for Tommy the culprit, Kevin wouldn't be bothering him at all. The boy would be feeling bad enough after the priest was done with him. "Thank you, Father," he said.

With the priest and Dulcie gone, Kevin focused on Kate and the wait.

"Will I need stitches?" asked Kate

"Could be."

"Will it hurt?"

"Maybe. You're a strong girl. You'll manage it fine." He looked toward the counter. "I'm going to check in with the nurse to see how much longer we'll be." He headed to the receptionist's desk. No one there. He tapped the desk bell. A single ping. A grey-haired nurse in a crisp white hat and uniform scurried to greet him. With a pleasant smile, she informed him that Kate would be tended to soon. Kevin expressed his thanks and turned back toward the waiting room. It was then that he spotted a young boy sitting beside Kate.

Hackles up, Kevin crossed the floor and stood in front of the newcomer.

Not so young after all. Sixteen, seventeen? The boy, thin as a rail, stood to his full height, maybe five-and-a-half feet, and put out his hand. "My name is Peter McGraw," he said, using his left hand to brush a lock of fine brown hair from his brow.

Kevin, surprised at the strength in the boy's handshake, stared into his brown eyes. Looked honest enough. Harmless. In fact, he looked somewhat familiar. "Have we met? Who's your father?"

"My father is Cornelius McGraw. And yes, mister, at the shipbuilding site. You were hammering away when my father and my brothers and me were delivering a boom."

Kevin raised an eyebrow.

"We built the jib boom for one of Mr. Palfrey's ships, sir. Red spruce, it was, cut from Connigan's Pond on the road to Colinet, and hauled out by bobsled."

"Hard work."

"Used to it, sir."

"What else do you do?"

Peter shrugged. "Lots of stuff. We chop ice in the winter and keep it in sawdust in the storeroom. We sell the ice blocks in the spring. We drive people across the Southeast Arm in the motorboat. Easiest way to get to Sunday Mass in Placentia. We sell fish to cargo boats too. Was on a Norwegian ship last year, delivering salmon."

"No school for you then?"

"Not since Grade 4, sir."

"Can ye at least read, you and your brothers?"

"A bit, sir."

Kevin nodded. A hard worker, this lad. "Reading's important, son," Kevin said and then paused. Not his business, this boy's education. "What are you at here? You don't look sick."

"Just waiting for my father, sir. He hurt his foot while we were hauling wood. I have to drive the motorboat."

"Ah, so you don't live in Argentia, then?"

"That's right, Sir. I live in Placentia, the Southeast. We had to come across the Gut to the hospital. There's no hospital on our side, not until the Commission of Government sees fit to put one there."

"That will happen soon enough. Lots of cottage hospitals shooting up all over the island. In the meantime, I'd like to thank you, son, for keeping my daughter company."

"My pleasure, sir. I cut me own head once." He lifted the brown wavy hair that had fallen back over his forehead and revealed a small half-moon scar. "My brother tossed the football at me and I dodged. Not soon enough though. The ball hit me in the head."

"Hmmm," said Kevin as he examined the scar. "Strange that a ball would make a mark like that."

"It wasn't a real ball, sir. We didn't have one so we were using a tin can." He grinned.

Kevin couldn't help but smile back.

"I have a scar, too," said Kate. "Wait a minute." She had been using her right hand to hold the towel to her head. She switched hands so she could show the scar on the back of the right hand. "Hey, it's a half-moon, like yours."

"Playing football too, were you?" asked Peter, still grinning.

"Of course not." Kate sounded indignant. "I got my scar when the water came and pulled our house into Miller's Pond."

Peter took on a puzzled look. "Never heard of Miller's Pond. Not in all my born days and I know every pond and river and lake and bay around here."

"But it wasn't around here. It was on the Burin Peninsula. A long time ago. Isn't that right, Dad?"

Kevin's breath hit a snag and he coughed it clear. Kate had been only three and a half years old when the tidal wave hit. How much did she remember of that day? He planted himself into a chair beside Kate. The best he could do was nod.

"Wait a minute," said Peter. "Was that after the earthquake? It was, wasn't it? I remember the earthquake. Me and my brother were putting the ducks in the barn when the rumbling set in. We slammed the barn door, ran to the fence, and jumped onto the bottom rail. We were sure the rumble came from the new motorcar up the street, and we were always dying to see the motorcar. But there was no motorcar. The fence started shaking beneath us and we got so scared we hightailed it to the house. Mother was on her knees praying something fierce and the dishes were dancing in the cupboards."

"Dishes dancing?" Kate giggled.

"You don't remember the earthquake?" Peter asked.

Kate shook her head. "I just remember being wet and cold and float-ing. My mouth tasted like mud. A nice man came and got me. I remember his hands because they were just stumps. Hardly any fingers at all. I went in his dory. Just me. Everybody else went to heaven."

"Your family?" whispered Peter. "Your family went to heaven?"

Kate nodded and went silent.

Kevin moved to the edge of his chair and hovered there, trying to keep from jumping into this conversation. All these years, he had never asked Kate what she remembered of that day. All these years. And now, a stranger, a mere boy, without any malice or fear of bringing up demons, just asked.

CLARA

CHAPTER 26

———◆———

WITH THE *ELIZABETH J* AT the ready and the next outing scheduled in a few days, Clara pored over ocean charts at her kitchen table. This was a make-work task, an attempt to keep busy the fingers that quivered as she slid them over lines marking coves and inlets. Clara needed to get back on the ocean before her nerves were rubbed raw altogether.

She had made a couple of trips this spring, carting goods from St. John's to local merchants around the bay, and she had encountered many men who were fishing and hauling and trading. But the man she wished to see had not appeared where he was supposed to be, in St. John's. On her last outing to the capital city, she had traipsed up the steep hill to Patrick's residence. When she found no one home, she trudged back to the vessel, weighted with disappointment.

And now, as she sat back in her chair, she pondered. What if she did not meet him on this next trip? Her plan for this season at sea had included their trysts. An unfulfilled plan would leave her with constant thirst and no way to quench it.

When a loud knock interrupted her musings, Clara jumped, inadvert-ently brushing a chart from the table. As the chart tumbled, she glanced toward the door. What on earth? No one around here knocked and no one used the front door, no one except priests and strangers. The locals just poked their heads in the back door and called out a name. Who could be here? Fallen chart forgotten, Clara rushed to the front of the house and flung the door open.

The visitor had his head down, salt-and-pepper cap perched on top of it. His arms were raised, leaning into the door frame. From his wool sweater to his wellington boots, he was all fisherman, like any of a hundred in the community. But he wasn't just anyone. It was the shape of him she instantly recognized, the way he had so often moulded that shape to fit into hers.

Her first instinct was to throw herself at Patrick, but she stepped back and, with a sweep of her arm, escorted him inside. When he was through the doorway, she hopped onto the stoop and looked around. No one in sight. She sprang back into the house and, heart pounding, put as much effort as she could muster into turning the key to the door, a key which had been moored in its lock for years, unused. No one ever locked their doors. But Clara's heart and soul were fired up by the presence and promise of Patrick, so she cast community custom to the wind and, after she heard the sure-fire click of the lock, she beetled her way to the back of the house. A little more exertion and that door was secure too. All the while, Patrick had been following her, meek as a lamb. She turned now and, not at all put off by his amused smile, launched herself into his arms.

"What are you doing here?" she asked when she could pull herself back from her want. "And why are you in that get-up?"

"The sea dragged me here," he said, blue eyes twinkling. "The clothes let me fit in."

"Fit in? Here? Why would you want to fit in here? You can't be thinking about staying."

"Why not? That husband of yours is still in England, isn't he?"

"Doesn't matter. People talk."

"So I'll stay at the Rectory."

"The Rectory?" Clara stepped back. She placed a trembling hand over her heart. "With the priest?"

Patrick laughed outright. He moved closer, so close that his breath was entwined with hers. "I'm not staying, but I am acquainted with your priest." His voice dropped to a husky whisper. "I was talking to him when we met years ago, remember?"

Clara remembered all too well. The heat of the memory fired through her and she leaned in until her cheek was against his, stubble prickling her face.

"You," he said. "I'm here for you. Isn't that enough?"

Having no quarrel with those words, Clara abandoned all caution. She took his hand and pulled him to the stairs, up the stairs, toward her bedroom. They were approaching the door, they were at the threshold, and then they were on the bed, she under him. He kissed her neck while wrestling her out of her dress. *Bang. Bang. Bang.* Could her heart beat that loud?

Patrick pulled away, jumped off the bed. Puzzled, Clara looked up. There he was, staring down at her, his finger over his lips.

"Patrick?"

"Sssh."

When the pounding started again, Clara jumped. *Sweet Heart of Jesus.* Someone was banging on the back door. A locked door. Someone was calling her name. Was that Dulcie's voice? Clara scrambled, buttoning her dress, and running fingers through her hair. She stumbled toward the mirror and shuddered at the sight—her hair all mops and brooms and her dress all buttoned wrong. With unsteady fingers, she undid the buttons. Patrick stepped in to help. She slapped his fingers away and completed the task herself. "Damn it all, Patrick," she spat at him in a throaty whisper. *Dear God.* Hers was the voice of a woman who had just stepped out of a brothel. She cleared her throat. "You wait here."

After one more check in the mirror, after securing her hair with bobby pins, Clara headed tentatively toward the stairs. She halted, went back, and pointed a finger at Patrick. "Not one word."

Patrick grabbed her arm. "I'm leaving on the train at four o'clock."

Clara was taken aback. Such a short visit. A few hours. "Why in heaven's name did you—?" The hammering came to the door again. With no time to deal with the whys of Patrick, she threw her hands in the air, then grabbed the doorknob and pulled the bedroom door firmly to. In an all-out run, she made her way down the hall, over the stairs, to the back door.

She yanked at the door, but it refused to budge. Damn it all. She struggled with the key and tugged again.

Dulcie Mullins was standing on the stoop, screaming. "Thanks be to God, you're home. What's going on with the locked door?" Fighting for breath, she peered past Clara.

"What in heaven's name? Is it Kate?"

At a nod from Dulcie, Clara snatched her coat from a hook and stepped outside.

"Sure and the blood was coming from her head," offered Dulcie, struggling for breath. "Thank the good Lord the priest was in, looking for the church dues. He took us to the hospital in his motorcar."

"Is she okay?" said Clara, fear clutching at her gut as she shoved her arms through the sleeves of her coat. "Is Kate okay?"

"I'm sure she'll be fine," roared a man's voice. Clara turned and tuned in to the fact that Father Mahony was yelling from his motorcar which was parked and rumbling just feet from the house. The priest sounded the horn and beckoned through the car's open window. "Let's get going," he called.

Without a thought for Patrick, Clara ran toward the car, Dulcie on her heels. As soon as they boarded, Father Mahony announced his intention. "I'll drop Dulcie off at home and then I'll get you to the hospital, Clara."

"Is Kate okay?" Clara asked again.

"Like I told you, I'm sure she'll be fine," said the priest. "A few stitches perhaps. Kevin is there already but he might be needing your help with the paperwork."

Father Mahony's certainty served to settle Clara's nerves. *She'll be fine. Kate will be fine.* After a few deep breaths, Clara turned her attention to Dulcie. "You don't mind going back to Kevin's instead of going to your place, do you, Dulcie? It would be good for Kate to have a meal or a cup of tea waiting when we get her home."

"A fine idea. Happy to make myself useful," said Dulcie. "Don't you worry about a thing," she added when the priest dropped her off at Kevin's.

At the hospital, Clara jumped from the car, barely registering the priest's voice saying he would come back to get her later. She ran into the waiting room where she found Kevin and Kate, Kate with a cloth to her head, both engaged in talking to a young boy. There was no panic here, surprisingly not a hint of it. In fact, there was an umbrella of calmness, one that brought her up short. As she stood there, she felt herself being drawn into its fold.

And so it was with slow, steady steps, that Clara walked toward Kate and Kevin and the stranger.

KEVIN

CHAPTER 27

———◆———

As CLARA APPROACHED, KEVIN STOOD and cautiously raised his arm, palm facing her. "Clara, Kate's doing fine," he said, deliberately keeping his voice low. "We'll see the doctor soon. This young man is Peter."

Clara's bewilderment was evident in her questioning eyes. Kevin understood but, needing to let the exchange between Kate and Peter play out and, not wanting Clara to interfere, he persisted. "Peter, this is my sister, Mrs. Clara Caulins." Kevin turned to Clara. "Peter and Kate were having a grand conversation," he said.

Clara blinked, clearly in a daze.

"About the tidal wave," added Kevin.

"The tidal wave." Clara took a deep breath. "I see," she said slowly. "It's nice to meet you, Peter."

The young stranger nodded.

Clara slowly faced Kate. "How are you?"

"I'm going to be fine." Kate said firmly. "But I wasn't then. That day on the Burin, I mean. Everybody else was gone. My mom and Jimmy and Marie and Joseph and Johnny." She counted them off, raising a digit for every name until all five fingers were spread wide. "Yes. That's it. Everybody but me and my dad. Dad was in the woods chopping logs for the winter, so he was safe from the water. Right, Dad?"

"Right," said Kevin, thankful that Clara seemed to have caught the gist of what was going on.

Peter's eyes were wide with curiosity and Kevin was sure he was going to ask more questions. In fact, he hoped Peter would ask. He hoped Peter would pry until Kate gave up every detail.

But that was not to be. A tiny, gnarled man clutching a cap emerged from a nearby doorway and hobbled toward them. "Time to go, son." He placed his cap on his head.

Kevin's heart fell. He let out a sigh, one that was echoed by Clara. An attempt to introduce himself to the old man was aborted when the man turned toward the exit.

"My dad's a busy man," said Peter.

"Sounds like he's a successful one, a man to look up to."

"Yes, sir, but you got to do your own growing, no matter how tall your father is." Peter stood, his eyes showing regret. "I have to be going. My father has no time for anything but the work. Nice meeting you, sir. You too, missus." He nodded and turned to Kate. "Bye, Kate," he said. After walking a few feet, he looked back. "You're a brave girl, Kate."

Kate said nothing, just raised her free hand in a tiny wave.

Clara plopped into Peter's vacant chair. Kevin figured that, just like him, she was mulling over the conversation. Would Clara ask about the tidal wave?

"He thinks I'm brave," said Kate.

Overwhelmed, fearing his chest would cave in entirely, Kevin looked to Clara whose eyes were piercing his. Certain she was awaiting a signal, grateful she was willing to jump in, he offered a single nod. The best he could do.

"I heard," Clara said to Kate. "Do you think you were brave?"

"No," said Kate. "I was upstairs that day and the rest of the family was downstairs. The water spit me back. Just like Nanny said when I came here. If the ocean had wanted me, it would have kept me. But it spit me back. It does that with lots of stuff." She reached into her pocket and retrieved a small, white stone. "The ocean can pound stones into sand if it wants to or it can spit them back."

Clara nodded. "You showed that stone to me when you were very little."

"I did?" Kate shrugged.

"The day we fixed Mrs. Fan, the day when her dress was torn. Remember?"

"Oh, yes. I remember. So I guess you know I got this stone the day that Daddy and me left. The ocean spit it back, just like it did to me. I keep it to remind me." She returned the stone to its place and patted the pocket as if to ensure that it was secure there. "I wasn't brave. The ocean just spit me back." She shook her head. "Ouch. Better keep my head still. That hurts."

Kevin put his hand over Kate's. When she raised her eyes to his, it occurred to him, for the first time, that his young Kate had old eyes As time worn as the earth itself. Withdrawing his hand from hers, he folded his arms and fastened his fingers over his biceps. His fingers whitened under the pressure.

"I wasn't brave that day, Dad," Kate said. "I was upstairs, that's all. And the rest of the family was in the kitchen. And I wasn't brave when the nice man carried me out because I saw Mommy under the rocking chair and I bawled my head off. But she was in heaven. And that was all there was to it."

A sharp pain gripped Kevin's throat. How selfish had he been all these years, thinking only of his own losses, while Kate remembered, while Kate suffered.

Clara dabbed at her eyes. She remained silent.

It took a few seconds for Kevin to find his voice. "You can talk to your Aunt Clara or me anytime," he said.

"Oh, I know that," said Kate, "but sometimes it's just easier to spill your heart to strangers."

"There's gospel in that," said Kevin, as his gaze met Clara's.

Clara nodded. "You're wise beyond your years, Kate."

The three sat in stillness.

It was Kate who broke the silence. "What did you think of Peter?"

Relief came over Kevin. Kate wasn't dwelling on the past. "I think you have lots of time for boys," said Kevin, thinking it the responsible thing to say. "The Tommys and the Peters of the world can wait."

"I know that." Kate seemed indignant. "But Peter is a nice boy, isn't he, Aunt Clara? I bet he wouldn't hit me with a wheelbarrow, accident or not."

"What wheelbarrow?" asked Clara.

Kevin filled her in, a brief description. "I think our Kate is a little mad at Tommy. Right, Kate?"

"Yes, I am. And I don't care if it is a sin!"

"It's just a feeling," said Clara. "Just let it be. It will go away."

"Are you going to give me a forgiveness lecture now, Dad?"

"Not a chance."

Just then, the nurse approached. "Kate Kerrigan?" she asked.

"No lecture," said Kevin. "Now you are going to see the doctor." When he stood with Kate, Clara remained seated. "Now *we* are going to see the doctor," said Kevin, indicating for Clara to follow as the nurse led the way to the examination room, to a meeting with the doctor, to a few stitches through which Kate sat very still, chin high.

CLARA

CHAPTER 28

———◆———

CLARA STEPPED FROM KEVIN'S HOUSE into the afternoon sunshine, grateful that she had declined the offer of a ride home from Father Mahony. Something was niggling at her and she needed the calming effect of a walk. Why was she ill at ease anyway? With Kevin back at work and Kate back at home in Dulcie's care, everything was normal again, wasn't it? Someone should tell that to her fluttering stomach. Was she overlooking something?

A few yards into her walk, that something jolted her. Patrick. Dear Father in heaven. She had forgotten all about Patrick. Would he be in the bedroom? Waiting for her? Ready for her? As she picked up her pace, the whistle of a train cut the air, a signal, she knew, that he was gone. Still she ran and thrust her way into the house and called out for him and combed through every room, all to no avail. Her heart sank with disappointment until, on her second pass through the kitchen, she spotted a sealed envelope on the table, an envelope addressed to Captain Clara Caulins. She grabbed it, raised it to her nose, and inhaled the scent of wild roses. Her scent. Her stationery. She broke the seal and unfolded the note: *Come to me on the sea.*

Six words. Nothing more. Pressing the paper to her heart, Clara sauntered across the kitchen. She lifted a stove lid. This note—evidence of sin—must burn. She held the offending piece of paper above the flame, barely gripping it between thumb and forefinger. All she had to do was to release it to the fire. But she couldn't commit. These few words were all she had of Patrick. What harm would one keepsake do? Robert wasn't around to find it. Robert was gone. Yes, long gone.

Clara still thought of Robert daily. Perhaps, after a while, she would only think of him when prodded, only when a meerschaum pipe, a tobacco pouch, or a leatherbound book came into view. Eventually, these reminders would become just things that were there, in the house, meaningless, a part of the everyday. Other thoughts would crowd in, other trinkets would find their way onto the shelves, in front of, or in place of, Robert's pipes and books, until finally there was nothing there to remind her at all. The connection, the obligation, would be lost. Would Robert return? She didn't know. If he did, she would deal with it. But now she had Patrick. And this note from Patrick. She pulled the treasured paper back and held it to her heart once again.

Clara scaled the stairs. She sat on the bed where, just hours ago, Patrick had warmed her heart and her life. She ran her hand across the white chenille bedspread and leaned into it. His aftershave. A hint of him, a treasure that would fade. Pulling herself away from the coverlet, Clara headed for her closet, for the hatbox in her closet, where she stored her treasure from the silver mine. She lifted the blue felt hat whose stuffing had been replaced by letters and placed this note, the most special of all, beneath all the others. She returned the hat to the box, replaced the lid, and shoved the box to the very back of the very top closet shelf. That would do for now. Secrets must be hidden. Robert was gone but Kate often spent time here. Kate must never find the letters in the hatbox.

As she closed the closet door, the painting of a schooner on the wall beside the closet caught her attention. Why was the painting askew? She must have bumped it on the way in. Shrugging, she straightened it. It gave some comfort, that painting. Captain Clara Caulins had her very own route to Patrick. No matter what, she would keep her schooner.

Clara let out a heartfelt sigh. A long day. Overwhelmed, she lay back onto her bed. She contemplated her days onshore and counted the days until she would be back on the ocean.

KATHLEEN

CHAPTER 29

IT IS A METRONOME, THE sea.

The North Atlantic rises and falls, ebbs and flows, the breath of a body, the pulse of a vein. Inhabitants of its shores mark time in the day-to-day humdrum of fishlines and traplines and clotheslines. Backs bent, minds bent upon survival, sunup to sundown. No note of the now, nor of the miracle that is every tree, every blade of grass, every tassel of dandelion. No realization that the seemingly unending monotony is but a finite lull. Paradise passing, unnoticed.

My Clara embraces the sameness, fixed in her daily chores. What she can't raise, grow, or sew, she purchases in St. John's or at the local general store. To some, the seafaring Clara is a heroine. *A woman at the helm. Can you imagine?* To others she is a delinquent, inserting herself into a man's world. *That one, a ship's captain. Have you ever seen the like?* Deaf to the lot of them, Clara goes on traipsing to and from the wharf.

Occasionally, she takes the *Elizabeth J* on a booze run to outports, transporting liquor, which remains in short supply. Mostly, she sails at the whim of the merchants, ferrying goods from St. John's to coastal communities. An able captain, my Clara, her ability at the helm honed at her husband's side.

The men of her crew talk time, tide, and weather but, at the command of Captain Clara, balk at idle gossip. On starry nights when the air is still and the sea subdued, I hover, a silent witness to these old sea dogs who, contrary to common belief, tell no tales. Robert and Clara's exploits are as guarded as a cloister of silent nuns. A wise leader, my daughter, well aware that a wayward word uttered on a small wharf in a small community suffers no neglect.

At home, away from the wharf, Clara reinforces the walls around her clandestine life by painting them with new images. She organizes a group of women to sew, quilt, and knit. There are people in need and there is warmth to be had in bedding and socks and mittens. Once or twice a year, Clara collects enough handmade goods to cart around the bay. A distraction, this, one that benefits the needy and shifts the gossip about Clara's gall to praise about her goodness. *A heart of gold. The soul of a saint.*

Kevin too has settled into routine. He has kept his bargain with God. He helps his sister plough, plant, and harvest. When Clara is at sea, he feeds her chickens and tends to her mare, Bessie. He fishes inshore. He maintains the snug house he built with his own two hands. He takes on additional work, plodding from one job to the next. Day after day. Week after week. Month after month.

On occasion, I witness a book in Kevin's hands and the stain of ink on his fingers. Imagine it, my Kevin, reading and writing. Surely that is an uphill hike for him. Is there healing in it? Will the jagged ridges of his soul fully mend? Maybe. But I believe the smile on his face is pasted there, a defence, a keep-away. At times, he seems tethered, a man who has accepted his lot. At other times, he is a man on a tightrope, picking up one foot and placing it in front of the other. Tentatively. Pause, balance, step. The brush of a feather could tip him.

My granddaughter Kate is a child who is not a child at all really. The trauma of her toddling years has made her an old soul. A sage. Wisdom for the ages. Her joyous exterior is to me a veneer for melancholy. Kate is there for her father, always ready to catch her father. She asks nothing of him and nothing about her mother or her siblings. As for her true lineage? I think it best that my Kate never knows. I'm not sure I can explain it myself: she is both daughter and granddaughter to Alphonse, daughter and sister to Clara, niece and sister to Kevin. What is she to me? Granddaughter? Yes. Stepdaughter? Yes. A Gordian knot. What will become of her if she learns of the tangle?

Through it all the sun traverses the sky, the seasons emerge and fade, the tide rises and falls. The sleepy fishing and farming village of Argentia continues its work of the everyday. I watch the flesh-and-blood Kathleen as she, the widow who has lost a loved one to the sea, plays the grieving role, her tongue silent, her eyes focused on the day-to-day movements of Clara, Kevin, and Kate. A wary look about her, a tautness. Ready to spring at any breach in the monotony of days. Day in, day out, everything's the same.

And then it isn't.

It is a still and shining early fall day when the airplanes appear. A squadron, military and grey, shaped like the cross of Jesus, crisscrossing the sky. The people of Argentia have no thought of a change in a way of life on this September day, upon this first witnessing of the planes. Many, having never set eyes on a plane, are magnetized by the sight, mesmerized by the wonder.

On the day of the airplanes, the ghost that is me takes flight. I am thrust to the sky, across the Southeast Arm to a tiny island meadow, the grazing ground of a small horse with short ears and a low-set tail. A New-foundland pony. It must be seven hundred pounds or so, maybe fourteen hands high, and it is chestnut in colour with a thick black mane. Usually good-tempered ponies, these, but this one is kicking and bucking and racing blindly this way and that.

A putt-putt sound catches my attention and I turn. Crossing the arm of the sea in a motorboat are two young men. The noise of their outboard motor crescendos as they draw closer. I recognize the boy in the bow: Peter. The boy Kate met at the Argentia Cottage Hospital. He is hatless, his brown hair blown back by the breeze to reveal a sharp point, a widow's peak. Not out of his teenage years and his hair is abandoning him. He wears a snug brown coat, patches on the elbow lovingly stitched. A young man who is still a boy in his mother's care.

"Bring her about, Nate," says Peter. Nate, a more weathered and mus-cular version of Peter, hand on the tiller, answers with a nod, not with a sound, even though Peter's eyes are cast forward, onto the sparkle of the water. Nate brings the boat parallel to shore. The motor cuts out and he tilts it up, out of the water. Both jump into the shallows and drag the boat onto the rocky shoreline. They scramble over the beach rocks onto an open meadow, its tall grasses moving in waves at the whim of the wind. As the boys plough through the meadow, skirting the occasional dwarfed pine, Peter grabs a strand of grass which he places between his teeth. They start toward a log fence, stopping dead when a rumble like that of distant thunder reaches their ears. They tilt their heads back and catch sight of a squadron of grey military planes emerging on the horizon. As the rumble becomes a roar, a frantic neighing comes from nearby.

"Aggie!" Peter cries. "Dear Jesus! The last time she jumped the fence, it took me two days to find her." He tears off. Nate is still transfixed, eyes to the sky.

When Peter reaches the enclosure, he bends to cross over the lower of the two rails. The horse cocks her ears forward, gallops to him, and comes to an abrupt halt in front of him. She rests her head on his shoulder.

Nate has his eyes glued to the sky as he makes his way toward Peter and the pony. Nate walks backward, circling then standing still, his head always tilted and eyes upward. "What the hell?" he says when he finally reaches the fence.

"I don't know but Aggie is scared to death. She ran to me. Can you imagine? I had myself set for a game of chase. She always takes off, darting, dodging, soon as I get close. Seems like I spend days trying to catch this horse."

"Like chasing a fart in a windstorm."

"Can't argue that one."

"You're the only one in the family that can get any good out of her."

Peter strokes the horse's long nose, then lowers his hand to her chest. "Her heart is pounding out a jig." He draws closer and hugs Aggie's neck. "It's okay," he whispers. "I'll take care of you." The horse lets out a whinny.

The squadron, having crossed the sky, is barely visible on the horizon. Its ear-piercing roar has shifted to a muffled hum. Aggie stays at Peter's side.

"What are them airplanes doing here anyway?" asks Nate.

Peter shrugs. "Not sure, but it brings surveying to mind. How many times did we have to check property lines on our land before even attempting to put up a fence? Those planes are likely surveying the land. And if that's what they're doing, they'll be back in an instant."

As if on cue, the airplanes bank and turn.

Peter maintains his stance beside Aggie who now appears totally calm. "Heard Dad and the b'ys talking over by the woodpile," he says. "They were saying the war is going to land on our doorstep. The Americans are coming."

"You mean here, in Southeast, Placentia?"

Peter shakes his head. "Just a few miles away. In Argentia."

Nate nods.

Peter strokes Aggie's mane. "Remember the time I took Dad to Argentia, to the cottage hospital?"

"Yep. What of it?"

Peter runs one hand down Aggie's fetlock and taps a hoof. The pony complies, shifting her weight. He lifts the hoof and checks for stones.

"What about the hospital?" Nate leans in, elbows on the top rail of the fence.

"Patience, b'y. I'm getting to it," says Peter as he checks the remaining hooves. The chore done, he strokes Aggie's mane and then, true to his word, gets to the rest of his story. "I met a girl there, in the waiting room," he says. "Kate was her name. Maybe thirteen, fourteen years old. She lost her home and most of her family to the tidal wave on the Burin."

"Oh. Yeah. After the earthquake. You told me."

"If them airplanes are surveying Argentia for a base . . ."

"Yeah?"

"Then what will happen to the people who live there?"

"I'm not sure, b'y."

The planes sweep back in the boys' direction, their growl growing to thunder.

"Better keep an eye on Aggie," says Nate.

"No worries. She's fine for now. And I'm not leaving until those airplanes are gone."

"I'll go back to the boat and get our lunchpail."

When the intruders disappear over the horizon for the final time, when their steady drone fades to silence, Peter leads Aggie on a stroll around the meadow. The pony is settled, happily fluking flies with her tail, when Peter bids her goodbye and steps over the rail. "I'll be back to check on her later," he says to Nate.

As they take to the motorboat, the scene fades. I see no picture, only sound—the slap of wave, the sputter of motor. Gradually all falls away.

Time slips back, a blink. I'm floating above the laneway to Clara's house, watching as she enters through the back door. She's in the kitchen, then she's on the stairs. She has one foot on the top step when the noise begins. A hum, then a rumble, then a roar. She shakes her head, as if trying to dislodge the ruckus. Running outside, she stands on the stoop, looking skyward at the zooming formation of military airplanes, grey as thunderclouds. When they near the horizon, they turn.

My Clara is a travelled woman, a woman who often sees aircraft when she is at sea. Rumours have filtered through the community, rumours about the war. That it will wash up on these shores eventually. What is she thinking as she watches these airplanes? Does she have any inkling as to what's coming? I wait as she remains on the stoop, body still, face set like stone.

I see a slight movement in her eyes, a mere spark, and I know what she's thinking. "Kevin!" The word seems ripped from her gut. My daughter knows the soul of Kevin, knows that, at times, a breeze could tip him, knows that the presence of the planes could cause him worry.

Clara bolts to the edge of the path and stops dead, an ear perked toward the barn, toward the frantic whinnying of Bessie. Clara casts a worried glance in the mare's direction, then tears off on foot toward Kevin's house. Clara has her priorities—she'll check on Kevin and Kate first. Bessie can wait.

Clara runs all out and seems all in by the time she charges through Kevin's door. "Kevin!" she calls. "Kate!" No response. The airplanes are roaring overhead, the windows rattling in their casing.

Her voice frantic, Clara calls out to no avail as she charges through every room in the house. She barrels into the backyard, coming to a halt when she comes upon a broken pitchfork lying on the ground. The handle is split, cracked right down the middle as if hit by a lightning bolt. Clara's fingers tremble as she brings them to her lips. "Where are they?" she whispers as she turns toward the sea, eyes searching the horizon.

My Clara leans into the ocean wind like a figurehead on a ship's prow. As gusts skirmish across her face, her hair tumbles into trailing ribbons. I breathe with her as she inhales, knowing, as she soon will, that the sea that will lead her to Kevin and Kate.

Seconds later, Clara bolts, aiming for the landwash.

KEVIN

CHAPTER 30

———◆———

Sɪɢʜᴛɪɴɢ Kᴀᴛᴇ ᴏɴ ᴛʜᴇ ʟᴀɴᴅᴡᴀsʜ, Kevin heaved a sigh and inched his way over the beach rocks toward her. She was fixated on the airplanes and took no notice of him. When the squadron flew into the sun, she tilted her head back, raised her hand to protect her eyes, and pivoted. Kevin sidled up to her. His touch to her shoulder was light. She jumped back, her hand falling from her brow to her chest.

"Dad! You scared me half to death."

He withdrew his hand. "Sorry, Kate," was all he could manage as he scrutinized her, waiting for her questions, wondering how in the name of heaven he was going to answer them when he had no energy left for any of it, for work, for ambition, for struggle.

A frown appeared on her fledgling face, a face too young for the fine lines it was wearing. "What's this all about?" She pointed to the sky. "What are airplanes doing here?" She rubbed the nape of her neck, then stretched, seesawing her head from shoulder to shoulder.

Kate's movements seemed slow to Kevin. Everything was slow. He was slow, like a slug crossing a pebbled path. He'd better speed up. Say something. Do something.

"I was just going to feed the chickens," Kate continued, "when I heard the noise." She stopped. She moved toward Kevin until the two were face to face. Too close for Kevin who cast his eyes down, locking his gaze on a beach rock.

Kate didn't back away. "Look at me, Dad."

Kevin raised his eyes.

"Out with it, whatever it is," said Kate. "What's going on?"

Kevin felt himself drowning in the depth of her gaze. "Never you mind feeding the chickens now at all. I just . . ." He was unable to form words to match his feelings, uncertain as to what those feelings were.

"You just what? Came to tell me about the airplanes? What are they doing here, Dad?"

Kevin said nothing. He felt himself yielding, his shoulders abandoning angles, slumping into curves. "Surveying, I think. That's what my years working construction tell me. They're surveying the land." Was that enough information to hold her? There were more questions behind the lines on her brow. Would she ask them all? Not likely. Not if she felt her curiosity would worry him. She'd hold back and tiptoe around him.

Kate sighed as she angled her head toward the ocean. She raised her fisted left hand and opened her fingers, revealing her keepsake from Burin—the small, white stone that the ocean had spat onto the landwash.

"They're talking about the war, Kate," Kevin volunteered. "When I saw the airplanes, I figured they were right."

"What's the airplanes got to do with anything?" Kate closed her fingers over the stone again, tight, her knuckles whitening.

"Not sure yet, but they don't survey land unless they got plans for it. Come on, let's go back to the house." He slipped an arm over her shoulders, intending to support her. Instead, he leaned. Kate buckled but regained her footing, making no comment. In silence, Kevin berated himself. This wasn't the right way of things at all, the adult depending on the child. He found himself wishing he could talk to Robert. But Robert was not here to rescue him this time. Kevin would have to figure this one out for himself.

Kate wrapped her arm around his waist and they stumbled off, the beach rocks skidding and clicking beneath their feet. A short distance on, the pair met Clara. "I've been looking all over," Clara began and then stopped. Without another word, she picked up Kevin's free arm and draped it over her shoulder. Kevin had two pillars now.

At home, Clara and Kate sat him down at the kitchen table.

"Will you make him some tea, Kate?" Clara asked.

Kate jumped to the task. "The kettle is still warm from the morning." She headed into the pantry. "I'll get some tea buns. Dulcie made a batch yesterday. Tons of currants in them. She churned butter too."

Kevin stared blankly at Clara who eased into a chair across from him. "The rumour mill has it that Argentia will be flattened, that we'll all have to move, Clara."

"I heard that too, Kev."

"What in the name of God are we going to do?"

"Whatever we have to. We'll survive."

"If it wasn't for Kate . . ."

Clara put her hand over his. "We'll be fine. I'll help you take care of Kate," she said.

"It will soon be time," said Kevin.

"Time? Time for what?"

Kevin didn't say. When all fell to sand, Mavis said, he would go. Or was it he could go? And go where? He didn't know. But wasn't that what was happening? Wasn't all about to fall to sand? Somehow he had the sense that Robert figured into all of this. Somehow, but how? "You're a good sister. And a good aunt. Thanks, Clara."

Kate placed a lead-glass butter dish onto the table. She removed the lid and dropped it, clunk. Kevin looked at the butter, a firm, golden circular glob with the imprint of a bird, a duck perhaps, in the middle. Dulcie's work. The image blurred before him, transforming into an image of his beloved Mavis, squishing butter through her fingers and shaping it into a wooden butter mould. A different design stamped onto the surface. a field of wildflowers. Mavis liked flowers. Then his Kate was there again, depositing lumpy tea buns beside the butter. Kate. His Kate. Back to the cupboards she went. Shortly, she returned, placing one hand lightly on Clara's shoulder, placing a teacup down with the other. "I'm glad you are here, Aunt Clara." She got a cup for Kevin and poured tea for both.

"You just have your tea," she said. "I need to be tending to those chickens." She darted for the door.

"Kate," said Kevin.

Kate halted, her hand on the doorknob. She faced him. "Yes?"

It was Kevin's intent to urge her to stay. But Kate's eyes—wide, round, and lit with fear—clipped his resolve. "Nothing," Kevin said. "Nothing at all. There's a new bag of chicken feed in the storeroom."

A sigh whooshed out of Kate as she eased through the door.

"My miracle child," said Kevin absentmindedly, a memory emerging through a swirl of confusion.

"Our miracle child," said Clara.

The echo of words prickled Kevin. He glared at Clara, wishing her, willing her to get off her arse and out of his house. He needed to be alone. A scream was forming, welling in his gut. He was supposed to leave Argentia, wasn't he? That's what Mavis said. What about Kate? Could he leave her, looking like she did, scared out of her wits? Could he leave her while he still didn't know who knit her, who she belonged to? Was he supposed to leave Kate now? *Get out, Clara.*

But Clara lingered, staring at her teacup, drumming her fingers on the table. She turned toward him, a slow tilt. When her eyes met his, she got to her feet. "I have to check on Bessie," she said. "Poor horse was frantic with the racket." Clara crossed the kitchen and went through the door.

Kevin sat still in the nothingness of it all. He picked up the teacup and brought it to his lips. Cold. He grimaced, put the cup back on its saucer, planted his hands on the table, and pushed himself up. He'd be better off knowing than hiding.

Six days of the week in Argentia, the community gathering place was O'Brien's. Upon entering the general store, Kevin smelled tobacco and sea salt and heard voices riddled with worry and fear. The men raised their heads and nodded at him, and he shuddered at the sight of their anxious faces. He stepped inside and to one side, out of everyone's way, and just hung there, back to the wall, slouched like he was suspended from a hook.

Once again Kevin was falling into a loop, past events echoing. This was just as it was days before the tidal wave when, at Artemius Nolan's merchant store in Burin, the offshore fishermen delivered news about the New York stock market crash. Once again there were voices of warning.

"Did you see them planes, Kev? They're planning to build a base here in case Hitler decides to send his U-boats to North America. Strategic defence, that's what they're calling it. Foolishness is what I calls it."

"Can you believe that Churchill gave Roosevelt our land, Kev?"

"We have to move away, Kevin b'y. Some shocking, it is. They're going to destroy all our homes to make room for the base."

Kevin needed air. He stumbled into motion, moving forward, closer to the sales counter, coming to realize it was the wrong direction, stumbling back, reaching a hand as he scrambled for the door. Once through it, he slammed it. He made a good show of marching down the road, just kept going down the road, foul words leaking through his lips like sewage leaching through the soil around an outhouse. Momentum kept him on the path to his own front door. He looked at his house, his second chance. In a blink, it would be flattened to sand.

Sand. When all falls to sand, Mavis had said in his dreams. Would he leave here then, like Mavis told him? The question hounded him. No answer evident. Would he go? Where would he go?

KATHLEEN

CHAPTER 31

———◆———

IT IS AN ACCOMPLICE, THE SEA.

The North Atlantic lies low, fingering the shore, while islanders lie in limbo. The reconnaissance airplanes have departed and the seagulls have reclaimed the skies. September slides on and the sea ushers in clear evidence of pending construction — a wave of floatplanes laden with lumber. Still, all residents are steeped in denial. When the ocean brings a battleship, the *St. Louis*, truth can no longer be ignored.

The war is coming to Argentia.

The phantom me is hollow, a flickering outline, watching Clara and Dulcie on the dock, their eyes wide at the sight of the monstrous grey battleship.

"Never seen the like before," says Dulcie. "The naval base is coming, just like they're all saying. They don't care who they're saying it to either. Old people and young ones alike, scared out of their minds. We'll all have to be leaving." Dulcie chokes back a sob.

My Clara's eyes are tear-filled. "How can we leave?" she says, the sadness pouring out of her. "What will the people do with their houses and hayfields and vegetable gardens?"

"Sure they're going to be destroying everything right down to the last piece of wood," says Dulcie, her voice sliding between whimper and wail. "Every last semblance of livelihood." She pulls a handkerchief from her apron pocket and dabs at her eyes. "There'll be plenty of work, they're saying. One of me sons got work, helping with triangulation, whatever that is. All I know is they hired him and his boat to transport them while they're triangulating." Dulcie buries her face in her handkerchief. "It's all too much," she mutters.

I watch my Clara turn her back on the grey menace of the ship. She stands as still as a stained-glass saint, eyes thrown out of focus, perhaps not noticing the meadow in her line of vision, its grasses and dandelions swaying without care, or the clapboard houses with their white-washed fences, their foundations firm and unaware of their fate.

"They're going to burn everything," says Dulcie. "Storerooms and stages and flakes. Even our homes."

Clara edges toward Dulcie, reaching a gentle hand to Dulcie's arm and holding it there. "Yes," Clara says softly. "That will happen. No time to grieve, no choice but to go." Clara's melancholy filters through me, giving my empty outline the dark of night and the weight of an anchor.

Since its inception, this community has been ruled by two entities: the Atlantic Ocean with its alternating benevolence and malevolence and the Roman Catholic Church with its consistent rite and might. Now, with a ninety-nine-year land lease given to the United States military, the powers are three.

In October, the USS *Bowditch*, a survey schooner, arrives with engineers who assess the harbour and land. Dulcie's words about plenty of work become concrete. There is certainly work to be had and men come from all around Newfoundland looking for jobs. This fishing-and-farming village of about seven hundred experiences an overwhelming influx in population, not only of island jobseekers but also of United States military who show up by the thousands until uniforms are as common as sheep.

Argentia residents scramble to come to terms with the trampling of their way of life. There is a gift here, the powers that be say. In the place of one lifestyle, in a place still struggling from the effects of the depression, a better life is coming. A gift, they say. The gift of war.

The first of the military to show up are skilled construction workers recruited for the sole purpose of preparing the place for occupation. In no time at all this Construction Battalion, the Seabees, erect an administration building and warehouses and bunkhouses. The ocean escorts in *The Richard Peck*, a passenger steamer from New York. It docks in the harbour and serves as residence for military and civilian workers alike. Some fishermen live in their schooners, travelling to and from Argentia in dories, others live in tents onshore, still others stay with relatives and friends.

Three months after the appearance of the reconnaissance planes, twenty-four families are given eviction notices. A stabbing dose of reality. Within a few months after that, all residents receive notice, all will be set adrift.

Where will they go?

KEVIN

———◆———

THROUGHOUT A WORRIED CHRISTMAS SEASON, people hovered, waiting for meetings to bring news of their fate. The arrival of the New Year did not bring new hope. 1941 would bring upheaval that would roll across their community, gradually ripping it asunder.

Kevin attended the meetings set up by the priest whose intent it was to keep his parish together. The priest had argued with government and Church about the best place to relocate and found what he considered to be a prime spot—the town of Freshwater, seven miles from Argentia.

When that announcement came, Kevin had it in his mind that it would be tough to grow as much as a potato in a rocky place like Freshwater. He kept his opinion to himself, preferring not to draw attention. A glance around the meeting room showed people nodding, willing to go along with the good Father. Who in their right mind was going to argue with the priest?

Kevin noticed a raised hand, a gnarled hand, seeking the priest's attention. "Father? Father?" Salty Joe Sallivan's voice.

"What will we do in Freshwater, Father?" Salty Joe asked. "Sure the ground is nothing but rocks. How can a man grow vegetables for his family or raise livestock in such a place?"

Kevin lowered his head. How many more people had that very same thought and were like himself, too cowardly to come out with it? Had to give Salty Joe credit. *It's just as well to say something as have it on your mind.*

But Salty Joe's concerns fell flat, the priest still insisting that Freshwater was the best place for all.

Kevin remained mute but vigilant. Of particular interest to him was his mother's opinion but Kathleen's face was stone, telling him nothing. Was she willing to move to Freshwater? Right off the bat? Without even shooting one question at the priest? Kevin caught his mother eyeing Clara who was nodding at every word the priest uttered. So that was it. Clara wanted to captain her schooner and that would likely mean staying in the region. Perhaps Kathleen was willing to sail right behind Clara's decision.

Kevin turned his thoughts to Kate. What about Kate? She could live with Clara and Kathleen in Freshwater. But was Kevin supposed to move there too, to be there for Kate? The more he fired that question into his gut, the less certain he felt about anything. A glance around told him that no one was going to fight the priest's decision, except for Salty Joe Sallivan. Where in the name of all that's holy was that man's courage coming from? Kevin looked at Salty Joe's wife, expecting her sharp tongue to snake its way into the mix. But she was silent, staring at her husband with teary-eyed respect.

"Well," said Salty Joe, feet planted, arms crossed, "I'll be taking my family to the Southeast and building a new home there. There's plenty of land and rivers so loaded with salmon you could walk across on their bellies." Mrs. Sallivan, all the edges of her angular face gone soft, put her arm through Joe's and drew herself close to him. With that, Salty Joe straightened his back and doffed his hat. Without as much as a "Goodbye, Father," he and his missus vacated the meeting.

The next day, Salty Joe and his family crammed into his motorboat which spluttered its farewell to friends and neighbours who waved from shore. Among the bunch stood Kevin, uncertain as to how he had found his way there, certain that he was reliving some dark hell. He remembered clinging to Kate as he dragged himself home to Argentia, onto this very dock, after the tidal wave. He was stooped and silent then. Same as now.

Salty Joe's boat churned the water. It distanced itself, diminishing to a speck on the horizon. The onlookers dispersed. Still, Kevin stood. Surely, someone, something would snap him out of this. He waited, all the while knowing that no one would. How could the community rally around Kevin when they were all as battered as he was?

A defeated Kevin wended his way home. He stepped up to the threshold of the house but he couldn't cross it. Yes, this was his home made by his own two hands, but it was built when he was living on hope and memories. What would be the point of going in now? He parked his butt on the steps and slumped, arms dangling.

Kevin was stranded, just like years ago when he was stuck on the stoop of his Burin Peninsula house. Then, he was waiting for his dead wife and children to come home; now, he was waiting for the military to burn his home. Eleven years ago his life was destroyed by water. Now? The powers that be had opted for the quickest method of destruction—fire.

Kevin watched day after day as one house after another went up in smoke. He sat as flames crackled, popped, and sizzled around him, as the odour of woodsmoke infiltrated his lungs, as thick, black plumes hurled upwards until they blocked the sun. His eyes glassed over, blurring out the sight of neighbours sagging away from burnt-out shells that used to be their houses.

When the residents voiced their anguish, the government conceded that burning, although fast, was too hard on the people. The work crews stopped setting fires then. They started driving bulldozers. Still, Kevin sat, witnessing people toss family heirlooms through the front doors of their houses while bulldozers roared through the back. As dust swirled in to replace the smoke, he wondered if he would ever get off this step. Did he even care? He was anchored, for Christ's sake, twitching but anchored nonetheless. They'd have to roll the godforsaken bulldozers right over him. If there was sign of God or Mavis left on the earth, it needed to show up. Otherwise, he was going down with this house.

It was sudden, the solid thump on Kevin's back that almost knocked him off the step. Mavis? He turned his head. A man plopped down beside him. Not Mavis. Disappointment flickered but didn't dwell, had no time to dwell because Kevin took note of a hand on the man, a clump of a hand, one thumb, no fingers. Jesus H. Christ. "Tom? Tom Murphy from the Burin?"

"Yes, b'y, Tom Murphy. Likely the last one you expects to see around here."

Kevin swallowed back a glob of emotion. "The house is coming down," he said, his voice shaking. "Can't do nothing about it."

"Two tidal waves is too much for one man," said Tom.

"Too much," Kevin echoed, the truth of it settling into his gut. He let out a pent-up breath. "What in God's name are you doing here, Tom?" he asked, bearing in mind that he had just been looking for his wife's ghost. Was Tom was real or a figment? Was Kevin's own head reliable at all?

"Like I always said, a man goes where the work is," said Tom. "This place is buzzing like a hive. The men are coming from all over."

Kevin nodded. Definitely Tom. Kevin's head was still set on straight.

"But the work don't want me at all," continued Tom. "Too old and too crippled. My sons now. Different matter entirely. Hired on, the both of them."

"What are you going to do?"

"Wait out the war on the Burin, that's what I'll be doing. Going back home on the coastal boat today."

"How's the missus?" Kevin didn't know where the question came from, but he knew the woman had been kind to him. Talking, like feelings, was a chore. It stuck in his craw. But the question felt right once it was out.

"Gone this long time, God rest her soul," said Tom, using the thumb of his right hand to make the sign of the cross. "The consumption took her."

More emotion gripped Kevin, a tightness in his chest. "Is there no end to the losses?"

"She was a grand one, my Mary. A grand one like your Mavis." Tom bowed his head.

Out of respect, Kevin waited in silence while Tom prayed. Kevin had no prayers left in him. He was worn out. Twice in his life, he thought he found a proper shore and, each time, he had hugged it. What now? He reached into his pocket, pulled out Mavis' travel sewing kit, and stared at it. What now, Mavis? He looked up to see Clara standing in front of him, her skirt streaked with mud.

"I don't like seeing you this way, Kevin," Clara said.

Tom Murphy raised his head.

Clara widened her eyes, no hiding her surprise. "Tom? Tom Murphy? What in heaven's name are you doing in Argentia?"

Tom didn't answer. He merely looked from Clara to Kevin.

Clara shrank back, a movement so sudden that it put Kevin on alert. What was going on here? Kevin fumbled his way to a standing position, dropping the sewing kit, leaving it in the dust while he scrutinized his sister.

Tom Murphy scrambled to his feet. He doffed his cap. "I'll leave ye to it," he said and walked away.

Kevin, his attention riveted on Clara, paid no mind to Tom's leave-taking. How could Clara possibly know Tom Murphy? As Kevin studied her, a red-faced Clara turned away, casting her glance to the ground. She folded her arms and pinned them against her stomach. She was as guilty as sin, he had no doubt, but guilty of what? Something to do with Tom? Kevin searched his brain. Maybe Kate had said something about Tom Murphy at the hospital the day she met that boy. What was the boy's name? Peter? Yes, Kate mentioned something to that boy Peter, and Clara was standing right there. But Kate hadn't said Tom's name. Clara's reaction to the sight of Tom had nothing to do with the hospital. Clara knew Tom Murphy, knew his face, knew the man. And the guilt of that knowing still owned her. Right now she couldn't even afford Kevin a glance.

The bulldozer belched and squealed as it thundered its way to the house a stone's throw from Kevin's. That house would go down. One more after that, then Kevin's. The machine paused. Its engine stuttered into silence.

Kevin could feel his face harden. "How could you be knowing Tom Murphy?" he asked. "I never said a word about the man." He stopped. He waited. Nearby a group of children were huddled, making mud pies and chanting.

"Humpty Dumpty sat on a wall, Humpty Dumpty had a great fall . . ."

Clara turned to the children. "Ye young ones go on out of that. It's not safe here with the bulldozer." The children ignored her. "Where's their mother at all?" Clara said, still staring after them.

"Look at me, Clara. Give me an answer, woman. How do you—?"

Clara raised her head to meet his gaze.

The bulldozer thundered back to life, gouging, ripping, trampling the next house in line. Its ruckus rumbled through Kevin, foot to forehead, culminating in a sharp pain that pierced his brow. Truth speared his gut and belched through his lips. "It's you, isn't it? You." His voice went feeble as he went on. "The unwanted baby Mavis took in was yours."

How Clara heard him over all the racket, he didn't know, but the shock on her face gave her away. She said nothing. The bulldozer went silent. Still not a word from Clara. She slowly stooped, retrieved the tiny sewing kit he had dropped, and straightened up. Using her skirt, she wiped dust from the top of the kit, revealing its pattern of pink flowers. "Handy for mending things," she whispered, her eyes tear-filled. She passed the sewing kit to him.

Kevin stiffened. *Handy for mending things.* Mavis' words. The nerve of Clara. He snatched the sewing kit and slapped her hand away. "Batter the hell out of here," he rasped, raw with new pain.

"I'm not going anywhere."

Kevin spat. The glob of saliva landed beside Clara's dusty shoe. "Well, I am."

"What are you on about?"

"There's no rhyme nor reason to me being here anymore."

"Kate needs you. That's the reason. She's as much yours as she ever was. This?" Clara spread her arms wide. "Wrong place, wrong time. That's all it is. We can't change this."

Kevin shook his head. "And who was in the wrong place, wrong time when the tidal wave hit? Would that have been Mavis and them babies? Or was it me?"

"You survived because God had a plan for you."

"A plan? You mean taking care of Kate?"

"You have been a good father to her," said Clara in a thin whisper.

"I'm no father to her," he said, his voice brittle. "And you're no aunt."

Again, Clara had no words for him.

"Kate is your daughter." He paused. "Yours, not mine." As soon as the words hit the air, he felt something snap. Was this it, the moment when he would fall apart altogether? He babbled on. "You wanted her back, didn't you? From the second I took her off the coastal boat. You wanted her back and I didn't want her near you." He went quiet then, sorting things out, letting the puzzle pieces slide together. All the while he stared at the sewing kit in his hand, Mavis' sewing kit. *Handy for mending things.* Was there anything left to be mended here? Was he done here?

Kevin had promised to take care of Kate and God had promised to bring him no more trouble. Had Kevin had misunderstood his purpose? Perhaps all God ever wanted from him was to bring Kate home to her mother. Well, he had done that, hadn't he? Kevin straightened his back. "For a while, Kate needed me," he said. "Not anymore."

Clara grabbed his arm.

Undaunted by the alarm in her eyes, he spoke his truth. "It's time for me to go."

"Kevin, you can't leave Kate. You're a wonderful father. Kate adores you."

"That's enough, Clara." He was done.

"Kevin, surely be to God . . ."

"No more." Sharp words. Were they enough to shut her down? His thoughts jumped to the letter from Robert, the one containing Robert's secret. He could spew all he knew about Robert's second family, couldn't he? No doubt that would get Clara off his back. He was coming up to the idea, fast, but then he eyed Kate in the distance. He swallowed back the bile.

"You'll always be there for her, won't you?" Kevin muttered, not raising his head. Did she hear him? Did it matter? He didn't bother to repeat it. He sighed, long and low, followed by a deep inhalation which packed his mouth and nose with dust. After a spate of coughing, he looked around. Layer upon layer of dust yet the potholes that dotted the gravel road were filled with muddy, watery gravy.

Kate barrelled toward them. "Aunt Clara! Dad!" She hugged Clara first. When it was Kevin's turn, he lingered, his arms around her. Over Kate's shoulder, he could see that Clara was waiting. He waved her away. When she didn't move, he repeated the gesture. Clara took a step backwards.

"I'll see you later," Clara said. "The both of ye, come to my house after the bulldozer . . ." Not bothering to finish, she slinked away.

"We will, Aunt Clara," Kate called without turning her head.

Kevin stared into Kate's eyes. How strange it was that, in the past, when he looked at her, he saw Mavis' face and his children's eyes, images that made his body buckle. Now he saw truth. Kate looked like her mother and that mother was Clara. And Kate was home, with her mother, where she belonged.

Kate yanked her father's arm. "Come on, Dad, we have to get our things out of here before they destroy the house altogether."

With an ear-splitting rumble and an explosive crash, another house gave way to the bulldozer. Kate dropped Kevin's arm and ran in and out of the house, gathering as many of their belongings as she could and depositing them in the gully beside the dirt road. Back and forth, back and forth. Blankets, dishes, chairs.

The bulldozer paused and grumbled, its noise fading as its motor was switched off. The operator jumped down from his perch and stood, arms crossed, looking at Kevin, waiting for Kevin. Kate stood by the side of the road next to a bundle of belongings.

His chin high, his steps sure, Kevin walked to Kate's side. Together they watched the bulldozer destroy the life he had built for them. When there was nothing left but rubble, he looked at Kate. Her glance connected. Without a word, the two turned away. Slowly, they loaded their belongings onto a truck provided by the American military.

"We'll be okay, Dad," said Kate.

"You're a fine girl, Kate. All of fifteen now, is it?"

"Yes."

"You know you got your nanny and your Aunt Clara and Dulcie."

"Mrs. Mullins is moving to St. John's."

"Well, your nanny and Aunt Clara then. You'll be living with them."

A box of dishes rattled as Kate scooped it up. For a moment, she stood motionless. "Where are you going?"

Stabbed by the raw hurt in her voice, Kevin couldn't look at her. "I was thinking I might be of more use across the pond. England." He blinked at this offhand response, trying to register the significance of his very own words. England? Where the hell had that idea come from?

"England?" Kate echoed. She dropped the box. "Sure there's no sense to that. There's all kinds of work right here. Men are coming from all over the island to build the base. Weren't you always about the work? You're as old as the hills. Too old for the military. How the hell are ya going to get to England?"

"Don't be swearing, Kate."

"Don't be talking to me about swearing when you're planning on leaving me."

Kevin saw her tears build and his own eyes brimmed in response. Damn. He had loved her like she was his for so long that there was no stopping the well of feeling. He opened his arms and she fell in. "We'll be okay, Kate."

She pulled away. "You'll be staying, then?"

And what was he to say here? My deal with God is done? He inhaled deeply, sucking in both dust from the house he had built and dust from the lie he had lived. Kate, as lovely as she was, was not his child. He loved her but she was not his. On an exhalation, he whispered another lie. "Yes."

She turned back to the chore, loading the truck.

He mirrored her to-and-fro activity of picking up and dropping off, all the while fighting the urge to break into a run. If there was truth in the words that fell out of his own mouth minutes ago, that urge would take him to England. What would Robert have to say about that?

Kevin's thoughts returned to Robert's letter, the one Robert had left for Clara, the one Kevin had never delivered. But he should deliver it, shouldn't he? He'd made a promise to Robert and he should keep that promise. Before leaving Argentia he would pass the letter along. But not to Clara. Not after all that had happened today. He'd leave the letter with their mother. Then he would start a new chapter, an uncertain chapter. Would he end up in England? Maybe. Maybe there, the world would have a purpose for him.

Kevin looked around, taking in the dirt and dust and debris. All had fallen to sand. Just as Mavis had said.

Alongside the road, children were still playing in the muck and chanting . . .

"All the king's horses and all the king's men couldn't put Humpty together again."

CHAPTER 33

———◆———

KEVIN TRUDGED UP THE PATH to his mother's. He paused to scrutinize her saltbox house, a house built by his father, the model for the one Kevin himself had built on the Burin. The image triggered memories but he instantly gave them their notice. *Get on with ye.* Sure he'd be dead on the spot if he let that pain in. No more of that. He was done. He'd left Argentia before and he could do it again. The women didn't need him at all now, did they? Kathleen, Clara, Kate—sturdy as oxen, the lot of them. They would survive and thrive in the new settlement of Freshwater. Still, he had to show up here, things to tell, things to give. The letter from Robert was scorching his pocket.

There was no such thing as a good point to start the telling. He waded in. "I can't be saying this to Clara." He gazed steadily at his mother who was rocking and knitting and staring at him all at once.

"Pull up a chair, son," she said.

He grabbed a chair from the kitchen table and planked it down in front of her.

"Now what is it you can't be telling Clara?" she said as she came to the end of a row of knitting and met up with a knot in the wool. She pulled scissors from her apron, cut out the knot, and rejoined the yarn. In seconds, the steel needles were flying again.

The click of the needles and the creak of the rocker grated on Kevin. Here she was biding her time knitting socks when the whole community was on the verge of demolition. Was there any rhyme or reason to it at all?

The bother of it boiled up and spewed out. "I'd be telling her that Robert was married already."

His words hushed both needles and rocker, his aim, he supposed. But finding no comfort at all in the silence, Kevin jumped back in to talking. "Robert got married in England years ago. I can't go into the details. It's all here." He pulled the letter out and shoved it toward her. "Will you pass this on to Clara?"

Kathleen took the letter, holding it mid-air between them. She looked into Kevin's eyes. "Robert has another wife?"

Kevin nodded. "All in the letter, Mom."

"And you're expecting me to give this to Clara?" She shook the letter, the waft from it hitting his face like an accusation.

He stood, backed away. "Can't face her with it, Mom." Kevin kicked the claw foot of the stove with the toe of his boot. "And that's all I got to say." He looked around. "You got a lot of belongings to move out. My friend Tom Murphy from the Burin is in Argentia. I'll get him and we'll get you started. Good enough?"

Kathleen drew the letter closer. As she inspected the exterior of the envelope, she dropped her knitting into an old basket beside the rocker. His insides prickling, Kevin stared at the basket, a fishing basket. He raised an eyebrow. Didn't that thing belong to his father? Why would Kathleen keep something that had the stamp of Alphonse on it? When Kathleen shifted in her chair, he turned his attention back to her. In a decisive action, she folded the envelope and put it into her apron pocket. "Good enough, son," she said.

Kevin sighed his way back into his chair. The hard part done, a promise kept, he eased into the moment, into the talking, holding onto each kernel of conversation like it would be their last.

CLARA

CHAPTER 34

———◆———

IT SURPRISED CLARA TO SEE the pathway to her mother's house filled with tables and chairs and dressers and beds. She threaded through the furniture to the door. Inside, the kitchen was empty with the exception of the rocking chair in which Kathleen had parked herself.

"How in God's name did you get all that furniture out of here on your own?" Clara asked.

"I'm still well able for it," said Kathleen, her voice tart, her hands tightening on the arms of her chair.

"Sorry. Meant no harm, Mom. But you have to admit it's a lot of work."

Kathleen let out a sigh. "Truth is, I did have help. Yesterday. Kevin and Kate were here."

"Here? The both of them? I asked them to come to my place last night but they didn't come."

"They were here, right enough. Along with Kevin's friend from the Burin, a man who hasn't much left in terms of fingers but he lifted and lugged anyway. Quite something, that Tom."

The mention of Tom triggered a wave of heat in Clara. She clenched her jaw. "Been searching for Kate and Kevin all morning," she muttered.

"Kate is around. She stayed with me last night. You're not likely to set eyes on Kevin."

"What do you mean?"

"He's gone."

"Gone? Gone where?"

"I think he left on the coastal boat with Tom Murphy yesterday."

"To the Burin? Why on earth would he do that?"

"It's not the Burin he's going to. I think he was looking to get away before he changed his mind. The good Lord only knows where he'll end up."

Kevin, gone? Clara needed to sit down but all the chairs were on the path outside. "Did he leave without a word for Kate? Without a word for me?"

"No messages," said Kathleen without a second's hesitation. "He left some money from his expropriation cheque though, money for us to use building our new place in Freshwater. Other than that, not a word. Not a note." She cast her eyes to the floor.

Clara's legs threatened to give way. In desperate need of a place to sit, she stumbled to the out of doors, plopped onto the doorstep, and wrapped her arms around her knees. Dear God. On the one hand, she was losing a brother. On the other, was she gaining a daughter?

The creak of a porch floorboard announced Kathleen's presence. Out the corner of her eye, Clara saw her mother's shoes, sensible shoes, usually shiny black, now grey with dust. With a single, flowing motion Kathleen sat beside Clara. "Isn't this what you been wishing for these last umpteen years?" she said.

Clara raised her head. "This is my fault." The wind brushed her face and she inhaled, seeking the calming scent of the sea. Grit flitted up her nostrils and she snorted it out. "I saw Tom Murphy at Kevin's house yesterday, recognized him from the Burin. Hard to miss a man with hands like that. Don't know where my head was at, but I called him by name without giving it a second thought." Clara couldn't put a halt to the quiver in her voice. "And Kevin looked like lightning had struck him down."

Kathleen reached for Clara's hand. "Calm down, Clara. Take a minute and get a hold of yourself."

"But he knows. After all these years, he knows." She turned toward her mother. "I'm sorry, Mom."

Kathleen met Clara's gaze. "The truth was bound to come out sometime."

Bleary-eyed, Clara stared at the tables and chairs and bedsteads lining the path to the house. Furniture in limbo, coated with dust, hoping for a new lease on life. "Will he come back, Mom? Will Kevin come back?"

"I put that very question to him and he was quick to say no. I asked him where he was going. He shrugged. Then . . ."

"Then what?"

"Then he asked me if I had a copy of his birth certificate."

"Birth certificate? Where was his?"

"Gone with the tidal wave."

"What did he want with his birth certificate?"

"Didn't ask. No need to ask. I saw a Royal Navy pamphlet poking out of his pocket."

"But he's too old to join up, isn't he? They don't take anyone over thirty-five."

"Easy to fix a birth certificate. But it's usually the young ones who do it, trying to make themselves look older."

"Huh. Kevin couldn't fix a birth certificate even if he had one. He can barely print his own name."

"You haven't been paying attention, Clara. Kevin can read and write. Sure and it was your Robert who got him on that road."

"Robert? How could that be? Robert's been gone this long time."

"I'm guessing they started eight, nine years ago. Kevin was dead set on learning to read and Robert on learning to build. They traded skills."

"Oh." Clara nodded. "So that's why Robert and Kevin were working together." Her thoughts landed on the door they had built as a surprise for her. The red front door. The joy of the red front door. She made an effort to smile but the weight of the moment stifled the memory and the smile never had a chance. "He still can't alter a birth certificate if he doesn't have one," she said.

Kathleen said nothing.

"Mom?" Clara grabbed her mother's arm. "Tell me you didn't."

"The man's been labouring under lies for years," said Kathleen softly as she patted Clara's hand. "He needs to live with truth and to live how he chooses."

"But the war, Mom? He could die!"

"You don't have to tell me what war can do to a man. Steal body, mind, and soul. But Kevin is fighting his own war. You think he wouldn't die here? Soon? A man can only take so much."

Not wanting to hear tell of any of it, Clara clapped her hands over her ears. Her thoughts stumbled, then changed direction, the worry that thrummed about Kevin replaced with concern for Kate. She dropped her hands to her sides. "Does Kate know?"

"I'm afraid not."

"Who's going to tell her?"

"Tell her what? That Kevin left without a word? That he is not her father?"

"That he left. It's not the time to tell her the rest, is it?"

"She never needs to know the rest." Kathleen's voice was calm, her words steel.

"Who's going to tell her that her father's gone?" asked Clara.

"Who do you think?"

Clara shook her head. "Dulcie Mullins and her family are moving into St. John's."

"Can't believe you'd even think of laying this on Dulcie. But, as you say, Dulcie's going to St. John's. It won't be her. Sure as suffering won't be me. I'm grieving Kevin's leaving for the second time. And who is left to tell her?"

"Me," Clara whispered.

"Yes, you, Clara. It's up to you." Clara felt the touch of her mother's hand on her shoulder. "There's only the three of us now. You, me, and Kate. We're a family. I'll be here for you but you should do the telling. Kevin would want you to do the telling."

The weight of it descended on Clara, pressing her down, down onto the porch step. "I'm terrified," she said. "I've always wanted full care of her. But not like this. Not without the title 'Mother.' How can I tell her that Kevin left her? I didn't wish for this."

"Her name was Clara, just like you . . ." began Kathleen.

Clara jerked upright. "For the love of the Lord God Almighty, Mom," she spat, "I'm not in the mood."

"No doubt about that. I got eyes on me," Kathleen said. She paused for a moment. "Truth is," she went on, "I have no idea what the names were in this story and no idea where I heard it."

"So that's it then?" Clara leaned forward, ready to vacate the step.

"Hang on to your horses. I can always see my way to the end of a story. You knows that for yourself."

With a sigh, Clara settled onto the step.

"That's better. Now I recollect that this story was about a couple who made a wish on a magic monkey's paw, wishing for money, two hundred pounds I believe it was."

"Did they get their wish?"

"Yes."

"So they lived happily ever after? That doesn't sound like one of your stories, Mom."

"Not done yet." Kathleen put her arm around Clara. "You see, they got the money all right. Their son got killed on the job and they got two hundred pounds in compensation."

"Oh." Clara wilted, her head dropping onto mother's shoulder.

"The people here wished for jobs and they got them," continued Kathleen. "But look at the cost. Every last family here losing their homes. Wishing is all well and fine, Clara, but you have to be careful what you wish for. Looks like you'll be getting your wish to care for Kate, but whether or not the word 'mother' will be attached to it, that's another thing entirely. It's up to you but I'm thinking that wishes have to be made with the good of all in mind," said Kathleen. She kissed Clara's head and then pointed to the end of the path.

Kate was approaching.

Clara straightened up.

Kathleen stood.

"The good of all," said Kathleen again as she headed into the house.

CHAPTER 35

———◆———

"AUNT CLARA, HAVE YOU SEEN Dad? I can't find hide nor hair of him." Kate stopped dead. She was so close that Clara could reach out a hand and touch her. And that's exactly what she did.

"Sit beside me, Kate."

"No, I won't." Kate pulled back and folded her arms. "If there's something I need to be hearing, just say it out."

Clara sucked in a breath and blurted the truth. "Good enough. Your father's gone."

"Gone? Gone where?"

"As close as we can figure, he's gone to war."

"You're lying."

Clara shook her head. "I wish I was."

Kate went silent. She edged toward the step and plopped down. "Then he lied to me. Dad lied to me." She turned toward Clara. "Why would he do that, Aunt Clara? He told me he'd stay."

Clara opened her mouth to answer but before she got a word out, Kate was on her feet again. She flung her arms wide. "Look at this place, more work here than ever. He was supposed to stay and take care of me. What am I going to do now?" She looked at Clara, waited for an answer.

Here it was, the opportunity Clara had craved for years. *Kevin left because he found out that you're not his but mine.* Guilt flowed through her veins as what she had wished for was standing right in front of her. Clara drew in a breath: *Be careful what you wish for.*

"You have me. You have your nanny," Clara said. *For the good of all.*

"But I am supposed to have my father, too. First the wave, now the war? It's not fair, not fair at all." She stormed into the house, calling for her grandmother, slamming the door behind her.

Clara remained on the step, wondering what Kathleen was saying to Kate, if anything. Should she follow Kate into the house, check to make sure that her own words aligned with Kathleen's? No. She'd stay put for a moment or two. Kathleen likely heard every word anyway. No need to worry. Clara had divulged no secrets.

The grey in Argentia was usually fog, a thin mist carried in and out on the wind. The grey now was dust, hovering, settling, seeping through doorways, lining tongues and throats and lungs. A coughing, hacking confusion of dust. Everything covered. Clothes, houses, and crops—a season's promise of crops—destroyed. What would happen to all of the people when the dust cleared? She didn't know. Their lives were torn like a page ripped from a storybook. With no ending to glimpse at, Clara fixated on the now. She had resisted the urge to blurt the whole truth. A sense of lightness filled her chest and she nodded. Her mother was right, as usual. Wishes must be made with the good of all in mind.

Standing, brushing the dust from her skirt, she made her way into the house.

KATHLEEN

CHAPTER 36

———◆———

IT IS A BATTLEGROUND, THE sea.

The sea lanes of the North Atlantic form the supply route for Great Britain, an island nation whose ability to fight, whose very survival, depends on imports, one million tons of them every week. Hitler, in his determination to keep provisions away from Britain, orders a blitz on the ocean supply chain. Thus began the Battle of the Atlantic which is unrelenting, lasting for the six-year duration of the Second World War.

The greatest weapons in Hitler's arsenal against convoys of supply ships are wolfpacks, groups of U-boats that skulk and strike, their torpedoes triumphant unless foiled by destroyers' depth charges. When the Luftwaffe storms the skies in support of the wolfpacks, British losses rise. When the British develop and equip their convoy escorts with radar and improve the killing potential of depth charges, the tide begins to turn.

I am but a shadow, heavy with dread, as I trudge after Kevin who is not long for Newfoundland now. I watch at the wharf in Argentia as he bids farewell to his friend Tom and boards another boat, a trawler bound for St. John's. From there, it's just a matter of time before he exchanges his own island for one across the Atlantic.

The air around me bristles, then needles, pricking me with self-blame. Why is it that my son feels driven to join a war? Why didn't I, as the corporeal Kathleen, call a halt to it when he told me he was going? For the umpteenth time, I sigh those questions into the wind as I remind myself that I couldn't have stopped him. Mothers long to wrap their arms around their children, keep them safe, keep them close, but sons and daughters have to fight their own battles. My Kevin must go. In his heart, there is something else for him, somewhere—a destiny of sorts, I suppose. And I, a ghost, one who knows the end of this story, of his story, also knows that awareness of the outcome has no bearing here. Every telling of this story is the same for the spectral me, minute to minute, nothing to do but to witness. It is part of my penance to wander as I wonder at the senselessness of Kevin fleeing to larger places with military bases, places like St. John's or Halifax or even Great Britain, when my home, his home, the deep-harboured Argentia, is being transformed into a strategic naval defence base, one that will play a major role in the Battle of the Atlantic, supplying anti-submarine patrols and allowing for the rendezvous of transatlantic convoys. Prime Minister Winston Churchill and President Franklin Roosevelt will meet aboard the USS *Augusta* in nearby Ship Cove, Placentia Bay, and from the Argentia naval base will issue a declaration that becomes known as the Atlantic Charter. An upwelling of anger infiltrates the phantom me. If this area is enough for the world's greatest democratic leaders, it should be enough for Kevin. Thousands of local men have been hired as civilian workers here, all sworn to secrecy as they raze and design and build. All skills required are well within Kevin's wheelhouse. Is it not enough that the living me suffered constant worry when Kevin the fisherman was on the ocean? Yes, my Kevin is accustomed to life at sea, to wind that goes from breeze to gale to hurricane. But fishermen perish with the cold. There are accidents. There is fog. And there is the ocean itself. Vessels lurch violently, pounded by icy, turbulent water until seams scream and rip. To all those concerns, I must now add explosions that create holes in hulls and make decks awash. Sailors in terror abide the heaving and crunching and flooding until jettisoned, along with cargo, into the deep. The bottom of the Atlantic is a graveyard, littered with skeletons of ships and souls.

At this moment, my disgust for the ocean knows no bounds. As for the sea itself? The Atlantic sits, silver, calm, almost nonchalant, as it funnels warships into Argentia and summons my son into battle.

KEVIN

CHAPTER 37

IT FELT FAMILIAR TO KEVIN, this skulking off to St. John's when faced with hard times. Isn't that what he'd done when he was just sixteen? Announced to Clara that he could get by on his own hooks and headed off? A boy seeking adventure. What he had found, in the middle of the grind of life as an ironworker, was the love of his life, Mavis. Kevin wasn't seeking love again. Even if it was out there, arms wide and waiting, he didn't think he could fall into it. Still, he was seeking something specific, but he didn't know what. Some reason for his going. Perhaps it was just that he had to believe there was something. Maybe he should have ignored the messages from Mavis and the help from Robert. Maybe he should have just put an end to his own misery back in the cellar when he had the chance. Was that an opportunity missed? Perhaps. But he was on a different path now, determined to see his way to the end of it.

St. John's wasn't as Kevin remembered. Yes, there were fishing boats in the harbour, but now they were outnumbered by naval vessels. And the streets were crawling with uniformed men. Would he end up as one of them? With a vague idea of being of service, he had brought along the copy of his birth certificate he had gotten from his mother. What better purpose could there be for him than to fight under the British flag? The magistrate's office was where he would enlist but he had another stop first.

When he was sixteen, he had stolen money for passage to Boston. Imagine the likes of him, walking into a shop on Water Street, lurking there, leaving with a few dollars a trusting customer had dropped beside the cash register. But this time, there was no need for larceny. Kevin had money from his own pocket, part of his expropriation cheque from the government.

With the memory of the theft clawing at him, Kevin made his way to the small shop on Water Street and stepped inside, cursing the sound of the bell over the door. He did not want to draw attention. He scanned the place and, satisfied that no one was paying him any attention, he strolled to the counter. There he deposited a few dollars beside the unattended cash register and immediately retraced his steps, picking up speed on the way. The clang of the bell above the door announced his release both from the confines of the shop and the sin on his soul. *Thou shalt not steal.* Feeling lighter, he wiped his hands on his wool trousers, adjusted his cap and, birth certificate in hand, ventured toward the necessity of breaking another commandment—lying to the powers that be.

Kevin, at forty, was too old to join the military so he had altered his birth certificate. It hadn't been much effort changing the birth date from 1901 to 1909. He considered using 1906 but that simple arithmetic would have made him thirty-five, the maximum age allowed. A little too obvious, that, so he opted for trying to pass for thirty-two. An acceptable sin this one, if the actions of the masses were any indication. Many were altering their birth certificates to get into the military, but the majority weren't men like him but boys, dying to get in on the action. It had never occurred to Kevin during his reading and writing sessions with Robert that the acquired skills would be used for this type of deception. All Kevin had wanted to achieve was the ability to read Clara's letters from Mavis, letters which disappeared from the silver mine before he could get back to them. Didn't matter in the long run. He knew everything he needed to know about Clara and Mavis. Nothing more to be done there. Nothing more to be said. No reason to stay.

He could leave when all turned to sand, Mavis had said in his dreams. And sure enough that had come to pass. Houses and barns and sheds and storerooms in Argentia all being mowed into the ground. And if the razing of the community wasn't enough to trigger his departure, the raising of a new flag was. Not just any flag, but the very flag he thought he saw on the north side years ago. The ghost flag. It whacked the wind right out of him in February this year to see the American Stars and Stripes flutter over Argentia.

Yes, he supposed he could go back to Argentia, stay *there*, work *there* in a different capacity, but *there* was the prison he had occupied for more than a decade. He was better off here.

As Kevin stood in line, he eyed the young men around him, all of them standing tall and straight and proud. An effort to pull his shoulders back brought a realization—his back was already as straight as a ship's mast. He smiled to himself. Perhaps this newfound youthful stance would help him get away with the lie on his birth certificate. A comforting thought, but one that didn't last. Doubt resurfaced when he raised his hands in front of his face and examined the scars, telltale signs of years spent hooking fish and hauling ropes. He hid his hands against his thighs. Not that that would do him much good. His face and neck would also be aged from exposure. He had scrubbed himself raw at the rooming house hoping to erase life's lines but it wasn't as easy as smoothing wood with sandpaper. A man like himself, ever on the sea in an open boat, was weathered and leathered, face burnt from the reflection of the sun against the water. What kind of idiot was he that he thought he could pass for thirty-two? But in deep now, he soldiered on.

The clerk at the magistrate's office glanced at Kevin's birth certificate, viewed Kevin with scepticism, and twirled an ink-laden stamp in his hand. He put down the stamp and tore up the application form. "I hate to destroy your hope of glory in war, mister, but you don't look nowhere near thirty-two and I can't be doing this. The Royal Navy's not going to take you but, if you're dead set on getting yourself killed or maimed, try the merchant marine. There's a ship leaving the harbour today, bound for Nova Scotia. From there, if you got any ocean learning at all, you can get yourself on a supply ship to Liverpool."

Kevin blinked, surprised that he was not the least bit disheartened.

In fact, he felt somewhat pleased as he reclaimed his birth certificate. A problem. An easy solution.

Next thing he knew he was in Halifax, waiting in a hiring line, hoping to sign on to a supply ship.

CHAPTER 38

———◆———

FROM THE BACK OF A slow-moving queue, Kevin observed the selection process. Were there no age restrictions other than being under sixty-five? Well, he fit that bill. No need to lie. He focused his attention on the castoffs who proved to be men of ill repute—the lazy, the grumblers, the deserters. Kevin raised his eyebrows at witnessing the deserters. Apparently these sailors just went on leave and didn't return. Was there no legal consequence for them choosing shore over ship? No prison time? How did men like that find their way back here? Better yet, how did they summon up the nerve to stand in a hiring line again? Kevin couldn't fathom it for the life of him, but the scene replayed over and over, each time punctuated with the stomp of boots and the slam of the door. When Kevin locked eyes with one of the castoffs, the man snarled, "What are you looking at?" Kevin lowered his eyes. A man had to pick his fights and this was not one he wanted. From then on, he watched only the feet of the men in front of him. One step at a time to the front of the line.

"So you were a fisherman?" asked the balding man with the pen in his hand.

Kevin nodded.

"Inshore or offshore?"

"Both. Dory and schooner. Seal hunt too."

"Where'd you get your dory?"

"Built it. Built many."

"Very well, you're hired. Next in line, please."

The newly-hired made their way to a nearby table where the captain and the shipping master informed them that, once signed, they were expected to sail for twelve months maximum with minimum rations and would be compensated one hundred dollars if they lost their kits in combat. Kevin signed the mariner contract, relinquishing his freedom, leaving the name of his mother as next of kin, knowing the likelihood of her being contacted in the event of tragedy was slim and none. The merchant marine wasn't like the navy where every detail of an individual was put on record. No, in the merchant marine he could go down with the ship and no one would notice. Or he could go on leave in some foreign port, find his own way about, and never return to the ship.

The next day, Kevin would be aboard a cargo ship working as a deckhand. It would be damn hard, hauling lines on the unforgiving Atlantic, but it would be familiar. He had always felt comfortable wrapped up in oilskins and wool sweaters, face to the wind that sang through the rigging. He'd love it even if he were in the bowels of the ship. Breakers or bilge water, made no never mind. Tomorrow he would be sailing on a fifteen-day journey to Liverpool. Tonight he was bunking down and visiting a local tavern on the Halifax waterfront.

The tavern was fogged with smoke and Kevin stopped just inside the door to get a sense of the place, which was stuffed with men and boys of all shapes and sizes, uniformed and civilian, bearded and bare-faced, gnarled and arrow-straight. All muttering and guffawing. Elbow room only, standing and sitting, guzzling beer, rubbing shoulders with each other and the unknown. The mood, like the room, was murky, the air vibrating with threat. Made sense, he supposed, that these men were on tenterhooks, that the slightest bump would launch the entire place into action. All of them, like himself, would soon be off on an adventure that could be their last.

He turned his attention to the bartender, visible in the slit between the shoulders of two heavies on barstools. He was a burly sort, the bartender, his left eye blackened, his nose twisted like a corkscrew, his lips soured in what looked to be a perpetual pout. One glance at the man was enough for Kevin who was never one for sitting in a pressure cooker. He wanted out of here. His idea of retreat was halted when the bartender caught his eye and grinned. Friendliness beamed, taking Kevin off guard. "A pint, sailor?" the bartender asked.

Kevin squeezed in at the corner of the bar and slapped his money down. The beer landed in front of him, froth rimming the glass and covering the counter. Suddenly, the bartender refocused his attention on the entrance. "We don't serve your kind in here," he said. Kevin looked up to see what sort could be turned away from this hash of people. The newcomer looked no different than himself but, in a heartbeat the crowd turned into a mob, menacing, threatening, and tilting toward the entrance. The newcomer's eyes widened, riddled with fear, and he flew back through the door into the night. "And close the door behind ya!" called the bartender. "Goddamn Jonahs," he added and all around nodded. "Bad enough they survive one torpedoed ship," said an unidentified growling voice from the bar. "Don't want them coming back on board with us, bringing their bad luck with them." As quickly as the disturbance started, it left and the room dropped into silence.

As if to fill the hole, music sprang up from one corner. A couple of fiddles, the clapping of hands and the singing . . .

The drums they do beat and the wars do alarm
The captain calls we must obey
Farewell, farewell to Nova Scotia's charms,
For it's early in the morning I am far, far, away.

Kevin hadn't heard this song before but it brought sadness to him as he supposed it was meant to do. He listened, watching the foam dissipate from his ale, sensing the stillness that engulfed the room. As the song faded, the silence eased back into steady chatter, low-key now. A shadow crossed between Kevin and the light above the bar and he looked up to see the bartender staring directly at him.

"I see you're not in uniform," the bartender asked. "The merchant marine for you, is it?"

Kevin nodded.

"I'm Joe." Towel in one hand, beer glass in the other, the bartender made a show of spit and polish. "And you are?"

"Kevin. Just Kevin."

"Well, just Kevin, there's someone here keeping a steady eye on you." The bartender tilted his head toward a darkened corner.

Curious. Kevin knew no one here. Was Joe the bartender having him on? Kevin looked at Joe who shrugged and headed to the far side of the bar. Maybe there was no joke. Kevin was curious enough to have a gander at the corner pointed out by Joe. A table, a single soul at it, merely a huddled shadow. Should Kevin approach him? The man at the table rose and threaded his way toward the bar. Kevin waited. When the shadow man was standing a foot away, when his hair glinted red in the rays of the light from the bar, familiarity sparked. Kevin stood.

"I thought I recognized you," said the man. "Crossed paths many times in Argentia. You're Captain Clara's brother. Kevin, right?"

Kevin grinned. "And you're Niall. First mate of the *Elizabeth J.*" He extended a hand. "What brings you here?"

Grabbing Kevin's hand in a firm shake, Niall grinned back. "Halifax is home," he said. "Thought I'd join up but they wouldn't have me. In merchant marine now. You?"

"Same."

"Off to Liverpool in the morning then?"

Kevin looked around. "I imagine the lot of us are."

Niall let out a sigh. "Grab your beer and come join me."

Kevin followed Niall to the small table in the corner. There the two talked time and tide, then turned to the topic of Argentia.

"The place will be demolished within a year," said Kevin.

"Robert sure got out of there at the right time," said Niall.

Kevin's interest perked up. "You heard anything from him? Robert?"

"Caught sight of him in the harbour yesterday."

"Here? In Halifax?"

Niall took a gulp of beer. He nodded. "Robert was talking to some captain and the two of them boarded one of the cargo ships. Going to Liverpool like the rest of us, I guess."

In the back of Kevin's mind, a door creaked open. Liverpool. Robert in Liverpool? Kevin sat with that while Niall nattered on. Then Kevin nodded a silent thank you to Mavis. No coincidence, his being here. He turned his attention back to his companion.

Niall plunked his empty beer mug on the table. "Another beer?"

"On me," said Kevin. He headed to the bar.

CHAPTER 39

———◆———

THE NEXT MORNING, KEVIN AND Niall met up and trudged their way to Bedford Basin, a large enclosed bay forming the northwestern end of Halifax harbour. In the light of the sun climbing over Citadel Hill, there was a clear view of the magnitude of a convoy, a horde of vessels of all kinds from converted trawlers to combat-ready destroyers. Kevin had seen many a vessel in his day but never anything like this, ships spread from harbour to horizon. It knocked the breath right out of him, bringing him to a complete halt.

"Something to behold, isn't it?" said Niall.

Kevin nodded. "Big as the ocean herself."

"It's deliberate, the broad front and the short flank, the perimeter protected by destroyers and corvettes, the middle occupied by supply ships. Hitler intends to defeat the island of Britain by cutting off supplies so our supply ships must be sheltered, kept out of reach of wolfpacks."

"Wolfpacks?"

"German U-boats. They lurk in small groups and attack from the side."

Kevin could have, would have figured all this stuff for himself but he found comfort in conversation. Made the situation more real, having someone to share it with. Someone he knew from a calmer world. Kevin nodded again and the two plodded along.

On the sun-bleached planks of the pier, they stopped. They were parting ways here, both in the merchant marine, each having been assigned to a different ship. The two shook hands. They held the grip and locked their eyes. Simultaneously they broke contact and moved on.

Kevin descended a rickety wooden ladder and boarded a shabby launch for a fifteen-minute ride to his assigned vessel, a supply ship whose cargo was being loaded from a barge alongside. The crates coming off the barge were large, solid, and labelled with "No Smoking" signs. Explosives? A shiver ran through him, lifting the hair on the nape of his neck. The launch clunked up to the ship. Shoulder to shoulder with two other sailors, Kevin scrambled up the wide rope ladder onto the supply ship, all the while wondering what he had gotten himself into. If not for knowing that Robert would be in Liverpool, he'd be tempted to high tail it the hell out of here, contract or no contract. As to what would happen in Liverpool, after Liverpool, Kevin had no idea. He just knew that he was meant to find Robert and that he would succeed. That was enough for now.

The convoy weighed anchor and, as the rumble of machinery coursed through him, Kevin eased back into life at sea. A comfort for him, unlike many around him who were so green that they didn't know enough not to spit into the wind. Kevin grinned to himself, watching wide-eyed sailors wipe unwelcome globs from their faces.

The only thing new to Kevin here was the idea of using a life belt, an idea which he instantly embraced. Both the life belt and a lifetime of experience at sea were gifts and Kevin felt gratitude as deep as the ocean herself. He supposed he should be thanking God or the saints. He didn't hold much with religion but Mavis would like it if he dropped a few words in God's direction. What harm would there be in that? He made the sign of the cross.

The convoy was long out of the basin, three days into its journey, when a stretch of bad weather had at it. Kevin had seen the feathered clouds of a front moving in and hoped it would blow past, but the Atlantic had other ideas. So it was going to be a battle, was it? Kevin had his sea legs well under him. Still, he was aware that there was no such thing as comfort when the sea got herself into a state. A sailor couldn't eat when the galley couldn't function and couldn't sleep proper while being clouted about in his bunk. The crew would be constantly black and blue, one bruise turning to yellow only to be replaced by another. Those on watch would have it the worst, hoping like hell no man got knocked overboard. Yes, the watch could spot a lost soul on the crest of a wave but then the sea would roll and take the soul down again to his doom.

As the storm raged, Kevin slogged his way along the deck, checking and securing lines. Just doing his job. And doing his best to stay aboard as the ship crested and dove. Eventually, the ocean calmed herself. Good. She'd given them sufficient grief for one day. He'd be below deck soon where dry clothes and hot tea were at the ready.

When a thunderous roar shook the vessel, Kevin clapped his hands over his ears. Had the storm rallied? He looked up. Apparently not. The sky was clearing, the wind waning, and the sun setting, its dying rays piercing the lingering clouds that rimmed the horizon. He peered over the starboard bow. A cargo vessel near the edge of the convoy was aflame, its red glare hurling a tower of smoke. Jesus H. Christ. His heart battering his ribcage, Kevin watched as the injured ship listed and surrendered to the sea, its seams ripping in a death wail indistinguishable from the screams of sailors who went down with it. Kevin slumped against the gunwale and slid down to the deck. Where were the destroyers and corvettes, the vessels whose job it was to protect the supply ships from the U-boats?

Kevin stayed low. After another explosion, this one muffled and underwater, he headed below deck where he heard mutterings about depth charges and U-boats. Most of the off-duty crew, quiet, shrouded in dread, stumbled to their bunks, not to sleep, but to get pencil and paper. A single voice piped up. "Have you got a letter yet? I haven't. What happened to the mail ship?" The voices multiplied then, all asking the same thing.

It didn't take much wondering for Kevin to figure that the attack triggered the conversation, that it had brought home their reality. All these young men could die at sea. The awareness was there when they signed on. But it's different, knowing something and owning it. And in the owning, everybody needed to write home.

Kevin thought of his family. Should he write a letter? To his mother? To Kate? Ah, Kate. Sure and he'd left her with a lie. A well-intentioned one, to appease her, wasn't it? He let out a sigh. Or was the lie only intended to make things easier for himself? He would write to her. Kathleen first, perhaps, to ask about Kate who was now living with her. Then Kate. He fumbled through his kit bag until he came upon the tools for the job. He had just put pencil to paper when a shadow fell across him. He looked up, into a pair of fear-filled eyes. Kevin said nothing, just tilted his head.

"I got no learning," said the hollow-faced young man, his voice a whisper, his eyes darting about, no doubt afraid he would be heard.

Kevin waited.

The young man leaned in, still whispering. "Can you write a letter for me? It's my mom, you see. She'll be worrying something terrible and I can't put no words to paper."

Lowering his head, Kevin blinked back a rush of tears. This sailor beside him hadn't seen twenty yet. Not a man at all but a boy who wanted his mother. Kevin patted the bunk beside him. "Just tell me the words." He licked the tip of his pencil.

The young man remained standing until he got "Dear Mom" out. Then he plonked down, radiating relief that slid right into the heart of Kevin, filling Kevin with a sense of worth that had long since vanished.

Would Kevin himself ever return from war? He didn't know. But he would write to his mother, to his sister, and to Kate. First, however, warmed by this new use of the literacy bestowed on him by Robert, he would write a letter for the young sailor. And for the one lined up after him. And for all others who asked.

As days passed, Kevin learned that all on board were dependent on mail to keep their spirits up, their need for letters second only to their need for food. They cherished every letter they got for as long as they could before they had to destroy it. Couldn't carry it forever aboard ships or in packs. It wasn't just an issue of space or weight, but of intelligence being leaked if men were captured. Despite knowing that strangers would edit every letter and would draw black lines through many words, sailors all sent letters, pouring their hearts out on paper, keeping content light, revealing no secrets. Letters were their lifeline.

KATHLEEN

CHAPTER 40

———◆———

IT IS A MESSENGER, THE sea.

The North Atlantic transports letters, swarms of letters of love and longing from both away and home. For those away, the focus is home, the simple things from home and at home. Mail, whether it contains wool socks, a fruit cake, or a message that Old Jim from down the road has fixed the latch on the backyard gate, somehow muffles the fear that armed forces are facing. For those at home, any message at all holds deeper meaning than the words on the page. The existence of a letter proves that a son or a boyfriend or a husband is alive. A future is possible.

The ocean conveys not only hope but also despair, the latter from those ill-equipped to confront loss or impending danger. "Dear Johns" come from sweethearts or wives who dread living alone and move on. "Dear Janes" come from boys or husbands who dread dying alone and move in with girls overseas.

The worst of the messages that the ocean brings are the letters and telegrams from the government announcing the killed and the disappeared.

In any case, letters pour, spilling from cubbyholes and kit bags and post offices, and piling up on supply ships and submarines and mine sweepers.

I am witness to my son Kevin as he writes letters. Not just for himself, but for others. It seems that, on this ship bound for somewhere, after years of torment, he is finding purpose. He is observing other lives, lives whose needs surpass his, lives of boys who posed as men to gain access to the glory of war and who now huddle in fear in the hold of their ship. My Kevin, who came late to literacy, is writing letters on behalf of young men who cannot read or write.

The air around me bubbles with pride as I reflect on the kindness of Kevin. Given a chance, he is assisting, perhaps reprising the role of father, one that he savoured until the tidal wave swept most of his offspring away. All of them really, when one considers that Kate is not his daughter. It was the shock of that truth that set him to wandering. He could not find meaning in staying, not for Kate, nor for the rest of his blood relatives. Is he experiencing that meaning in pledging to help strangers? The breeze sighs in quiet affirmation.

For some, despite the glut of mail crossing the Atlantic, there is a scarcity. Time and time again, mothers and wives and girlfriends, lips frozen into smiles, wait in line for letters only to be met with disappointment. Quite the contrary for my Clara, who seems unconcerned by the lack of letters from Robert. The only written message from him is one he gave to Kevin who, in turn, gave it to me with a request that I pass it on to his sister.

But the Devil, with the help of a blast from my tea kettle, worked his will on the sealed envelope and its inflammatory contents fell into my hands. The first few lines made me writhe. It stated what Kevin told me, that the British gentleman Robert was married already. With children, nonetheless.

I put flame to paper.

I rejoiced as the letter burned.

Alas, perhaps I should have ploughed my way through to the end of it. But there is no remedy for regret in this realm of ghosts.

My attention slips back in time, to Clara, to her experience with a letter of eviction.

CLARA

CHAPTER 41

———◆———

WITH KEVIN ON HIS WAY to God knew where, the onus for moving the rest of the family had fallen to Clara. She dealt with Kathleen's furniture, getting help from the military, stuffing it into her own barn until moving day when another military truck would haul all to the site of their new home. Kate, with her own home razed and Kevin gone, was dividing her time between Kathleen's and Clara's. Today, Kathleen's house was slated for demolition, so Clara's would become home for a brief time.

Clara reached to the back of the bottom shelf in her kitchen cupboard to retrieve a cheque, an expropriation payment. "Can't forget this," she said. "Two thousand two hundred and sixty-one dollars." Shaking her head, she pocketed the cheque. "As if that's going to be enough to make up for the loss, right, Kate?" Met with silence, Clara looked around. "Kate?" A memory flickered. Kate was off to watch the razing of her grandmother's house. Kate had asked Clara to go with her, but Clara didn't have the heart for it. "Where's my head at today?" Clara muttered.

Sighing, she resumed rummaging. The next item she came up with was the eviction letter from the Department of Public Works. She yanked it from its envelope and, for the umpteenth time, blurry-eyed, she pored over the passel of words.

> I enclose herewith a copy of an order which I have made under the Defence (Requisitioning of Land) Regulations with respect to an area of land in the vicinity of Argentia.

I am informed that you are the owner of the land which is situated within this area.

I regret to inform you that it will be shortly become necessary to take possession of this property. It is necessary to take possession immediately of all of the land within the area upon which there are no buildings erected and the Order which has been made authorizes this to be done. It is not intended to take possession of any building immediately and this is not authorized by the Order. It will shortly be necessary to acquire buildings, but again you will be notified again before this is done.

Under the Order which has been made agents and contractors of the United States Government may go upon your land immediately to start construction work. I hope the entry on your land by the United States Authorities will not cause you serious inconveniences at the present time. It is absolutely necessary as a war measure.

I should be glad to receive from you a claim for damages which will be caused to you by the expropriation of your property. Such a claim can be dealt with by direct agreement or, in due course, by the compensation board set up to deal with such claims.

Yours faithfully,

Commissioner for Public Utilities

"Serious inconveniences," Clara muttered as she tossed the letter onto the counter. "Sure there's nothing inconvenient at all about being dispossessed of your home and your life's work, now is there?" A heft of hurt bore down on her, throwing her off-kilter. She leaned into the cupboard shelf, resting her forehead against her arm while she eyed the floral pattern on the rug beneath her feet, a rug that her own mother had hooked. Clara pictured Kathleen's bony fingers, unwavering as they yanked strand after strand of stubborn yarn through a prickly base of burlap. The memory blurred as did the red roses on the rug. The hurt inside her swelled and, with an apparent mind of its own, surged up through her, exploding in an ungodly wail.

When the scream was done, Clara was done in, limp, all the good wrung out of her. She continued to lean, steadily breathing into the stillness that followed. What was it she herself had said to Dulcie? "No time to grieve, no choice but to go." Clara let out a deep sigh. Like everyone else, she would just have to get on with it. She pushed away from the cupboard, grabbed the expropriation letter, and struggled with the urge to burn it. If destroying the message could change its meaning, she would do it. But it wouldn't make a drop of difference, now would it? She shoved the letter back into its envelope. Well, if she couldn't destroy this one, what about the other letters she had to deal with, the long-saved letters from Mavis? The ones in the hatbox in her closet. With Kate away, now was as good a time as any. She put the expropriation letter into a box marked "Papers" and headed for the stairs.

Resting at the very top of the hatbox were several pieces of birch bark from trees in Bannerman Park. Clara smiled as she set these aside. She removed the ribbon holding Mavis' letters and fanned them out on the bedroom floor. She counted them. Twenty-five, just as she remembered. Should she keep them? Destroy them? Clara lingered over the decision, choosing a letter, reading it, trading it for another, all the while hugging her memories. She glanced at the one note she had from Patrick. A slow sigh slid out. She missed him, often pictured him, and recently thought she actually caught a glimpse of him in Argentia. Could Patrick be here? With a shake of her head, she dismissed the notion.

Clara gathered up all the letters and took them to the stove. Was she doing the right thing? Did she owe it to Kate to tell her the truth? Not now, but someday? Memories of Alphonse flashed. The blush that rose to her face had nothing to do with the heat from the stove in front of her, everything to do with the heat of sin behind her. Would she ever have it in her to tell Kate the truth? As she stoked the stove, her anger steeped, gathering momentum. Perhaps some secrets should not be revealed. She held the first letter over the flame. She paused. She pulled it back. Perhaps she could wait a while longer.

Setting the letters from Mavis to one side, Clara turned to the note Patrick had written on the day she had left him to help Kate at the hospital. She would keep this too. This was her only message from Patrick.

Back in her bedroom, with the letters safely stored in the hatbox, she gathered the pieces of dried bark she had set aside and headed to her desk in the front room. As she dipped the nib of her pen into the inkwell, she recalled the tryst in the darkened park when she and Patrick had stripped bark from the birch trees. Here, in her house which was on its last legs, she abandoned all thought of loss and indulged in longing by writing love notes to Patrick. Perhaps she would send these letters to him. Perhaps not. She sat in joy until a creak from the back door jolted her. Was she expecting someone? She dropped her pen, wiped her ink-stained fingers on her apron, and headed for the stairs.

"Mrs. Caulins? Anybody home?" A man's voice.

Clara stopped in her tracks, her heart dropping. She had indeed been expecting a visitor. She had forgotten. There was another letter that had slipped her mind completely, the one from a farmer in Southeast, Placentia. Where had she put that letter? She couldn't recall. Taking a deep breath, she called out, "Coming." Slowly, she made her way to the back door to face the farmer, to face another loss.

The man at the door was here to buy her mare.

CHAPTER 42

———◆———

CLARA TOSSED AND TURNED BUT sleep wouldn't come. Her impending evacuation kept her busy through daylight but left her brooding through darkness. No slumber. Just struggle. One night, all in with the effort, she got up, shrugged a coat over her nightclothes, and pulled gaiters over her slippers. She tiptoed into the dark, closing the door silently behind her, leaning on it, giving her eyes time to adjust to the ribbon of light from the moon. A deep inhalation brought a stink that snatched her breath away. Damn. How could she have forgotten?

The night air at this time of year should be rich with the fragrance of wild roses. But the rose bushes that had flourished beneath her kitchen window, which mirrored those in her mother's garden, were gone, uprooted by bulldozers days ago, their remnants lying, dying, mixed with mud and rock at the side of a trench that surrounded her house, a trench dug to hold waste pipes and cables. No scent of roses, only the stench of muck. Clara crinkled her nose and kept her eyes forward, not daring to look at the failing flowers. She lurched toward the thin plank that joined both sides of the trench and held her breath as she scurried from one side to the other. Then she inhaled again, seeking and finding the faint smell of the sea. Thank God for the sea. No amount of machinery could lay waste to that. She stood still, listening to the throb of waves.

Clara held no animosity toward the young Americans, the Construction Battalion, who filtered into Argentia daily. They were only doing their jobs, preparing a community for occupation. She knew that the naval base was needed for the protection of North America. She knew that the naval base would provide work for the unemployed masses of Newfoundland. Yes, she knew all this. But how did she feel about the destruction of her home? Clara couldn't lay a finger on a feeling. She had bundled her emotions like dirty laundry and was dragging them along, refusing to sort through them. The result was numbness. She could deal with numbness. Numbness allowed her to function.

Clara continued her trek to the barn, anticipating the pleasure she always found in her night-time jaunts to check on her beloved horse Bessie. Halfway there, she faltered. How stunned was she at all? Her beloved mare was not in the barn. Bessie was gone, sold to that farmer from Southeast, Placentia.

Regardless, she stumbled on. She sniffed the air as she approached Bessie's stall, seeking comfort in familiar scents. Noticeably present was the odour of hay mixed with damp and manure. Noticeably absent was the smell she needed, that of Bessie.

On a hook on the far wall of the stall hung an old harness. Clara went to it, breathed the blended smell of horse and leather. Assailed by remorse, she wilted against the wall and slid down, slumping on the hay-strewn floor. Could she forgive herself for letting go of that animal? "You be good to her now," Clara had said to the farmer and just walked away. Bessie had neighed, calling to her but Clara had not turned back.

And now, here in Bessie's stall, triggered by scent, all Clara's numbness gave way. Grief owned her and she let it wail.

It was hours before Clara followed the moonlit path back to her house.

The next morning Clara removed her rose-decorated bone china from the kitchen cupboards. Her eyes were a blur of red and yellow blooms as she placed each piece on the table in preparation for packing. The china barrel was waiting. Where were the newspapers? She was about to go on the hunt when Kate entered.

"Good morning," said Clara.

"Where's Nanny?" asked Kate.

"Up and out. Gone to the landwash."

"Again? How many times does she need to stare at that ocean?"

"She's lived here her whole life. There's comfort in the sight and the sound of the sea."

Kate nodded. "Leaving is hard for all of us." She stepped closer. "I heard you crying last night."

"Really, dear?" Clara picked up a china teacup and eyed it for flaws.

"I've been so busy thinking about Dad that I never gave you a thought." Kate's voice was weighted with apology.

Clara put the cup back on the table. She faced Kate. "I'm fine."

"But you went out, to the barn, didn't you?"

Clara sighed. "It was just habit. I was going out to check on Bessie."

"Bessie's gone," Kate whispered.

"Some things are hard to get used to."

"Did you get any sleep at all?"

Clara managed a hint of a smile. "You're kind, Kate."

"No, I'm not. I'm just used to checking on my father. No end to the number of times I crept into his room at night just to be sure he was there. Sometimes I'd put an extra blanket on him."

"Then you are definitely kind and caring."

Kate shook her head. "Not kind. Selfish."

"What on earth are you on about?"

"One night long ago, I woke up wet and alone. Shaking with the cold. After that, when darkness came, I was afraid to close my eyes. Terrified I would wake up alone again. I couldn't bear the thought of losing Dad." Kate cleared her throat. "So, every night, I checked on him, not because of him, but because of me."

Clara reached out her arms and drew Kate in.

"No amount of checking made a difference," Kate said. She pulled back a little and, eyes tear-filled, studied Clara's face. "I couldn't keep him here."

"I'm not going anywhere," said Clara.

A small smile spread across Kate's lips. "Do you mind if I keep checking on you?"

"You go right ahead," said Clara. "Me and Nanny too." Clara inwardly cautioned herself to control the tremor in her voice. It wouldn't at all do for her to crumble. Not when Kate needed her. "Where did I put those old newspapers?" she said hurriedly. "I'll never get the dishes packed without them. I'll be right back." With that, Clara escaped to the stairs, up the stairs, to her bedroom where she leaned into the dresser.

At the sight of herself, the fright of herself in the mirror, she gave a start. Only thirty-two and as old as the hills. Her long, brown hair, usually popping with pin curls, was pulled into a bun. Were those wisps of grey, protruding from it? She knew she looked shorter these days, with her rounded shoulders. When had she started slumping? Was that how women got dowager's humps? Did they just curl over with the worry of the world? She looked down at her faded, tattered dress, one that she would usually have relegated to the scrap bag. It was stained with dirt and tears. Not a good example for Kate at all. Clara could and would do better.

After a quick change into a clean dress, Clara tucked every hair into place and made her way down the stairs. Remembering her quest for newspapers, she darted into the parlour, grabbed a stack, and then marched into the kitchen.

"We'll get through this." Clara put the newspapers on the daybed and began wrapping china, dinner plates first. "I got you to take care of and take care of you I will—you can rest assured, Kate." Clara worked as she talked, talked as she worked, fearing the let-up of one or the other. There could be no break, no pause, no place for a chasm to form. If a hole fell open in front of her, she would surely fall in. There was no telling if she could get herself out. "I can't believe that it's been months since the government letter of eviction showed up. The contractor building our new home in Freshwater says it will be ready in October, but I have my doubts. Those builders have more work than they can handle."

A sideways glance at Kate put a halt to Clara's flurry. All the while she had been prattling, Kate was sitting at the table, body still, head bent. With a deep breath, Clara pulled out a chair and plopped into it. She took Kate's hand. "You're a strong young thing, Kate Kerrigan. Your father knows that. He knows you can take care of yourself. Now, we'll be rooming in Placentia until the new house gets built in Freshwater. I need you to help me, Kate." Clara shook Kate's arm. "Kate, are you listening?"

"Yes," said Kate, not looking at Clara.

"Good, because I'm going to be needing your help with the door."

Kate's eyes were full on Clara now, questioning.

"Kevin and Robert built that front door and it'll be a cold day in hell before I let anyone demolish it. We can unscrew the hinges, swaddle the door in quilts, and sneak it into the transport truck that the Americans are providing. There's no time to waste here, Kate. We have to get to it. The bulldozer showed up one time before, the time it dug that godforsaken trench. It will be back any day now to mow down the house. Go get the toolbox from the shed while I get this china packed."

Kate obliged, moving across the kitchen but abruptly veered toward the parlour, to the window in the parlour where Clara had placed a lighted candle.

Curious, Clara followed, leaning against the door jamb, watching while Kate stared into the candle flame. A draught from a cracked seal in the window casing caused the flame to flicker and Clara to wince. Just days ago, she had attempted to repair that casing. Such folly. The house would be razed but its window would be sealed. Clara shrugged. What was Kate doing?

Kate stuck a finger into the crack in the casing. The flame stood at attention. "Seems to me we have a choice," said Kate. "As to what will become of us, I mean."

Clara looked curiously from Kate to the candle. Such a candle was usually placed as an eternal flame, a memory of the departed. Clara had lit this one as a sign to the community that she was a loyal wife, awaiting the return of her husband.

"The truth of it, Kate, is that we don't know. All we ever know is the now."

Kate toyed with the draught, allowing it in, blocking it again. "We can fall or we can rise," she said. She turned, her back straight, her eyes bright.

"Nobody's going to tell us we can't take the door that Dad and Uncle Robert made. I'll get that toolbox." She brushed past Clara, depositing a quick peck on her aunt's cheek.

Remaining in the doorway, Clara listened as Kate scrambled into her coat and boots. The door slammed. Kate was on her way to the shed.

Clara took one more look at the candle. A sham, that candle. Its purpose wasn't to prove loyalty but to hide lies, to disguise her adultery. What lengths would she go to at all? Was her desire to keep the door another sham, another attempt to show the world that she was a loyal wife? What if Robert never came back? Could she, would she, keep the *Elizabeth J*? The only truth she had was the one she just told Kate: all we ever know is now. And in the now, Clara was an imposter. A liar.

Clara stepped up to the window. With a whoosh of breath, she extinguished the flame. Done. She'd let the candle cool before packing it.

CHAPTER 43

ON MOVING DAY THE FOG slid in one finger at a time until it held Argentia in the palm of its hand. The rains came in a deluge. The trench around Clara's house transformed, inch by inch, into a moat. The squish and squelch of mud formed a drumbeat, erratic, syncopated, unlike the steady, unperturbed rhythm of the sea. There was no end to the mud, to shoes sucked down, to brown sludge on clothes and brows and hair.

It was through this that Clara, Kate, and Kathleen trod as they emptied Clara's house, the last house of the three. They lugged everything, one piece at a time, across the moat on a wooden plank that served as a walkway, a walkway which eventually caved under repeated use. Clara was on it when it collapsed, carrying a small box of crocheted doilies that were flung into the water. Clara, unhurt, was up to her knees in mud. Two members of the United States Construction Battalion rushed to assist. After they helped her to solid ground and retrieved the box, they scrounged up a new board, a wider one, and put it in place. Clara thanked them but she wouldn't turn her eyes to them. As she stamped her feet to rid them of mud, the two servicemen offered to help carry out the household goods. Clara put up a hand in protest. She still did not afford them a glance.

Earlier, while she and her family carted and hauled, Clara eyed the two lonely figures smoking their cigarettes and leaning on a bulldozer. Just biding their time until they could snuff the cigarettes and topple the house. The nerve of them. She should give them a good piece of her mind. She was coming up to doing just that when a fragment of memory floated, a memory of a very young Kate asking if houses got lonesome. *Not if you kill them first.* The thought had Clara spewing more bile. She would spit at the servicemen before she'd speak to them. She glared. Would have hawked up a glob if not for the restraining hand of Kathleen on her arm.

"We bear you no ill will for doing your job," Kathleen said to the young men. "But you should take to your heels. When we remember this day—and we are not likely to forget—we don't want to see the faces of the men who destroyed our homes, for whatever reason."

Mud squelched as military boots trudged off.

"Thanks, Mom," said Clara. The proper thing to say, she supposed. She turned her attention to her own shoes, which were mud-caked like the box of knitted doilies that had landed in the moat. She retrieved the box, put it in the truck, and marched back into the house, grateful for the newer, wider plank laid by the two servicemen. She sighed. Like her mother said, they were just doing their job.

Step by step, load by load, they emptied the house and filled the truck. Kathleen and Clara pull a tarp over everything and a serviceman took up the wheel. Clara sat on the passenger side with her mother and Kate huddled beside her. She cracked the window and stuck her head out so she could see her house one last time. What she saw was the bulldozer, rumbling and grumbling, on its way to meet up with the front wall of the house. There was a gap where the door should be. Clara took heart in the knowledge that the door that was buried at bottom of their belongings in the back of the transport truck. There was no going back. She pulled her head in and rolled up the window.

"They have started already, haven't they?" asked Kate, her hands clasped tight in front of her.

"No sense in folding your hands to pray," said Kathleen. "The deed is done."

"Not praying." Kate opened her hands, revealing her small white stone, and then closed her hands over it again.

"Lots of rocks where we're going, Kate," said Kathleen, gently.

"Something to hold onto," said Kate. "It reminds me of Dad. I wonder if he remembers . . ."

"He's not like to forget."

The truck managed the muddy potholes well for the seven miles from Argentia to the entrance of Freshwater, and they continued, shimmying as they navigated the U-shaped road through the community. The plan was to offload their belongings, storing them in a shed on Clara's property, and then check on the progress of the new house. When they got to the curve which was the peak of the highest hill in Freshwater, Clara expected to see the foundation for her new house. Sure enough, it was there and a few framing boards had been put up. Other than that, there was nothing but the shed and a field of rocks and mud, the barrenness broken by the occasional bush, shrub, and stunted fir tree. Work on her house had clearly come to a halt, but why? When Clara spotted a group of men sawing and hammering, she got out of the vehicle.

"We're building this here tilt to give us a place to hole up while we build our own homes," one of them volunteered before she got a greeting in. "Hoping to have them done before the winter sets in. Them contractors have more jobs than they know what to do with; they're abandoning the small projects. They got much bigger fish to fry. I see you got yourself a shed for your belongings. Hope you brought along a good padlock. Do you have somewhere to live, missus? It'll be a long wait for the construction crews."

Clara nodded. "A temporary place. A boarding house in Placentia."

"Where's your mister then? In the wars?"

Clara nodded again. A nod of convenience. Truth wasn't required.

"Too bad. No man to help you. All of the men around here have to get off their arses, pardon my language, and get this work done or else their families are going to freeze this winter. No time for come-day-go-day, God-send-Sunday laziness now. I got me a new baby coming in a couple of months. My missus and my other seven children are living in a rattrap of a house with nary a bit of heat. Cracks in the walls and windowsills, big enough to let in a moose. The snow will be coming in across the floor. Now, if you'll excuse me, I got to get meself back to work. Good luck to you, missus."

As Clara turned to head back to the truck, she heard a familiar voice behind her. "Missus?" She froze. Footsteps approached, did not stop, slid past, but a voice whispered in her ear. "I'm working on the base. Living on the *Richard Peck*."

"Patrick?" The word slipped out of Clara, unbidden. On its heels came warmth and gratitude. He was here. After all this time. And no one would question his presence. Half the men on the island had shown up looking for work. No fear of scandal at all. Aching for him, making no attempt to throttle the feeling, Clara slogged back to the truck and climbed aboard.

"Who is that man, Aunt Clara?" asked Kate.

With a wince and a wave, Clara dismissed the question. "It's going to be a long time before we have a home here," she said. She let out a sigh. Her gratitude, just seconds old, slid right into guilt, the guilt of sin and secrets. Despite that, she found herself anticipating time with Patrick. No odds about how. She'd find a way. "The contractors are hired, but it seems they have overextended themselves," she continued, determined to keep on track and keep her companions oblivious. "They've abandoned our project in favour of a bigger one."

Disgruntled, no time to dwell, Clara thought of the crew of her schooner, able builders all. "Perhaps my crew would like the work."

"Some of them, in their free time, maybe," said Kathleen. "But aren't they working on the base?"

Clara let out a groan. Her mother was right. Like other civilians, some of the crew were razing houses, building barracks, and excavating peat—millions of cubic yards of peat—which would be replaced with air-fields. Others, like her first mate, had gone home, back to Nova Scotia to join up. "Build it ourselves if we have to," Clara said as the driver pulled up in front of the storage shed.

Under dim skies, all three moved belongings from truck to storage.

The last item was the salvaged front door which fit in comfortably on its side, its bright red the only note of cheer amid the beige of barrels and crates.

Kate threw a quilt over the lot. "How long will we have to stay in Placentia?" she asked.

"No telling," said Clara. "We may have to hire more men to do the building."

"Hired men will be fine as long as they have somebody to lead them," said Kathleen.

"I can handle that," said Clara. "I'll just have to learn this construction business myself."

Kathleen laughed. "I'm sure you could. You're a strong woman, Clara Caulins. I'll caution you though—it's a man's world."

"That is of no consequence."

"Can I help, too?" Kate asked.

"You can go to school," said Clara. "Heaven help us all. You haven't been inside a classroom in months."

"No one goes to school in summer."

"I meant months before that. They closed the school much earlier than usual. We haven't even seen the inside of a church in weeks."

"No fault of our own," said Kathleen. "They demolished the Holy Rosary Church in April to make way for runways."

"It boggles the mind," said Clara. "We never saw an airplane in Argentia until last September and now they're building runways."

"I heard that the priest plans to have the church in Freshwater up and running before Christmas," said Kate. "Perhaps he's the one you should talk to him. If anyone can set a fire under those contractors, Father Malony can."

Kathleen sniffed. "We'll manage."

The three climbed back into the waiting truck which lumbered out of freshwater and onto Jerseyside Hill overlooking the town of Placentia. Clara took in the view, a shingle of a community, its church steeple prominent against the grey sky, its smattering of houses, hugged by the sea. Like all those who lived and toiled at the whim of the sea, Clara took its beauty for granted. Not the truck driver though, who slammed on the brakes, wrenching all three women forward, then back again.

"What in God's name ails you?" said Kathleen.

"Nothing at all, ma'am," the sailor drawled. "Just taking in the sights. One of the finest views I've ever seen. My apologies." He shifted into gear and headed down the hill to the shore. At the motorboat crossing, he took his leave.

Clara paid twenty-five cent fee for the crossing and, bone weary, the three handed their suitcases over and boarded for the short, choppy ride. On the other side, they hiked the mile or so to the boarding house whose colours—yellow with dark green trim—brought to Clara's mind the paint job on a dory. She took in the side yard with its struggling lilac trees and thorny rose bushes. At the far end of the yard was a barn-shaped shed and a bevy of sawhorses. Not far from the house sat the pinnacle of the community, the Roman Catholic Church and, next to that, a convent. "The land of saints and scholars," muttered Clara. "That's Placentia."

"Maybe some saints, some scholars," said Kathleen. "Sinners too."

"Let's hope we don't meet up with them. The sinners, I mean," said Kate.

At that moment, the heavens opened, releasing shrouds of rain. The trio scurried toward the back door of the house.

CHAPTER 44

———◆———

THE ATLANTIC WIND SPAT NEEDLES of rain at the exposed faces and bare hands and thinly-stockinged legs of Clara, Kathleen, and Kate as they huddled on the stoop of the boarding house.

Clara knocked, long and loud.

No response.

"Try again," said Kathleen.

Clara raised her fist again. Before she could land a thump, the weather-beaten door groaned open.

"Come in out of the wet before ye gets soaked." A woman's voice came at them, pleasant enough.

Suitcases in hand, Clara, Kate, and Kathleen ducked inside.

"I'm Virginia Wittier," said the landlady as she closed the door behind them and angled her hefty frame toward them. She wiped her hands on the skirt of her bibbed apron. Clara peered at the woman, whose face was shadowed in the gloom of the dreary porch, where the one window offered little light on this dull day. Adding to the murkiness was dark paint, a drone of brown on doors, floors, and walls.

Virginia reached an arm up and tugged on a string. A single, dangling bulb glared, bringing the woman's face, round, red-cheeked and robust, into full view. Her hair, streaked with grey, was pulled into a loose topknot which looked as though it could unravel at any second. "Knew you were coming so I made plenty of pea soup and dumplings." She grinned.

The smell of the promised meal wafted. Good Lord, Clara was hungry.

Surely her mother and Kate must be starved. Virginia's welcome triggered not only Clara's appetite but also a sense of relief. Perhaps they were in luck. This could be a haven, a safe place to wait out the construction of their new home. She extended a hand, preparing to offer introductions.

But Virginia wasn't looking at her guests at all now. She was gazing toward the room behind them. Her expression turned sour.

Clara withdrew her hand. She followed Virginia's gaze.

There was dimness at first. Then a bulb glared and the kitchen burst into view. In the centre of the kitchen, hovering beneath the light bulb, was a stocky teenager, his brown hair slick with oil, his plump face pock-marked and scowling. Virginia tilted her head toward him. "That is me oldest, Bartholomew. All of sixteen."

Virginia shoved past Clara, Kathleen, and Kate to the kitchen door-way. She leaned on the door jamb and sucked in a breath "What do you think yer doing, just standing there?" Virginia bellowed. "Get yer arse out to the woodpile and chop splits for the stove."

Staggered, Clara twitched with an urge to leave. But where on earth could they go? It was a nudge from her mother's elbow that had Clara switching places with Kate, putting Kate at the centre of the trio. That would do for now, flanking the girl. Clara straightened her back to match the tower of strength that was Kathleen. All three stood on the sidelines while Bartholomew, spittle forming at the corner of his mouth, moved closer, apparently intent on a face-to-face with his mother.

"Are ye out of yer mind, old woman?" Bartholomew said. "Be damned if I'm going out in that downpour. It can wait 'til tomorrow." He spun on his heel but he didn't get far. Virginia rushed him, raised her right arm, and brought her outstretched hand down full force on the side of his face with a resounding smack.

In unison, Clara, Kate, and Kathleen flinched.

The bulk that was Bartholomew remained as solid as the floor he stood on.

"Get your lazy arse out of this house this instant," Virginia screamed. "Take yer younger brother with ya and, so help me Jesus, ye better not come back until ye has enough wood to keep that stove ablaze for the night."

Bartholomew turned, fists raised. He drew his right arm back. A gasp from Kate had him snapping his head toward the sound. Still in fight position, the imprint of his mother's palm coming into focus on his face, he leered at Kate.

Clara and Kathleen edged closer to Kate until the three moulded into one, no light between them.

"All right, all right," Bartholomew yielded and, fists still clenched, stormed toward the door. "Benjy, get yer arse out here and help me."

"Darn well better be all right," Virginia yelled. "Can ye imagine the likes of him, turning on me like that? Me own son!" She shook her head and looked back toward her guests, her voice returning to buttery smoothness. "I'll be showing you to your room. Then I'll get you tea and biscuits to tide you over until supper." Virginia headed into the kitchen. "Where did them biscuits get off to? Lu-u-u-u-cy!" Virginia was hollering again.

"They were on the chesterfield, Mama." Lucy entered the kitchen from the far door, penitently holding up the bright red Purity box which her mother snatched with one hand while she swung at the child with the other. Lucy was a wiry waif, more agile than her brother. Virginia missed and, when her target took off, Virginia went on about her business like nothing happened.

"The saints preserve us," muttered Kathleen.

Kate tugged on Clara's sleeve.

"Shh," whispered Clara.

Virginia lobbed the box of biscuits which landed squarely on the table where it stalled as if under threat of death if it slid an inch. The trio of visitors didn't dare move either.

"Come with me." Virginia beckoned them. "Keep yer boots on. But wipe them on the mat. Take a lamp with for later." She pointed to a quartet of kerosene lamps on a porch shelf.

Clara, Kathleen, and Kate stepped forward. Clara handed her suitcase to Kate and picked up a lamp, then followed Virginia into the kitchen, past a large rectangular table with a floral oilcloth cover and along a wall of dilapidated off-white cupboards at the centre of which was a small sink. A simmering cauldron of soup sat on the stove on the right side of the room and socks were dangling from the pipes above.

They filed into the hallway and up a narrow flight of stairs to a large bedroom with three cots and a closet. Virginia opened the closet door. "Blankets on the bottom shelf if you wants one." She then kicked at a bulky object. "Only other thing in here. A useless piece of junk. Careful you don't trip. Throw it out or take it when you're going." As she was leaving the room, she said, "Don't be moving the beds unless you wants to be rained on. Them buckets is on the floor for a reason."

With Virginia gone, Clara, Kathleen, and Kate stood looking at each other.

"I'd like to be able to move these beds closer," said Kathleen.

"We have to avoid the leaks," Clara said. "Are you okay, Kate?"

"For the time being."

For the time being. Well said. Clara nodded, comforted by the fact that they were all in the same room. She examined their surroundings, the single cots with their wrought-iron headboards and footboards and the large bay window that looked out onto a dirt road. Dodging buckets and pots, Clara headed across a creaking floor to inspect the closet.

About three feet deep, five feet wide, and rife with the smell of mildew, the closet contained a single rod and, on the left, a trio of shelves. Clara looked down at what Virginia had called a piece of junk. A typewriter. Curious, Clara bent to poke at the keys. A few stuck. Likely reparable. Certainly usable. She would keep it. A new skill for herself or for Kate. She moved the treasure to a back corner of the closet and covered it with her coat.

As Clara placed her suitcase on the top shelf and took a step back, she stumbled. Recovering, she looked down at strewn fragments of linoleum. A kick at a single piece revealed a gap in the floor where jagged floorboards struggled to reach each other. The kitchen below was visible between the cracks. She returned to the bedroom. "Be careful where you step," she warned. "Broken floorboards in there. Could easily fall through."

At supper, Virginia sat at the head of a table of eleven—Clara, Kate, Kathleen and seven children. Her jaws grinding, Virginia voiced a stream of complaint. "Only three hundred thousand people in this godforsaken little country and twenty-two thousand of them gone off to Europe to fight for His Majesty," she said. "No conscription or nothing. Volunteers, the lot. Desperate for military wages, they were, what with the people here starving in their beds."

Clara looked Virginia over. No sign of lack on that woman's frame. When the woman ceased her rant to slurp her soup, Clara turned toward Lucy, a tiny child—maybe seven—her face freckled, her eyes brown and fear-filled. Clara smiled. Lucy looked away. Clara took a sidelong glance at Bartholomew whose cheek was red and whose eyes were focused on Kate, leering at her. A shudder crept through Clara. Her spoon clattered against the bowl.

Virginia started in again. "Don't make life no easier for those of us left at home without a man to do the labour, now do it? Wish me arsehole of a husband thought things through before he took off to war and left me here with all these worthless young 'uns to take care of. You'd think Bartholomew there would pick up the slack but he's a no-good like his father." She turned to Kate. "What's your name again?"

Kate parted her lips but Virginia didn't wait for an answer. "Men are a useless lot," she said, "but I'm sure you figured that out for yourselves."

Indignant, Clara glanced at Kathleen who sat quietly pressing her lips together, a subtle signal. Clara kept her mouth shut and ate her soup.

In their room, a still dejected Clara managed to light the kerosene lamp but then just stood in place, feeble as a newborn. What was she supposed to do next? Before she knew it, Kathleen stepped up, her face close, her voice soft. "If the burden of hope is too much for you right now, Clara, I'll hold it." Kathleen took the lamp from Clara's hands. "It don't matter who holds the light as long as it's lit, isn't that right, Kate?"

"You're a wonder, Nanny," said Kate. She smiled.

Clara dropped her shoulders but immediately hitched them up again.

She mirrored Kate's smile. Just in time too, for Kathleen chose that instant to turn up the lamp's flame, placing Clara's face in full view. Wouldn't do to put her disappointment on display for Kate to see. "Thanks, Mom," Clara said, as she let out a soundless sigh. In silence, she pondered their presence here.

How many lamp lightings? How much time? And how would they slog through?

KEVIN

CHAPTER 45

———◆———

TIME WAS A SLOW CHAFE on the passage to Liverpool. Kevin knew in himself that the going out always seemed longer than the coming home but, in the wake of the U-boat attack, he wondered if they would make it to Liverpool at all. As for getting home? Try as he might, he couldn't see that far. His focus was on getting to England, on finding Robert.

While on duty, on deck, Kevin let the wind have at him, blowing the stink from his body and the worry from his brain. Worry can own a man and Kevin had no intention of bidding the Devil good morrow until he met him. Below deck, in the crowded hold, he helped sailors write letters but turned a deaf ear to their eager chatter about shore leave and flophouses and pubs. He couldn't see the excitement of it. But they were young, Kevin reminded himself, and he? He was on the wrong side of forty now, perhaps wising up, perhaps wearing out. In either case, his sea legs were as steady as a man of twenty. If the ship made it to shore, his land legs would show up and he would move on.

As the scheduled two weeks dragged to a close, the vessel approached the River Mersey which led to Liverpool. Any hope of catching sight of the port city was dashed. It was night and not a speck of light was visible from shore. A murmur of explanation coursed through the ship. Blackout rules, well enforced, were in play.

In the darkness, in an anchorage well away from populated areas, the crew steadily unloaded cargo onto barges. At the blare of an air raid siren, all hands halted, a mere gasp, then jumped back to work, their pace feverish.

Enemy planes rumbled, roared, and thundered, their vibrations rattling the very bowels of the ship. As screaming bombs detonated, ribbons of searchlights streaked the sky and anti-aircraft shells whistled, bursting like fireworks. Throughout the din, the work of unloading continued, with the crew who had been anxious to go ashore now wishing they could go back home. A long night, a tremulous night, all hands shaking.

It was daylight before the all-clear came, bringing with it the quiet sighs and whispered prayers of the crew. Once the docks were pronounced secure, a harbour pilot from the port authority boarded the ship and ferried it down the Mersey into Liverpool.

Shore leave was granted to all but a skeleton crew whose job was to load ballast that would keep the ship upright on the return journey. Kevin counted his blessings that he wasn't among that crew as his plan revolved around abandoning ship. He gave the vessel the once over as he left, searching his soul for any hunch about returning to it. He shrugged. This ship was no odds to him at all now. As for the young men he met here? A different kettle of fish entirely. But he couldn't utter farewell without arousing suspicion. He silently wished them fair weather and turned away.

As he trod the wharf, Kevin shot thoughts of thanks toward the heavens. It was a blessing, a veiled one, that he was too old to join the Royal Navy. He recalled the hiring line for the merchant marine and the lesson he had learned while waiting in it. Merchant mariners signed onto a ship and often walked away in some strange port. If he had been admitted into the Royal Navy, his every movement would have been tracked. Now? He could abandon ship and no one would look for him.

At the end of the wharf, he hesitated. The debris that fretted the shoreline stirred his memory. The tidal wave. His stomach churning, he turned from the coast toward the city where piles of smouldering rubble choked the streets and layers of thick smoke dimmed the sky. A sickening stench brought on a spate of coughing. Hand over nose, he clambered through ruins and stones and streets with no names, each step carefully placed to avoid the litter of bits of furniture and shingles and broken toys. Burning embers flitted around him like fireflies and a coat of dust covered every vacant space. How the hell would he find Robert in this mess? He stumbled upon a bald and bearded old codger gripping a wooden mallet, a short-handled one that any boatbuilder like Kevin himself might use to drive caulking into plank seams. A strange thing for the fellow to be hanging onto. No boat building going on here amid this, now was there?

The old man met Kevin's eyes. "An awful stink, burning flesh, burnt-out buildings. Believe it or not, you get used to it. You be looking for something?"

Kevin lowered his hand and coughed some more. Before he could get a word out, a siren blared. He looked up. "An air raid? In broad daylight?"

The old man chuckled. "Hitler don't know no time of day, lad." He tugged on Kevin's sleeve. "Follow me to the shelter."

Bewildered, Kevin trailed along, keeping an eye on his leader who showed no fear, just gripped the handle of his mallet and trudged at a steady pace, demeanour calm and destination sure.

The devastation all around had Kevin pondering the point of this particular raid. What the hell was left here to destroy? He spotted a tenement building or two, still intact, surrounded by mounds of wreckage. While sirens shrieked and airplanes rumbled, anti-aircraft guns started up, their ack-ack cackling through the ruckus. He looked at the crowd he was following, all the people for whom the Blitz had become a way of life. Like the old man, they showed only a steady trudging determination to get out of harm's way.

As they descended steps into the shelter, Kevin caught a glimpse of a familiar figure up ahead. Robert? Could that be? He couldn't tell. Inside, he squinted, trying to make sense of fuzzy shapes of people lumbering into this passage, a long passage that gradually dimmed to the blackness of a mine shaft. The arch-shaped ceiling and stagnant air bore down on him. Dear God. A man could suffocate in here. He continued following the old man with the mallet who eventually disappeared into the crowd. Kevin found a free spot against a wall and leaned back. As his eyes adjusted, as kerosene lamps were lit, solid images emerged through the stench of mould and urine and fuel, images of benches lined up against walls and people filing along, filling them in. Once seated, some women opened books and, in the glow of kerosene, read to clusters of small children. Some dragged knitting from woven bags, others pulled rosary beads from apron pockets. The men, old or lame or both, sought comfort in flasks. Then there were those who appeared to be permanent residents, people with pillows and blankets and a space claimed as their own. When explosions shook the walls, all manner of pebbles and dust rattled loose, showering huddled people who covered heads and books and knitting as best they could. Between the blasts, all calmly resumed their chosen activities.

Kevin cast his eyes over those sitting against the wall opposite, steadily scanning, only stopping when he came to a man at the end of a bench, newspaper in hand. Definitely Robert. Although his heart leapt, Kevin did not approach. A waiting game, this.

It was later, when the all-clear sounded, that Robert, head down, brushed past. Kevin followed, threading his way through a swarm of people into the smoke-filled air. Only when a pocket formed in the crowd, when those moving past paid him no mind whatsoever, did Robert stop. An abrupt, full halt. Kevin was a few feet away now and already smiling in anticipation of a friendly greeting.

Robert turned, his face taut. Hands deep in his pockets, he glanced all around, taking in the crowds, the movements. Then, only then, did his lips curve upward. "You look taller than I remember," he said.

"I stopped slouching," said Kevin.

Robert nodded. Then he sighed so deeply that Kevin sensed him sink.

As Robert walked on, Kevin fell into step beside him. "What have you been at for the last couple of years?"

"Long story."

"I got time."

Robert stopped and stared. "What the hell are you doing here, Kev?"

"Merchant marine." No need for more words. Not yet.

"I was praying when you showed up," offered Robert. "Strange, that, don't you think?"

Kevin didn't answer. His thoughts were locked into long-ago dreams about Mavis, dreams in which she said Argentia would fall to sand. It had. Dreams in which she said he would find a new purpose when that happened. And he had. Here. Now. "Where are we going?" he asked.

"We? I don't know about you but I have to make my way to France."

"France it is then."

"Kev, I'm going to Dover to find someone who's skilled enough and fool enough to help me row the English Channel."

"I can row the best kind, all day and all night long. You know that yourself."

"It's dangerous, Kevin. And I can find willing rowers."

"Anyone you'd trust more than me?" Kevin asked, owning the truth in the question.

A pain-filled whine pierced the air. Both men turned. Kevin looked toward one of the tenement buildings he had noticed on the way into the shelter. Its façade was gone. For an instant, Kevin recalled a dollhouse he had built for his oldest daughter, Marie, a dollhouse with no front wall. All its tiny, handmade, perfectly shaped furniture visible. In the exposed skeleton of the tenement, however, the furniture was in fragments, chairs and tables and beds, some pieces dangling, tangled in ragged blankets.

The whine sounded again. This time Kevin found the source, on the ground in front of the fractured tenement. Hovering over the trembling body of a bloodied, dusty, white puppy was the old codger with the mallet. Kevin watched as that mallet rose and slammed down on the head of the injured creature. Kevin winced. The old man leaned over the animal, nodded, and bowed his head, his lips moving as if in prayer. In turning away from the scene, he caught sight of Kevin and moved in close. "War's a hard thing," he said. "Sometimes mercy is the only thing." Gripping his mallet tight, he plodded away.

Both Kevin and Robert watched until the man with the mallet vanished in a screen of smoke. On the heels of the man's walking away, the tenement building rumbled, then tumbled, a landslide of debris. Moving to a safe distance, the two witnessed shattered stone and plaster and glass collapsing into yet another mound.

As the dust stirred and settled, it occurred to Kevin that, all his life, when things had crumbled around him, he had fled. Fights with his father had him running to St. John's where he boarded a ship to Boston. Delighted with meeting Mavis, yet dissatisfied with the life of an ironworker, Kevin ran back to Newfoundland, to the Burin. After the tidal wave, he bolted again, this time home to Argentia. And, when he found out the truth about Kate? Well, he was here, wasn't he? In England. In the midst of war, a bleak future staring him down. He cast a glance toward the ocean. The merchant ship with its ballast crew would be making the run back to Nova Scotia before long.

With certainty in his step, Kevin moved toward Robert. "As I was saying, anyone you'd trust more than me?"

Robert shrugged. "This way."

The two set out through the wreckage.

CHAPTER 46

---◆---

THE TRAIN TO DOVER WAS packed with soldiers, dazed young men gripping kits and rifles and sitting in silence, cigarettes dangling from taut lips. Plumes of smoke rose and hovered around them like burial shrouds. Kevin and Robert edged past without acknowledgement and sat on a bench seat at the back of a car.

The train stuttered into motion, the clack of the wheels, the cadence of rails, a steady rhythm, oddly comforting to Kevin. Not long into the journey, he turned to Robert. "So, the last two years then? You want to fill me in?"

Robert fidgeted, looked around. "We'll talk in Dover," he said.

"Oh." Kevin caught the gist. Not safe. "Good enough." But another matter, something personal, was pulling at him like a riptide. Again he faced Robert. "Why did you marry Clara?" he asked, then cringed. Could he pull the question back? He didn't want to. Anyway, it was out there now, sitting between them, a lead-in to what he really wanted to know.

Robert sucked in a deep breath and slowly released it. "We've had this conversation."

Kevin pushed on. "Did you know that Clara'd had a child?"

Robert went quiet. Stayed quiet.

Then he put his hand up, palm toward Kevin. "Please . . ." He dropped his arm and let his voice fall to a whisper. "There are scars on a woman's body that no husband should talk of, scars that no brother should know of." He gave a brief nod. "Enough said."

Enough said, indeed. Clara didn't tell. But Robert was her husband. He knew. Memories of his Mavis and his children floated through Kevin then but pain jolted in too. He dismissed the images. That past was no longer a place he could comfortably go back to. He thought about Argentia and Kate. "Kate is the face and eyes of Clara," he said under his breath.

"I heard your father say that many times," Robert said.

Kevin jerked upright. "My father?"

"Yes, your father. Alphonse."

Ambushed by a discomfort he couldn't explain, Kevin squirmed. Did he want to pursue this? No. He did not. But whatever was buried at the base of this uneasiness wouldn't stay put. "I feel like I'm missing something here, some bit of information about Clara. Not sure why. Not even sure if I need to know it."

"How did Clara take the news?"

"What news?" Kevin asked, his concern derailed by Robert's abrupt question.

"The news in the letter I left with you. You gave Clara the letter about Elsheva, didn't you?"

"Not a chance. Gave the letter to Mom. Asked her to pass it on."

"And do you think she did?"

"Six of one, half a dozen of the other."

Robert shook his head. "If Kathleen reads that letter, she'll think me a demon."

"No doubt. Either that or she'll pray for the Devil to take you." He shrugged. "What do we do when we get to Dover?" he asked.

"You still want to go with me?" Robert turned, his gaze fixed on Kevin. Kevin nodded.

A slow smile spread across Robert's face. He leaned back into his seat and let out a sigh. "In Dover, we find a pub and hatch a plan." After looking around the railroad car, he fished into his jacket pocket. "Can't say much here, but you'll need papers like these when we're in France."

Kevin looked over Robert's shoulder. "Do I need to speak French? Jesus! The only French I know is a few words I picked up on the island of St. Pierre."

"No. No. You just have to be silent." When someone asks for your papers—*vos papiers, s'il vous plait*—you show your papers."

"And how the hell do we get to France? Dangerous in the English Channel, isn't it?"

"Dangerous everywhere."

Kevin eyed the somber young men on the train. He said nothing.

"We'll talk in Dover," offered Robert, shoving the papers back into his pocket.

"Good enough." Kevin faced the window. He focused on the rolling green of the British countryside, a sight for sore eyes after the devastation of Liverpool. Almost a miracle that war hadn't touched down here. Kevin took it all in, the thatched roof cottages, the granite walls, the horses and carriages, the stables and coach houses and cobblestone streets. Like an old picture book of Kate's, a happily-ever-after book of princesses and toadstools and fairy godmothers. Pure magic. But when the train passed through coastal towns where horizontal coils of barbed wire fenced the beaches just above high-water level, the magic disappeared. Kevin turned back to Robert.

"I'm thinking you're not all that selfish, that perhaps you rescued Clara to make up for not helping your wife and children. And I'm thinking that perhaps I'm meant . . ."

"To help me?" Robert leaned in. "A penance for not being able to help your own wife and children?"

Kevin let the questions shiver through him. "A man can hope."

CHAPTER 47

In Dover, Kevin and Robert were again witness to a city in shambles, its houses and tenements and factories ravaged. "Another port city," Robert said. "Hitler is wreaking havoc on any place that moves equipment, men, and supplies." Kevin could see that for himself and had no need for explanation. But not so for the group of soldiers within earshot, young men, boys really, their faces pale with shock. A couple of them nodded, absorbing Robert's words.

"You'd think the enemy would have the common decency to stick to military targets," Kevin said, as they left the train station.

"Probably would if they could, but equipment is not that accurate. Night-time raids are mostly dead reckoning—guesswork. Civilians killed everywhere." Slowing his pace, he tilted his head toward a building just yards ahead. "The pub," he said.

Kevin scrutinized the wood-framed stucco structure with its steeply-pitched roof and thick brick chimney.

"Not a word until we're settled in," said Robert.

Kevin nodded.

Inside, Robert led the way to a tiny room with a single frosted window above head height, a window that allowed light in for the patrons but prevented outsiders from seeing in. "Perfect place for a private meeting," remarked Kevin.

"Built for just that. Privacy. For anyone wanting to grab a pint without being noticed. Could be the wealthy or the priests or even the coppers.

Women too. So-called honourable citizens can't be seen in public bars. They want to escape their worries in secret. Beer costs more in snugs, but it's worth it for the privacy."

Kevin ran a hand over the oak table, its dark grain echoed on the walls of the snug. Secrecy all around. Kevin nodded. "You going to tell me what we're doing?" he asked, taking a swig of beer. It was warm beer. Very warm. Not what he was used to because he had chilled his beer in the cellar but the buzz that crept through him was familiar so he kept right on drinking.

"I know where my children are," began Robert.

"Berlin?"

Robert opened his mouth but promptly shut it again when the door to the snug swung wide. In barged the stout bartender, dropping off stew, forks, bread, and more beer. He parked his empty tray on the edge of the table and wiped his hands on his stained apron. "Anything else, gents?"

Robert shook his head.

Grabbing his tray, the bartender exited, hauling the grudging door toward its jamb. With a scrape and a click, the door found home.

As the steam from the stew flavoured the air, Robert stayed quiet.

Kevin opened his mouth to restart the conversation. Robert pointed a finger and perked an ear toward the door. When the thud of the bartender's footsteps faded, Robert continued. "They were," he said in a whisper.

"Not now?"

Robert shook his head. "In 1939, I tried to locate Elsheva. Not a trace. Then I got a message from her."

"How the hell did that happen?"

"Not important. It's the why that counts. Our sons were on Kindertransport to England and she wanted me to take them in. They stayed with me, and then I took them to Canada when London was no longer safe."

"What about your daughter?" asked Kevin.

"Ruth is in hiding in France, according to Elsheva. She has sent me details of where she is. I'm going to go get her."

"And where is Elsheva?"

"Maybe in Germany?" Robert shrugged. "I am not sure where she is now."

Kevin hesitated. Thin as an eggshell, that lie. Should he poke at it? With a sigh, he let it slide. Robert would tell him what he needed to know when he needed to know it. "So we row the Channel and after that?"

"If we get separated, it's every man for himself. I'll hunt for you. But Ruth is first. She has to be first. It haunts me that I didn't help her when she was a baby." Robert lowered his head. "Every man is guilty of all the good he did not do."

"Whoever said that had the gospel in him." Kevin took a slug of beer.

"Voltaire, a French philosopher, said it. Two or three centuries back."

Kevin breathed an exasperated sigh. "Never mind that. If you do find Ruth, then what? How are we going to get her out of France? What can one man, or the two of us do?"

Robert lifted his head and stared straight at Kevin. "One man can change the world for the better or, in Hitler's case, for the worse."

"You're a bloody font of wisdom, aren't ya?" said Kevin. His wisecrack got no response. Kevin didn't let the silence sit. "So when are we going to France?" he asked.

Robert picked up his fork. "First we eat. Then we'll talk about rowing the Channel."

Eat first? Kevin's hunger for details beat that of his need for food but he complied. At least, long enough to spear a potato. "What kind of boat?" he asked.

"Good enough," said Robert who then put down his fork. "Remember Dunkirk last year? A flotilla of small vessels made their way across the Channel and I think we can do that in a single boat. This is a tonnage war. A couple of fishermen in a small boat, in the dark of night, they'll likely overlook."

"Aren't there U-boats in the Channel?

Robert hunched his shoulders and, releasing a sigh, let them fall. "Yes. But it's troop and supply ships they're after. Not small craft."

"What kind of small boat?"

"Can't use a motor. Too noisy. Can't use sails. Too visible."

"A skiff then? How far?"

"About twenty-one miles at its narrowest point."

"We can do that. At an easy pace. How's the wind on the Channel?"

"You know as well as I do that the wind and the sea will whip up a storm if they have a mind to. With a bit of luck, we'll make it. We have to bide our time, travel on a moonless night, and muffle the oars."

"So," said Kevin, "we pad the oarlocks, coat them with a bit of grease? It helps if you wet the oars beforehand too."

"Easy enough."

"Sounds like you've had some help planning this."

Robert nodded. "And that's all you need to know about that."

"What about mines? Aren't there mines in the Channel?"

"Yes, but mines are magnetic, meant to react to metal hulls, which we won't have. Either that or they're likely set too deep to affect a small boat."

"Likely?"

Robert shrugged. "We'll have to be careful." He retrieved his fork. "We won't see much good stew once we're on the run in France."

Kevin chewed on the information as he downed every morsel of stew. That done, he wiped the bowl clean with his bread.

KATHLEEN

CHAPTER 48

———◆———

IT IS AN IMPOSTER, THE sea.

On moonless nights the North Atlantic merges with the sky, no sign of a line that marks their meeting. It is into this black ink that missions are launched, missions that have no chance in the light of day. The ocean, on the face of it a cooperative entity, welcomes all who venture into the dark.

I am a wisp of shadow here, mingling with the sooty stream of smoke from the kerosene lamp which lights Kevin's fingered path through the lines of a book. Kevin, hunched in a corner of some flophouse in the bombed remnants of a British town called Dover, is reading Dickens again, *A Tale of Two Cities*. My son's life journey has led him to this, to the Dickens' protagonist who finds his life's purpose by creating a covenant, by offering to relinquish his life to save that of another man.

It is not a new idea, this covenant. Dickens himself compares his hero to Jesus who offered his life for the good of all. A Greek myth floats into memory, that of Damon and Pythias, two friends who loved each other so much that one was willing to give his life for the other. In this Greek myth, the tyrant Dionysius of Syracuse is so moved by the devotion of the friends that he mercifully frees both men.

In the Dickens' tale, the French Revolution's guillotine shows no mercy and the hero Sydney Carton seeks none. Believing he is doing something that is better than anything he has ever done, he dies in place of his friend Charles Darnay.

And in Kevin's story? My Kevin is going to France to help his friend find his Jewish wife and child. France, where Jewish people are rejected like pestilence, where posters everywhere denounce them, where they must register at local police stations and have the word JUIF stamped across identity cards. Just last year thousands of goose-stepping German boots clacked on the Champs-Elysées in a parade of sleek horses and shiny machinery and coal-black swastikas.

I cannot fathom the depths of the struggle Kevin is going through, all to help Robert, my imposter son-in-law. Yes, Robert rescued Clara. He also betrayed Clara. Is it for me to judge this man? It's fuzzy here in the afterworld but the truth is still etched somewhere in my shadow.

Kevin has lied for Robert, has kept the secret of Robert's wife and children from Clara. Is he also willing to die for Robert, all to help Robert save his wife and child? The air around me shivers with dread. If caught during their mission, there will be no redemption for either man. Hitler shows no mercy.

In my living years, I knew only that my son was searching, that I could not stop him. In my living years, I condemned Robert, burning the letter he left for Clara. And as ghost, I hover helplessly as the tale of Kevin and Robert untangles.

Time jumps forward into blackness. The scent of the sea fills my senses and there is a trembling in the atmosphere. At first, I can barely discern movement along the shoreline so I focus harder. Clad in black from their woollen caps to their rubber-soled shoes, Kevin and Robert carry what little they need in rucksacks. They are not alone at first. Other men, silent men, slide a rowboat into the tide and then disappear back into the shadow of the shoreline. Kevin and Robert insert the oars into padded oarlocks. Muffled rowing, barely a sound.

Kevin once told me about moonless nights at sea, nights so quiet that he could hear the beat of his own heart. It's his heart I focus on now, not a steady pulse but a racing thump, fuelled by exertion and fear. Could their rowboat, a mere skiff, be sunk by U-boats or strafed by Luftwaffe? Perhaps.

In any case, here Kevin is, determined, and here I am again, a floating spectre, stranded in a never-ending limbo and destined to watch. On this night, the sea starts out stagnant but within minutes it pushes up little waves shaped like chevrons, waves that lap at the boat in teasing fashion. The rowers ignore the taunts, just steadily dip the oars, the edge of the blades noiselessly slicing the water, the retraction barely above the sur-face, no time to drip before the blades are dipped again. The ocean, not signing off on being snubbed, engages the westerly wind which increases the waves to whitecaps and spits them at the vessel. As the boat rolls and pitches, Kevin and Robert are knocked about, not an unusual occurrence in a churning sea. Undaunted by the whip of the wind and the clunk of oil-soaked debris against the planks of the boat, they move forward at a steady pace.

I'm unclear about what happens next. Does an oar nick a floating mine that blows the boat out of the water? Or has the ocean that lured them simply turned traitor? There is a roar of sea and a spurt of water and then nothing. I wade through the darkness, looking for life, or in absence of it, souls. But there are no bodies, no spirits. Time slips by and daylight slips in. I skim the surface of the now tranquil sea, the seemingly safe sea, searching, searching. I catch sight of a fragment of an oar which will take its place among the flotsam and jetsam of the war-ravaged channel.

There is nothing more.

KEVIN

CHAPTER 49

———◆———

WHEN KEVIN CAME TO HE was freezing and sodden and lying prone, his face pressed against the grainy metal bed of a galloping truck, his body lurching at every rut in a gravel road. An intake of breath brought such a stench of sweat, tobacco, and urine that it induced an urge to retch. He swallowed hard. The bile stung his throat and seared its way back down through his chest. Where the hell was he? He opened an eyelid, just a slit. Visible through a stripe of lash were black boots and a rifle, the butt of the gun resting just inches from his face. The wearer of those black boots sat on a bench at the side wall, close enough to kick Kevin's head in.

Was this a Nazi truck? How the hell had he wound up in the hands of the Nazis? Hold on a minute. Perhaps he wasn't with the Nazis. He could be back in England. Or perhaps he made it across the Channel and was with the French Resistance. One of the black boots budged and Kevin caught sight of a crate behind it. An ammo crate, stamped with a swastika. Jesus H. Christ. Where the hell was Robert?

Kevin hammered his way through memory. He and Robert and friends of Robert had lugged a rowboat to the shore of the English Channel. In silence, he and Robert had boarded and set the oars. Their helpmates launched the boat into the deep and then slipped back into darkness. Kevin and Robert had rowed, shoulder to shoulder, their rhythm steady. Then what? Then nothing. Then Kevin was here. Kevin was here and he had to get out. Was he injured? There was no sense of sting or stab. How many Germans were in this truck? The only human sound was the wheeze of the one on the bench. Only one, no more, except for the driver. Apparently, no more prisoners either. Perhaps Kevin had been picked up alone on the shoreline by a truck on patrol.

He focused his squint toward the rear of the truck which was an open arc. Kevin could barely make out the shapes of trees and what looked like farm buildings. He could jump out, couldn't he? If the jump didn't kill him, he would run. But how much time would he have to get up and out before the soldier could bring his rifle to his shoulder and aim? Seconds. That's all he would have. Seconds. Kevin would do a countdown. On three. He would go on three.

One . . . two . . .

The prattle of a machine gun broke his count. The truck swerved, its gears ground to a halt, its horn sounded, an unceasing alarm. A mental image of the driver, dead, the weight of his body leaning on the horn, triggered Kevin to move. He was up and gone, throwing his body forward, hitting the ground with a smack, rolling onto his feet, and running into a field alongside the road. Bullets screamed past. He stooped but did not stop. An explosion shook the ground, throwing him off balance. He dropped. Down for now. Panting. No pain. No sign of blood mixed with the mud at the base of the wheat. He scrambled to the side of the road and lay flat, peering over the top of a berm. The truck rumbled, then ruptured into flames. Kevin ducked his head. When an agonizing scream pierced the ruckus, he looked up again. Through a rising column of black smoke, a figure emerged, arms raised, the bulk of him on fire. Kevin maintained his position, body flat, eyes glued to the burning German soldier who fell to the ground a few feet away. Amid a rain of soot, their gazes met, the soldier's eyes a magnet of fear. Kevin's gut twisted at the sight of this man, not a man, really, this German enemy, but a boy. He was just a boy. A boy in pain, whose shrieks penetrated the roar of engines and rattle of gunfire. The smell of burning diesel and burning flesh flooded Kevin's nostrils and stung his throat, a stench so strong he could taste it. He couldn't cough. Couldn't move. Couldn't take his eyes off the boy. "Mutti," the boy cried. "Mutti," he repeated, this time a whisper, his last whisper before his body shuddered and went still.

Kevin dragged himself away from the berm toward the tall grass, crawling, rasping, all the while seeing the image of the dying young man crying for his mother. That German soldier was his enemy, yes, but he was no different than Kevin. They both loved their mothers. Kevin lay still in the grass while a door to his past squealed open. His own mother's voice came at him, a retelling of the death of the baby Jimmy Kerrigan. Alphonse had murdered Jimmy she said, killed his own child to save him from the fate of war, the fate of dying in battle while calling for his mother.

At the time of the telling, Kathleen's story had served to solidify Kevin's lifelong anger toward his father, Alphonse, that shell-shocked, crazy old man, a man of low moral fibre. No sane person could think like Alphonse did, could do what he did. No one, no how, no way. No logic for it whatsoever.

But now? Kevin had just seen the logic. It didn't matter what country you came from, what God you believed in. Dying young soldiers cried for their mothers. Alphonse's madness had roots in truth.

Kevin put his head down. He raised his fist and repeatedly pounded the ground, silent sobs escaping from his chest. Heaving and panting, he heard nothing but the roar of the fire.

When he lifted his head, all was still. Gone was the roar of flames and the rattle of gunfire, all replaced by a steady ringing in Kevin's ears. What also fell away was Kevin's anger toward his father. Just melted like the spring ice on Miller's Pond in the Burin. Breaking, drifting, gone.

Suddenly, he sensed a presence and he looked up to see a dark, thin figure. All he could make out was the pistol, pointed at his head.

"*Qui êtes-vous?*"

Kevin raised a hand. "English?"

"Who are you?"

"I'm from Newfoundland."

"Where?"

"Newfoundland. British colony. Off the east coast of Canada."

"Canada. All right, then," the man replied. Better get out of here, mate." He put away the gun and extended his hand. Kevin grabbed that hand, the pull of which launched him to his feet.

"My friend?" Kevin asked. "Where is my friend?"

"Not here. Only you and those dead Germans," said the boyish-faced man. You are lucky to have been in my drop zone. Help me hide my parachute. They'll be looking for us."

Kevin was paralyzed.

Another man materialized, this one huge, dressed in black, a beret on his head and a small machine gun slung over his shoulder. His face was smudged and deeply lined by time and sun. "I am Bernard," he said. He extended a meaty hand to the Englishman. "There was only supposed to be one. Who is this?" he said, looking suspiciously at Kevin.

"He's all right. He's coming too, at least for now."

"*D'accord. Allons-y!*" Bernard turned.

The Englishman moved forward, beckoning Kevin to follow.

At the edge of the field was a parachute, which they dragged and rolled and stuffed into a ready-made shallow grave hidden in a nearby copse of trees. Kevin was unable to focus on anything but the feel of the parachute. It was as smooth as the bolts of satin Clara bought to make dresses for Kate. Such a waste, this, piling dirt over beauty. He caught himself thinking these things, these silly things. Was he taking leave of his senses? Was this some kind of dream?

"I don't know what the hell you're doing here, but you'd better stay with us for now. You can explain yourself later." His rescuer passed Kevin a knife. No dream here at all. Kevin drew the weapon from its sheath. Baffled, he looked back at the man.

"The blade is black so it can't catch the light at night," he explained.

"Oh." Kevin shuddered. He swallowed hard as he clipped the knife to his belt.

"If you have to use it, go for the ribs and aim up. The point is sharp, the blade double-edged. Will cut through anything if you use enough force. Can you handle this?"

"I'll do what I have to," Kevin replied, the truth of his words sinking into him like a stone.

"Very well then. Bernard here is Maquis, the Resistance. He'll take us to a safe house." The trio slinked through fields, heads low, stopping and dropping at the slimmest sound, and waiting for stillness before starting up again.

Their progress was slow, and Kevin's lips were peeled, split, and blistered from the dryness, and his throat was raw from thirst but he didn't complain. No one did. Throughout the day and into the night. No words at all.

As a rooster crowed, they came to the edge of a village and, for a while, lay in the field with their eyes peeled. When Bernard pointed his finger forward, they stood and advanced, walking at a leisurely pace, one that put Kevin on edge. Shouldn't they be hurrying? Running like madmen? But that wasn't to be. Head down, his toe to the heel of the black boot of the Resistance leader, he plodded as expected looking up when they came to a stop at a stone cottage, an explosion of flowers in its front yard. Pink and yellow and purple. Kevin had never seen anything like the dangling purple flowers on the climbing vine which wound its way up a trellis and across the edge of the thatched roofline. They walked the cobblestone path around the house to the back. and Bernard knocked on the door. It opened and a woman poked her head out, her brown hair falling diagonally across her face. She smiled at Bernard. "*Bienvenue*," she said, then beckoned all to enter. Inside, in the kitchen, the aroma was bacon, and the table was set. Two small children sat on chairs, staring curiously at the visitors.

A buzzing sound cropped up in the distance, faint then swelling, like an approaching swarm of insects. Kevin froze, barely able to breathe.

The Englishman perked an ear. "Planes. Definitely German," he warned. "We need to hide now."

As the buzz grew to a roar, the children whimpered. Their mother hurried them to an internal door. As Kevin ducked low to follow, he recalled the day the reconnaissance planes appeared in Argentia. On that day there was wonder, but no fear. This was different.

Something on the floor caught Kevin's eye, a white stone, similar to the one Kate had brought with her from Burin, a stone the size of a robin's egg. Kate. Had he done right by Kate? He hoped so. Without thinking he picked up and pocketed the stone, a scared man seeking hope in a pebble.

A hand gripped his arm. "Come, *monsieur*." Bernard pulled him towards the open door to the cellar and down sturdy wooden steps. The others were at the far wall, where the woman was standing in front of some shelving. Kevin couldn't understand why she was tapping and banging at the wall in a strange way, then she lifted a shelf and a hidden door swung open, revealing a tunnel.

The woman prompted them forward, a sense of urgency in her voice now, one which Kevin understood. If the Germans found the parachute, they would come searching the fields and farms and cottages. She was putting her life and the lives of her children in danger. As he stepped into the tunnel behind the Englishman, he remembered the tiny white stone he had taken in a moment of panic. What kind of man would even think of stealing from these brave people? He pulled the stone from his pocket and passed it to her. The woman cradled it in the fingertips of her left hand and, with her right hand, twisted its top. It opened and from within she produced a miniature rosary which she held up for him to view. "*Regardez, monsieur.*" She reassembled it, placed it in the palm of his hand, and closed his fingers around it. "*Que Dieu vous protège,*" she said.

"May God protect you," the Englishman translated, prompting Kevin to look at him. "She wants you to take it with her blessing."

"Thank you." Awash with emotion, Kevin added "*Merci,*" hoping he said the word right, knowing that pronunciation didn't matter. It was a French word. It fit the bill.

The woman patted his hand.

"I leave you now," said Bernard. "Follow the tunnel. You will find others at the end. Wait there, *deux semaines.* We will need time to get clothes and papers. *Au revoir.*"

"Wait," Kevin said. "My friend was on the boat with me. Can you find out where he is, what happened to him?"

"I do not know, *monsieur*," said Bernard. "I can try." He headed back the way they came.

Kevin and his new companion entered the tunnel, darkness engulfing them as the entrance closed behind them.

"Get out your torch," said the pilot.

"What torch?" said Kevin, visualizing a long stick flaming at one end.

"Your flashlight. I assume you have one?"

"Oh." Kevin reached toward his belt. "I did. I guess it's somewhere in the channel."

"I'll be on light duty then. I'm John, by the way."

"Kevin." The two acknowledged each other with a nod.

They set out, bodies stooped to accommodate the five-foot height of the wet, slippery tunnel. As the smell of mouldy earth charged up Kevin's nostrils and the sound of dripping water echoed in his head, he was thrown back in time to the silver mine in Argentia. But the walls in the Argentia mine were walls he knew, the shape, the distance, the safety. He was in the unknown now with a stranger, trudging forward, stopping every few yards to reassess, use light, and move on. When they came to the end of the tunnel, they waited in stilted silence, the air stifling, leaning on a wall of caked mud framed in by wooden planks. So slow, the ticking of time. What day was it anyway? "What day is it?" Kevin asked.

"It's Sunday." The pilot paused and then added, "You're clearly not military. What on earth are you doing here and how did you end up in the back of a Jerry lorry?"

The question triggered a memory, that of Kate at the hospital the day she had stitches, Kate telling him it was easy to spill your heart to strangers. Could he do that? Just let his whole story tumble into the ears of this willing stranger? He peeled himself away from the mud wall support and poured out the story of his English friend who needed help in rescuing his Jewish daughter hiding in France.

"Is your friend Jewish?"

"No. His wife and children are."

"So he's the friend you asked Bernard about?"

Kevin nodded. "I hope to find him. All I know is we were rowing the Channel, then I was in the back of a German truck, and now I'm here." He stopped. There was nothing to add.

Their support wall rumbled. They jumped, stepped back. The wall slid open and an elderly man directed them through a wine cellar, row upon row of bottle after dusty bottle, the racks stacked from floor to ceiling. There was no imbibing, no stopping at all. Another hidden door, another tunnel that led to the cellar of another farmhouse. A small woman appeared, bringing bread and cheese that the two men scarfed down. Then she took Kevin's measurements. "*Pour les vêtements*," said their hostess.

"French clothes, so you'll fit in," explained John.

Kevin nodded. He looked around. Against the far wall were three cots with thin mattresses, woollen blankets, and iron frames. A haphazard pile of wooden chairs occupied another wall. In the middle of the room sat a small square table made of rough-hewn boards. To the right was an arched cellar door with a latch and a padlock and, high on the right, a horizontal window. Not much else.

Nothing to do but rest and watch the cycle of night and day.

It was in the heat of the last day of their wait that a knock came to the exterior cellar door. Cautiously, John unlocked the padlock and edged the door open. Over his shoulder, Kevin took in the sight of the woman on the stoop, the sun catching her face. A brief, revealing moment of light. Strange, her eyes—one brown, one green. He'd never seen someone with two different-colour eyes before. She dipped her head and the image was gone. She was about Clara's height and had dark hair, which was curled into two rolls that met above her forehead like a "V." A victory roll, Robert had called it in England when Kevin had seen a woman with the odd hair-style. All business, this woman pushed the door open and stepped into the cellar like she owned the place. Then she locked the door, turned to face them, and removed her trench coat to reveal a Red Cross uniform on a bony frame.

"I'm a nurse," she said. "You may call me Eva." She looked from Kevin to John and back. "Which one of you can drive an ambulance?"

"I'm an RAF pilot," said John. "Can fly or drive pretty much anything."

Eva turned to Kevin. "And you? Are you on an intelligence mission too?"

"A mission of sorts, ma'am. Came to help my friend find his family. Rowed the Channel. Something happened and I wound up in the back of a Nazi truck. John here and the Resistance helped me escape."

"You're damn lucky." Her voice softened. "What happened to your friend?"

Kevin felt a gush of emotion. He shut it down. He knew that if Robert was still alive he was likely searching for his daughter. But knowing and saying are two different things. When he spoke, the calmness in his voice surprised him. "I have no idea where Robert is."

Eva said nothing. Kevin watched as she raised one hand to brush a stray hair from her brow. She trembled, a slight movement and then, inhaling deeply, Eva slid away from the moment, leaving Kevin feeling unsettled.

"Well, gentlemen," Eva said, sweeping a now rock-steady hand through the air, "it's you and me and my ambulance. As I said, I'm a nurse. I can, therefore, travel into the city." She focused on John. "Do you know your way around Paris at all?

"Somewhat." He stood and presented his hand. "My name is—"

She shook her head. "Sit down and listen carefully." She pointed to the wooden chairs.

Kevin and the pilot looked at each other.

She stepped back, arms crossed.

Shrugging, both men obeyed.

"I neither want nor need to know your names," Eva said. "The only name you have is the new one assigned to you. I have brought your papers which you must study: name, address, *arrondissement*. I have brought clothes." Clasping her hands behind her back, she began pacing. Back and forth, back and forth, continuously, a sideways glance at them every now and then, no doubt attempting to gauge their reaction. "We are driving in to Paris where two others will join us."

"Who?" Kevin asked.

Eva raised a hand. "Need to know basis only. From Paris, we will head south where we will meet a guide who can take us over the Pyrenees, the Freedom Trail. Do you understand?" She faced them full on.

John nodded. Kevin did not.

"You have a problem?" she asked him.

"Who will join us? In Paris, I mean?"

"As I said, need to know basis. No need here."

"What I need is to find my friend Robert. And his daughter. She's called Ruth, and she's in hiding somewhere here in France. Then the Pyrenees."

Ignoring him, Eva turned to the pilot. "You are fluent in French, *oui?*"

John nodded.

She angled her head toward Kevin. "And you, *monsieur?*"

"No." Kevin twigged to the snub, but he wasn't about to be put off. "I promised Robert I would help him find his daughter Ruth."

"*Eh bien,*" Eva continued, "he will be the ambulance driver and you will be a patient—an unconscious one—we are transporting to the city hospital. Understood?"

Kevin looked around. Hadn't he said the words out loud? Why the hell was this woman not hearing him? Kevin couldn't leave it alone. "Yes, but I have to find—"

Eva leaned in. "It's in God's hands now." She stood straight. "All in God's hands."

Kevin could do nothing but blink.

CHAPTER 50

———◆———

FLAT ON HIS BACK IN an ambulance, Kevin owned his role as an unconscious patient. He had faked unconsciousness before, as a prisoner in that German truck, his body motionless as he squinted through the open rear of the vehicle. No view now. All dark in this panelled truck with its rear doors shut tight. The stretcher beneath him offered no comfort and his body bounced as the rumbling wheels met ruts in the road. As ordered, he didn't move, not a stir, until allowed out for a stop beside a country hedgerow for bladder relief. There, he saw rolling fields, all green and grain, before darting back into position. No dallying. Too dangerous.

The clamour of the city came soon enough—the shouting of people, the roaring of vehicles, and the pounding of jackboots. It was the boots, their synchronized marching, that set Kevin's heart to hammering. Must be a sea of swastikas flooding the streets. How the hell had he gotten himself into the likes of this? The sweat poured off him as the ambulance inched forward. So slow. But slow was good, wasn't it? Yes, slow was good. As long as they weren't stopped. Kevin hoped they wouldn't be stopped, he wished they wouldn't be stopped, he prayed they wouldn't be stopped.

The ambulance jerked to a halt.

"*Vos papiers, s'il vous plaît.*" A request to the driver. The exact words Kevin had expected. Seemed civil enough. All in the plan.

Papers rustled. Kevin kept his eyes closed. Not tight. He had been warned not to squeeze his eyelids but he had to keep them closed, no matter what. Eva was doing the talking. There were no words from their driver, the pilot John. Kevin willed the young John to remain quiet. *Don't let your tongue cut your throat, b'y.* As John's silence continued, Kevin's concern fell away. A young fella but a wise one, the pilot. Wisdom did not require wrinkles.

Papers were being folded now, returned. Feet stomped alongside the ambulance. The back doors rattled, hinges whined, and a gust of air brushed Kevin's face. "*Vos papiers,*" someone screamed. Kevin kept his eyes closed. The front passenger door opened and slammed. The click of quick footsteps. Eva had gotten out? Eva with the different-coloured eyes? He pictured her, her hairstyle now bangs not a victory roll. She wouldn't dare raise her head and stare straight into the eyes of the police, would she?

"*Non, non, non.*" Eva's voice was determined. Not an ounce of fear in it.

Kevin remained taut as Eva talked on. He had no idea what she was saying but whatever it was silenced the inquisitor. The hush held, a dropped curtain, everything muffled. When would they close the damn doors? Something, a hand, grabbed Kevin's foot. Kevin did not cry out, did not move, and did not open his eyes. Another extended silence, followed by a disgruntled snort and the slam of the ambulance doors. Kevin's heart was in overdrive as the front passenger door opened and someone, hopefully Eva, slipped into the seat. He held his breath. Was it Eva? When he heard her call, "*Merci,*" he stifled an exhalation of relief. Not yet. No movement yet. The key clicked into the ignition and turned. The engine did not respond. Kevin imagined the pilot, his hands shaking. The key again. The engine revved but did not catch. The third try brought a rumble.

And then they were out of there, rolling onward, minutes later stopping. Was this another request for papers? Was this their destination?

"*On arrive,*" said Eva, the prearranged cue.

Kevin's breath came out in a whoosh.

The trio abandoned the ambulance in the shadows of an alley and moved silently through the dark to their safe house.

CLARA

CHAPTER 51

———◆———

ALL NIGHT LONG RAIN DRUMMED, seeped, and trickled, its errant drops ping-ing and plopping into buckets and pots that dotted the bedroom floor. In the background of the thrum and plink, welcome to Clara's ear, was Kate's steady breathing and sporadic wheezing from Kathleen. They were asleep, they were safe, for the moment. Clara drifted and surfaced like a guard on duty, anticipating daylight with each awakening. But the darkness on this, weeks into their stay at the boarding house in Placentia, seemed to persist beyond all reason. For a drop of comfort, Clara thought on Patrick.

On the very day she moved here, she had run across him. After that, she figured he would locate her. And he did. Clara had moored the *Eliza-beth J* in the harbour and boarded it one day to find him waiting for her. She was startled to the point of calling on the saints but she was quick to calm and to query, the questions being about why he'd left St. John's.

"The wind changed," he said. "Lots of work here. Easy lodgings. Easy to get close to you."

With that, she had let the questions slide, choosing to relish a future of his rowing up in a dinghy in the dark while she waited, lulled by the sway of the schooner.

When Clara opened her eyes for what seemed the hundredth time, the sun was streaming in, owning the room. Clara glanced toward the other two cots. There was no sign of Kathleen or Kate, their beds neatly made up. Clara threw back her covers and shivered. No doubt mornings were a challenge in this old house. Regardless of sun, the steady diet of damp from ocean wind invaded one's bones. She hurried into her clothes, made her bed, and headed away from the chill toward the heat of the stove.

Kate was huddled beside that stove. No sign of another soul.

"Good morning," Clara said. "Where is everybody?"

"Virginia's in the shed. Nanny followed her. Don't know where the children are." Kate glanced at the porch door, then inched closer to Clara. "I don't want to stay here anymore," she said, her voice edged with unhappiness and a touch of fear.

Clara froze in position like she was fastened to a wall. *Breathe. Just breathe.* "The house in Freshwater is nowhere near finished," she said as soon as she could speak.

"I know, but I thought . . . I hoped . . ." Kate's voice trailed away. She drew her sweater around her.

"I'm sure we'll be able to move before Christmas," Clara offered while her mind was searching for other solutions.

"But that's months away."

"You want to tell me the exact problem?" said Clara.

Kate didn't respond. She again fixed her eyes on the porch door.

"Kate?"

Kate let out a sigh. "The other night, I was half-frozen so I got up to get a blanket from the closet."

"And?" Clara prompted.

"There were voices in the kitchen—Virginia and Bartholomew. Couldn't help but overhear."

Clara nodded. "Not surprised. Those broken floorboards."

"My name came up. That and the tidal wave." Kate began wringing her hands. "How on earth did they know about that?"

Bitterness pricked Clara's throat. "The whole of Placentia Bay knew the story of how Kevin survived and brought you home. No end to tongue wagging when it comes to misfortune." She berated herself. What had she done, bringing Kate here?

"I stayed still until the light in the kitchen went out," Kate continued.

"I was about to leave the closet when the light came on again. I peered through the cracks. Bartholomew was staring up. He said, 'Looking for me, Kate? I'm waiting for ya.' Scared the daylights out of me. I ran back to bed." She turned to look at Clara. "He's always given me the creeps but I didn't mention it. It's different now. I don't feel safe here."

Clara put her hand out, palm forward. "Just let me think," she said, truly needing time to calm herself. *Fury doesn't breed common-sense reactions.*

"I'm sorry if—"

"Nothing to be sorry for. A lot less suffering would occur in this world if people just spoke up." A rusty memory scraped its way into Clara's mind. As a child, an abused child, she herself harboured guilt and shame that wasn't hers to begin with. And she told no one. She was having none of that for Kate. Apparently, Kate was having none of that for herself. Was each generation a brighter version of the past?

"I'm sorry for bringing you here, Kate. This house is no haven."

"I don't blame you, Aunt Clara."

"No one to blame but Bartholomew. Important thing is that you spoke up. And my job is to help." Clara eased into clarity. The solution appeared. "How do you feel about living on a schooner?"

"What?"

"We're moving today."

"Really?"

"Go get your grandmother."

Kate wrapped her arms around Clara, hugging her tight. "Thank you."

"Never mind that now. You get all our things packed. I'll find us a ride to the Gut and we'll take the motorboat back to Jerseyside. Won't be hard to get to the schooner from there." Clara shooed Kate away but then called her back. "Kate, don't tell your grandmother about this. She'd make short work of that Bartholomew."

Doubt glimmered on Kate's face. "Nanny is too old to do anything against a brute like Bartholomew."

Clara folded her arms. "Your grandmother never let the march of time prevent her from doing what she has to and she never will."

Kate shrugged. "I'm sure there's more to that but I'm not asking."

"Good, because I'm not telling," said Clara as Kate headed off. "Now when you're packing," Clara called, "make sure you put that typewriter beside our suitcases."

Clara listened for Kate's footsteps on the stairs. No such sound came for Kate was back again, her face flushed, her eyes flooded. "Aunt Clara, I have to confess that I already told Nanny about Bartholomew. She said I should tell you, that she'd keep Virginia busy for a bit."

Clara let out a small laugh. "No surprise there."

Kate exhaled long and slow. With a dramatic wipe of her brow, she hurried off, her footsteps pounding the staircase. Clara nodded. She was proud of Kate. Kathleen, too.

Clara breathed more easily knowing that she had come up with a good solution. But a grain of sadness had emerged too. Yes, she, Kathleen, and Kate could manage aboard the schooner until the house was done. But she had just lost the ideal hideout for herself and Patrick.

KEVIN

CHAPTER 52

———◆———

IN THE DEAD OF NIGHT, in another dank cellar, on the edge of a bare mattress on a stone floor, Kevin sat, head down, his mind reeling from the events of the past few days.

Eva approached. Setting her lantern on the floor, she plopped cross-legged beside him and delivered a sigh so deep it must have wrangled its way from the very pit of her. Then silence. Kevin waited.

"All right, friend of Robert," she said, "what promise did this Robert make to get you to follow him here?"

Unexpected, the hope that surged through Kevin. Perhaps she was interested in helping him after all. "No promises," he said. "Not a darn thing. Why do you ask?"

"Why are *you* here?" she said instantly. "Before you think of putting me off again," she added, "let me assure you I have no time for anything but truth."

Kevin exhaled, yielding. Clearly it was her way or no way. "Good enough," he said. "Lost my family in a tidal wave. Wasn't there to help them. Robert rescued me from the hell of it. Figured if I could help Robert's family, I could ease my own guilt."

Eva nodded slowly. She tapped a cigarette from her pack and offered it to him.

He raised both hands, a refusal. She shrugged.

Kevin watched as she struck a match, introduced the cigarette to the flame, and drew a breath. The paper sizzled. Smoke wafted. With a flick of her wrist, Eva extinguished the match which she tossed across the floor. All fine-tuned movements, all done without peeling off her gloves.

"So tell me," she said. "What do you know of Robert's sons?"

"They're safe, in Canada," Kevin said at once, then stopped short. The truth took root at his core: "Your name isn't Eva, is it?"

"No, friend of Robert, my name is not Eva. And I am not French. I am German."

Kevin's thoughts whirred and lagged, pulsing with questions. He opened his mouth, and Eva raised a hand to silence him.

He paused. Had she planned this? This moment of telling. If so, answers were not far off. He could wait. He would wait.

"My sons are safe," Eva said with a sigh that spoke of relief. "I only wish I had placed my daughter on Kindertransport to England with them. How selfish was I, how foolish to think Ruth would be safe with me. I soon learned," she said, her voice brittle and cracking, "I soon learned that I was wrong." She slid a gloved hand across her eyes, cleared her throat, and went on. "I got involved with people working against Hitler and the Nazis and I forged documents to hide the fact that my daughter and I are Jewish. Friends helped me get my daughter out of Berlin, into a safe place, a convent in France."

Kevin hung on her words, grappling with them, wanting to know more. How the hell had she herself gotten away from the Nazis in Berlin?

"But France isn't safe," she continued. "The Nazis will herd, move, and massacre the Jews here just as they are doing in Germany, Poland, and Austria. The Vichy collaborators will allow it. I have to get Ruth out of France." Eva stopped speaking.

Kevin let the silence sit. At the sound of scampering in a corner, he turned his head. A mouse, there and gone in the darkness. After a few more moments, Kevin nudged a low question into the quiet. "And where does Robert fit into all this?"

"If he survived, he will be trying to reach Ruth." She shrugged. "But there's no way we can know. I must get to my daughter and get her out of the country."

"I understand," said Kevin.

"I'm sure your do. Any man who has lost his family would."

Kevin nodded. "Do you mind telling me how you got away from the Nazis in Berlin?" he asked gently.

"They came for me, three of them. 'Please come with us, Frau Cotter,' one said, a nice as you please." She sucked on her cigarette and blew out a long stream of smoke. "That was the name I was using at the time. I knew if I obliged, I was done for, so I stalled, offering them coffee. One requested *café au lait*, like he was in a restaurant. I pounced on that, saying that I was out of milk and had to borrow some. I left through the back door."

"They didn't chase you?"

Eva shook her head. "Maybe they waited. Maybe they didn't. Possibly they were not keen on what they were doing. Germans are not all bad, you know. So terrified of being reported and killed that they just do whatever it takes to survive. Never blame *all* Germans for this. The very first help I got was in the home of a German man."

"He got you out of Berlin?"

"Not that easy. I was there for six months, moving from house to house, in one place for a maximum of two weeks, pretending to be a cousin, a visitor."

"Two weeks?"

"After that, visitors have to register with the local police. Sometimes the neighbours didn't even know I was there. But one day, I got caught. All it took was a squeaky floorboard. Someone reported it."

"Weren't you scared?"

"Fear is nothing compared to hunger. Have you ever been hungry, friend of Robert?"

"I suppose so," said Kevin. "Certainly on this trip."

Eva laughed, a low chortle. "This is nothing. You'll see. I was hungry all the time. Sometimes I'd get a bit of food and it felt worse because once the stomach juices start flowing, the body wants more food. The constant ache, gripping at your gut. Hunger owns you. You can't think about anything else. You are always standing in line hoping for food, always carrying empty bags, always walking, forever walking. Nobody drives here except

Germans and if you don't have a bicycle, you walk. You can take a train but you are under curfew."

"What about help from England?"

"I did ask for help for my child," she said, her voice low, taut. "I got word through a French policeman, a man who couldn't send a letter that I had written but he could write one himself."

"Kind of him," ventured Kevin.

"You are naïve, friend of Robert. Well-intentioned, I'm sure, but naïve. Morality went out the window with the invasion of the Nazis."

"Meaning?"

"Humph." The grit returned to her voice. "The cost of that kindness was sex, in the backroom of an abandoned café."

Startled, Kevin shot a look of doubt. Fleeting, but she caught it.

"It's true, friend of Robert," she said. "I learned that if I need help, I should ask a woman. Women can be trusted. Women are the strength of the Resistance."

Kevin didn't doubt that for a second. He was looking at that strength in Eva. He nodded. "How do we get to your daughter?"

"It won't be easy." Eva dropped her cigarette and stomped it with her boot. She removed her gloves and tossed them onto the mattress. She rested her hands on her knees.

With a sidelong glance, Kevin watched the light from the lantern play over the backs of her hands. Calloused hands. Like a dockworker's. When she slid her hands back—a slight movement—she brought them into full view. Kevin's gut twisted. Eva's left hand was missing two digits, just like his friend Tom Murphy. But Tom's misfortune had been the result of an accident. And Eva's? Kevin swallowed hard as he stared at the two tiny knobs where her ring and little fingers should be.

"Interrogation is not pleasant," said Eva.

Staggered, Kevin gawked full on, no apology.

"Sometimes I wonder if it is the killed who are the lucky ones," said Eva. "Those who survive trauma and torture will live with the hell of it forever."

When Eva pulled her hands from the light, Kevin responded with a sigh of relief. Damn hard to look at. Damn hard to look away too. He slumped, juggling thoughts about what he ought to say. He had nothing. Nothing but a lump of words wedged in his throat.

Eva retrieved her gloves and slipped them back on. "I stuffed the left one," she said. "Looks normal, doesn't it?" She held her hand out, fingers splayed.

Kevin didn't answer.

Eva dropped her hand. "I didn't mean to shock you," she said, "but I had to be sure you understood. You're in danger here."

"*Me?* What about you? What about your husband and my friend—Robert? He crossed the Atlantic to save his family."

Eva sniffed. "*Oui, en effet,*" she said. "Too little, too late."

In the abrupt hush that followed, Kevin slid away from her, a good foot away.

Eva rose from her cross-legged position without even reaching a hand to the floor to push herself up. Sitting, then standing.

Effortless.

Kevin thought of Clara. A wiry woman, iron-clad.

"After we claim my daughter, we will make our way to the mountains," said Eva. "Train is the easiest, but we can't travel that way. Too dangerous. I am too distinctive, my hands, my eyes. You cannot speak French, and the two people we will be escorting are far too important. We must make it on foot to the Pyrenees."

Eva picked up her lantern. "What you need now is to take a page from that pilot's book." She pointed to John who was curled up in another corner. "Sleep. In the morning, I will tell you what you need to know." With that she was gone.

Kevin dropped back onto the mattress and closed his eyes. Was Eva right? Was it the killed who were the lucky ones? The last image he saw before fatigue took over was that of the young German soldier he had watched dying. The soldier was gone, and Kevin was stuck with the image of his death forever.

CHAPTER 53

———◆———

WHEN KEVIN LOOKED UP FROM his mattress again, light was streaming through a cellar window and Eva was standing over him.

"Good morning, friend of Robert. *Réveillez-vous!*"

Kevin sat upright, rubbing his eyes. "Slept like the dead. Can't believe I slept at all."

"Bodies sleep when they need to. It is time," she said.

"Time for?" said Kevin.

"Time to go."

John shrugged and yawned and scrambled to his feet. "Good morning." Locking down his emotions, Kevin headed to the toilet. When he returned, Eva and John were sitting on wooden chairs in the far corner of the cellar. With them were a couple Kevin had never seen before.

"These are the two people I told you about," said Eve. "You can call them François and Jeanne. They will be coming with us to the Pyrenees."

Kevin slid into the remaining empty chair.

"It is vital that you act normal as we make our way through the city to the outskirts," Eva was saying. "Friend of Robert, Pilot, make sure your watches are set to one hour ahead. The whole of France is on German time now. *En peine de mort.* Deviation could mean death." She stopped, while they did as they were told.

"The streets are swarming with soldiers and with informers who will not be wearing German uniforms. Trust no one. Keep your head low. Follow where I lead. Above all, do not show fear. Fear is a giveaway. If anyone asks you for help, ignore them. Beggars and businessmen alike. Just walk on. Pay no mind to children who may claw at your clothes. Walk on. You must look like you belong here. You are not tourists. You must not stand out. Nothing must appear new to you. Your life depends on this. Understood?"

Eva handed the pilot a silk map, which he placed a secret pocket hidden in his coat's lining. "Silk doesn't rustle like paper," he explained to Kevin, who looked confused by the odd document. "And it handles the rain well."

"If we get separated, you will need that map, Pilot," Eva said. "I assume you have a compass too?"

John nodded.

"Keep that hidden, too."

Eva stood and faced them all. "Courtesy of the owner of this house, we will eat before we go. And I advise you, eat well. We don't know where the next meal will come from."

The clack of a latch and all turned to see a couple, both grey and spry, both clad in black, enter the cellar door. The trays they carried held tea, bread, butter and jam, and a dish of peeled hard-boiled eggs. They set their gifts of food on the floor and walked away.

"*Merci*," said Eva.

The host turned and smiled. "*Bonne chance*." The woman with him nodded. "*Reste en vie*," she said as they both exited.

"Stay alive?" the pilot asked.

"It is as common as 'farewell' in the underground," explained Eva. "Stay alive. It is what we all want." She grabbed a piece of toast, shoved another toward Kevin.

CHAPTER 5 4

ONE AT A TIME AND serpentine, a low-key quintet made its way through Paris streets slick with rain. Kevin brought up the rear and kept an eye on those in front who trailed Eva through clusters and lines of people. So many lines. People waiting for bread, waiting for buses, waiting for trains. Kevin couldn't help but be skittish as Eva bisected those lines. Heaven forbid the invisible thread that connected them be cut.

The air stirred around Kevin as bicycles, countless bicycles, rushed past. He noted baskets on handlebars. Were the cyclists smuggling black market items like eggs and meat? Maybe they were working for the Resistance, transporting guns and dynamite. According to Eva, Resistance workers operated in constant fear as they were considered terrorists. Informants were paid. Informants were everywhere. Kevin felt the fear himself now. How people lived with this shivering sensation inside their guts day after day, Kevin didn't know. But then, he himself had lived in a state of numbness, no feelings at all, for a long time. People did what they had to, he supposed. From what he could discern of shoes and ankles and skirts, many of the cyclists, possible Resistance fighters, just like Eva said, were women.

A bicycle's brakes squealed, its front wheel stopping just a hairsbreadth from Kevin. He jerked to a halt and turned to the rider, a dark-haired woman wearing what looked like a skirt but was slit up the middle, like pants. Their eyes met. Hers flashed fright. She muttered something, an apology perhaps. He spun away, kept walking, heart pounding. Dear God. How stunned was he to let his attention stray like that. Had he lost the thread? Where the hell was John? Oh. He spotted the pilot. Relief was instant. Still, he berated himself. *Look at what you almost went and done.*

When gunfire shattered the air, Kevin did not react. He was full-on focused now. Not a ripple on the surface of him, not even when the hum of voices around him surged to screams and the shiver in his gut swelled to dread. Had to do what he had to do or he would get them all killed. Tortured first, then killed. He just kept plodding, not changing his pace, as they made their way along the Seine to the outskirts of the city. Welcoming the peace of the countryside, yet still wary, they slogged onward.

For days they walked, aware of trains whizzing by, wishing they could board, yet knowing trains had to be avoided. Trains meant requests for papers. They slept in fields of tall grasses feathered by breezes and rustled by mice. They stole eggs from squawking chickens in tiny coops in muddy barnyards. Sun and wind partnered to burn faces and crack lips. Mosquitos stabbed and pimpled them, head to toe, but the resulting itch was nothing compared to the growing hunger. Eva was right about the hunger. There was little Kevin could do except notch his belt tighter.

After two weeks of endless trekking, they reached the southern border of the Dordogne region. They were resting in a field, distantly overlooked by the walls of a small medieval town.

"We must have a brief delay to our journey here," Eva announced. "Before we continue to our rendezvous."

John, François and Jeanne all looked confused and concerned. Only Kevin nodded, understanding.

"Why? What's wrong," John asked. "We should be heading straight there."

"There is something I must do. We must collect one more person to join us for the final leg of our journey," said Eva. "We must go to a convent near this town. It is run by an order of Franciscan nuns."

"Who is so important that it interferes with our mission?" the pilot demanded.

"My daughter."

331

There was no more discussion.

Eva led them along a country lane to a creamy-coloured stone building whose iron gates creaked and whose slanted shutters screamed for a lick of paint. Eva tapped on the convent door while the others hid around the corner, pasting their backs to the wall. At Eva's beckoning, Kevin, John and the couple scurried through spitting rain and to the inside where they met a tall, angular woman whose wizened face was pinched with worry.

"*Je suis la Mère Supérieure ici, Mère Angélique,*" she introduced herself. "*Comment puis-je vous aider?*"

Kevin took her in, her clothes not so different from those he had seen on nuns in Newfoundland—floor-length, dark habit tied at the middle, this one with a rope, not a leather belt. The rosary she wore was pretty much the same as those back home: huge, black beads that dangled from her waist. All around was an air of the sacred, just like he remembered from church. Crucifixes on every wall, and statues in every alcove—Jesus, Mary, Joseph, and the namesake of the order, St. Francis of Assisi. He attempted to listen as Mother Angélique spoke to Eva but it did him no good at all. Kevin's spirit sagged until John sidled up to him, whispering bits of translation.

"The Mother Superior is saying that priests brought Jewish children here," John offered. "Safe for a while, pretending to be Christians. Warned not to reveal their heritage to anyone. Even here, there are children of wealthy Catholics who are collaborating with the Germans. When the Germans started knocking, they were first looking for Resistance fighters, and then they looked at the children. They were suspicious of their dark hair and eyes, and forced the nuns to hand them over."

As Mother Angélique talked, she absentmindedly fingered her rosary beads. Her tale finished, she led the group into a makeshift dormitory with row upon row of empty cots.

Eva walked forward and sat on the edge of one of the beds.

"*Qui cherchez-vous, madame?*" asked the Mother Superior.

"Ruth," said Eva. "*Ma fille,* Ruth."

This Kevin understood. Eva and the nun exchanged more words, and

Kevin saw the relief in the eyes of both the women. Then he heard a name he recognized, Elsheva, followed by another, even more familiar: Robert Caulins.

John whispered to Kevin. "A man named Robert Caulins took Eva's daughter away, just before the German soldiers came. He used a password—Elsheva—which is why the Mother Superior knew that it was safe for the girl to go with him. He said he was heading toward the Pyrenees, so we may be able to catch up with them."

Eva asked the nun another question, nodding her head at the answer. Then Eva turned back to the group. "We must go. The longer we stay here, the greater the risk. We don't want to bring any trouble to these good sisters. My daughter isn't here and she is on her way to safety, I hope and pray."

CHAPTER 55

FROM THE CONVENT, THE GROUP resumed their trudge along winding country roads edged by low bushes and bounded by golden fields. With every breath, Kevin inhaled the soothing scent of new-mown hay. A peaceful place. Easy to slip into the comfort of it, like falling onto a pillow, but there was no allowance for a letup in vigilance. The slightest sound—a scuff of gravel, a snort of a horse, or a grumble of wheel meeting road—sent all three scurrying. Masked by brambles or haystack, they watched in silence as cars and carts and cattle travelled past.

This well-practised routine changed when, at the appearance of a horse-drawn hay wagon, Eva left her hiding place. Startled, Kevin leaned forward. John clamped a hand on his shoulder and Kevin yielded, resigning himself to the waiting, the watching.

Eva skipped over a ditch and stood in the road, fixed and facing the approaching wagon. Its driver, a squat man with matted strands of hair dangling beneath the edges of his tweed cap, reined the horse to a halt. Eva strode up to the dappled mare and, with one hand stroking its muzzle, looked at the driver. "*Bonjour*," she said. Nothing more.

The driver doffed his cap and launched a grin. "Ah. *C'est bon de te revoir.*" He swivelled his head, eyeing the road and fields around her. "*Le pilote et ses passagers?*" he asked.

It was rare, the smile that spread across Eva's face. "*Oui, et un de plus.*"

"*Un autre?*" The driver shrugged. "*D'accord.*"

Without turning, Eva raised her arm and crooked her finger, beckoning her companions.

Kevin released a sigh. The four abandoned the bushes, clambered aboard the hay-filled wagon, and tunnelled in. The wagon trundled along and, in the comfort of its sway, Kevin drifted, coming to with a jolt as a wheel hit a rut in the road. Light no longer streaked through slits in the hay. Night? How long had he been asleep? The slide of branches against the sides of the wagon meant they were on a different road. Narrower. A lane forged in a forest perhaps, one bulging with spruce trees if the smell was any indication.

When the wagon stopped, Kevin scrambled out. Stupefied, he brushed away bits of itchy, dried grass from his neck and squinted into the light of a puffed-up moon.

"No." Eva was in front of him. "Not you. This is the pilot's stop." She stepped aside.

There stood John the pilot. wearing a dark, heavy-leather jacket lined with sheepskin. A flight jacket. Was John leaving? "Where did you get the jacket?" A stunned thing to ask but it was all Kevin could muster.

"The Maquis are a resourceful lot," said John, as he moved to Kevin's side. "This is my mission, Kevin. Had to keep you in the dark. But now?" His voice dropped to a whisper. "There's a plane for me nearby. I'm flying François and Jeanne to England. Safest way to get them off the continent. They have vital intelligence for the Allies."

He grabbed Kevin's hand and pumped it up and down. "I'm sure you'll find your friend. And Eva will find her daughter."

Then he and the couple were gone. Through the trees, into a field.

Kevin turned to Eva. "You knew about this?"

"Of course. It was my mission to get them here. Wartime." She shrugged. "Secrets must be kept at all costs."

Images of Eva's mutilated fingers jumped into Kevin's mind. He shuddered. *At all costs.*

Back aboard the hay wagon. while Kevin was mulling things over, the abrupt roar of an engine tore through the night. Kevin stiffened. No doubt it was John's plane that was revving, then thundering down some makeshift runway, its growl shifting to a hum when it took to the sky. Kevin held his breath as he tuned his ear for anti-aircraft fire. There was none. The sound of the plane faded and Kevin began to breathe easy. John and his precious cargo were on their way.

It was still dark when Kevin, at Eva's signal, exited the wagon again. This time, the wagon rolled away instantly, not a word out of the driver. Kevin took in their surroundings. The spruce trees were well behind them, a medieval farmhouse in front, and weathered outbuildings off to one side, their greyness taking on a silver sheen in the moonlight. All was quiet. A windless night.

"I'm going into the barn. You wait here," said Eva as she headed off.

"But—" he began.

She waved him off. "Need to know basis." She looked around. "Safe house. We're fine."

Kevin put both hands up in front of him. He took a step back. "Good enough." Eva knew what she was doing. He watched her walk the few yards to the double doors of the barn. She opened one just a crack, slid through, and brought the door to behind her.

Kevin scanned the area. Not a soul. Not a sound. Not a movement. His attention turned to his aching body. Too much time cramped in the hay wagon. As he stretched and twisted to ease the discomfort, his hand slid across the sheathed knife attached to the left side of his belt. *Damn.* John's knife. Should have returned it. Too late now. He patted the hilt of the knife. It had been a rough few weeks but at least John was safe. Perhaps that was an omen, a good one. Perhaps they would all be safe. He took a deep breath, easy in, easy out.

Spotting a rain barrel at the far side of the barn doors, Kevin sauntered toward it. He slid the lid open and bent forward, scooping water into his hands and slurping it down. The icy water chilled his fingers and dripped between them, plopping back into the barrel. Thirst slaked, he hauled his sleeve across his face, rested his arm on the arc of the barrel, and straightened his back.

Facing him was the sturdy figure of a man, pistol in hand. "*Nicht bewegen*," the stranger rasped.

Kevin's chest tightened. He drew a quivering breath.

CHAPTER 56

———◆———

KEVIN HAD LET HIS GUARD down, had let go of the whine of fear that had riddled his body for the length of this journey. A stupid move. *Be afraid and you'll never meet danger.* Well, he was afraid now. Fear coursed through him like a riptide. He had to block it. If fright got the better of him, the intruder would get through him to Eva. Sobered by that thought, he steadied himself.

Kevin's arm still rested on the barrel, the tips of his fingers on the hilt of the knife at his waist, his touch on the knife triggering a memory of John's words. "The blade is black so it can't catch the light at night." Extending his fingers, Kevin coaxed the knife into his hand, palming the hilt, blade down. He sidled to his right, away from the barrel and into the moonlight. There he paused, just inches away.

The intruder brandished the pistol. He snorted and spat and reiterated, "*Nicht bewegen!*"

Kevin slowly lifted his left hand, a gesture of compliance. A stalling tactic. *Wait a fair wind and you'll get one.*

The barn doors clattered and as the intruder turned to the sound, Kevin lunged, knocking the gun to the ground and ramming the knife into the man's ribs and up, just as John had instructed. The target dropped. Kevin recoiled.

Eva stepped from the barn. Beside her loomed a hulking figure holding a lantern. He turned to Eva. "*Celui-ci est* Kevin?"

Eva nodded. "Kevin, this is Louis."

Louis put the lantern on the ground. "*Bonsoir*, Kevin. Get your knife. Might need it again. Spies everywhere," he grumbled. "Third one this week. Help me move the body."

It was a time for doing. Kevin extracted the knife, wiped it across his pant leg, and sheathed it. Silent, Kevin gripped the legs of the spy. Grunting, Louis hefted the torso. When the two had stashed the body between the barn wall and the rain barrel, Eva helped them cover it with hay.

With a gesture of his hand, Louis led Kevin and Eva through the tall double doors, past rough-hewn walls and gated horse stalls, over creaking floors strewn with straw, every board and joist withered with age, the stench of urine-soaked hay and dried piles of manure. Evidence of animals, but not a horse, cow, or goat to be seen. "Where are all the animals?" asked Kevin, not even realizing he had said that out loud.

"Louis sold them," said Eva. "All of them. To get us through the Pyrenees."

"Louis is coming with us?"

Eva nodded.

Louis led them to the far side of the building, where he grabbed a rusted spade and scraped at a mound of hay until the rungs of a ladder emerged. Waving off Kevin's offer of help, he lifted the ladder, lugging it and leaning it against a wall. Ensuring it was steady, he climbed. At the top, he raised a swarthy arm and pushed against the ceiling. A crack appeared. Hinges groaned. The opening widened. The farmer stepped to the top rung, leaned forward. "*Allors-y!*" he whispered into the depths, "*Maintenant!*" He climbed back down the ladder and held it steady.

There was a beat of silence then a rustling sound. A teenage girl started down the ladder and then paused. "*Un moment,*" she whispered. She climbed back up. Shortly, she returned with a small child whom she coached down, rung by rung. Kevin looked at the girl, clearly Eva's daughter Ruth, and then at the boy with the dark hair and tiny limbs. When the light from the lantern met the little boy's eyes, Kevin flashed on a memory of Kate, the haunted eyes of Kate after the tidal wave. He remained locked in the memory until Ruth raced past. He snapped to the present and saw Eva embrace her daughter, now at the foot of the ladder and holding the boy. Scuffling noises overhead transformed Kevin's moment of joy into a razor of fear.

Louis looked toward the loft and waved away his concern.

As he watched Robert descend the ladder, Kevin's urge was the same as Ruth's, to rush forward in greeting but he clipped that desire. He stood back, waiting as the scene unfolded. Eva and Ruth, clinging to each other, the boy now hanging onto Ruth's leg, Robert gazing at the trio. When Ruth pulled herself away from her mother, she introduced Robert. "Mother, this is the man who rescued us from the convent. His name is—"

"Oh, I know his name." Eva folded her arms and stared at him. Finally she nodded. "I can forgive all when you save my child." She put out her gloved hand. Robert grasped it. They stood, eyes locked while Kevin watched. Was it that easy? Forgiveness?

When Robert finally turned to Kevin, he smiled and said, "Good to see you made it, Kev."

Ruth introduced her mother to Pierre, the little boy who wouldn't let go of her leg. "He's an orphan, brought to the nuns to keep him safe. He followed me everywhere, and so I 'adopted' him. When Mr. Caulins came for me, I refused to go unless Pierre came too." She gave the little boy a reassuring hug.

There was no time to linger, no time to share news. The group headed out for their next destination, a village in the foothills of the Pyrenees.

CHAPTER 57

———◆———

THE VILLAGE WITH ITS STONE houses and small alleys was set against a green backdrop of deciduous forests and rolling fields. Like Kevin's home in Argentia, the place was timeless in its slow beat. But there were mountains here, not hills. And the sound he was accustomed to—the pulse of the ocean—was replaced with the thunder of a river, a wide river which allowed a view through the village and offered a clear line of sight to the peaks of the Pyrenees. A free view to the Freedom Trails. On the other side of those mountains was neutral Spain.

In one of those huts, they met their guide, Manuel, a mountain of a man whose square, reddened face was as pitted as a dartboard. His dark hair was pulled into a ponytail and he had a jagged, greying beard. A working man, evident to Kevin in the patched knees of coarse pants and the threadbare elbows of a black wool sweater. There were the hands too, the scars on the hands, proof of nicks and cuts. Kevin knew all about physical work and the scars it left.

Manuel distributed sturdy peasant clothes and rope-soled shoes. "Traditional Basque footwear," Eva explained. The plan was to start through the hills at dusk, weather permitting. This morning, they would attend Mass in the village church.

Kevin automatically dipped his fingers into the font of holy water and made the sign of the cross. An ingrained action, as was his genuflection before entering a wooden pew in the middle of the church. The kneeler banged as he lowered it. He looked around. A smaller church than he was used to but the altar, pulpit, and statues were all there. A few lit candles at the front cast a glow on the altar. The stained-glass windows towered and the smell of incense hovered. He dropped onto the kneeler, elbows on the pew in front of him, head down. He joined his hands and stifled a yawn.

He was alone. Early. Intentionally. Here for Confession. Kevin had not felt the need to confess before. But now? He had killed a man. And seconds later, he had dipped his hands into a rain barrel to rinse the blood. Yes, it was an act of war, but Kevin wasn't about to risk any chance at heaven, at seeing Mavis. His body trembling, he sneaked into a confessional and rattled off a "Bless me Father." After a rehash of the last few days, he let the sin fall out. Sudden. Swift. No reaction from the priest. Not a word. Kevin knelt still, waiting. He'd never known a priest to be at a loss for words. When the words did come, in French, Kevin blinked. How stunned was he at all? Sure he must have been behind the door when God was handing out common sense. Of course, the priest spoke French. The Father never understood a word of Kevin's confession. With a quick "Amen," Kevin was out of the black box and back to his pew where he sat, head down while the rush of embarrassment slid from his face. He'd just have to do his own praying, a self-assigned penance, as it were, and hope for forgiveness.

He hadn't prayed in so long that he didn't know where to begin. He reached into his pocket, pulled out the small oval case containing the rosary. If memory permitted, perhaps these tiny beads would guide him through. Perhaps Kate could trace the same path through this rosary someday. How could he get it to her? Uncertain. All he knew was it would connect them somehow. He started in the prayers, surprised at how easily the words fell from his lips. A steady rhythm.

As he finished the rosary, he heard footsteps in the aisle, familiar footsteps that stopped at his pew. Kevin smiled. Robert was here. The answer to his question. Robert would take the rosary to Kate. Kevin shifted from kneeling to sitting and slid across the pew to make room.

Robert sat.

"Eva is a strong woman," Kevin said, a respectful whisper. "Or should I start to call her Elsheva?"

"My wife is indeed resourceful. She could have managed without my help."

"Perhaps, but you saved your daughter."

Robert let out a satisfied sigh. "I told you that if we were separated, I would find her first. Remember?"

"Proper thing too. If you had waited, she would have been swept away by the Nazis." Swept away, like his own family. *Swept away.*

"True. But I wouldn't have made it here without your help. I never meant for you to get picked up by the Nazis. Lucky the Resistance found you."

"Getting picked up wasn't hard. Not as hard as killing." He paused, expecting a scrape of guilt. None came. He moved on. "There's nothing left now except for you to find your way back home. With your family."

The priest approached the altar for the beginning of Mass. Kevin and Robert slid from the pew and went to the back of the church. In an alcove, Kevin showed Robert the tiny oval rosary case. "I first set eyes on this when I was diving under a kitchen table in a safe house. Thought it was a stone."

"It's not?"

"No." Kevin twisted it open to reveal the rosary.

"Huh. Pretty clever. You took it?"

"Steal it, you mean. And no, but I was going to. The missus of the house gave it to me with her blessing."

"Why did you want it?"

"It reminded me of the pebble Kate carries, a souvenir from the Burin."

Kevin placed the rosary back inside the oval case and twisted the case shut. "I want her to have this, to know that not everything is as it seems, that blessings show up when you don't expect them." He passed the case to Robert.

"Why don't you give it to her yourself?"

"This is for you to do," said Kevin, the truth of his words spearing him. "When you go back to Canada for your sons, perhaps you can make your way to the island of Newfoundland."

"But we're going over the Pyrenees together," Robert said. "You can give the rosary to Kate."

Kevin slid past the protest. "I also want you to take this." He pulled the travel sewing kit, Mavis' travel sewing kit, from his pocket. "Please give this to Clara. Tell her I said it's handy for mending things."

Robert gave him a puzzled look. "Handy for mending things?"

Kevin nodded. "Exactly."

"But you're coming over the Freedom Trail with us."

Kevin let out a needed sigh. "I'll make a start. But I'm not altogether sure I'll make my way to the end of it."

Robert still hadn't taken the sewing kit. Hands up. Refusal. "We are all going to make it to freedom." He looked steadily at Kevin.

Kevin met his gaze and locked on.

Robert took the sewing kit. "Handy for mending things?"

Kevin nodded. "Handy for mending things."

"No point in arguing. I'll give these things back to you when we get to safety."

"Good enough then." Kevin nodded.

CLARA

CHAPTER 58

———◆———

IN THE FALL, CLARA AND her family were still stalled in the predicament of having the build of their house on hold. They weren't alone in this situation. Others had to bide time with relatives in neighbouring communities or hole up in makeshift shacks on Old Settlement Hill in Freshwater. At least Clara's family had a home—her schooner moored in the harbour. This, of course, meant she couldn't meet Patrick aboard, but he and she were doing grand anyway. Makeshift shacks proved to be make-do environments for all manner of activities.

Clara often slogged her way to and through Freshwater, her mind churning. Could she, Kathleen, and Kate make a go of it here on a craggy hilltop? The site for the house had come to her in the lottery, and she had had to accept it, but her heart sagged from the loss of a proper piece of land. Hard to fathom that Freshwater was only seven miles from her original home when the terrain was so foreign, rock after rock—boulders, for God's sake—spiking through ground like fractured bones through skin. How could anyone grow a potato or a turnip in the likes of that? And the size of the lot? She'd fare better with a postage stamp. No room for a barn or livestock. A few chickens maybe, but they'd dull their beaks pecking at stones. The only familiar things were the whip of the wind and the scent of the sea. Small comfort to her now.

Clara looked forward to sailing the *Elizabeth J* again, to running goods from merchants to outports. But that wouldn't occur until things were settled and she needed income now. All monies from expropriation cheques—hers,

Kathleen's, and part of Kevin's—were earmarked for the new house that would be home to the three of them—Clara, Kathleen, and Kate. Money from rum running would remain stashed, something to fall back on. As for new money? Clara would avail herself of the bounty brought by war.

Jobs were available on the base for women who could type. With that in mind, Clara grudgingly acknowledged her gratitude to Virginia. Despite the nightmare stopover at that woman's boarding house, Virginia had given them a gift—a cumbersome, clattering, typewriting machine. Yes, the thing had two broken keys, but that was no odds to Clara. Someone would mend it. A new skill was in the offing for both her and Kate.

With thoughts of her rock-ribbed land, her skeletal house, and her crippled typewriter jangling her last nerve, Clara felt the need for a distraction. One look at Kate, languishing aboard the schooner, her face sagging, told Clara that Kate needed it too. A life of worry was no life at all for a young girl. There was no need for concern about Kathleen for the moment as she, after some pondering and no disclosures, had up and boarded a train to St. John's. All Clara knew was that her mother went to visit Dulcie Mullins.

On a clear day late in October, with Kate in tow, Clara hiked past a smattering of houses in Jerseyside and stood at the head of the path leading down Jerseyside Hill to the Placentia Gut. From this vantage point, they eyed the silver ripples of the Gut and the town of Placentia on the other side, a town formed on a mere shingle of a peninsula that jutted bravely into the Atlantic. The dominant building in the town was the Roman Catholic Church, its spires almost touching the heavens. A grand view, this small town wrapped in the arms of the sea, backed by evergreen hills, and capped by a cloudless sky. Worth the trip all on its own. But it was not the town or the Church or the Gut that Clara and Kate had come to see.

Until this fall, the only way across the Placentia Gut was by boat.

Recently, the American military had rigged a pontoon bridge—a wooden deck supported on shallow-draft boats and anchored by concrete blocks. The old-timers of the area, wise to ocean currents, laughed at the folly of the floating bridge, knowing that if the Atlantic had any say, and it would, that bridge wouldn't last jig time. Still, the bridge was the talk of the place and the people were determined to walk across it while they had a chance.

As they stood on the hill, Clara eyed Kate who had been in a pout, oddly silent during the hike. When Kate pulled her keepsake pebble from her pocket, Clara let out a sigh. Kate was remembering her life on the Burin Peninsula again. That was all it was. Kate's face would brighten soon. Clara waited, hushed, as Kate rolled the pebble between her fingers. But in the next instant, Kate flicked her fingers and her precious memento went pop, pop, popping against jutting rocks as it made its way downhill.

Clara gasped.

Kate turned to her, her face hard. "Did you ever meet my mother Mavis?"

Clara went cold. "Whatever brings that on?"

Kate glared, eyes wide and watering in the wind. "Thought that if you never met her, you might perhaps have written a letter or two?"

A shudder ripped across Clara's chest. *The letters. The letters from Mavis.* Should have burned them. But she had stowed them. On the schooner. Safe, she thought. Beneath her bunk. *How stunned was she at all?* Sweet Heart of Jesus! Had Kate seen the letters?

When footsteps clomped on the path behind her, Clara spun toward them, ready to take on anything other than Kate's questions. The steps belonged to a young man, boy really, vaguely familiar. Short and rail-thin, clad in a wool jacket and pants, elbows and knees patched. It was Kate he was eyeing and he whipped off his salt-and-pepper cap as he called her by name.

"Kate, is it?" He put out his hand. "Do you remember me? Peter McGraw, from the hospital." When Kate didn't respond right away, he pulled his hand back, ran trembling fingers through his thinning brown hair, and kept right on talking. "You remember we met one day at the Argentia Hospital? When it was a hospital. Too bad they had to dismantle it this year. But they're building a new one in Placentia."

Kate stepped forward, offering her hand and a smile. "Peter. Nice to see you again. And you remember my . . . Aunt Clara?"

The slight hesitation over the word "aunt" pricked Clara at her core. "Good to . . ." Clara's voice rumbled with phlegm. She cleared her throat. "Good to see you again, Peter."

"How are you, Peter?" Kate asked, moving a little closer to him.

Relief flickered through Clara. She stepped aside.

"Working on the base," said Peter. "What about you?"

"Moving to Freshwater, as soon as our house gets built."

Peter pointed to the pontoon bridge. "You going to walk across?"

"That's the plan," said Kate.

"Mind if I come along?" Peter asked.

"Not at all," replied Kate.

"And you, missus?" Peter turned to Clara.

Clara gave a quick nod. "You're from the Southeast, if I remember right." Her words came easy this time so she continued. "You still live there?"

"No. Too far from the job. I was in a rooming house in Jerseyside for a while but now I'm aboard the *Richard Peck*. That's the ferry they brought from the States to use as a barracks."

The three ambled down the path on Jerseyside Hill, Clara trailing Kate and Peter and content to be in the back as it gave her time to mull. It wasn't only Kate's questions that were niggling. Something else was rising alongside them. What was it? Something Peter said maybe. Did Peter just say he was living on the *Richard Peck*? Clara halted. Patrick McMurty was living on the *Richard Peck*. What if the two met up and talked up a storm? Kate's name would come up. And her own name would follow. Clara shuddered. She felt her knees weaken.

Kate turned. "Did you hear? Peter says he can fix our typewriter. Are you coming?"

Clara jolted forward, but her mind kept stirring, seesawing between two worries—Kate reading letters, Peter meeting Patrick. Then she chided herself. What was she doing imagining the Devil when there was no sign of the beast? Managing to put a pause to her thoughts, she sucked in a breath and let it out. Somewhere in the outflow, another notion cropped up. *What if Robert returned?* That one stopped her breath altogether. Head light, skin clammy, she tripped over her own feet, barely managing to come to rights. If she didn't still herself now, both in mind and body, she'd tumble over the hill altogether. "You go on ahead. I'll catch up," she said as she parked her butt on an embedded boulder, the rounded top of which was several inches above ground.

Kate and Peter barely acknowledged her. As it should be, Clara supposed. A couple of youngsters, right delighted with each other's company. Didn't matter. Clara needed time to herself.

What did Kate know, or think she knew? Had she found the letters? Clara sat, dazed and wondering at her walled-in secrets. Were there cracks in those walls?

Clara turned her attention to the sea, the shine of it blinding, the wind from it biting. What had she done, telling so many lies for so many years? *Built a rod to whip her own back.* Nerves raw, she took deep breaths, sucking in as much salt air as she could. A good idea this, slowing down, sitting down. She couldn't fall off the ground.

Still, the ground was shifting beneath her feet.

KEVIN

CHAPTER 59

———◆———

KEVIN WAS LAST IN LINE as, at dusk, the group started their trek on goat trails over the Pyrenees, trails mentally mapped by Basque shepherds over generations, trails unknown to occupying forces. Provisions were small—a piece of meat, some sugar, a slice of bread—and the journey was to last two days. Between Manuel at the front and Kevin at the rear were Ruth, Robert carrying the French boy, then Eva, and the farmer Louis. The rule was silence. The pace unhurried. Walking sticks tapped steadily. Ferns flanking them swished at their passing. Littered leaves crunched beneath their feet. Toes thudded into tree roots crisscrossing the path. By dawn, the trees became sparse and scraggly and then they were gone. In alpine tundra, they climbed and crawled and slid over rocks and boulders and ice. Cold and hungry, they crept onward.

They were on a rise when the sound of a bird call brought Manuel to a halt. He beckoned. All responded, the spaces between them folding in like the bellows of an accordion. He spoke to Eva. "The call was a warning," said Eva. "A search party is onto us."

"Can't we speed up?" asked Kevin. "Get away from them?" He clapped his hands over his ears to ward off the wind as he waited for her translation.

"They won't stop. They'll keep coming until they capture someone."

"I'll lead them away," said Kevin. "You all go on."

Eva placed a hand on his arm. "You mustn't do this."

"No." Kevin looked into her eyes and then cast his glance to her fingers, gloved fingers, two missing. He touched her hand. The gesture was enough. He didn't need to add words. But he did. "You must get away. At all costs."

Her eyes, one green, one brown, were wet. "*Merci*," she said. "Thank you, friend of Robert."

Kevin turned to Robert, saw little Pierre on his shoulders and his daughter, Ruth, leaning into him. He nodded at his friend, and said softly, "Stay alive." Kevin released the sheath with its knife from his belt and set it on the ground. Then he was gone, bounding down the mountain. So much faster this tumbling, running, sliding. He came to a fork in the trail and took it. Then he slowed down, cocked an ear. The crunch of footsteps.

Someone was following him.

Kevin was playing his part. He was meant for this, to lead the enemy away. The group needed Manuel, their guide. The group owed Louis, the farmer whose sacrifice had paid for their freedom. Robert, Elsheva, and their daughter needed sanctuary.

His thoughts on Mavis, Kevin kept going. How had his heart kept pumping without her all these years? *Until death do you part.* Not enough, that. The path back to her was here. To Mavis, to his children, to another realm, the destination that he had wanted for a long, long time.

When he reached a point where he thought the others were safe, Kevin stopped running. He was taken without a scuffle by tired troops and led the rest of the way down the mountain into a waiting truck, one at the back of a convoy.

Kevin clambered in and plopped onto a bench. He looked into the faces of the others aboard. Strangers all. As soldiers lowered the canvas flap and laced it tight, darkness fell over the interior. The vehicle revved and grumbled, its tires spitting gravel as it bounced along. Kevin thought of Robert. He could imagine a future for Robert and his family, possibly raising the young French boy. He could see Robert going back to Argentia, passing along the rosary and the sewing kit. Robert, sailing with his sons back to England. Pleasant thoughts, all, interrupted when a distant rumble caught Kevin's attention. As the sound steadily grew to a thundering roar, Kevin knew they were alongside the river.

When the truck stopped and the flap was lifted, he and the twenty or so others were ordered out at gunpoint. One and two at a time, they stepped down. Kevin was last on, first off, and edged toward the riverbank, eyeing the swirl of eddies and whitecaps as the swollen water powered past. He looked around. No animals, not a bird to be seen. The ground beneath him was a mass of sand and silt—river deposits. A recent flood, no doubt. Rivers and oceans. Destroyers all. On a nearby bush, he spotted a broken spider web. A deep sigh fell out of him.

He had done his best to take care of his own, but the sea broke him. After that, he managed to take Kate home to her mother. Then war came at him. Broken again, he strived to help Robert and he had succeeded. He had saved a family. Not his own, but a family nonetheless. Robert and Elsheva and their daughter Ruth were free, on their way home.

The bolt-action sound of rifles cut the air.

Kevin turned.

In the light of the morning sun, in a single glance, Kevin took in the hard faces of the captors, their eyes cold and grey like a winter sea. The roar of the river fell away as the soldiers raised their weapons.

Rifle reports bit the air and men fell. No flailing arms. No crying out. Just dropping like flies.

A sting in his chest and the ground claimed Kevin. He stared into the blue sky and, in his last breaths, struggling breaths, he thought of his mother.

KATHLEEN

CHAPTER 60

———◆———

IT IS A BYSTANDER, THE sea.

Without ripple of regret, the North Atlantic ferries fathers and sons into the snares of Hitler. Cold to the fate of the people it carries and the families who wait, the sea looks on, its icy fingers lapping both the shores of home and the shores of war.

Like the Atlantic, the ghost of me is bystander to goings-on, both at home and away. Unlike the sea, I am distraught, a quaking mist. My community of Argentia is reduced to sand, its houses and barns replaced with airfields and barracks. The familiar wharf that has hosted many schooners, skiffs, and coastal ferry boats is now lined with warships, battle-grey and battle-ready. There is nothing the people can do other than to evacuate. And they do. In my living years, I was among them.

Today, in my afterlife, I observe my daughter Clara and my granddaughter Kate who are standing on Jerseyside Hill and staring at the pontoon bridge spanning the Placentia Gut. I remember that the very idea of the pontoon bridge prompted old salts to warn that it wouldn't last jig time. I remember that jig time turned out to be two months, after which the wind reared, the Atlantic jeered, and the bridge was shredded, pieces of it strewn up and down the coast.

I also recall that the flesh-and-blood Kathleen was not with Clara and Kate on this day. The living me was off to St. John's under the guise of helping Dulcie settle in. The truth of it was that I was seeking release from guilt.

In my living years, I deemed the killing of my husband, Alphonse, a justifiable deed. At the same time, I harboured a nagging fear that the Lord and His Commandments would see things differently. In St. John's, with the help of an anonymous priest in an unlit booth of an unfamiliar church, I managed to have the weight of the deed lifted from my soul. One would think I'd cling to that lightness, without relapse, for a lifetime. But like the pontoon bridge, my soul floated for jig time.

As I hover now, I ponder my presence. Why am I trailing Clara and Kate? Maybe this is a gift, a pleasant outing?

Then a voice calls me, shattering all hope of maybe.

A shock of memory propels me into denial. I grasp at Clara's skirt in a pitiful attempt to stay put. The voice comes again.

Kevin's voice.

The wind sweeps me away, shepherds me across the Atlantic into a chain of mountains that climb to dizzying heights. The peaks are solid and snow-capped, sawtoothed silhouettes against a cobalt sky. Mystical and mystifying. Do I know this place?

The morning sun breaches the summit, blushes through clouds, and gives shape to a huddled line of people who are sliding, scrambling, struggling to scale the highest ridge. One of the group casts a backward glance and I catch a glimpse of a haggard face. Robert? I urge myself onward, closer. A downward blast of frigid air barricades me. I witness only the icy fog of breath, Robert's breath, as he disappears over the mountain top.

As Robert's face lingers, as fragments of images adhere, I am flooded with foreboding. Given a choice, would the rising sun retreat, sink back behind the peaks rather than shed light on what happens here? A useless question. The sun persists as mandated, climbing and climbing. The scene plays out.

From the foothills comes a volley of popping sounds that bounce from peak to peak until their echoes fade. A gust of air ushers me down, down, down to a rugged road that rambles through a lush valley. In a clearing near a raging river, the breeze stalls, locking me into a pocket of air. The sun turns its focus on the clearing, highlighting it, daring me to look.

Scripted like the sun, I have no choice. The air around me shakes violently, throwing images out of focus.

What do I see? Logs? Is that what is piled in the clearing beside the river? Of course it isn't. I am making a game here. A delaying tactic. Distracting myself with memories from my living years when it was the job of fathers and sons to head into the woods in the fall to cut logs, to stockpile them, and then to return in the winter with horse and sledge to cart the logs home. I remember the sweet scents of sawdust and turpentine and recollect pleasant evenings in the kitchen, my husband stoking the stove with splits from those logs and Kevin—or was it Clara?—doing lessons at the kitchen table, while I rocked and knitted. I recreate sounds—chair creaking, needles clicking, fire crackling. The comfort of home takes hold.

Abruptly, the air stills itself. In a blunt calm, under a blazing sun, the images on the ground come into focus.

In the light of acceptance, I see bodies, Kevin's among them. I can only watch as, flat on his back in a mound of sand, he struggles to speak. "Mom," he says, "I'm going home."

Jarred, agonized, I am useless, a bystander, there when Kevin opened his eyes for the first time, here as he closes them for the last.

Kevin is soundless, motionless, a puddle of red forming around him. His blood gurgles and swells and mixes with blood from a huddle of bodies to form a pool. Rivulets branch off, running downhill, darkening as they mix with the brown of the sand in their rush to join up with the river.

An engine revs and I turn. A grey-drab military truck tears away from the scene, spewing dust, its canvas flap flailing. The thunder of the vehicle dies out and a hush sets in. Air currents cart me higher.

A cloud brushes by, spinning me around to behold the spectre of my son. I sense the touch of his hand in mine—a short-lived, yet eternal, rush of love—as he sweeps away, upward. The sun sparks, sending golden threads that lift him, drawing him higher and higher. In the weightless moment that follows, I smile my way toward him, ready to go with him. A thundercloud materializes, plugging my path with the steel greyness of the battleships in the harbour at home. I launch the heft of my spirit against the cloud, slamming it, then swing wide in an attempt to circumvent it. It blocks me at every turn. A hopeless endeavour, for this is Kevin's redemption, not mine.

Kevin's choice, Kevin's soul, Kevin's destiny. His story ends here.

My destiny is to continue the telling. I know this and the knowing, the owning, has me frantic, clawing at the edges of the scene in an attempt to escape its sting. I implore the universe to whisk me away and it complies, drawing me down, like the lifeblood of Kevin, into the river. Unfamiliar, this travelling in water in lieu of air, but who am I to question the determined current that takes me from the Garonne River to the Bay of Biscayne to the Atlantic Ocean? Once in the Atlantic, I intuit the inherent mercy of the universe. It is showing me in its own way that the ocean, the giver of all life, has a way of reclaiming the same. Wherever I go, wherever the ocean goes, part of my Kevin will be there.

Through crests and troughs and billows, on a sea voyage that spans a ceaseless cycle of seasons and racks my hollow spirit with grieving, the Atlantic Ocean takes me home.

On a glistening day, I slide into Placentia Bay and find myself floating alongside the temporary bridge, the pontoon bridge that spans the Placentia Gut. From my perch on a spit of foam, I catch sight of my daughter on Jerseyside Hill and I am instantly baffled. How can Clara be in the same time and place that she was when I left? Haven't I been gone a long, long time? Clarity comes when I recall my spectral state. In the world of ghosts, time is arbitrary, shapeless, without rhyme or reason or sense of sequence. I was there. I am here.

Eager to distance myself from the angst of my travels, I turn my attention full on Clara who flops onto a boulder like she's been struck by the hand of God. The air around me sighs in exasperation. There is no hand of God in this at all, only the threat of truth that takes all the use out of Clara. Would love to talk to her, but any attempt would be wasted for there is no bridge, temporary or otherwise, between my lower world and her living one.

What would I say to her anyway? *Why trust this shadow man you are seeing? What of your husband, Robert, if he returns?* Another sigh comes as I replace *if* with *when.*

I look for and locate Kate, her brown curls bouncing and gleaming, as she makes her way across the pontoon bridge. I am familiar with the young man—Peter—who accompanies her. I remember him from the hospital when he comforted Kate. I remember him from the day of the airplanes when he calmed his horse. Seemed fine enough on both occasions.

Is he steady, this Peter, a rock like the Apostle Peter, whom Jesus selected from the Twelve? Where will Peter be when Kate learns about the death of Kevin, the man she called father all her life?

And will Kate, my Kate, ever learn the secrets around her birth?

I slide close to Kate, hoping to hear a whisper from her but it does not come. Not yet. Just as well. I'm already bent by care.

Weariness washes through me. I crave a respite from this story. It is coming, I know, a lull. It is programmed. Any second now, the wind will scoop me up and sweep me to sanctuary in some coil of a cloud. Would that I could hide there forever from the sin which doomed me to the hell of repeated telling.

Better yet, would that I could reclaim my soul . . .

———◆———

Dear Reader,

Thank you for taking the time to read *Of Sea and Sand* and its predecessor *Of Sea and Seed*. If you enjoyed these books, please consider telling your friends or posting a short review. Word of mouth is an author's best friend and is greatly appreciated.

My best to you,

QUESTIONS AND TOPICS
FOR DISCUSSION

- At the heart of *Of Sea and Sand* lies upheaval. In the world of the Kerrigan family, war was something that occurred far away, not on their doorstep. Did it surprise you to learn that, on the east coast of what is now Canada, a whole community was uprooted during the Second World War to make room for a strategic US Naval Base? Have you ever experienced a moment of great turmoil in your life, a moment when you knew things would never be the same?

- Kevin believes that the job of a man is to take care of his own and harbours guilt that he wasn't there to save his family from the tidal wave. Is guilt justifiable here? How are Kevin and Robert alike in their feelings of guilt and in their quest for redemption?

- The self-sufficient Clara appears to be at the cutting edge of twentieth century social change. She is also immersed in secrets that begin leaking out. Kevin learns her deepest secret and leaves. How do you think Kate will react if she finds out? How are you at keeping secrets? Have you ever held one that you wish you hadn't?

- At this point in the projected trilogy, Daylon has given starring roles to not one, but three characters. The journey of the umbrella character, Kathleen, winds throughout the entire series: Book I, *Of Sea and Seed*, focuses on the journey of Clara; Book II, *Of Sea and Sand*, focuses on the journey of Kevin. It follows then, that Book III, *Of Sea and Soul*, will focus on Kate's journey. What predictions do you have about Kate?

- The ghost of Kathleen Kerrigan has been set adrift, doomed to atone for mortal sin by telling repeatedly the story of her downfall. Would you, if you could, redeem Kathleen from this relentless, repetitive ancient mariner journey?

READING/VIEWING LIST
THE KERRIGAN CHRONICLES TRILOGY

———◆———

Andrieux, J. P. 2009. *Rumrunners.* St. John's, NL: Flanker Press.

Anonymous. 2003. *Eine Frau in Berlin (A Woman in Berlin, Eight Weeks in the Conquered City).* Germany: Eichborn AG, Frankfurt am Main

Argentia 282 Coastal Defence Battery Municipal Heritage Site. Canada's Historic Sites. https://www.historicplaces.ca/en/rep-reg/place-lieu.aspx?id=6122

"Behind Enemy Lines, Story of British Commandos in WWII." 2001. Netflix Documentaries. https://www.netflix.com/ca/title/80114588

Bond's Path and Southeast Come Home Year Committee. 2006. *An Armful of Memories.* Placentia, NL: Transcontinental.

Bedard, John. 2017. *Thetford Park (Halifax to Liverpool on a coal burning ship stuffed with ammo).* Canada: Independently Published.

Berman, Kathryn. n.d. "Hidden Children in France during the Holocaust." The World Holocaust Remembrance Center. https://www.yadvashem.org/articles/general/hidden-children.html

Cashin, Peter. 2012. *My Fight for Newfoundland.* St. John's, NL: Flanker Press.

Collier, Keith. 2011. "Cottage Hospitals and Health Care in Newfoundland." Newfoundland and Labrador Heritage Website. https://www.heritage.nf.ca/articles/society/cottage-hospitals.php

Collins, Gary. 2013. *The Gale of 1929.* St. John's, NL: Flanker Press.

Collins, Gerard. 2011. *Finton Moon.* St. John's, NL: Killick Press.

Crook, Flight Lieutenant David, DFC. 2015. *Spitfire Pilot: A Personal Account of the Battle of Britain.* Amazon Digital Services LLC.

Duke, Darrell. 2013. *Thursday's Storm: The August Gale of 1927.* St. John's, NL: Flanker Press.

Duke, Darrell. 2018. *An Irish Tale of Leaving.* Newfoundland: Stagehead Publications.

Duley, Margaret. 1941. *Highway to Valour.* New York: The MacMillan Company.

Evans, Calvin. 2014. *Master Shipbuilders of Newfoundland and Labrador, Volume 2.* St. John's, Newfoundland: Breakwater Books.

Everts, Lee K. M. 2016. *The Placentia Area: A Changing Mosaic.* Placentia: Lulu.com.

Fitzgerald, Jack. 2005. *Newfoundland Disasters.* St. John's, NL: Creative Publishers.

—. 1989. *Strange but True Newfoundland Stories.* St. John's, NL: Creative Publishers.

Freshwater Come Home Year Book Committee. 2002. *Freshwater Come Home Year*. Freshwater, NL: Robinson-Blackmore.

Goodall, Scott. "The Freedom Trail (Chemin de la Liberté): WWII Escape Route to Spain. " https://www.ariege.com/en/discover-ariege/occupation-and-resistance/freedom-trail. Accessed June 25, 2018.

Gooley, Tristan. 2016. *How to Read Water: Clues and Patterns from Puddles to the Sea*. North America: The Experiment, LLC.

Halliwell, Sarah and Cooke, Tim. 1995. *Eyewitness War: Personal Accounts of World War II*. London: Marshal Cavendish Books

Hanrahan, Moira. 2006. *Tsunami: The Newfoundland Tidal Wave Disaster*. St. John's, NL: Flanker Press.

Hershco, Dr. Tsilla. 2007. "The Jewish Resistance in France During WWII: The Gap between History and Memory." http://jcpa.org/article/the-jewish-resistance-in-france-during-world-war-ii-the-gap-between-history-and-memory. Date accessed Aug 2, 2018.

Higgins, Jenny. 2007. "Great Depression—Impacts on the Working Class." Newfoundland and Labrador Heritage Website. https://www.heritage.nf.ca/articles/politics/depression-impacts.php

Higgins, Jenny. 2006. "Royal Navy.' Newfoundland and Labrador Heritage Website. https://www.heritage.nf.ca/articles/politics/royal-navy.php

Higgins, Jenny. 2006. "Argentia." Newfoundland and Labrador Heritage Website. https://www.heritage.nf.ca/articles/politics/argentia-base.php

Holocaust Encyclopedia. Kristallnacht. USA: United States Holocaust Memorial Museum. https://encyclopedia.ushmm.org/content/en/article/kristallnacht

Houlihan, Eileen. 1992. *Uprooted! The Argentia Story*. St. John's NL: Creative Publishers.

Johnston, Wayne. 1999. *The Colony of Unrequited Dreams*. Toronto, Ontario: Vintage Canada.

Kitts, Kathy H. 2013. *The Minesweeper's Letters*. USA: Kitts Family Publications

Lannon, Alice, and McCarthy, Mike. 1991. *Fables, Fairies, & Folklore of Newfoundland*. St. John's, NL: Jesperson Press Ltd.

"Life in the Shadows: Hidden Children and the Holocaust." USA: United States Holocaust Memorial Museum. https://www.ushmm.org/exhibition/hidden-children/insideX/

Neary, Peter. 1988. *Newfoundland in the North Atlantic World 1929-1949*. Kingston and Montreal: McGill-Queen's University Press.

Neary, Peter, ed. 1996. *White Tie and Decorations: Sir John and Lady Hope Simpson in Newfoundland, 1934-1936*. Toronto: University of Toronto Press.

McKenna, Brian. Director. 2016. "Newfoundland at Armageddon." CBC Documentary. Gala Film Productions. Morag Loves Armageddon Inc. https://www.cbc.ca/documentaries/specials/newfoundland-at-armageddon-1.5092119

"No Price Too High: Canadians and the Second World War." Morningstar Entertainment. 2004.

O'Connor, Joe. 2016. "The Myth of Beaumont Hamel: How Newfoundland's tragic death march became a noble advance." Canada: The National Post. https://nationalpost.com/news/canada/newfoundland-beaumont-hamel

Power, C. Olive, ed. 2012. *Bridging Places & People from Big Barasway to Ship Harbour.* Placentia: Placentia Intertown 2012 Come Home Year Book Committee.

Raley, James. 2013. *I Fell four Miles and Lived: Missing in Action—WWII.* USA: Jamesgate Press LLC.

Romkey, Bill, ed. 2009. *St. John's and the Battle of the Atlantic.* ST. John's, NL: Flanker Press.

Rosbottom, Ronald C. *The City of Light under German Occupation, 1940-1944.* New York: Little, Brown and Company, 2014.

Simon, Marie Jalowicz. 2014. Underground in Berlin: A young woman's extraordinary tale of survival in the heart of Nazi Germany. Canada: Alfred A. Knopf.

Strowbridge, Nellie P. 1988. *The Newfoundland Tongue.* St. John's NL: Flanker Press.

"The Placentia Area." Decks Awash: The Placentia Area Volume 17, No. 3. St. John's, NL: Memorial University of Newfoundland, May-June.

"Underfire: The Untold Story of Pfc Tony Vaccaro." 2016. HBO Documentary. Max Lewkowicz, Director.

Walsh, Barbara. 2013. *August Gale.* USA: Globe Pequot Press.

"War Junk: Juno Beach." 2015. Season 3, Episode 1. https://www.history.ca/shows/war-junk/video/juno-beach/561452611642/

"World War II Great Escapes: Freedom Trails, The Pyrenees." 2017. CBC Documentary Channel.

Yardley, Jonathan. 2014. "A History of Paris during Nazi Occupation." Date accessed August 2, 2018. https://www.washingtonpost.com/opinions/a-history-of-paris-during-nazi-occupation/2014/08/29/fce9e112-222c-11e4-958c-268a320a60ce_story.html?utm_term=.e792b4fee2b1:/

Young, Ron. 2006. *Dictionary of Newfoundland and Labrador.* St. John's NL: Downhome Publishing Inc.

—. 2005. *Downhome Memories.* St. John's, NL: Downhome Publishing Inc.

Acknowledgements

First and foremost, I am grateful to my father, Andrew Lannon (1922–2019) who sparked this particular writing journey when he told me a true story about a little girl who survived the 1929 Newfoundland tsunami.

Thank you to my husband, David, for his love, support, and encouragement throughout all my creative endeavours. He is my soulmate, my joy, my rock.

Thank you to "Tea & Critique" partners, Fran Brown and Mary Keane, for their invaluable input. Great writers, great friends, greatly appreciated.

Thank you to: Ron Young, founding editor of Newfoundland's *Downhome* magazine; Paul Butler, author of *The Good Doctor*; Nellie Strowbridge author of *Ghost of the Southern Cross*; and Darrell Duke, author of *Thursday's Storm* for their generosity in taking time to read and endorse the first book of this trilogy. An extra thank you to Darrell Duke who is writing about the same area during the same era and who is gracious in sharing his knowledge of the time.

Thank you to Brian Rodda at www.roddawrites.com for creating the inset map of the Avalon and Burin Peninsulas of Newfoundland.

Thank you Kilmeny Jane Denny for her superb editorial skills, excellent advice, and overall support throughout the publishing process.

Thank you to the Newfoundland Archives Department of The Rooms Museum in St. John's, Newfoundland, for taking the time to respond both by email and phone to my concerns regarding the publication of the evacuation letter sent to all Argentia residents.

Thank you to *Downhome* magazine to which I have subscribed for years. It is a constant source of information, entertainment, and inspiration.

Thank you to "Land and Sea," the TV series from the CBC whose episodes, too numerous to detail, have inspired me.

Thank you to Argentia Facebook Group members Donald Lannon and Gerry Dollmont for taking time to respond to my research questions.

Thank you to the Writers' Alliance of Newfoundland and Labrador for advice and support.

Thank you to the Federation of British Columbia Writers for information and support, in particular to past president Ben Nuttall-Smith, author of *Secrets Kept, Secrets Told*, for his ongoing encouragement.

Thank you to British Columbia's Chilliwack/Abbotsford bookstore The Book Man (www.bookman.ca) for its enthusiastic support of local authors.

About the Author

Annie Daylon was born and raised in Newfoundland. She studied music at Mount Allison University and education at both the University of Manitoba and the University of British Columbia (M.Ed.). After many years teaching, she delved into her passion for writing. Annie lives in the British Columbia Fraser Valley with her husband, David, and their dog, CoCo. You can find out more about Annie at www.anniedaylon.com